Other Books by Caroline Ailanthus

To Give a Rose

Ecological Memory

Bifurcation Events

A Novel By
Caroline Ailanthus

ISBN 978-1-62806-401-8 (print | paperback)
ISBN 978-1-62806-402-5 (ebook)

Library of Congress Control Number 2024904773

Published by Salt Water Media
29 Broad Street, Suite 104
Berlin, MD 21811
www.saltwatermedia.com

Cover artwork and interior illustrations
by the author Caroline Ailanthus

For Tom Wessels and Charles Curtin,
my friends and teachers,
without whom this book would not have happened.

Someone cut down my favorite tree
along with the shadow that used to hang over me
No one keeps a secret like a sunny day.

-Douglas Morea, Tom Soukup, in *untitled song*

Contents

Author's Note

If you see the excellent movie *2001: a Space Odyssey*, pay particular attention to the scenes set on the moon. In one of them, Earth is visible briefly in the lunar sky—looking quite unrealistic. It's the only glaring special-effects failure in the whole show, and it happened because Stanley Kubric didn't know what Earth looks like from the moon because nobody did. He and his team had to guess. And less than a year after that movie came out, everybody in the whole world found out that the guess was wrong because somebody went to the moon and took a picture. Poor Kubric had less than one year in which his masterpiece could plausibly seem to be about the real future.

And wouldn't you know it, the same thing happened to me. In the summer of 2019, I published a book set twenty years after a terrible pandemic, and less than five months later....

My guesses were pretty good actually, but I wrote about a world in which COVID-19 never happened—my fictional pandemic is a surprise in a way we can no longer be surprised. We can never again have a future that does not contain COVID-19 in its past.

Like Stanley Kubric, I must press on.

Although I have allowed what I learned from COVID to enrich this second book in the series, I have chosen not to update my fictional future. *Bifurcation Events* remains consistent with *Ecological Memory*. It is a second visit to the same world.

You don't need to have made the first visit yourself yet. Both books are designed to stand on their own. I was even going to repeat (and expand) the essays on science I included with the first book, as they apply here too, but this one is long enough as it is. So I'll just let you know that everything that isn't obviously fiction is as realistic as I could make it, except for the campground above the little beach at Long Pond. It's not there yet. I do recommend you check out the annotated reading list at the back, and that you do so *after* you read the book, as it may contain some spoilers.

I suppose it's not a spoiler to say much of my tale is set on Mount

Desert Island—I mean, there it is on the cover, that's Long Pond and its hills. It's a place I've spent a lot of time and know quite a bit about, largely thanks to Tom Wessels, who introduced me to the island, and Chris Seymour, my wonderful husband, who has hiked most of it with me and generally made my visits there possible.

But there's more to the tale. Tom didn't just teach an awesome field-studies course I happened to take, he's also stayed involved, answering questions and exploring little-known places off-trail with me. And Chris isn't just my partner—he's also a wildlands firefighter who has shared fire videos and training materials with me, answered questions, and reviewed my scenes. And after I found the ruins of Barberry Ledge, the house that my fictional Cranberry Ledge is based loosely on, I went back with both Chris and Tom and listened in as they analyzed the site together. There is no greater privilege.

If I thank Charles Curtin for everything I should, I'll only embarrass him. Instead, I'll just acknowledge that I stole some of his lines. Again.

Rowland Russell showed me how to treat *place* as foreground rather than as background, a perspective that drove much of the development of the book. Plus, he has always encouraged me as a writer in ways large and small, and his existence is good for my soul.

When I was a child, Elisabeth Curtis taught me how to edit and how to care about writing well. She also became my friend. When she was dying, I showed her as much of the draft of this book as I could because I just had to. And she read it. My dear Elisabeth, let me adapt a phrase of A.A. Milne and say Penny Darling would be my gift to you were she not already your gift to me.

My parents, Kass Sheedy and Douglas Morea, are both writers and helped immensely with planning and plotting and figuring out how to revise this book (plus, they ARE my parents). Martha VanderWolk is not related to me at all but did likewise. When in doubt, ask Martha.

The late Betty Seymour, my mother-in-law, was a genealogist (among other things) and explained how Kevin could find his great-grandmother. Lauren Leonardi provided Spanish translation. Jamie Capache did Quebecois translation (yes, Andy's Quebecois is supposed to be bad). Sarah Zavaski was my cover model (though she does not look like that). The rangers at Acadia National Park, especially those of Seawall Campground, did much to make my research even possible (the pig should not be taken personally, I swear, I just needed a name). The staff at Southwest Harbor Library provided all sorts of resources, from research assistance to much-needed water. Many other people gave me brief but pivotal help in various ways, notably Christine Christensen, Max Sparrow, Logan Clevenger, Ryan Crosby, Steve Chase, Jan Quick, Denise Caignon, Mark McConchie, Will Brussard, and the late Jeremy Schvetz. I'm sad you're gone, Jeremy.

Joel Parthemore, Ada Kerman, Jamie Capache, Karen Chelquist, and my parents and Martha all beta-read for me and provided valuable feedback. Rachel Brice proof-read.

And then there is the staff at Saltwater Media, Steph, Patty, and Andrew. Without them, this book *could* exist, you just would be unable to buy it and read it.

And you *have* bought it and will read it, so thank you! A book is communication; it begins with a writer, but it only fully comes into existence when someone reads it.

Part One

Part Two

A Cold, Uncertain Dawn

Elzy woke to cold, the scent of cold, of snow, of tent fabric. The coldness felt good on her hot skin. Confusion. She wasn't in her room…? The child fell asleep again before she could figure it out. Nothing seemed worth thinking through. Her head hurt. Her chest hurt. Her tummy hurt. Her breath wouldn't come right. She slept again.

She woke. Daddy feeding her soup. It tasted funny. Daddy had put something in it to make her feel better. Try to have *some*, he said. You have to stay hydrated.

Where's Jamie?

Shh, said Daddy.

Consciousness came and went. She snuggled down under blankets in her sleeping bag, shivering, then struggled out of her bag and threw off the blankets, burning up. In the daytime the walls were luminous. She was in a tent. She kept forgetting that. To poo she had to go outside and squat in the snow. She always had to poo. Her butt hurt. Her breath, reflected back at her face from the inside of her sleeping bag, burned her eyes. She had a moment of clarity, of fledgling analysis. *I have a fever, so my breath is too hot for my eyes.* And *my sleeping bag is wet because I'm sweating even though I feel cold. It's because I have a fever.* But mostly she couldn't think much. Then she had to poo again.

3

There had been other people. When she was awake enough to think through anything, she could remember that. The camping trip, not to either of the campgrounds, Blackwoods or Seawall, but to a spot way up in the woods they had to hike to, carrying all their stuff, so much stuff, all of it heavy, uphill through the snow, with Daddy and Jamie and those two women who were Daddy's friends and their kid who was Elzy's own age but seemed sort of shy or maybe stuck-up and then started coughing and turned blotchy.

I'm going to remember everything for Show and Tell, when we get back to school, Elzy had said.

We're not going back, Jamie had told her. You don't know anything.

She hated it when he got that superior tone, just because he was older, but he was right, she hardly knew anything, and that was almost OK, because he would explain it all to her eventually. He always did.

But then everybody got sick, spotted and blotchy, and the others went into separate tents or something because they weren't around anymore, and everything got confusing, and Elzy couldn't think right or breathe right and now she had to go poo again.

Daddy?

Daddy had been gone a long time. She went to sleep while he wasn't in the tent, and when she woke up, he still wasn't there.

Daddy?

When he got back, he looked tired and sad and sort of gray in the face. He sat down on the sleeping-pad, just like he used to sit on the edge of her bed back home. He asked all his questions. Are you warm? Cold? Hungry? Thirsty? How's your tummy? He felt her forehead, asked her to breathe deep so he could listen. This time when she breathed, she didn't cough, though breathing still hurt. She didn't really feel like talking. She sort of fell asleep but not really. Nothing much was really anything these days. She lay there, sort of sleeping but not really, and Daddy rubbed her ear so she felt a little better. After a while, Daddy spoke.

It's just you and me now, kid, he said. But don't worry, I can take care of us. We have plenty of food, plenty of ammunition, I know lots of wild plants we can eat, and there's deer here. We can have a garden, too. You'll like having a garden. There's fish in the lake. I'll teach you to fly-fish, how about that? No one will find us. We'll be safe here. Don't worry. But there's one thing I need you to do for me, Elzy, Elzita, Elzy-Elzy-Girl. I need you to just not die. Not now. Because I need to have somebody to care for. I can't do this alone.

The inside of the tent smelled cold and musty, and the daylight through the tent walls was starting to fade.

Elzy never afterwards remembered him saying that, but for the rest of her life, when she thought about those weeks in the tent while one world, one life, ended, and something else began, she wondered if something just like that had been said.

The Crack in Everything

Christine Pennington had music in her head all the time. She did not initially realize most other people didn't. She would have preferred if it was always the classical material she was rather proud of honestly liking, or the rarefied music of the spheres, but as often as not it was the Everly Brothers, the Phantom of the Opera, The Beatles' White Album, or some other pop-music-type thing. Adults kept saying all that was "before your time," as if she shouldn't like, or even know much about, stuff that came out before she was born, but that wasn't a very fair standard as she wasn't even ten years old yet.

She could make music herself if she wanted to. She had a piano and took lessons during the school year, when she lived in the city, where her parents "worked in the garment district" (that meant something to do with clothing, so she hadn't bothered to find out any more about it). Living in the city meant going to museums, eating soft pretzels with mustard from street carts, and riding the subway with her father, always in the front car so they could look out and see where they were going.

In the summer there were no more lessons because she lived with her grandparents (and sometimes her parents, when they could "get away") on the farm in the Hudson Valley. She still had to practice, though. They had a piano, actually a nicer one than she had at home, a lovely old thing with worn keys and a rich voice. Living on the farm meant reading whatever she liked, not just the stuff her teachers told her to read, sleeping and then waking with the window open with all the wonderful smells and sounds coming in, and tramping around through the fields and the woods where she could listen to things and be by herself.

Or being with her best friend, Krista, who lived nearby and could come over to play most days.

Sometimes she'd go over to Krista's and then there would be a problem, because when Krista's parents called either of them by name, both girls would turn around. But problems have solutions. Krista's parents quickly learned to use her whole name, Christine Pennington, and then just her last name, Pennington, and then just Penny. She liked being Penny. There were an awful lot of girls at school with names like hers, all the Kristins and Kirstens and Kristys, and none of them were called Penny but her. Also, anytime anybody called her Penny, she'd think of Krista, whom she could not see during the school year (a Major Tragedy), and who'd called her Penny first.

In the summers, she and Krista could tramp around the woods together and find bird nests or build forts or lay on the ground looking up at the trees and talking.

"If I learn the guitar, too," she was saying, "I can play it on stage when we go on tour, in case the concert venues don't have pianos." They were going to be the next Indigo Girls and felt they needed to get all this planned.

"But I can't play *any* instrument!" Krista wailed. "What am I going to do?"

"You can just sing. Lots of acts have someone who just sings. Or I can teach you to play something."

"I could draw the concert posters and stuff," her friend said, after some thought.

"That's right, you could."

Between the two of them, Krista was acknowledged the better draw-er.

Gramma ordered them into the bathroom to de-tick as soon as they got back, but there were places they were too shy to inspect each other, and before long Krista got a weird, bright red rash on her butt and had to go to the doctor.

"I'm going to die a deadly death," she announced.

"You will eventually," Penny agreed, by way of comfort, "but not today, and not because of that tick."

Between the two of them, Penny was acknowledged the more sensible one.

When she turned ten, Penny had her long, black braid cut off and given to some organization to make a wig for a kid with cancer. She wished she could meet the kid and wondered what it would be like to sit and talk with somebody wearing *her* hair. Thus shorn, turning or shaking her head felt really different. She liked the difference.

"I finally understand what *light-headed* really means," she told her mother.

"No, you don't," her mother said.

When she was twelve she learned that noticing stuff outside and knowing about living things is called *natural history*, and that there are scientists who do it full-time. She and Krista, who preferred microbiology but would generally do as Penny told her, embarked upon their scientific careers by catching as many fireflies as possible and diligently writing down the number caught every night. They stopped when Penny's mother asked a couple of questions and they realized they actually had no idea what they were doing. Science, evidently, was more difficult than the documentaries made it look.

When she was fourteen, Penny learned that her grandparents had sold off the big crop field. A developer was going to build a shopping center on it. The beautiful land her family used to *feed people* would become an ugly old row of box stores! Grampy explained that money was tight, and farming didn't pay as much as it used to, because of climate change and other things, but Penny would not be consoled. She hadn't even been consulted. This was a Major Tragedy For Real This Time, and so in rage and in mourning she shaved her head. She really wanted to shave her eyebrows, too, as she'd read somewhere the Ancient Egyptians did when they lost their pet cats, and a farm is as important as a cat, isn't it? You can't eat cats. Well, you could, but she wouldn't. Anyway, she had a feeling the eyebrow thing wouldn't fly with her mother. The shaved head wasn't exactly popular either, but there was a line, and she knew where it was.

Penny also refused to go visit the maimed and damaged farm. Instead of seeing each other in person that summer, she and Krista spent hours on the phone talking about farmland conservation and environmental activism and also the lyrics to various songs by Dar Williams and Ani DiFranco and which of the male lifeguards at the pool where Krista worked might be good in bed. Not that either Penny or Krista had any experience whatsoever in that regard.

Krista did come visit for two weeks in August. They ended up sitting on the fire escape together, breathing in the muggy, New York City night, with a bottle of wine Krista had smuggled in and the guitar Penny was learning to play. Penny gamely took an experimental swig, but the transgression unnerved her. She quickly passed the bottle back. Krista, whose parents weren't Mormon, experimented more extensively. The guitar chords gradually became more confident, more fluid, more like music.

"Wine, women, and song," announced Krista and giggled, a bit off-kilter. "I guess we're the women."

"No, we're the singers," Penny replied, sharply. "For us, it's wine, *men*, and song." She, like Dar, had resolved to be the seer, not the seen.

That September, her hair grown out at least far enough to approximate respectability, Penny started high school—a Catholic school at her father's insistence. He had been raised Catholic, and while he had converted to Mormonism for the sake of Penny's mother, he still thought the Catholics provided the better education. Penny found she agreed. The nuns were strict but fair and introduced Penny to actual reason, a skill and a discipline above and beyond her habitual mere reasonableness. Unfortunately, the nuns themselves seemed not to actually use the powers of reason they taught, since they believed the most twisted things—so did Mormons, she realized. In fact, the more she thought about it, the more religion in general came to seem like a pretty raw deal to Penny. She read up on feminist history and theory, Goddess thealogy, mythology and ritual design, and Earth-centered spirituality. She learned to read Tarot cards and found a meditation hall where she could sit zazen. After two years she relented and returned to her grandparents for the summer, but she wasn't a child anymore, so everything, not just the old-cropfield-now-shopping-center, was different. And her grandparents didn't approve of her new interests any more than her parents did. When she got home in the fall, she tried to dye her hair purple, but it wouldn't take on her natural black.

"When I'm *old* I'll wear it purple!" she announced, poetic reference deliberate, anticipating gorgeous and dye-able milk-white locks.

"If you live that long," said her mother, darkly, joking yet not joking.

"Could be worse, Mom," Penny replied, quite seriously. "I could be turning into a Republican." There, her mother agreed. For all their narrow piety, Penny's parents were the progressive sort of Mormon. They went so far as, when she started experimenting with kitchen magic, to be glad she was learning to cook.

She graduated high school with honors, then announced her intention not to go on Mission. She was formally leaving the Church. Instead, she took up her own sort of Mission, backpacking from the Delaware Water Gap to Mt. Katahdin on the Appalachian Trail, then thru-hiking the Adirondack Trail southbound, making a big circuit. On the way, she taught herself to play the flute. It fit in her pack nicely, and its voice seemed to match the forest somehow.

Of course she would go to college, but she wasn't sure what she wanted to go *for*. The old dream of forming a musical duo with Krista had hit a major snag in that Krista wasn't actually interested in making music. Not for real. She was going to be a dental hygienist. Anyway, Penny had realized that becoming a professional musician would entail spending a lot of late nights playing in crowded, stinky bars, so that was out, but what was in? Her plans for herself swung wildly. She would be a ridgerunner on the Appalachian Trail. She would join EarthFirst! and handcuff herself to trees—it would be glorious. She would be a Buddhist nun. She would be a school-teacher. She would be a large-animal vet and go work in a zoo, caring for endangered species. She would be a light-house keeper and play her flute in duet with the cruel and crashing waves. She managed to apply to several colleges without first making up her mind.

She chose a small school in New England with a program that consisted entirely of supervised independent studies. It meant she could earn a liberal arts degree while living anywhere and doing anything, provided she had time to read and write and could plug in a laptop computer and get to a post office occasionally. She spent an entire semester studying Leonard Cohen lyrics as literature—the rhythm of the line about the break, no, the *crack* the light comes in especially appealed to her. She spent another semester reading up on the scientific basis of miracles. She read Rilke. She read Rumi. She read Pablo Neruda. She learned how to properly cite papers and how to spell "rheumatism," a word that had previously eluded her. She got serious about Buddhism but strictly on an impermanent basis. Through all of it she ran the blue prayer thread of music almost without meaning to, and she was mildly surprised to discover afterwards that she'd gone to college for music after all.

All during her undergrad days and for a few years afterwards she worked a series of interesting jobs for next to no money in interesting parts of the country. She was a field hand on small, organic farms in Vermont,

Maine, Utah, and Washington (the western part, near Seattle). She spent a season as a kind of shop assistant for an artists' collective in Boston where she called herself an intern and learned how to Dumpster-dive for food. In Philadelphia, she tutored at-risk children in English, history, and geography. When she learned her grandparents had let most of the orchard go for a housing development, she did mushrooms for the first time with a man she'd met along the way, and she cried. She got a job in a hostel in Flagstaff, Arizona, where she attended puja every week for a Hindu goddess whose name she afterwards could not recall and also visited a women's sweat lodge in the desert outside of town. She went to Big Pine Key, Florida, to work in another hostel, and bicycled to the grocery store through limestone-white puddles in the outer bands of a hurricane and later did more mushrooms. She spent way too much time sitting on her luggage in bus stations at three AM, and when she had to call the IRS to ask what state she lived in for tax purposes, she knew she didn't want to be psychologically homeless anymore.

Turning in the air of her life like a boomerang—she actually thought this, *I am turning in my life like a boomerang, or maybe a comet!*—she returned to her parents' apartment in New York to re-group. There she spent a couple of weeks pretending to look for a job while actually reading lots of Ursula K. LeGuin books ("Mom, I've decided I want to be Ursula K. LeGuin when I grow up." "Aren't you grown up already?" "Evidently not, since I am not yet Ursula K. LeGuin"), then awoke one morning knowing in her bones that she should teach music.

Penny took a couple of classes that she felt her earlier studies had neglected, then started a masters' program in education with licensure. She expected to get a professionally important piece of paper out of the deal, and did so, but she got something else, too.

"You're not as...flighty as you used to be," was the way her mother put it.

"Your convolutions have straightened out," her father opined.

But they were both wrong, or rather, not entirely right. Rather, she had discovered the ability to focus, as if it were a muscle she'd always had but just hadn't known how to use on purpose before. Now, she could flex it—or not—any time she wanted.

When she finally got a job teaching band to elementary school students, she found she loved the work but disliked her employer. She particularly hated the school building, which smelled funny and had no natural lighting. But, she reflected, the kids couldn't leave, except by getting older, so she would try to stick it out with them.

By then she was married and living in a rather upscale apartment on the other side of town with a truly odd man—literally, as his initials spelled ODD: Otter Delano Darling. "Otter," of course, was a nick-name, but nobody, not even his parents, called him anything else. Her friends didn't approve, telling her she should take more time to enjoy herself while she was young, but Penny thought she could enjoy herself quite well with Otter. Anyway, having grown up Mormon, she didn't think twenty-six was all that early to get hitched. She thought of herself as quite grown up now, and it was Otter's maturity that drew her to him. He was fourteen years her senior and acted like it—he had *renter's insurance*, for crying out loud! He had an established career and everything! Guys her age mostly still seemed like boys, but Otter was a real man.

Penny did not at first realize how her marriage, far from solidifying her adulthood, would undermine it, placing her always in close relation to someone more experienced, better prepared, and more resourced than she. And whenever she learned another layer of personal responsibility, he would pick up some new thing she hadn't thought about before, edging ahead of her again. But she'd been a slightly precocious child for such a large portion of her life that it took her a while to realize she was still being treated as one—by her husband and by all his family and friends.

Not that her marriage wasn't also grand.

Otter was a Quaker, a psychologist, and an activist. He expanded her world just by being in it, opening her eyes to social justice, local politics, and an entire vocabulary of personal growth, development, and interpersonal connection. They attended organizational meetings, had lunch with people who served on the boards of various non-profits, and marched in demonstrations carrying signs. And they talked to people, all sorts of people. Arabic Muslims, some of them the pampered scions of super-wealthy families, others shell-shocked refugees. Graffiti artists, some legal, some not. People who were mentally ill and open about it. People who attended protest marches in electric wheelchairs, shouting slogans by repeatedly tapping an icon on their speech synthesizers. People experiencing homelessness but not by choice. Penny was startled to realize that she'd spent her life thus far simply not seeing whole swaths of humanity. Chastened, she resolved to unlearn the habit of ignoring, to root it out again and again as needed, and Otter heard her resolve and honored it.

Mornings, she'd wake an hour or two before Otter did, wrap herself in her bathrobe, put the coffee on, read some Rilke, some Snyder, or maybe something by Terry Tempest Williams, write in her diary, and then sit zazen for fifteen minutes. She charted the course of the year by when in all that process the sun would appear in the kitchen window and how the yellow-white rectangle of sunlight would make its way across the floor.

With Otter, she went to talks and lectures and concerts. With Otter, she subscribed to magazines like *The Atlantic*, *The Smithsonian*, and *The New Yorker*. They bickered amicably about who would get the *New York Times Book Review* first. They attended religious services, though not always together, since Penny had no wish to become a Quaker. Instead, she joined a nearby Unitarian Universalist congregation that took in pagans and agnostics and whatever Penny was these days and let them be. Afterwards, she and Otter would discuss their respective spiritual pursuits over comically over-complicated coffees. They had a joint bank account, but also each had their own, and Penny started saving her own money rather than spending that of her parents. She and Otter almost never left the city. It felt like they almost never went outside.

And somewhere along the way, quiet, bookish, self-possessed Penny became shy. She never had been before.

She was aware of that last change and puzzled over it. Problems have solutions, but the obvious solution—to hop on a bus and go thru-hike the Pacific Crest Trail or something—wasn't really what she wanted to do. Not anymore. No other solutions occurred to her.

Into her confusion came a pregnancy (it *really* should not have been a surprise) and a tragedy, a Real Tragedy I'm Not Being Melodramatic This Time—the deaths of Penny's grandparents, one after the other in quick succession.

Negotiating grief and pregnancy at the same time was difficult. The matter of inheritance just made everything harder.

The remnant of the farm, just the house and two acres of land, plus the wooded part that had a conservation easement on it, had been left, not to Penny's father and uncle, but to the three grandchildren, Penny and her cousins. There was a little money, too, plus some insurance, but not much. The assumption, clearly, was that the cousins would sell the property and split the proceeds among them, a nice little windfall after taxes and so forth. Penny said no.

"I want the place," she said. "I want to live there."

"Sure, buy me out, then," said one cousin.

"You can have my share for free," said the other, "but you'll have to pay my share of taxes and everything, too."

So Penny talked to her husband. He agreed in principle, even though it meant upending his life and re-organizing his career, but said she had to make it happen. For a shy person, even a newly-shy person, making things happen proved difficult, but she buckled down. "Taxes and everything" turned out to be a problem, since the place needed a lot of work, and property tax, heating, and maintenance costs were all going to be high for a rickety old house sitting on what would otherwise be prime commercial real estate. They had some money set aside, but not enough. So she talked to her parents and uncle. She talked to a lawyer and to one of the non-profit people she'd met over lunch, someone from an agricultural land trust. She talked to the historic structure preservation people. She talked to her banker. Very little of that helped. She called Krista to complain about the whole situation.

"Great! When can I move in?" Krista said.

"Next Tuesday, at a quarter to four."

"I'm serious."

"Then....I think I am, too."

Krista had been living with her parents, saving up to buy a house. She had a good job at a local dental office, and had already saved quite a bit, enough to fill the hole in Penny's budget. Krista did indeed move in on a Tuesday, though it was a Tuesday several months after that phone call, and she and Otter became joint breadwinners for the little family while Penny stayed home with the baby, the vegetable garden, the surviving remnant of the apple orchard, and a couple of big, old hickory trees and two walnuts.

The place was a raw wound of assaulted memory, so much gone, just a narrow patch stretching back to the woods with the development on one side and stream with its wooded strip on the other, then the hated shopping center on the other side of that. Penny swore never to use that shopping center and never to be friends with anyone from the development, but of course she upheld neither oath for long. She did her best to heal by tending her garden.

Soon, there was a second baby (another girl) and a pet pig named Wanda. Penny had wanted a dog. Oh, how she had wanted a dog. She had always wanted a dog (an Irish setter, ideally, though she wasn't sure why), and she'd never had one, for reasons she could not now understand. But Otter was allergic. So they got a pig. Wanda lived in a fenced run with a little wooden hut, not in the house as a dog would have, but spent much of her time free in the yard with her human family. When Penny and the girls took her on walks to the woods for acorns and other goodies, the animal graciously pretended not to be strong enough to rip the leash in half. She was a good pig.

Having the pig meant finding a vet willing to treat a pet pig, which proved tricky but doable. That's how Penny and Otter discovered two other couples, the Wojciechowskis and the Clevengers, who also had pigs, a sow and a boar respectively. And since pigs really need the company of other pigs, soon they were all arranging porcine play dates and meeting each others' friends and children.

Penny found a new UU congregation to belong to (one that actually included both a Buddhist study group and an amateur adult choir), and she took on a few private students, but even after the girls were both in preschool she did not seek a job. She had one—making a home for five people and a pig.

It occurred to Penny that life might just be like this now, that the part of her life where things changed rapidly and a year or two constituted a long time might just be over. She had very mixed feelings about that.

Then the pandemic happened.

Penny was the first person she knew to get sick, which ought to have been impossible, but there it is. That was when the new disease was starting to cause serious problems in New York and a few other cities, but for most people the pandemic was just a story on the news, one it was still possible to pretend would go away so everything could return to normal. For Penny, the disease felt like a really bad flu, with the added features of pink-eye, diarrhea, and a tight, itchy, blotchy rash across her cheeks and forehead. The worst of it was over after a couple of days, with only some residual weakness and shortness of breath, and she'd done such a good job of keeping herself isolated that she hadn't infected her family, a Minor Miracle, surely.

Alright, I can handle this, she thought, her mind on whatever difficulty and disruption the ongoing public health crisis might bring. And, to her surprise, she *could* handle it, even when, two weeks later, Otter, then the girls, then Krista all got sick within two days of each other, leaving Penny the only one in the house able to get out of bed for more than a few minutes at a time. She knew not to fear getting sick again—you couldn't, it was like chicken pox or measles that way—but it was a lot to keep up with, especially as her own lungs still weren't quite working right.

And then it got worse.

Otter woke her at two AM, unable to catch his breath, burning hot to the touch. Even as she called 911, she watched his lips start to turn purplish.

The paramedics came in their masks, their shields, their gloves, and their weird, drapey suits, and they gave Otter an oxygen mask, started an IV line, and took him away with them. Krista assured Penny she was feeling a little better and could manage, so Penny drove off to the hospital, following the ambulance.

That night, talking to doctors and nurses, she learned a great deal that she wished she had not had occasion to know, including scary words and phrases such as blood-gas analysis, perfusion, decompensatory shock, and cytokine storm. Around eight in the morning, a very tired, very sad doctor asked her for permission to sedate and intubate Otter.

"I gotta level with you, though, most people who get to this point never wake up."

Penny let that sink in, but it wouldn't sink.

"Why don't you ask *his* permission?" she asked, focusing on the one part of the situation she seemed able to grasp.

"Because he can't answer. He's not getting enough oxygen to his brain to think."

"Can I see him?"

"You've already had the disease? Then yeah. Just sign some paperwork and suit up, so it won't get on your clothes. Come on."

And so on she went.

She tried to ask Otter what he wanted, unwilling to believe he couldn't meaningfully decide, but the words wouldn't come. He looked at her.

"Breathe!" he whispered, begging. He didn't have the air to say anything else, though he was on oxygen already. Her face crumpled.

"Intubate him," she said.

She had to leave the room while they did it, but she was allowed back in afterwards. He looked like he was sleeping, except for all the equipment plugged into him. She sat on the edge of his bed and took his hand.

Oh Darling, she said, though not aloud. *I promised till death do us part, but I didn't think it would happen so soon.*

For the next six hours she became a volunteer nurse's assistant with a single patient, watching monitors, switching out IV bags, double-checking procedures. Not that she'd had more than fifteen minutes' training in any of that, and probably even them asking for her help was illegal, but in the two weeks since her own illness the plague had intensified exponentially, and the hospital was now over-run. Any pair of properly-gloved hands was put to work.

When it was over, Penny kissed Otter's hand and went home, but she could not weep, nor even sleep yet, because she could not wake Krista. She couldn't wake the girls, either, who both lay sweat-damp in soiled, stinking sheets. She called 911 again.

I am getting way too good at this, she thought.

The paramedics came and pronounced both girls badly dehydrated. They thought Krista had passed out shortly after Penny left, meaning the girls had been virtually hemorrhaging moisture through diarrhea without adult care for almost twelve hours. IVs started, the girls were taken away.

The paramedics wouldn't take Krista.

They did set her up with a portable oxygen concentrator, an IV for rehydration, and an injection of something or other, but they wouldn't take her in.

"We can't do anything for her that you can't do here," one of them explained, sounding funny through layers of protective equipment. "She needs oxygen, and if she needs more than this concentrator can deliver, we can't provide it. We've got people dying in hallways waiting for a ventilator. We just don't have any more."

"One just got freed up," objected Penny. Her own calmness struck her as surreal, but then everything was surreal now, since she'd had two hours of sleep in the last thirty-two and couldn't remember when she'd last eaten or drank. And she was a widow. She kept forgetting that part.

"I know," said the paramedic. "But it has already been reassigned."

"So, what, you can just decide not to treat people now?" Anger flared into her voice.

"Field triage, yes. As of—oh, God, *when* did I come on shift? Eight, nine hours ago." When she opened her mouth to argue and nothing came out, the paramedic reached as though to place a gloved hand on her shoulder, but of course did not. Nobody touched anybody anymore. "Eat something. Drink water. Sleep. Take care of yourself so you can take care of your friend."

And the paramedics were gone.

Penny did as she'd been told. When she woke it was dark outside again. She got up, turned on some lights, grabbed a granola bar, made some coffee. Her phone rang. She answered it. She said yes and no and I understand, even though she didn't, and, numb but still handling it somehow, went upstairs to check on Krista. She switched on the room light and found the IV bag empty and Krista's eyes open and blinking.

Penny took out the IV line as she'd been taught, putting pressure across the pinprick wound with some gauze and then taping the gauze down, then checked the flow rate of the oxygen, made sure Krista's cannula was properly positioned so it wouldn't fall off, then sat down on the bed and took her friend's hand. She was exhausted in a way no sleep could fix, too exhausted for capitalized tragedy of any kind, light-headed for reasons that had nothing to do with her hair. Reality had gone strangely flat. There were indeed cracks in everything, she could see them now, all over, but the light seemed to be leaking out, not in. Insatiably hungry darkness nibbled, gnawed, beckoned—but those lyrics brought no comfort, for neither the intricacies of Leonard Cohen nor the harmonies of the Indigo Girls played in her conscious mind. Far beyond coherence or relevance, the music in Penny's head at that moment consisted of a single line from a Flintstones Children's Vitamins commercial stuck on endless repeat.

"I'm going to die a deadly death, aren't I?" Krista said, her voice full of sad irony. Penny grunted, a single *chuck* of a chuckle. She felt a twitch of a smile.

"Not today," she replied. "Not this week, not this year. You can't. There were only three tickets out of this house, and all three of them have been used." Did Krista even know what that meant? Penny could feel her friend's eyes on her face, but glanced away. "So, you'll have to stay here with me."

"Alright, I will," said Krista, after a pause.

And she did.

Gradually, Krista recovered. Penny "made arrangements" for her husband and children. She tried not to worry about not being able to get her parents on the phone. She made a batch of pumpkin bread, and it made her cry. Everything made her cry, it seemed, except the deaths of her family. For that she had no release. Getting through each day felt rather like learning to ride a bicycle, that moment when she'd realized she was balancing, proceeding down the road on two wheels for the first time, without really knowing how or why. When Krista didn't need the concentrator anymore, Penny returned it and the other medical stuff to the hospital and went shopping on the way back. She didn't need anything, she'd made a point of stocking up weeks earlier, plus all the canning she'd done from the garden, but she had a feeling she shouldn't dip into the emergency supplies yet. She kind of wanted to add to her long-term supplies, actually, but at the store she realized so did everyone else. The shelves gaped bare, almost whole aisles empty—no toilet paper, no duct tape, no pasta, no canned beans, and no meat.

"People are buying up meat?" she asked, incredulous. Meat wouldn't keep, so why hoard it?

"No," said the shelf-stocker. "The meat-packing plants are closed. There's nobody healthy enough to run them."

"Then this is a day no pigs will die." She'd always liked that book, but had not expected to be able to use its title in real life.

"Oh, they'll die," the stocker told her. "There's nobody to feed 'em, either."

Penny left the store with a week's worth of whatever food she could find, a compromise between her competing impulses. She was furious and grief-stricken about all the pigs, everywhere.

When she got home, she found Krista sitting at the kitchen table, stirring and stirring and stirring a cup of elecampane tea, staring off into space. As Penny started to put away the groceries, Krista seemed to come back from somewhere very far away.

"They're running out of food, aren't they?" Krista asked. "Bill called." She meant Bill Wojciechowski, one of the pig-people. "It's going to get bad."

"What do you mean, it's going to get bad? It *is* bad."

"It's going to get worse. Penny, have you noticed? There aren't any delivery trucks on the road anymore. There aren't enough healthy drivers. How is anybody going to recover if they can't buy food? Or if they can't get gasoline? Gas comes on trucks, too. And once people do get better, how are they going to start delivering food again if they don't have gas? How will they start delivering gas again if they don't have food? And look at us—if you had a job, you wouldn't be at it. You'd be home looking after me. That's *two* workers out. Across the country, a *million* people are sick right now. How many are out of work looking after them? How many are recovering but still too weak to work? Next week, all those numbers will be bigger. There's no, there's no stopping it. *Can* you turn off a country and turn it on again?"

A million?

Penny turned and tilted her head, as though listening for something. She often did that when she was thinking, though she was unaware of the habit.

"We should call Bill back," she said. "See if he has any ideas. We have to do something."

So they called the Wojciechowskis. They also called or texted their other friends in the area. They got very few responses. Most of those who did answer thought Penny and Krista were over-reacting, that the idea of the country "turning off," as Krista put it, was simply another one of the alarmist, often paranoid ideas sweeping the country. Conspiracy theories. Fake news. Wake up, sheeple.

"First of all, I would never refer to anyone as *sheeple*," Penny said, on her dignity. "It doesn't even have a natural singular form."

"I think it sounds cute," opined Krista. "Sheeple would be fuzzy and, you know, bleat."

"The threat's real, though. We're not making this stuff up."

"That's what all the conspiracy theorists say."

But of course the Wojos took it seriously, Bill having been the one to warn Krista in the first place, and the Clevengers (the other pig-people) took it seriously, too. So did Brian, Rosa Clevenger's friend and ex-husband, and Amanda, Lee Clevenger's best friend. At first, none of them, not even Bill, had any idea what to do, but they all thought they ought to do it together, and that it ought to involve a large amount of food.

"We have enough for two months," Penny said, "for eight people." They were all meeting in her dining room over coffee.

"I think with all our supplies added in it will be enough for three months, maybe four," put in Bill. "But we need enough for six, until the garden gets going. And we need a garden. A big one."

"I have a garden" said Amanda.

"I have one too," said Penny. "And fruit trees."

"I feel like we need to consolidate," put in Krista. "If we're going to end up living in Mad Max World or something, we're going to need a little defensible kingdom. We need something we can all be inside of." She made a box-like shape with her hands.

"I'm not sure I like the implications of that," said Penny. "Defending ourselves inside of something means keeping everybody else out. What's going to happen to *them*?"

"Die, probably," said Amanda. "Us or them. What? If we're going to be living in a dystopia, we're going to have to start thinking that way."

"I can't believe this is happening," muttered Penny.

"Alright, but I am *not* riding a motorcycle and calling myself a Vulvalini," insisted Rosa, referring to a group of warrior women in one of the Mad Max Movies.

"'Vulvalini' is plural, anyway," put in Brian. "You'd be a Vulvalino."

And so, swinging erratically from practical discussion to the edge of breakdown to plain goofiness and back again, they gradually evolved a plan.

They all squeezed into Penny's house, the others leaving most of their stuff behind in their old houses, which they hoped to keep and return to, after whatever would happen finished happening. They brought all their food, though, and Amanda, Brian, and Lee brought their hunting weapons, a varied arsenal of bows and rifles. They planned also to watch for human thieves, if it came to that. The Wojos brought their children's climbing structure and reassembled it in the backyard, although they could not bring their children—they'd sent their three daughters to stay with relatives in Wisconsin, back when getting away from major population centers seemed sensible. Now, with the travel bans in place and gas supplies becoming intermittent, there was no way to get them back.

"If you build it, they will come?" said Bill, half-mocking himself. All of them had children's things but no children. At least the Wojo girls and Rosa's teenage son with Brian were probably still alive. There were other losses, besides children, too. At least one of them would break down at least once a day.

There wasn't much to do, and what needed to be done mostly could not be. The funerals had to be postponed indefinitely because of the ban on public gatherings. The ashes of Otter, of Brian's husband, of Penny's girls, of Rosa and Lee's baby, all sat in simple urns on the mantle-piece, a melancholy row. Penny had no way to check on her parents, who still hadn't answered their phones or emails, because the city was on total lock-down and you needed a permit just to be on the streets there—except nobody seemed to be issuing permits, or at least the relevant officials weren't answering their phones or email. Krista was in the same situation, as her parents had gone to visit friends in the city just before the lock-down order came, and nobody had heard from them since. The police, now critically short-staffed, refused to do wellness-checks anymore. Pleading made no difference.

At least the pigs were settling down together. There was plenty of pig feed. And Lee, who had worked in an auto shop (until it closed for the pandemic) and still had access to its equipment, built a serviceable wood-fired cook-stove, enough rain barrels for every corner of the house and the barn, and an indoor barrel for holding melted snow. On Penny's recommendation, he also built a mesophilic composting privy, though nobody used the privy as long as their well-pump kept their indoor plumbing working. Krista recovered enough to bicycle into the office where they were still doing some emergency dental work. When she got home, she mostly slept. Rosa integrated the book collections of five households into a semi-organized library, and Penny and Amanda put their heads together over their seed collections and garden diagrams and thought about spring.

And outside the traffic on the road got lighter and lighter.

The world was growing quiet. Nobody traveled, except sometimes by ambulance. Nobody did much online or answered their phones. TV and radio stations were, one by one, going off the air or switching to news-only, but there wasn't much news because there weren't a lot of reporters. On clear days, Penny could look up at a blue sky absolutely clean—there were no jet trails, none at all.

"I had thought the end of civilization would be more dramatic," she said one day, looking up.

"Do you remember my cat?" asked Krista, in response.

"Of course I remember your cat."

"When he died, I was there. He didn't meow, or struggle, or anything. He was just breathing. And the breaths got softer and softer and farther apart. And then there just weren't any more."

"Otter kept breathing, because of the machines. Or—he kept being breathed, I suppose. This isn't bad, actually, as apocalypses go."

Two days later, the electricity went out and did not come back on.

The remaining weeks of winter passed and became spring. Only indirect signs, distant implications, suggested the horror going on in the world beyond their home. A great column of smoke rose in the distance in the direction of New York City. Gunshots sounded, some near, some far. Possibly people were hunting, possibly not. Twice, people approached the house and tried to look in the windows, but Amanda ran them off, gun in hand. Once, somebody in the distance screamed. An oddly well-organized mob systematically removed everything edible from the shopping center. Before Penny and her house-mates could make up their minds to risk joining in, the mob went away again and left everything quiet. In the housing development next door, nobody moved—no dogs barked there, no children laughed or shrieked, and at night there was no glow of candle or torchlight. Amanda went to reconnoiter and reported the place abandoned, its locks not hard to force (she'd been a lawless youth). They all went over together. Penny was surprised, and a little disturbed, by how much she enjoyed methodically stripping the hated housing development of its goods. She lit the last of her store-bought incense in honor of the people whose canned goods and toilet paper she helped take. The spring that year was beautiful, dry and warm and clear.

Spring became summer. Deer walked across the empty main road to graze on the unmowed median strip. Birds and bats took advantage of the insects growing up on lawns and fields that never got sprayed. Bill and Lee each brought home a big buck. Both sows turned out to be pregnant (it really shouldn't have been a surprise) and soon produced twenty-three piglets between them. Young pigs after weaning need either very high-quality forage or prepared feed. As there wasn't enough of either, the fate of the piglets didn't require much discussion.

"I'm sorry we can't leave you even one," Penny told Wanda one evening, speaking mother-to-mother and feeling terrible. The pig looked up at her, hearing the sympathy but not understanding the reason for it.

All of the meat, pig and deer, became the responsibility of Tin Wojo, Bill's wife, who was as passionate about preserving food as Penny and Amanda were about producing it. Her real name was Kristin, but the others called her Tin—early in their mutual acquaintance, she'd insisted that she was KrisTIN, not KrisTA. Besides canning and fermenting and drying all sorts of vegetables and fruit, she made sure no molecule that had once been part of a living animal ever went to waste.

The much-expanded vegetable garden, the apple and nut trees, and the nearby forest fed Penny and her housemates and fed also the deer and the pigs that fed the humans in turn (once the piglets were weaned and slaughtered, both sows promptly got pregnant again), fed them all

23

gradually but finally in glorious abundance. By winter, the kitchen, pantry, and basement were all full of food again.

Through winter, there was again very little to do. Penny missed working in the earth, but the earth was frozen more days than not. Instead, she took up her reading. She went for long walks in the woods, hoping not to meet any trespassing hunters. She spent hours every day playing the piano, filling the house to overflow with the grand, rich voice of her grandparents' old, worn instrument. She sat on the stairs by the window and tried to decide exactly what color to call each patch of snow.

And she took up meditation again. She wasn't sure when or why she had stopped. It came to her, meditating and re-reading her old copies of *Tricycle* and *Shambala Sun*, that yes, all her pain of the past year followed directly from having been attached—to her husband, to her daughters, to various friends, to her daily life as it used to be. And yet, she would not have willingly forgone the attachment in favor of less pain now. She wasn't sure she wanted less pain, actually. Pain meant something. Anyway, she couldn't see how painlessness by itself could be any sort of point at all. Was pain, then, distinct from suffering? Was the attachment to her girls not the sort of attachment the Buddha had meant?

The others came and went through her solitude. She liked them, and her liking impressed itself on her mind, quiet and simple as her fondness of the worn, dusty, utterly familiar floorboards of her grandparents' house, or of the dried grasses—two kinds of *Setaria*, the tubular timothy, and the lovely pink thing whose name she did not know—that Krista had put in an empty vase and set on the edge of the bookshelf months ago. Krista herself was like that pink grass, both in her loveliness and in her essential mystery.... It was only with those Penny knew best that she could appreciate how little she knew, how little anyone could know, about another human being. And yet these others surrounded her. Krista, yes, of course and always, but now also Bill, compassionate butcher of piglets; Lee, still touchingly vain about his old racing bibs and high-end shoes; Brian, once a professional chef, but now, to salve his grief, learning everything he could about apple-growing; Rosa, salving hers by unflagging, even neurotic, helpfulness; Amanda, with her smart-ass mouth and her vast skill with plants grown for seasoning, medicine, and joy; Tin, with whom Penny had once spent long afternoons in a kind of sisterhood of stay-at-home mothers, together pursuing one or another intricate skill last practiced by pioneer women—it had been a Quixotic, totally impractical, group of hobbies, once.

Funny, Penny had always had trouble feeling any kind of belonging to anything of which she herself could not be the center—and she wasn't the center of much, only her own life. But now, just now, and for the first time, the thought occurred to her that a circle is defined by its periphery as much as by its middle. It came to her that perhaps the church of her childhood had been right in that salvation is only ever achieved together.

Spring came again, spring with the feel of the warming earth in Penny's hands and the sound of the bees in the apple blossoms. Digging, planting, transplanting, weeding, the others helped sometimes, but Penny wanted most of the work for herself, as much as she could do. Tending her garden, leaning a moment on the sweat-darkened handle of her shovel, there were times she could see the light come upon her at last, not in place of, or despite, or even necessarily because of the brokenness that she knew now would always be, it's just that sometimes there was light for a moment, light shining off the trees along the little stream or filtering through the hickory or apple leaves or glowing through the rosy mist that sometimes lifted from the damp earth first thing in the morning. She liked being out there to see it, to catch those rare moments when she *could* see it. Usually she still couldn't.

She was out tending her garden when an outsider, a woman named Melanie whom Penny knew slightly, came to talk and to begin the process of assembling something new.

There was no going back to the quasi-rural sprawl that had existed before the pandemic. The old community had died. Too many of its people were dead or otherwise gone, and that essential economic fact, the automobile, was gone, too. Any houses that had been left untended (including those left by Penny's housemates) had been looted, most left open to the elements and now uninhabitable. But about a thousand people, mostly in little multi-family clumps on newly-made subsistence farms, had survived within ready walking distance of each other. Some had lived in the area before—some Penny knew—while others had come in from somewhere else, refugees seeking food and safety, going to ground as Penny and Krista had in the last days of the old civilization. They began by trading seeds, breeding stock, and supplies. Penny's group traded piglets for corn with which to feed their remaining animals. In time, they hoped to also trade for some chickens. The trading quickly evolved into a weekly farmer's market (in the parking lot of the hated, now defunct, shopping center) with a basic town government to organize it. And soon, there was something that resembled a church.

The church started with the funerals.

There were no funeral homes left, nor were any of the members of the new community a clergy member of any kind, yet services could not be put off indefinitely. So first one family, then another, gathered with friends new and old to say a few words before scattering ashes, those who had ashes to scatter. Some families had bones, bodies discovered in empty houses after the ambulances stopped running. These they burned in bonfires, the light bright on attendees' faces through the long night. Afterwards, the ashes of the wood and of the people mixed were raked out, dug in, and planted with flowers. Everybody, regardless of their own religious affiliations or lack thereof, would join in whatever songs or prayers might bring comfort to the bereaved, whether those prayers were Protestant, Catholic, Jewish, or something written by Starhawk or even Tolkien. Sometimes there were no remains at all, only a near-certainty that someone had died (of those still in the city when the food trucks stopped coming, there was no rumor of survival), and a need for closure. In this way, Penny let go her husband, her children, her parents, and Krista's parents, who were very nearly hers as well. All gone.

Afterwards, some part of the assembled, mostly those not immediately bereaved that particular week, would remain and sit and chat over food and drink about what they believed or didn't believe about life, death, meaning, and everything else.

The funerals didn't stop, even after all those who had died in the pandemic and the silent year following had been given rest. There were also the more recent dead—many of them, since there wasn't much anyone could do when someone got really sick. There were no doctors, and the supplies of medicine had already run out. But there came a time when the prayers and the songs and the discussions following the private meetings of mourning developed their own momentum, their own structure, and most of the town, including the atheists and agnostics and independent spiritual types, attended every week to be held in that structure together.

When someone suggested they form a choir, Penny joined eagerly. Despite the ongoing funerals, despite the pervasive and persistent brokenness within her and around her, she felt something beginning, something good. Just before heading off to choir practice for the first time, she shaved her head yet again, this time not in mourning or in protest but in celebration. She poured a cup of water over her head to rinse away any clinging hairs, patted dry with a towel, and dropped her severed tresses in the compost. Then, feeling free and unencumbered, she went to be with others and to make a joyful noise.

When someone else suggested, two weeks later, that the community also create a children's choir, Penny spoke almost before she knew what she was going to say.

"I can do that!"

And just like that, she had a job again, of sorts.

It was very different than any other job she'd had before. She wasn't being paid, for one thing, there being no money anymore. For another, she had no boss, no employer. There was nobody at all to tell her what to do or how and when to do it. Should she put in forty hours per week? Sixty? Ten? Who should be in her class, and what should she teach them? "How to sing," yes, but singing could be the tip of a very large educational iceberg, or it could be a free-for-all that didn't require anything but an adult to hand out sheets of lyrics and play piano accompaniment. Penny had never before been truly in charge of anything except her own self. In the years of her marriage, she hadn't even had that very often.

"How am I going to make all these decisions?" she asked herself.

"Pretty well, probably," herself answered.

And she did.

The community then had only eight-hundred-some residents, forty-three of whom were under the age of fifteen. Most of these were older than ten, the pandemic having killed the younger children disproportionately, and Penny decided she'd rather deal with a big age-range than leave the few younger kids out. Thirty came to the first practice, then forty, then all forty-three, and then the number started dropping off again, eventually stabilizing at twenty-five. That answered the question of whom she would teach.

What she would teach was harder. Mica, the youngest, the town's one five-year-old, couldn't carry a tune in a bucket (though he'd happily sing "Do-Re-Mi" over and over and over again all day long), whereas twelve-year-old Aja had a voice like a Gospel singer. It would have been simple to hold auditions and include only those who could meet a certain standard, but Penny had no stomach for telling anyone they weren't good enough to learn. She wanted to treat musical literacy the same as literal literacy, as the right of anyone even remotely capable of it, irrespective of whether they would ever be any good. But she also wanted to promote the pursuit of excellence, and how was she to set a high bar when plainly each of her twenty-five charges would need a different height? She could solve the problem any way she wanted to—she had no school administrators peering over her shoulder, no relevant precedent to follow, and as a volunteer she could not be fired. The little town had only one qualified music teacher, and she was it.

Finally, she settled on offering individual voice lessons to all choir members and then using group practice to integrate, rather than push ahead, all the different voices. That meant putting in a lot of hours, so many she could no longer get much gardening in. Her housemates gladly picked up the slack. She held voice lessons at the house, group practice at the church, and started the kids in on a collection of popular children's hymns from half a dozen different Christian denominations. Because that's what a children's choir director is supposed to do.

Jesus loves me, this I know, for the Bible tells me so. Rise and shine and give God your glory-glory. This little light of mine, I'm gonna let it shine, let it shine, let it shine, let it shine. The kids, especially the younger ones, liked the songs, and their singing was cute, but there was little challenge for the older kids. Worse, the more Penny thought about the matter, the more disingenuous the songs seemed—though ostensibly religious, they expressed neither the mystery of the Ultimate, nor the longing of humanity. They were not the songs Penny herself sang to her God, whoever or whatever that God might be.

On the other hand, anything real enough to express either God or humanity was also likely to offend some parent or other. No two families had the same rules or expectations, but all of them thought they were right.

Finally, she settled on the Everly Brothers. Their sweet, obsessive love songs made very fitting hymns, and she didn't see how anyone could object to such innocent lyrics. Plus, the close harmony would be a fine challenge for some of the older and more talented kids, while the others could sing a simpler version as back-up and thereby replace the instrumental line. Although Penny played the piano or the guitar during practice so the kids could follow the tune better, she liked the idea of a cappella performance.

When "Devoted to You" raised nothing worse than a few eyebrows (and quite a lot of compliments), Penny decided to push the envelope a little farther.

The shift wasn't absolute nor did it ever slide into secularism. Some of the children's hymns stayed in rotation, and some of the new additions were traditional adult religious music from a variety of faiths. But the repertoire swelled with more and more "accidental hymns," as she sometimes called them.

Jimmy Buffet's "La Vie Dansante"

Dar Williams' "Playing to the Firmament"

The Beatles' "Let It Be"

When Aja sang an R&B-laced version of U2's "I Still Haven't Found What I'm Looking For," with the rest of the choir singing, wordless, as her back-up band, some in the congregation wept openly.

All this took time, months and months to get to the point where choir could begin to sound beautiful, rather than merely cute. And all through that time more and more kids were spending more and more time at the house, largely because it had become impossible to keep to an appointment schedule for the lessons. The kids were all emotionally fragile for obvious reasons, and sometimes one or another would show up for the lesson either unable to focus or unable to hear any kind of critical feedback as anything other than personal criticism. The lesson would end early, sometimes before it began. Or the lesson would go long as the kid co-opted the session to tell extended, rambling stories about a missing parent or a dead sibling or some harrowing adventure involving evading police or hiding from bandits, something that might be made-up but, alas, probably wasn't. Or everything would go fantastically right, the music would take over, and neither teacher nor student would be willing to stop. Before long, parents simply dropped kids off for the day. Anyone not currently in with Penny would play together, go pet the pigs, noodle around on the piano, or read whatever they found on the bookshelves. The other adults of the household would keep an eye on them, befriend them, make them lunch, or just allow them to exist in the state of benign neglect in which so much of the best of childhood happens. When Penny discovered a trio of ten-year-old boys studiously reading "*Our Bodies, Ourselves*," she figured she was doing something right.

"It's good having kids here again," said Krista over supper. The last kid had just left, and the housemates were all comparing notes for the day, a tradition they'd recently evolved.

"I guess I built it and they came," said Bill, referring to the children's climbing structure, which had been getting a lot of use lately.

"It feels like we're becoming something," observed Penny.

"Oh, we're something, alright," said Amanda, sarcastic.

"No, really. We're not a school, we're not a daycare, we're not the neighborhood hang-out, and yet we are becoming all three. Or something."

"We're aunts," supplied Krista. "Communal aunts."

"And uncles," put in Brian.

"Communal aunts, I like it," agreed Penny.

"And uncles."

"We could be an auntfarm," suggested Tin.

"And an unclefarm."

"We're aunts *and* uncles," acknowledged Rosa.

"Ankles," supplied Amanda. They all laughed.

The anklefarm (Penny was sad that the name didn't stick) remained the primary place for kids to be, when they were not at home, for several years. Meanwhile, the community of Walmart kept changing, becoming better organized, more cohesive, less focused on mere survival, more connected to the outside world. Medicine, including some antibiotics, filled the pharmacy again. A police force of sorts developed, and a fledgling criminal justice system. There was a committee on the disbursement of abandoned property (Penny asked for and received the land of the hated housing development, but not the houses or their remaining contents) and another committee to decide on which traveling healers should be allowed to practice in town in exchange for food or clothing. The dental office was open again, as Krista and another hygienist offered regular cleanings in barter for eggs or peaches or whatever people had. Sometimes a dentist would visit and work with them for a bit. And still every Saturday evening after the market there was the non-denominational religious service, following or followed by various discussion groups—seminars or salons or meetings, the names and formats varied, but they were all basically the same idea.

Somebody would bring food, while somebody else brought a topic of conversation, usually some community issue or sometimes an intriguing passage of text. There was usually alcohol, sometimes pot, but neither to excess. Nobody had a source of caffeine, yet, though rumor had it some farmer up in the mountains was working on the problem, trying to grow black tea. Each group had five or six regulars, plus a varying cast of drop-ins. Regardless of the specific topic of the week, the conversation was always about the same thing: what the hell kind of world could do what theirs had just done?

Two very different answers gradually emerged.

Some held that the pandemic and its aftermath must have been the doing of a just and loving God trampling the grapes of wrath exactly as long predicted. Others insisted that no such God and no such wrath exists, that the universe is impersonal, amoral, painful—and yet beautiful, intricate, worthy of attention and praise. Other viewpoints, those marked by cynicism, inconsistency, or indifference, mostly sorted themselves out, evolving into either of the other two. Everybody had a sudden need to believe in something, just to keep going.

Penny, though not quite an atheist, was among the most committed to the idea of the impersonal world and among the very few who could find real solace in it. She tried to explain how and why, when other people asked. Some believed her. Among the most prominent proponents of the other, theistic, view was a woman named Alicia, a newcomer to the area (she had arrived during the pandemic, just before the collapse), mother of two young sons, and a breeder of goats and chickens. Penny initially disliked the woman. Alicia was not only a Baptist Bible-thumper but also the leader of a growing—for lack of a better word—clique. Another woman from the same farm, Shania, would sit next to her in discussions, echoing and anticipating Alicia's points like a fourteen-year-old mean-girl toady. Of course, they were polite and tactful at all times, presenting a flawless friendliness of affect that somehow made it worse. But while Penny continued to dislike Shania, she came around on Alicia.

Again and again, Penny and Alicia began a discussion on diametrically opposing sides and then finished up still in diametric opposition—and yet each had changed her position, sometimes radically. Alicia believed the most twisted things, but she explained her beliefs intelligently, even logically, and she asked probing, clever questions. Penny would leave the conversation at the end of the evening with the disconcerting feeling that everything she'd thought to be true and right and important might not be. She'd sit with the feeling, get comfortable with intellectual uncertainty, and return to the table carrying whichever ideas could still stand on their own two feet. Alicia's questions were food for thought, always.

Penny could never shake Alicia's foundations in return. It bothered her. Though eager to understand any point of disagreement, the woman was too sure, too logical, too fast to construct a counterargument, to ever be surprised into true receptivity. And yet she listened, never letting Penny's persistent disagreement make her adversarial, drinking in Penny's points and using them to water her own growing ideas—which had long since ceased to be strictly Baptist, or even really Christian in any traditional sense. In fact, Alicia was becoming convinced that a new, *non*-traditional form of Christianity was at hand, that a new revelation was in progress and would change everything. As an ex-Mormon, Penny found the notion reassuringly familiar, though she didn't exactly agree. The new Christianity seemed to be a good deal more inclusive than the old one—at Alicia's request, Penny taught her Tarot and the basics of ritual design from the Western Occult Tradition, and lent her several books by Joseph Campbell and Karen Armstrong.

The town organized work crews to grub up the asphalt in the shopping center parking lot (it went into an empty PetCo for storage until needed for road repair) and seeded in the beginnings of a pasture. The stripped and soured dirt needed fertilizing before it would grow much of anything, so everybody was encouraged to pee upon it at their nearest convenience, a civic duty Penny enjoyed way too much. Work crews also disassembled the town's abandoned and increasingly decrepit houses, grubbing up driveways and even some roadways as they went, storing all the material in one or another abandoned commercial building. The process started with the hated housing development, leaving at last a vast, broken, muddy field dotted with patches of overgrown lawn, landscaping plantings, and a few surviving apple trees, spared years ago by the developers to look pretty in now-vanished backyards. Brian then led his own work crews in replanting the place, not as an apple orchard but as a food forest, a scattering of apples, pears, quince, cherries, peaches, but also edible natives—hawthorns, Juneberries, mulberries, persimmons, paw-paws, brambles, wild grape, wild cherries, hickories, hazels, walnuts, white oaks, beeches, blueberries, all interrupted and aerated by miniature, flower-filled meadows meant to feed rabbits, honeybees, and deer.

Penny walked through the clumped plantings, imagining how they'd look when they were grown, feeling the sun in her hair and on her scalp (that was the year she kept the left side shaved and let the right side grow) and listening to the flirting and the boasting of birds.

And more and more of the town drifted right, following Alicia's persuasive, persistent logic. Penny was at first curious about the process, then alarmed, but these were her friends. She assumed nothing could really change their interdenominational camaraderie until the day she walked into her discussion group and found that the suggested topic of conversation was *her*.

The problem, it seemed, was Dar Williams' "Mercy of the Fallen," which Penny had recently introduced to the children's choir. Its themes of humility and mercy had seemed much more Christian than some of the other material she'd introduced, and it didn't mention sex anywhere, so she hadn't anticipated an issue, but apparently some of the parents were concerned. Of course, Alicia and Shania took the lead in explaining matters, faultlessly polite as ever. They had *three* impressionable young people on their farm (Aja and her father lived there, too), all of whom were in the choir, and to have them singing a song that seriously questioned the existence of a singular, apprehensible truth might confuse them seriously, I'm *sure* you can appreciate our perspective?

Well, yes, the lyrics could be interpreted that way, but Penny saw that as a feature, not a bug. Surely, anybody with any sense of the realness of *God* would understand humans cannot fully know the infinite? Isn't that the whole point?

But it wasn't the point, not today. The point was, Penny, you fucked up.

Not that anybody said it that way, but the implication was clear. Alicia and Shania were ringleaders, but soon most of the group seemed to be politely brandishing pitch-forks. Not all attacked, but none defended Penny.

Penny had never done well with true animosity, or even real disapproval—shaving her head to shock her parents had been one thing, but her parents had loved her. Among authorities whose favor might be conditional, she'd walked the straight and narrow, except when principle demanded she do otherwise. She'd never even seriously sassed a nun. Now, she sat upright and attentive as the others' words ran together in her mind, feeling the shame of any child lectured by greater power. Until something inside her, quite unexpectedly, snapped.

I've buried my children, she thought. *These people can't do anything to me.*

She stood up.

"I don't have to take this," she said. She left the room.

Alicia caught up with her in the coat-closet.

"I'm sorry, Penny," she said, catching at Penny's sleeve. "None of that came out the way I wanted, and we all got carried away. You're doing a great job, we all think so, and if I didn't respect your perspective, I wouldn't bother to offer you mine. Will you stay and talk with us?"

"Not today," Penny told her, but then relented enough to face Alicia and speak candidly. "I do my job the way I see fit. That's the only way I know how. If you don't want to send your sons to me, don't send them. It makes absolutely no difference to me. Tell the others that, won't you?" And she put on her coat and left.

She went home and found everybody out at their regular this-that-and-the-others, so she took advantage of the emptiness of the house to clean the place top to bottom while singing the few lines she could remember of "My Give-a-Damn's Busted" over and over and over again, sometimes very loudly. When Krista got home, Penny made both of them mint-and-ginger tea and explained the whole affair.

"I don't really know what happened," she admitted, speaking of her sudden snapping.

"Do you know why babies don't get gum disease?" asked Krista.

"I've never thought about it." Penny had learned long ago that Krista's randomness always had a point.

"It's because they've hardly done anything with their mouths. They haven't had a chance to get gum disease. It's only older people who eat weird stuff and skip their six-month-cleanings and forget to floss and have vulnerable mouth-ecology or whatever who get it. Then you go and get treated and learn better habits and whatever, and you get back close to where you were to begin with—a healthy mouth. But it's not the same. Before, you were healthy because nothing had happened to you. Now, something has happened to you, but you're healthy because of what you did about it."

Penny nodded, acknowledging the metaphor.

"I feel like a bad-ass all of a sudden," she said.

"You always were a bad-ass. You were a bad-ass when you were eight years old."

Penny thought about this, recalling terms she had learned from Otter like "primary narcissism" and "secondary amenorrhea," in which *primary* meant you had not yet grown out of something, and *secondary* meant you had returned to it but for a new and maybe unrelated reason.

"I am now a secondary bad-ass," she said, trying the words out on her tongue. "I like it."

No family pulled their kid out of choir after all, and in time Penny did try to explain her choice of songs to the concerned parents, with some success. But a line had been crossed. She briefly considered teaching the kids "The Christians and the Pagans," but quickly saw there was no point in that. She thought about a few other Dar Williams songs, then settled on "Daniel Barrigan," the song about the Catholic priest so committed to peace he was arrested for stealing and burning Vietnam War draft files.

"Let them *try* to pretend Jesus wasn't a revolutionary," she declared, though not out loud.

Nobody tried.

Thus encouraged, Penny began more deliberately choosing songs that said things the kids' parents might not want them to hear. She'd always had a double motive in selecting her material, going back to when she'd taught them "Bye-Bye Love," a strangely upbeat song about heartbreak. Ostensibly, the song was a means of practicing harmony (it wasn't hymn-like, and therefore wasn't for performance), but she'd wanted to give the kids the language to talk about their losses and pain. Now, as the majority of the community (and all the parents, except Mica's father) shifted right, she worried increasingly about what these kids weren't hearing at home—messages of female empowerment, inclusivity, the value of diversity of all kinds. She started introducing practice material, songs not for performance in front of parents, that provided the messages.

It was a tricky thing. Though no longer caring about approval for its own sake, if she drove parents away through too much radicalism, the kids would suffer. She could not, for example, take a few kids aside and say "hey, you're clearly gay or trans or something, so when your parents tell you that's not OK, don't believe them." Outwardly, she had to respect the silence, the firewall of ideas, that left each misfit child alone, believing themselves to be the only one of whatever each of them was. If she did otherwise, they really *would* be alone, unable to find, for example, hidden away where no child could find it except that all of them would, that one copy of *The Atlantic*, or that one novel by Margaret Wander Bonnano, or the framed photograph of Brian and his husband, the one where Brian's face was not recognizable but the love and tenderness of the two men shone clear. It gets better, she was trying to say, it gets better than anything I can do for you now.

She could say that by offering to them her home. And she could sometimes take a step or two beyond by using music to insert certain ideas or phrases into their consciousness, nothing they'd notice now and report back to their families, but maybe something would pop back into their heads later, when they needed it.

Her efforts did not go entirely unnoticed by the parents. And as more and more of the community drifted into the conservative movement, the fact that Penny showed no sign of following began to arouse suspicion.

"People are starting to talk," Krista warned her at breakfast.

"Talk about what?" asked Bill, buttering his hash-browns.

"Me," explained Penny, then glanced away and muttered "sorry I haven't been to church, I've been practicing witchcraft and becoming a lesbian." It was the text of a t-shirt or a bumper-sticker or something she'd seen once.

"But you do go to church," objected Rosa.

"And you're not a lesbian," added Amanda.

"Not as far as *I* know, anyway," hedged Krista, making Bill smirk. Krista, of all people, would know.

"I said 'becoming,' OK?" insisted Penny. "I've got almost everything down. I've got the flannel, I've got the cargo pants, I've got the hair." Hers was relatively quiescent at the moment, neatly trimmed and boy-short. "I've got the super-short finger-nails....It's only the having-sex-with-women part I'm not there with, yet."

"You're not the only one," said Amanda, who was bisexual and had not managed to get anyone into bed for a very long time.

"I always found the having-sex-with-women part difficult myself," put in Brian. "No offense, Rosa."

"I always said you'd make a terrible lesbian," Rosa shot back, then grinned at her ex-husband.

"Let them talk," advised Bill, returning to the subject. "By the time they get around to deciding they don't want you around their kids anymore, there won't be any."

Any kids, he meant. And he was right. At least in what had become the town of Walmart, not only had no very young children survived the pandemic, but none had been born in the first five years afterward. That meant even Mica would grow out of the children's choir before the oldest of the next cohort grew into it. Already, the choir had shrunk from the original twenty-five to just thirteen, five of whom were teenagers and likely to move on any day now. But all thirteen could behave like professionals and sing like soloists, and Penny strongly suspected that if their parents pulled them from choir, they'd all keep showing up at her house anyway. So she went for broke, pushing excellence, pursuing holy transgression, determined to run herself out of a job properly—but preferably slowly enough that she would find herself fired from an empty classroom. She had to get the timing right.

In that spirit, before the teenagers left, she finally had the group perform a program that included "Closer to Fine," an Indigo Girls song that, *as its very point*, argued explicitly against a singular, apprehensible truth. Some of the words and phrases were what Penny would have written about her own life, had she been in the habit of writing poetry, and had Emily Saliers not written it first. She did not talk about herself with the kids, it would have seemed unprofessional, but sharing that song and certain others were the closest she could come. The song worked well, emerging powerfully from the mouths of babes, a growing near-crescendo of sound and meaning.

"You did it," said Krista afterwards. "You finally did it. For real."

"Yes, I suppose I did," Penny replied, thinking, as Krista must be, of afternoons in the woods when they were eight. "*We* did."

But the ending of the choir did not happen as Penny had anticipated. Endings never do.

The last teenager left in the choir, a 15-year-old boy whose voice had not yet changed, was murdered.

At least, his family said he was. Certainly he disappeared. Certainly some of his clothes and a great deal of blood were found off in a pasture where he'd gone alone to check the fences. His horse came back without him. It was the first violent crime in the little community since the year after the pandemic, and it shook everybody. No body and no perpetrator were ever found.

Penny privately had her doubts. Why would anyone kill Geordi? Frankly, she thought the only person likely to do so was Geordi himself. He'd always been a clearly disturbed child, far too obedient and unobtrusive, and lately working way too hard to pretend to be straight. Sometimes, when he thought nobody was looking, he would make a curious gesture that looked way too much as if he were pretending to slit his wrist. Watching him go about his life had been rather like watching an impending train-wreck, yet another reason why Penny wished Otter were still alive and could please just tell her what to do. Children in crisis had been his department, not hers. Watching Geordi, she had felt very much alone. But if Geordi *had* killed himself, where had his body gone and how? More likely he had run away and staged the whole thing, but that was a possibility his mother would not raise. Why not?

What kind of woman would rather think of her son as dead—*murdered*—than as a run-away? Who gives up hope so easily? A woman who wanted to preclude other people's curiosity might. A woman who did not want the child found and questioned might. It had always bothered Penny that while Geordi had, in the first year or two of the choir, told stories about his missing father, no such stories emerged from Adam, his brother. In fact, Adam quite calmly and happily told anyone who asked that he had no father and had never had one. Also, Geordi didn't look like either Adam or their mother.

Their mother was Alicia.

Vague suspicions were enough to end a friendship, an ending that saddened Penny much more than she had expected. Vague suspicions were also enough that Penny chose never to mention to anybody that she thought Geordi might still be alive—let the boy run, if that's what he needed to do. But suspicions were not enough to absolve Penny of her grief. She had not known Geordi well, but he had been a fine singer and an attentive student, and anyway the loss of any young person always ripped open the wounds of her own losses. He *could* have been murdered. She would never know. And any way you sliced it, she had been in a position where she maybe could have done something, but she hadn't known what to do, and the probability that nobody, not even Otter, might have known either didn't really help.

And so the children's choir was over for her. Penny didn't do anything overt to pull the plug—there were still eight kids who counted themselves as members and wanted to continue. But her heart wasn't in it, and they could tell. Possibly, they knew why. Finally, the kids themselves ended it, organizing a farewell concert under the direction of Aja, now a grown woman and long since shifted over to the adult choir. For the first time, Penny attended a performance from the back row. She did not want her kids to be able to see her weep.

Forty years old and once again out of a job, Penny was not sure what she was going to do next. She went back to full-time gardening while she thought about it, and gardening became what she did for a while.

By then, the food-forest was starting to produce—the new trees were still too young, but the various berry bushes were doing well, plus the populations of rabbits and deer and turkey had increased. Penny left the management of the forest to Brian, but she happily took her turn harvesting, usually going out alone before the others were up, eating two berries for every one she dropped in her basket, bringing home raspberry leaves for tea. Thanks to the forest, the farm had, for the first time, more food than its residents needed, so Penny used the abundance to buy and then feed a dog. She named the little border collie mix Ada, and found her an absolute joy.

With that half-grown puppy, both of them muddy, squirrel-chattered, be-leaved and be-seeded from crawling and rolling through the undergrowth, she found herself laughing. It felt like it had been sixty million years since she'd last really laughed. She did not intend to go without laughter ever again.

The curious thing was that she'd *bought* the dog, rather than trading for her. Money existed again, though it wasn't dollars—the new system took some getting used to, but the world was showing definite signs of growing a new civilization. There was even some electricity, mostly from micro-hydropower, and a basic sort of internet. Over the internet came news; two of the Wojo girls had survived, as had Brian and Rosa's now-grown son. Reunions would have to be postponed a while yet, since there was no easy way to travel long distances, but, *inshallah*, would occur.

And then, besides gardening and playing with Ada, Penny found herself building a house.

It was a small thing, made of salvaged boards and cinder blocks, straw bales, and stucco, out in the food-forest. Rosa, though now in her early forties, had decided to start another family and was pregnant. She and Lee intended to have more, so clearly the old farm-house would soon be too crowded. The plan was for Brian to move with them and be a third parent, much as Krista had been for Penny's girls, but all of them would come back to the main house for dinner and sometimes breakfast. Mortaring together salvaged bricks for the chimney or stuccoing over a load-bearing straw bale, Penny put another item on her long list of things she had not expected to do but was nonetheless doing. That, too, made her laugh.

The Clevengers weren't the only ones having babies. A dozen other families had reproduced, and more would soon do so. The new question was, did the town need a school? Some people answered yes, without hesitation. Others argued that the town's first batch of kids had all been home-schooled and had turned out alright, so why not continue that way? Still others thought something more should be offered the kids but weren't sure *school*, as it had existed prior to the pandemic, should be it. A few questioned whether the whole thing might be moot—did anybody in town actually know how to create an educational institution?

Penny, as usual, was willing to invent something, but found her efforts rebuffed. She was still unpopular among certain powerful people. Lee and Rosa had better luck, since nobody wanted to exclude any of the community's parents, but Brian found himself shut out entirely. Most of the others refused to even acknowledge him as a member of the Clevengers' family. Nobody said so directly, but Brian was fairly sure his new and obvious romance with Mica's father had something to do with it. Penny was so outraged by the injustice that she didn't take any time to mentally capitalize anything, but marched herself off to the town's new library and talked her way into a part-time volunteer position as its director. By the time the new learning center opened, the library had a rich children's section with lots of children's programming and an inclusive vibe. Penny personally made sure that books about families of all shapes and sizes and orientations occupied the shelves. No child would be dependent for educational resources on an institution that denied the legitimacy of their family.

The learning center and the children's library were both designed to provide resources and community to homeschoolers. They were more formal versions of what the anklefarm had been. But as the new cohort of kids got older, it became clear that teenagers would need something more.

Homeschooling worked well for subjects like reading or basic math that all the parents knew and could teach, but not all families included someone who understood pre-calculus or basic chemistry, and while everybody agreed that kids ought to learn CPR, there was no one in town who could teach it. The town would have to hire teachers from some other community, and you can't hire teachers if you don't have a school. And since Penny was the only one around with a master's degree in education, the others more or less had to swallow their politics and ask for her help.

Of course, since circumstances called for re-thinking education from the ground up, most of her academic training was close to irrelevant, but she didn't remind anyone of that. Instead, she and several interested others formed a committee to explore the matter, and by talking to parents, talking to people in other towns doing similar things, and brainstorming together, they developed their own version of the six-year boarding-school model already being pioneered elsewhere.

It was another, though altogether more pleasant, of those moments like learning to ride a bicycle, Penny becoming aware she was competently doing a thing she still did not quite see how she could do. She, Otter's diffident young wife, patient reader of the New York Times, was now making decisions that would directly affect the future of the entire town, co-coordinating the efforts of dozens and dozens of people.

She declined a permanent teaching position. By that point she'd been without a boss for some fifteen years and didn't want to go back. She did drop in every other Friday to teach music, and she took on private students as well, but never again as many as in the days of the anklefarm. Mostly she served on the board, a position that involved quite a lot of arguing. She got very good at it.

More arguing followed after Bill resigned as their farm's representative to the Town Senate and Penny agreed to take his place. She was promptly elected by the Senate to serve on the Executive Council, where she worked largely to oppose and contain Alicia, who was also on the Executive Council and trying to pack the Judicial Council with people willing to impose religious law. State government was still largely hands-off, and there was no Federal government at all, so each town was nearly free to do as it pleased. Penny felt a duty to make sure her town did not do certain things.

Though still not chatty or gregarious, she suddenly seemed to be everywhere, at the library, at the school, at the town leadership offices, and even at Krista's dental office, where she helped with the paperwork every Tuesday and Thursday. People would see her go zipping by on her bicycle or striding along down some corridor or other, the same fast, long-legged gait she'd learned trying to keep up with her father on the crowded city streets, back when cities had crowds and crowds had cities.

There were problems, of course. But problems have solutions and, failing that, she could always complain about the problems to Krista.

"So, why doesn't Caitlyn just *come* to me?" she asked one fine, autumn morning, not expecting an answer. "It would make things so much easier." Caitlyn, Shania's grown daughter, had an issue involving a conflict between library procedure and her son's disability accommodations. The library employees had not been sure how to handle it and bounced it up to their immediate supervisor, who had bounced it somewhere else, all according to protocol but without result. Penny, who had no patience with protocol or hierarchy for its own sake, thought just talking to the director—herself—would have made more sense.

"She's afraid of you," explained Krista, almost apologetically.

"What? Why? How?"

"Well, half the town kind of is."

"Pff. What*ever*. It's because I'm tall. I'm tall, and I'm shy, and when a tall person doesn't talk much, that reads as intimidating somehow."

"Yeah, except I don't think you're shy anymore."

"What*ever*."

"Well, you kinda have to deal with it."

"I'd never hurt anyone, though. How can I be scary?"

She was scary because she wasn't scared. Not anymore.

At least the kids weren't scared of her. By then, there were four kids running around the farm and farmhouse and occasionally breaking things by accident. Three of them were Clevengers, the fourth—and this time the surprise was quite legitimate—was Krista's son. She'd gotten pregnant back before the new boarding school opened, she never would say by whom. The pregnancy was high risk, given Krista's age and several health issues, and she nearly died giving birth, but afterwards she gently chided Penny for worrying.

"I'm not leaving until after you do, remember?"

The baby latched and began to suckle, his tiny face serious, even studious, as he learned about taste and food and living. Newborns are serious beings by nature. They aren't children yet.

Penny did not believe anyone, even Krista, could keep a promise not to die, but she smiled and said nothing about that.

"What are you naming him?" she asked instead.

"Pryderi. He's Pryderi Pennington Mongeon."

"*Pryderi?*"

"Hey, you're not the only one around here who's read the *Mabinogion*."

More recently, the two surviving Wojo girls, now young women, finally got back into town and moved in, and Braxton, the grown son of Brian and Rosa, brought his family to settle nearby. So Braxton's young son joined the rabble most days too.

Penny found herself acting like something between an aunt and a grandmother to all of these people. She loved having children in the house again, though something about their presence hurt, too. The gaps her daughters left in the world were still so obvious she could almost see the holes. She didn't expect those gaps to ever heal over, but she had decided she was OK with the company of ghosts.

Through all these years since just after the collapse, Penny had been attending services at the abandoned church. She stayed in the adult choir, too, which now included many of the young people she'd once taught, and she still participated in her discussion groups whenever she had time. The right-shift of the town hadn't impaired the collaborative, open-minded vibe—the conservative contingent had simply stopped attending, choosing to meet separately in their own way. Those who remained were progressive Christians, playful agnostics, curious atheists, Scientific Pantheists, New Agers, Goddess-worshipers...basically anyone who liked the community aspect of church but did not want a preacher telling them how to think and feel.

The group was small now, but they were in communication with similar groups in other towns, all of them trading ideas and resources and hands-on help. The whole thing had the feel of a gradually rising tide. Krista called it a movement, a comment that somehow prompted Penny and Bill to simultaneously start spouting extensive quotes from Arlo Guthrie's "Alice's Restaurant."

Penny wasn't a leader in the movement. There were no leaders, not really. But she offered what she could. The others said she asked good questions, so she asked more of them. Sometimes she made suggestions. The others liked her "accidental hymns," so she sometimes brought in sheet music left over from her work with the children's choir. Looking over her old papers, she remembered the days back when ordering teaching supplies was impossible and computers wouldn't work. She'd had to write it all out by hand and from memory, just hoping she got it more or less right. No wonder it all took so much time. She fingered the paper of her hand-made hand-outs and found it already starting to yellow. One day, she borrowed one of the newly-refurbished computers from the library and began transcribing all of it, making corrections and additions as she went. She added more songs, more historical context notes, and some of her favorite poetry, snuck in some truly stupid jokes (best kind!), and printed it all up, bound it, and gave away copies. While she was at it, she typed up and bound copies of the notes she'd been taking at meetings. She sent copies of both to the discussion groups in other towns, just to keep the conversation going.

All these discussions and meetings no longer had as their sole objective the rediscovery of the meaning of life—though that pursuit continued. Now the participants also sought to support each other, to explain themselves to others who might be interested, and to stick up for people whom the conservatives might otherwise try to push around. Because the conservative contingent, too, had become a movement transcending any one town.

Both movements even had names. For years, now, the conservatives had been calling themselves the Society of the Lord of the Tribulation (others called them "Tribs," behind their backs), while the liberal or progressive group chose the name, ECA, short for Earth-Centered Alliance. The choice had not been without contention, and almost a dozen possibilities had seriously vied for dominance, but Penny, for one, had been glad when "Earth-Centered Alliance" won out.

"I feel like earth *should* be at the center," Penny offered. "It's the one thing we all have in common." She was thinking then, not of the Pale Blue Dot, the Spaceship Earth, but of soil, the good, rich earth in her hands, the ultimate source (with the sun and the air) for all food, the reliable, walkable ground.

For years, ECA had gotten along as a rather casual movement of people trading ideas over drinks or online, but eventually some kind of semi-formal structure proved necessary, and somebody organized a kind of constitutional convention at a farm in the Adirondacks owned by a family named Grayson. That was just after Pryderi was born, and when it was clear Krista was going to be OK, Penny agreed to be one of the delegates from her group. It was the first time she'd left town since before the pandemic. She had heard the rest of the world still existed, but seeing a little of it herself pleased her.

The objective of the meeting was to decide on an organizational structure and to formalize the core principles by which ECA would know itself different from that which was not ECA, but Penny did not think of herself as doing anything to actively pursue those objectives. She was there to see what happened and to speak her mind if she thought of something, but everybody else seemed to have everything well in hand. She volunteered to take notes, just as she did in the meetings at home.

Of course, she could not be everywhere at once, so when the convention broke up into committees, she asked the note-takers from the other committees to give her copies. She soon discovered very few people were as good at taking notes as she was. Often, there was little other than a list of attendees, an agenda, and a list of decisions made. But why were those decisions made? What other ideas had been floated? Who said what? The information would be useful later, so she filled in the gaps by conducting interviews. Sometimes nobody had remembered to take notes. Sometimes two or three people took notes and they differed. All of these conversations seemed too important to lose.

Afterwards, Penny volunteered to use her notes and the various documents created by the committees to formally write up the proceedings. The process took a lot longer than she'd expected, and while she worked, two committees continued to meet online and hash out major issues left unaddressed by the conference. She was on both of these (the Coordinating Committee and the Theory and Practice Committee), so when she finally finished with the conference proceedings, she went ahead and added a year of committee meeting transcripts as well. She'd compiled a record of ECA's collective mind thinking itself into existence.

She sent it out electronically, and someone suggested she have it printed. Correcting and formatting it, plus correcting, formatting, and once again expanding the Accidental Hymnal, and making arrangements for printing and distribution of both took several years, years while the boarding school opened and she served on the Town Executive Committee and the kids started getting big. Getting funding for all that work and all that paper proved particularly difficult. The infant civilization still had very little in the way of cash. But she, and a small group of friends and allies, managed to pull it off.

When the printing house finally started sending out copies to interested ECA circles, it felt a little like giving birth and sending your kid off to college all at the same time—not that she knew what either was really like. Not that she would ever know. She returned to her garden.

Penny was in her early fifties. Her hair was quickly turning gray now, and she dyed it (with indigo) successfully for the first time. The remaining black strands still resisted the dye, but the gray ones turned blue-black, and the white ones turned blue-green, and she sat on her garden fence looking up at the clouds with her multicolored hair sticking up in back like the down of a baby bird. It came to her then, not for the first time but never without surprise, that this new world, the one without fossil fuel or plastic or deforestation, was where she would spend the rest of her life. It was the real world, now.

Not that the world seemed strange anymore on a day-to-day basis, and not that she was complaining. Penny had made a very good life for herself, her friends, her community. Was that good life *in spite of* or *because of* the uncapitalized tragedy that had ax-blowed itself across her life and her world twenty years ago? The question, she knew, could do no good to think too much on. Anyway, there had been cracks in everything long before she'd found out they were there. The pandemic hadn't made them, and every good life in the history of everything had been lived either in ignorance or in awareness of those cracks.

Christine Penny Darling looked up to where a large cloud boiled and billowed, growing so fast she could sit and watch it change. No jet trail marred the sky, there were no jets anymore, and though various drones existed, she could see none at the moment, only birds. The light on the tops of the storm cloud glowed pale lemon yellow, now with a faint hint of peach as the long afternoon shifted towards evening.

There was still music in her head.

No Matter How Far Down

Luc Cote drove through the night in a red, beat-up cargo van, trying not to think. He thought anyway. The guys he'd taken the van from— were they still lying in the snow, or had they been found and taken to a morgue somewhere? If they'd been found, then his wife had been, too. He very much did not want to think about that. Nothing Luc had ever done had *ever* worked right, except when he did wrong things. He was very good at doing wrong things. At least he hadn't let the bastards get away with it.

Quarter tank left. That should see him across the border, at least.

He'd been back on the road a little over two hours now. The roads had been all but empty, but at this time of night that was almost normal. The van drove fairly well—the handling was decent, the gas mileage not terrible, and nothing smelled weird or made noises it shouldn't. The radio wouldn't work. The heat barely functioned. He knew nothing whatever about this vehicle, having only made its acquaintance that evening.

"Made its acquaintance,'" he mocked himself, speaking aloud to drown out his mental chatter. "I *stole* it, is what I did. There's no point in lying to You."

He addressed his God in French, in Quebecois. He always spoke to God in Quebecois, when he spoke to Him casually like this. It was the language of Luc's family, the language of his childhood. To pray formally, he would switch to Church Latin. He loved the sound, the feel, the structure of that sacred tongue. As for English, the third language in which Luc was fluent, English was just for business.

"Does it matter, morally, that I stole it from thieves?"

He supposed not, considering everything else he'd done that night. He'd done it all to stay alive, and to stay alive now he was running, running just south of west through darkness punctuated by painted lines and reflective dots, mile after mile, like the world's most boring video game. He just didn't understand what was so important about living, why he couldn't have let himself die when he'd had the chance.

"I'm a fuck-up," he admitted. "I've always been a fuck-up, I'm still a fuck-up, and, let's just face it, Father, I'm always gonna be a fuck-up. You sent Your Son to die for my sins, for what? Maybe *I'm* the rock You made and can't lift, huh? I did *everything* You told me to do, everything, for ten years, everything they said to do in the rooms. I thought I was pulling my act together. And then just a *little* temptation and *bam!* Look at me now. Or are You gonna try to tell me this was Your idea? That You got me up off that pavement? Maybe, maybe it was. It sure didn't seem like my idea. But why? Why, Father? Did it escape Your attention that I'm a fuck-up whose family is *dead?* Dead or dying? So what's the point? Huh? Cause I'm gonna need to know eventually, if I'm gonna follow Your plan. Or is *this* Your plan? Is this Your fucking plan, that I just keep *going?*"

Luc did not always have a foul mouth. He was not an especially crude person, but he wasn't going to pretend God didn't know he was thinking those words. Call a fucking spade a fucking spade, when talking to the omniscient. He wiped his nose on the back of his hand and tried to pull himself together. He had a long road ahead, and he wasn't even sure yet where he was going.

Fifty-six years old, blond hair going cigarette-ash gray at the temples, Luc Cote still looked like a Hollywood leading man. Tall, slim, blue-eyed, with an expressive but narrow face and a thousand-watt smile, his charm had been his stock-in-trade for decades, a thing he had honed until he could turn it on quite consciously. He tried not to do that anymore.

How had he spent those charming decades?

He was not thinking over the story of his life. Real tortured reveries aren't that organized. Instead of a story, with scene after scene in rational order, like a movie, the scenes play on shuffle or repeat, full of bugs or distorted by weird, ill-advised filters, and the user can't change the settings. But over the course of that long night, most of his life did play through his mind at least once.

Luc was born in America, in Detroit. His father, Andre, had come to work in the auto industry back when the American car was king. After a few years, Andre brought over his wife and young son, Philippe, and then the couple set about having more babies like the good Catholics they were. Luc was the fourth out of five. He hadn't learned English yet before the new plant opened in Montreal and the family went back home. Becoming American had never been Andre's plan.

Getting sick hadn't been Andre's plan, either.

Luc remembered his father getting clumsy. The man tried to deny it, resisted concern or sympathy, but then there was the day he tripped over his own feet getting up from the breakfast table, hot coffee all over the kitchen, and Maman put her foot down. Diagnosis took awhile, and there were a couple of misdiagnoses, some hopeful, some not, but the final answer—that was bad.

Papa had welder's disease, a form of early-onset Parkinson's caused by manganese poisoning. No cure and, at the time, no real treatment. The plant was good about letting Papa retire early with his full pension, it was a good Union job. His good Union job as a skilled welder is what killed him.

That pension had not been enough to support a family of seven—or, rather, six, since Philippe was out of the house by then, away in Chicago. And Maman couldn't get a job because she had to stay home and take care of Papa. And so Philippe started sending money home instead of saving for college. Marrying that pretty Jewish librarian was the closest he'd ever get to the educated class. The next year, René and Michelle both got jobs, part-time, low-wage jobs for teenagers, the best they could do. No fun extra-curriculars for them, it was all about survival. The year after that, Luc got a paper-route, but really he was too young to have his plans interrupted much by changed circumstance. By the time he and Francine were old enough to work, René was eighteen and bringing in real money. Luc was free to put his time into getting some impressive grades.

He just had to watch his papa die.

"That can't be why I'm like this, though," he said. "You put Michelle though exactly the same thing, and look at her—she's a saint. Probably literally, by now." He thought about that a moment and amended himself.

"No, Michelle's not there yet. What she's doing takes longer. Anyway, I'd know if she died." He thought for another moment, wondering if that were true. "If, uh, *when* she dies, will You tell me?"

But he had no right to ask for favors.

Michelle, his big sister, closest to him in age, both more and less like him that any other human being he'd ever known. She had none of his darkness, none of his ruinous heat, yet she could say "we are both sinners" as if she truly saw no difference between them. And she, more than anyone else in the family, shared the one true, passionate love of his life. They had played at religion the way other children play house. They'd talked about joining religious orders the way other teenagers started garage bands. And she'd done it, becoming one of the sisters teaching math at the Catholic high school. As for Luc....

Serving as an altar boy, playing CYO sports, later being in charge of inventory for the church soup kitchen, none of that changed—only hid—the fact that he was smoking and drinking even as a teenager, that he often shoplifted for the thrill of it (never anything very valuable, mostly candy bars, but still), that some of the pranks and stunts he and his friends pulled were cruel or dangerous, that he threatened or sometimes actually hurt anyone younger than him or smaller than him who tried to get in his way. All the adults, when they learned anything of what he was doing at all, dismissed his activities as harmless fun, boys being boys, and at the time he thought of it that way himself. He hadn't realized then what his "fun" foreshadowed.

But, driving along in the beat-up old van, he smiled, thinking about the overly-religious little boy he'd been. He remembered sitting on his bed, not old enough yet to read but leafing through his children's Lives of the Saints books, looking at the pictures and thinking someday he was going to be just like that, and *then* his parents would be sorry for sending him to his room all the time—the irony of such holy vindictiveness would escape him for decades. Plotting constantly to get his own way and raging when he couldn't had not exactly been Godly behavior.

What made him smile now—and what hurt—was not how often he'd been bad but how very much he'd wanted to be good.

When Papa died, it was a kind of liberation for all of them, Papa included. Requiem aeteman, requiem aeteman dona eis, Domine, yes, Lord, *perpetual* light, free of that corrupted, fibrillating body that failed him....

As for the rest of the family, Maman went to work tutoring kids in science and math and didn't need support from her children anymore, so Michelle quit her boring but well-paid job in retail to begin the process of becoming a sister. Francine got that shit internship that she loved for Parks Canada instead of something sensible. And Luc spent another year at home, waiting tables and saving his money, before enrolling in college, his eye set on the seminary. Of course, liberation made no difference for René and Philippe. René had no need of freedom—he liked his job working for some auto mechanic friend of Papa's. He learned the business, moved up, and eventually married the boss's daughter and bought the old man out. And Philippe had no freedom at all. As soon as Papa stopped needing him, his son turned out to be a retard or some shit like that. There never would be time or money for Philippe for himself, not nunc, not semper.

Much of Luc's thinking involved words like *retard* and *fag*, or their Quebecois equivalents. He knew they weren't polite to *say* anymore, but he really didn't see why. Or care, frankly.

For one thing, he firmly believed that "fags" did not exist. Oh, there were men who had sex with other men, sure, but Luc did not believe it was in their special nature to do so. After all, *Luc* had always desperately wanted to have sex with men, just as he'd wanted to do all sorts of other things he knew he should not, such as bed other men's wives. He assumed all men experienced such temptations. And he'd resisted temptation.

Until he hadn't.

It was his first time with anyone, and some of the best sex of his life, but thirty years later, Luc still regretted it. If only he and Greg hadn't been left alone that night. If only they hadn't been drinking. He still wanted to know why God hadn't rescued him from himself.

Why hast thou forsaken me?

Luc was capable of believing that nothing and everything was his fault simultaneously.

The miles sped by, the faint hum and vibration of the engine and the road lulling him into the bad neighborhoods of his mind, places he knew he should not go alone, but he had no one left to go with anymore.

He noticed he'd sped up, his bodily tension giving him something of a lead foot. He slowed down to just under the speed limit. He hadn't seen a cop in hours, but there could always be an exception, and he really did not need police attention right now.

Follow the little laws strictly, when you're breaking the big ones. That had always been his rule.

He'd quit the seminary and went looking for a nice girl to marry. He could keep his hands off men, no problem, but to live without sex had suddenly seemed like doing without breathing. And he'd had some honor in those days, some integrity. He didn't want to be a priest who did things no priest should do. And so he'd gone to work in his brother's garage, a messed-up situation if there ever was one.

Luc had firmly believed then, and halfway believed now, that being an auto mechanic was alright for someone like René, but Luc had *talent*. He had *drive*. He had a (rather unmarketable) degree in philosophy and a flare for painting, so why should he have to accept some grease-monkey telling him what to do? So he mouthed off to the boss, his brother, had words with his co-workers who thought they were better than him. He didn't always bother showing up for work. But when he did work, he did a good job, and when René confronted him he'd turn on the charm and clean up his act for a while. There were good months, sometimes a few good months in a row, but everybody was surprised René waited so long to fire him.

Except Luc. What surprised him was that even if you hate your job, being fired is so humiliating you'll punch your own brother in the jaw.

They'd never really reconciled after that, and now they were out of time. Luc, mulling through his life as his fingers on the wheel went numb from the chill, became so maudlin and so guilt-ridden that he suddenly got defensive and started shouting.

"I never *said* I was going to be a mechanic for the rest of my life!"

But there was no one in the van to hear him but God and his own cold-nipped ears.

He'd worked for René for five years, five lousy years, and though his brother gave him decent paychecks, he'd been more or less broke the whole time, even towards the end when he was also selling paintings regularly. Where *had* the money gone? He hadn't spent all *that* much.

"I bought *painting supplies*," he insisted. "I paid the rent. My first car was that crap station wagon, and I kept it forever. I didn't get the sports car until—"

But he had invested in nice clothes, took women on extravagant dates, tried coke—no, the coke was later, when Célie was snooping around in his finances.

"I still don't know why she cared, I mean, I paid the big bills, the essentials, why shouldn't she have been responsible for everything else? She *liked* her career as a nurse. What the hell was her problem?" Except he knew what her problem was.

Man, she'd been a great chick in the beginning, though—smart, practical, and wholesome, with a *sweet* body, a really nice ass, breasts he'd wished he could sculpt in marble, the real full package. And she'd liked him, she'd really liked him. He'd never known why, nor had he ever been fully clear on whether he truly liked her back, but he'd thought for a while that her admiration of him would be enough. He'd felt like a better person around her. But....

"The bitch cheated on me, almost as soon as we got married. I guess she had couple of good fucks and decided she wanted—"

No, that wasn't it, that was actually what *he'd* done, more or less, and if she'd ever been less than faithful, she'd given him no evidence of it at all. But he'd worried. He'd seen how men looked at her, and the thought that she might say no if asked, that what she wanted actually mattered at all, had not occurred to him. He'd questioned and tested her loyalty obsessively for months, convinced the other guys must all be laughing at him for not being able to keep his woman in line, until her first pregnancy mollified him. At first, something about the pregnancy itself reassured him—they were becoming a real family, inviolable—and then he simply stopped thinking about whether Célie was cheating on him. He was too busy trying to keep her from thinking he was cheating.

"I never *meant* to start, though," he told his God. "If I hadn't had so much wine at that dinner with that art critic—what was her name? Hell, I can't even remember her name. Of course, You're going to tell me I shouldn't have had dinner with her at all. You're right, of course You are, but I didn't know that then. I didn't know I'd be so damned weak."

And yet he smiled at the memory, even now. Her body was like Célie's, only different, her responses like Célie's, only different, and the incredible, miraculous intimacy—no more polite distance, no more rules—of being able to let his hands go where they liked, to touch her so as to make her want him....

"Oh, God, tell Célie I'm sorry!" he cried, appalled at his sudden arousal. Sinning in his heart.... He tried to think of something else. Célie wasn't even dead a day, yet.

Of course that art critic had not been the last. He would swear off cheating, go to Confession, do his penance, and then sooner or later he'd get a little over-served again, or something else would happen, and he'd end up in a motel somewhere or in somebody's bed or in the back seat of a foggy-windowed car, feeling weirdly betrayed afterwards, as though he, rather than Célie, were the victim in the situation, a mental distortion he didn't even notice for years afterwards. He alternated between charming away Célie's suspicions, wining and dining her as seriously as he did his illicit women, and lashing out at her for her distrust, because couldn't she see he meant it this time?

And when he wasn't feeling guilty, he felt like a super-hero.

By day, he was a mild-mannered auto mechanic, a responsible young father, an active member of his church. By night he was a glamorous and increasingly successful artist, an imbiber of fine wines, a lover of beautiful women. He was too slick, too good, to ever get caught.

The bridge over the St. Lawrence lay ahead, the bridge and the border. He'd been thinking, when he'd set out that afternoon, when he and Célie's had set out that afternoon, that he'd cross on some unguarded back road somewhere, but there was no practical way to get to an unguarded crossing given everything else that had happened. His blood-pressure rose. He schooled himself in calmness, in composure. There were no other cars around. The lights looked garish after the blackness of the long road.

Almost, he thought nobody was going to challenge him. The border was still closed, but most of the guards in charge of closing it must be dead, sick, or home caring for the sick and the dead. That's where almost everyone was, these days. The young man who hurried out at last did not seem too terribly competent.

"Do you have a permit, sir?"

The man spoke in English. Luc replied in kind, in the American accent he'd learned to mimic for short periods only.

"I had one," he said. "They let me across to go see my wife. She was visiting family when the border closed, and then she.... I didn't know I'd need a permit to get back."

"Well, let's see your original permit, then."

Luc allowed blank terror to play across his face.

"I, I don't know where it is. I, it's just...."

"She didn't make it, did she?"

"No, sir. She didn't." Luc did not bother to *act* grief-stricken, he simply allowed himself a moment to feel his real grief, his real exhaustion. The truth always made the best lies.

"Go on, go home," the border guard said at last. "I'm sorry about your wife."

"Thank you, sir."

The kid never even asked to look in the back of the van.

He'd gone west originally, avoiding population centers and the complication of mountains, but now he ran almost straight south through New York State on I-81. He had to find a place where spring would come sooner. Already he'd gone far enough that there'd been some melting during the day. Patches of new ice reached across the road. He wished he could sleep.

He refilled the gas tank from one of the containers in the back. He'd thought the inside of the van was cold, but outside the chill crept under his collar and woke him up. He urinated in the crusty snow on the side of the road, hoping his pecker wouldn't freeze, took a couple of swigs from his water bottle—he was saving the last of his coffee—and climbed back in the driver's seat. He sang for a while, his voice nothing to get excited about, but nobody was listening except the One Who is omniscient, and God already knew Luc wasn't a soloist. Schubert's *Ave Maria*. *Time of Your Life*, by Green Day. *Dancing in the Dark*, by Bruce Springsteen. *Take It Easy*, by the Eagles. *Ode to Joy*, sung loudly in badly-pronounced and only half-understood German. He sang whatever popped into his head. He wished the radio wasn't broken. He wished the heater worked. Hours later, in Pennsylvania, he pulled into an empty truck stop, topped off the gas tank again as the first faint hint of dawn enlarged the sky, and got in his sleeping bag at last.

Sometime later, he woke and poked his head out of his bag. Broad daylight, but still frigid. And the truck stop still looked deserted. He couldn't risk staying much longer—as the only occupant of the parking lot, he might attract attention, either from police or from criminals, he didn't know which would be worse. Without getting out of his bag, he breakfasted on one of the sandwiches he'd packed yesterday (only yesterday?) finding it frozen but edible. Bless us, oh father, with these, thy gifts. His water-bottle was frozen solid and doubtless useless for the rest of the trip, he had no way to thaw it, but his last thermos of coffee was still merely icy. Through Christ's bounty, amen. By the time he was done eating and drinking, he was so cold he had to withdraw entirely into his bag again for a while. Shivering in the warm, sleep-scented dark, he prayed. He could sleep or wake any time, the years of alcohol and drugs seemed to have scrambled whatever circadian rhythm he'd once possessed, but these familiar prayers made it morning for him.

Oh Jesus, through the Immaculate Heart of Mary, I offer You my prayers, works, joys, and sufferings of this day in union with….Gloria Patri, et Filio, et Spiritui Sancto. Sicut erat in principio, et nunc, et semper, et in saecula saeculorum….Pater Noster, qui es in caelis, sanctificetur nomen tuum….ave Maria, gratia plena, dominus tecum. Benedicta tu in mulieribus….God, grant me the serenity to accept the things I cannot change, the courage to change the things I can, and the wisdom to know…. Lord, I am now willing that thou shalt have all of me, to build with me and to do with me as thou wilt. Relieve me of the bondage of self that I might better do Thy will. Take away my difficulties that victory over them may bear witness to those I would help of Thy power, Thy love, and Thy way of life. Car c'est à toi qu'appartiennent, le règne la puissance et la gloire. Thy will, not mine, be done. World without end. Amen.

Amen.

Amen.

Amen.

It's still fucking *cold*.

Amen.

So, praying, he fell asleep again, then woke in a panic to what sounded like somebody knocking on the driver's side window.

But there was nothing. No one was there. He never found out what the sound was.

Treating the incident as a close call and a warning, he shook off sleep for real this time, went outside to piss on the pavement, there being nobody around to offend, then got out his atlas.

Looking at the names of towns and highways and national forests, he saw no particular reason to head towards any one of them. He figured he had enough gas left to cover about four hundred miles more, so he used his hands as a kind of compass to see where those miles might take him. Pennsylvania, Ohio, West Virginia…. His eye swept over Marietta, Ohio, and some vague buzzer of familiarity went off in his brain.

Marietta, Ohio? Why should some bumblefuck place in Ohio be familiar to him? After a few seconds, he remembered. His eyes lit.

"Fish," he said. Within minutes, he was on the road again.

In daylight, he felt less inclined to reverie. Instead, he thought about where he was going and what he'd have to do when he got there. He figured his chances of making his plan work were close to zero, but his chances would have been even smaller doing anything else. He wasn't worried about it now.

"I guess You've finally granted me serenity, huh?" he said, mouth twitching into an amused smile. "It works if you work it."

There were a few cars out on the road now, though not many, and very few with out-of-state plates. He wondered how many of them were driving on stolen gas, as he was. He guessed that soon everybody would be stealing or stolen from until there was no more gas. Then what would the thieves and fornicators do? Most would probably just die, unless they had a plan. He had a plan. But instead of congratulating himself he was surprised by a wave of sadness. A woman passed him, her car full of stuff. Did *she* have a plan?

So he did have a heart, at least occasionally. Huh. The more you know. He crossed himself the same way he might when an ambulance drove by. In nomine Patris, et Filii, et Spiritus Sancti. Amen.

Prayer kept him focused, kept his mood up. He wasn't sure he had a right to pray anymore, and the thought hurt him more than any rejection by a woman, any estrangement from a put-upon friend, ever had. But the habit and rhythm of memorized prayers had the advantage of almost saying themselves, whether he felt like saying them when he started or not. He said the Rosary, his right thumb and forefinger counting imaginary beads, right palm resting on the fake-leather steering wheel.

But as the miles fell away and the sun rose behind him, he thought again about his wife and how and why she had died. Her death was only the last of a long string of stupid, awful, unfair things that had happened to her, and the only one he couldn't have spared her simply by ceasing to be a jackass.

Or maybe he could have spared her that one, too.

Just before the birth of their third child, Rosalie, Célie got a little too curious about finances and started looking through Luc's credit card statements and other records. That was a couple of years after René fired him. He'd been working a series of increasingly demeaning jobs (car-wash attendant, bus-boy, dish-washer) to supplement what he made from his art, with long periods of unemployment between hires. His wreck of a resume seemed much less forgivable to hiring managers now that he was in his thirties. But he *did* have an income, and yet the family subsisted almost entirely on Célie's salary. When she found out why, she took the kids to go stay with her parents. She wouldn't talk to him again until after the baby came. Luc denied everything she couldn't prove, wept with genuine remorse about the things she could, and swore up and down he'd never do it again. And he meant it. Being found out was actually a kind of relief. The lying and the cheating were over. Things would be different. Célie could see his sincerity and moved back home. For a time, everything was good between them, really good. He was starting to do more shows, selling his art for better and better prices.... He even stayed monogamous for a couple of months, but then after that decided that if he just treated Célie and the kids really well when he was with them, then what he did when he was not with them wouldn't matter.

Célie disagreed.

If she hadn't become so damned frigid, he told her....

He regretted that. He worked hard and won her back again. The cycle repeated itself. The kids were afraid of him. Damn little ingrates. *I'll give them something to be afraid of!* he told himself, but he hardly ever followed through on that thought, not much, anyway, and instead he did his best to win them back, too. He succeeded, for a while.

And then one of his girlfriends found out about his other girlfriends, and the vicious bitch went to his wife and told her everything. Célie filed for divorce.

"You can't divorce me, we're Catholic," he told her.

"Catholics can't commit adultery, either," she reminded him, dryly. "Luc, in the eyes of God and in my heart we will always be married, this is true, but if secular law is the only way I can get some peace and some child support, then so be it."

She got the house in the suburbs. She got the kids, except for supervised visits on the weekends. She got most of his remaining pride. A week after the divorce was finalized, he was sitting by a pond in a park thinking when, in a fit of rage, he took off his wedding band and threw it as hard as he could—except it slipped from his fingers and fell at his feet, as if he'd been fake-throwing a stick to confuse a dog or something. He stooped at once to search, intending to throw it again, then searched more diligently, intending to put his ring back on and keep it. But it was no use. Regardless of his motivation for searching, his wedding band had buried itself in a thick layer of autumn leaves, and all his rummaging among those leaves served only to move the buried ring around and make it harder to find. He searched. He searched again. He searched fruitlessly and frantically and finally wept, cursing himself, his knees and fingers cold in the mud of the all-but-icy shoreline.

More than twenty years later, driving west, now, Luc Cote rubbed his thumb along the place where his wedding band used to be. He'd already poured the last of his gas into the tank. He knew there would be no more after that, whatever happened. His van would shortly become a small storage shed on wheels.

Losing Célie had meant not only losing her income but also gaining the responsibility of child support, a legal obligation even he couldn't justify evading. Even in the crappy little apartment he'd taken, he couldn't make the rent.

He sold paintings, he borrowed money from friends and siblings, it still wasn't enough. His dealer suggested he take a quick little trip across the border. He agreed.

And drug-running agreed with him.

He started slow but soon learned the ropes and started hauling more product more often. Some substances went north while others went south, so he had a cargo on both directions of every trip. His dual citizenship was a definite advantage. So was his skill at lying and his ability to make just about anyone like and trust him, at least until they got to know him better, which of course border guards never had to.

In fact, for the first time in his life, Luc felt like he was really good at something.

"I was good at *lots* of things," he protested, turning south again now, towards Marietta. "I always got good grades, and there's painting—and fucking, obviously…." You don't sell your soul for a piece of ass and not get very good at taking your piece. The thought prompted a rueful smile. But the thing was, underneath his loud and charming megalomania, he'd never *felt* like he was good at anything because he was always getting in trouble, and he never knew why. He didn't know why he did the things he did, or, really, why other people minded. Sometimes he honestly believed he was being screwed out of his just deserts by some sort of conspiracy of unappreciative, perhaps jealous, losers. Other times, he was equally sure he was simply and fundamentally broken. He still felt both ways often, but back then the poles had been especially extreme. As he grew out of his childish faith that *of course* the creator of the entire *universe* must consider Luc His most excellent creation, the concept of original sin had come to make a lot of sense. Even at his most successful, he'd always felt like a fraud.

But as a drug-runner, he actually *was* a fraud, that was the whole point, and he was good at it. The danger excited him, sharpened him. With boredom finally conquered, he became canny, focused, disciplined in a way he had never been before. He never had close calls, never got his hands dirty with any aspect of the business that wasn't his, and never stopped learning how to do his job better. His clients trusted him. He could get as much work or as little as he wanted.

He even invested in a kind of career development, taking self-defense classes (ironically, the kind offered by the police), several types of martial art, and advanced first-aid. He found a gun range and learned proper care and safe handling of several kinds of weapon, and he practiced until he became an excellent shot. He did not buy a gun. He did not want a weapon to complicate any encounter with the police, nor did he want an assailant to take his weapon from him and shoot him with it. If a situation went bad, though, he wanted to be able to take his assailant's gun.

And on supervised Saturday after supervised Saturday, he watched his kids grow up largely without him. He watched his wife move on with her life. He felt himself getting used to being a criminal, slowly giving up the dream that he might somehow make himself into a good boy.

He stopped going to Mass. His faith in God never wavered, but his faith in God's forgiveness fell, broke. There seemed little point in going to Confession anymore when he knew for a fact he was going to sin again. His honest intentions to do otherwise evaporated like mist from the river in sunlight, and he was tired of trying to believe that this time would be different.

He could not stand the inside of his skull anymore. In any moment of silence or peace, the guilt for his drinking and his screwing would rise, and a strange, childlike grief would follow. He still loved God so much it hurt.

When he had money, he spent it, mostly on alcohol and drugs, but also on ostentatious luxuries meant mostly to impress women. He seldom paid for sex directly, preferring the thrill of the chase, the game of seduction, everything that led up to the moment when he could finally sink into another human being and be, for a few minutes at least, less entirely alone. To hire a prostitute was, in his opinion, only a step or two above masturbation, which was in turn only a step or two above pointlessness. And yet sex of any kind, even by himself, seemed to have more going for it than pretty much anything else. When he didn't have money, he begged loans from family and a dwindling number of friends until he could sell another painting or organize another trip across the border.

When he wasn't on the road, he painted. High, drunk, or occasionally even sober, he daubed on paint furiously, his apartment throbbing with hard rock or sometimes techno, living in a fever of art, creating some of the best work of his life.

He burned like a magnesium flare. He hoped that when he burned out, it would at least be quick, that it wouldn't hurt too much. He didn't like to think at all about what might happen after that.

What happened was that one day he confessed all of it to his sister, Michelle. If Célie had seen the best in him and loved him, Michelle had always seen the worst and still loved him. And just then, he'd needed desperately to be seen. He told her everything, all the shameful, horrible, ugly bits, and she listened and told him she would pray for him. He thanked her, but felt sure no prayer for *him* would be heard. And yet, a few days after that, without actually intending to do any such thing, he walked in to an AA meeting.

Luc did everything the guys in the rooms told him to do. He prayed, he got a sponsor, he worked the Steps, he went to meetings, he did service (mostly washing coffee mugs after meetings), and he read the Big Book. They didn't tell him specifically to start attending Mass again, but he did it anyway. He couldn't put more than thirty days of sobriety in a row, and he kept up his work as a drug runner. He needed to make a living, after all. But he kept coming back to the rooms. He kept trying again to get and stay sober. He didn't know why.

The turning point came while he was attempting yet another "searching and fearless moral inventory." This time, his method was to write out his life story, to get it out on notebook paper where he could look at it and it wouldn't turn slippery. And when he looked, what he saw was that every time he'd written about some new low in sexual immorality, he'd first written the words *I got drunk*. He'd always told himself that he couldn't have a problem with sex, since he only acted out sexually when he was drinking. Once he really stopped drinking, he'd figured he'd also stop screwing around. Now, he suddenly saw it differently—could he have been drinking *in order to have sex?*

His sudden clarity appalled him. If sex was his addiction, and he drank as a means to that end, then until he could give up sex, he was going to just keep on drinking, and nothing else in his life would ever get better.

Give up *sex?*

He wouldn't. He couldn't. God couldn't expect him to, no way. He had *needs*, he had a *right* to meet those needs. He shouted objections, alone in his apartment, shaking his fist in righteous anger at the ceiling. At other moments, in other moods, he cried out very differently. He couldn't do it, he was tired of trying, please, Father, don't make me try and fail again. And soon he was back to self-righteousness.

And yet, that very week, he walked into a meeting of Sex and Love Addicts Anonymous.

He didn't like it. The group met in a church basement otherwise inhabited by stray cats, to the extent that the whole place stank of tomcat piss, a stink that seemed weirdly appropriate for the child molesters and fornicators and fags he found himself among—some of the latter even seemed proud of their proclivity, and the other group members would encourage them to get "married" and other bizarre things. There were atheists and Protestants, even a couple of honest-to-goodness witches, all of whom thought they could lecture *him* on spirituality. And how was he supposed to quit objectifying women in a group where he was encouraged to refer to his lovers as *drugs of choice?*

And yet he kept coming back. New habits of thought from both his programs made their way into his skull, largely through repetition—the meeting formats required, and talking with other members encouraged, frequent quoting of program literature and program slogans and truisms, and all of it seeped into his brain and took up residence there when he wasn't looking. Let go and let God. Easy does it—but do it. First things first. Keep it simple. Nothing is so bad that a drink won't make it worse. Think, think, think. If you point your finger at someone else, three more are pointed back at you. Attitude of gratitude. One day at a time. He heard stories from people who'd done what he had done and worse, and yet had somehow come back from that darkness. They gave him a sense of hope, but also a kind of urgency—because none of those men had come back just by wishing or promising or intending to do so. They did it only by changing their lives.

And for the first time in his life, Luc got, not just exhortations *to* change, but some practical advice on *how* to change his life. It started with sobriety (they used the term in SLAA, too. Luc would have said *chastity*, but these people seemed not to know the deeper, more technical meaning of the word, mistaking it for *celibacy*, which wasn't an overall goal of most members). You didn't work the program to get sober, you got sober in order to work the program—working the program *kept* you sober and repaired your life. From there it was a matter of doing service, being honest with yourself, trusting God, and working the Steps.

The elevator to recovery is broken; take the Steps.

The people in the rooms knew what sort of advice he needed because, unlike all the other people who'd ever told him to shape up, they were like him. Some of them were, anyway. Luc didn't think the mere fact of sharing an addiction conferred much in the way of kinship—he'd been a screwed-up alien long before he ever took his first drink or had his first fuck. He was something other, something deeper than an addict. But some of the people here were that same something, too, and knew how to live as such.

What they knew was service.

Luc had, of course, heard about twelve-step groups, especially AA, long before he'd ever been to a meeting, and he'd always thought that the idea was to go to meetings and make phone calls and so forth to get help. Now, he realized that he and most of the rest of the world had had it back-wards. The thing to do, most of the time anyway, was to go to meetings to *give* help. By trying to help others, an addict could earn a daily reprieve from an incurable illness, a reprieve very specifically contingent on serving God by helping addicts. There are atheists in the twelve-step movement but, as Luc learned, the movement itself is not atheist. God is its central principle. He liked that. And it worked. Washing coffee cups, setting up folding chairs, listening to some sad-sack bitch and complain, all of it built a kind of muscle-memory of empathy for him, a new habit of thinking about others that left him slightly less quick to fly off the handle when things did not go his way.

But while he could build his sobriety on service, he couldn't build his life there. He was not like those old-timers who would profess gratitude for being addicts in the first place, claiming that the necessity of performing service to stay sober had become the key to meaning in their lives.

No matter how far down you've been, you'll find your experience can help others. Words to that effect were recited, from the Big Book of AA, at almost every AA meeting and not a few SLAA meetings. As if that made it OK. As if that made the darkness make sense.

"If I am an addict so that I can help some newcomer," he explained to his sponsor, "and you're an addict so you can help me, and someone else was an addict so he could help you, then why was the first addict an addict?"

"You think too much," his sponsor told him.

Luc was grateful, but only for his sobriety, not for his addictions. He saw his addictions and other issues purely as limitations, as illnesses, problems he had to spend the larger part of his time and energy dealing with, lest they break out and destroy his life again. What a waste. What a pointless waste. And he had to face that waste without alcohol or drugs or sex or even daydreams about his own grandiosity to make it bearable.

But the guys in the rooms said, "fake it till you make it," and Luc was good at faking things. Faking sobriety kept him actually sober, until something better could come along.

He faked his way to sobriety in both his programs for a very long time.

Sobriety in AA meant no alcohol, period. Sobriety in SLAA could mean anything a member thought it should mean, and it could change as needed. There were those who counted even sex dreams as slips. There were many who were sexually active with their spouses. There were a few who felt free to have sex with whomever just so long as they made a point of praying first. For Luc, it was simple; he would not have sex outside of marriage, nor would he masturbate. He figured any impulse that drove him to break the rules taught by his religion were probably the wrong impulses to act on. And since his wife wouldn't talk to him, much less have sex, he figured that meant no more sex for him.

Celibacy was a lot easier to contemplate now than it had been in his twenties, since, in all fairness, he'd probably already had his share. One day at a time, anyway.

Eventually, a couple of guys sat him down and convinced him he had to change careers. He'd listed lying and manipulation and flirting with strangers as defects of character, hadn't he? How was he supposed to become willing for God to remove them if they were job requirements? And what about "whenever anyone, anywhere, reaches out for help, let the hand of AA always be there—and for that I am responsible." He couldn't be responsible for aiding others' sobriety when he had a financial stake in their using hard drugs, could he? Well, no, but…. He argued, he resisted, he temporized. They waited.

"OK, fine," he huffed. But he'd *liked* running drugs.

Money wasn't the problem. Now that he was no longer paying for booze and motel rooms and coke, he found bills much easier to pay. He almost didn't need a second job besides his art, though there were still gaps between sales that made him nervous. He'd never learned to budget, nor did he ever know how long a gap would be. And so he delivered pizzas for a while. Then a guy he knew from the rooms hooked him up with a job painting "inspirational" images for a start-up Christian greeting-card company. The work they wanted was insipid and dull, but it was a regular paycheck, and the boss knew he was a recovering addict and was cool about it.

The problem was boredom. Luc had developed a healthy respect for his need for excitement—his monster needed to be fed, and if he did not feed it, he knew it would someday feed itself. And so he took up marksmanship again, enjoying the challenge. Working out at the gym got the endorphins running and left his body sweetly tired, sort of like sex. The gym had classes, and he signed up for kick-boxing, then for jujitsu. Soon he was entering competitions, doing well for a man in his fifties. Then one of the younger guys in his dojo turned him on to paintball. Paintball was play, but it was serious play. Some of his team-mates were army reservists and retired military. They refused to lose to, as they put it, "some team of pimply-faced, untrained geeks," and so they trained their own team-mates mercilessly. From them Luc learned tactics, team communication and discipline, and how to move and hide in the woods. The sport demanded his whole body and mind, and every weekend gave him a new opportunity for either shame or glory, depending on how well he could rise to the challenge—and yet the adventure wouldn't put him in a grave or a prison cell if he messed up. It was fun. He couldn't remember when he'd used that word before, except as a euphemism for sex. He liked *fun*, he decided.

Paintball and God together kept Luc sober.

There is a Step, Step Nine, where an addict is supposed to make amends for his wrongs (or her wrongs or their wrongs, but Luc thought in the universal masculine and rarely spoke to women anymore anyway).

Luc approached this step with trepidation, imagining a lot of difficult conversations and doors slammed in his face. But he did imagine that he'd be forgiven eventually, and that the people he'd wronged would be grateful, eager for his apologies, once he'd really proven his sincerity. That's not what happened.

A few people did accept his amends—some more easily than Luc thought he deserved. Some had forgotten the incidents he tried to make amends for or refused to admit he'd done anything wrong in the first place. That was frustrating. But a large portion of those he had harmed shut the door in his face, not out of anger or hurt, but simply with an air of tired irritation.

"Frankly, my dear, they don't give a damn," his sponsor told him.

"How am I supposed to make amends if they won't friggin' *talk* to me?" he asked, indignant.

"Luc, man, nobody owes you a chance to clear your conscience. Pay the debts that you can pay. Fix the broken things you can fix. Let the rest keep you humble."

So, he did.

He began paying down his debts to his friends and family, the loans he'd never expected to repay at all. He publicly corrected the lies he'd told about other people. He did the right thing, whenever he could tell what that was. He no longer expected to be forgiven. Mostly, he wasn't.

Luc counted his sobriety as a miracle, the literal kind, a grace from God. To simply be able to get angry with someone and *not* fly off the handle, or to pursue something he wanted and *not* resort to manipulative bullshit or threats in order to get it, these, too, were miracles beyond his understanding. But he wasn't happy. His friends in the program told him that if he just kept coming back, if he practiced gratitude and did enough service, that his life would make sense, that he would develop the self-satisfied glow a lot of the old-timers had. He kept coming back, and he did the service work, and he practiced gratitude, and still he felt as though his life had been pointless, just one big, stupid mistake.

He kept going anyway. He kept up with his studies in jujitsu and aikido, lifted weights, practiced kick-boxing moves for cardio, and got very good at paint-ball. He made friends. He had fun. First one, then another, then all three of his now-grown children started having lunch with him occasionally, one-on-one or in a group. He answered their questions about his life honestly and listened to their anger and hurt. He didn't try to win them over. They kept having lunch with him. His blond hair started turning gray. He developed crows' feet. He celebrated birthdays he hadn't expected to ever see.

Most of it still felt pointless. He had nothing important he could give to anybody, no way he could be any better than slightly less bad.

If nothing changes, nothing changes, as he'd been told, but sooner or later everything changes, and the next change was a big one. Only, it didn't seem like anything big when it began. He noticed it first on the news feed on the home page of his internet browser. The feed was just a series of photos and headlines that never stayed put long enough to actually be read, but one headline caught his eye, and he had to wait through the cycle three times before he finally managed to read all of it and understand what it said.

New measles-like disease found in New York City.

That looked bad, so he clicked on the link and learned that five people initially diagnosed with unusual break-through cases of measles (they'd already been vaccinated) actually didn't have measles at all, based on genetic tests run on samples of their virus. It was some other virus in the same family, an unidentified morbillivirus, for which existing vaccines would be ineffective and about which nobody knew anything. That sounded really bad, but as Luc had no reason to go to New York and didn't know much about medicine anyway, he decided to let somebody else worry about it.

But then a few days later, the news got worse—the same mystery disease had also appeared in other major cities, thirty of them, all around the world, within the same two-week period. And some of the victims were dangerously ill. A few had died. Predictably, the usual suspecters started drafting conspiracy theories, and while they did kind of have a point (*thirty* cities? All over the world at the same time?) Luc had enough crazy in his own life already, and none of the cities were in Canada, so again he let somebody else worry about it.

The week after that he saw, on the news, a graphic that scared him. It was a map of North America showing all the outbreaks of the new thing in red. The largest red spot was in New York, of course, but there were smaller spots in almost every major American city, plus a scattering of even smaller red spots between the cities—and in parts of Canada. It looked like the continent itself had measles. Luc thought it was time to start worrying, except he didn't see what good his worrying could do.

And people were dying.

Estimates of the mortality rate varied widely. Estimates of how quickly the disease was spreading varied just as widely. Interpretations of what it all meant varied, too, and everybody had an opinion, whether they were qualified to analyze the situation or not. There were calls to close the borders, calls to forcibly quarantine sick people, and calls to do literally nothing at all because achieving "herd immunity" would soon take care of the problem. Public health authorities tried to inject notes of sanity into the discourse, but they, as yet, knew almost nothing about the new disease.

In late December, Canada did close the border with the United States and banned travelers from a long list of other hot-spot nations, but since the disease was already inside the country and had been for weeks, that seemed a little late. Anyway, the United States had not yet taken any definite measures—its president seemed more worried about his ratings than public health—and so Canadians could freely head south and return, carrying more of the virus back in with them. Just before Christmas, official word came banning multifamily gatherings or any public gatherings of more than ten people. By then, the virus had been sequenced and some of the basic questions had preliminary answers. Epidemiologists thought the mortality rate might be as high as 20%. Luc attended his 12-step meetings online and by phone. Midnight Mass was online, too, but something was wrong with the audio, and he couldn't hear anything. A deacon came by to give him Holy Communion at home on Christmas.

The day after that, the deacon got sick. A week and a half later, so did Luc.

Supposedly, his was a mild case. He had no real trouble breathing and didn't need to go to the hospital. He barely even got the rash. And yet for three days, Luc could not get out of bed except to stagger to the john. He lived alone and asked no one to come tend him, lest they get sick, too. He lay in bed, out of his head with fever, and watched the half-moon, waning that week, slip on down the sky past his window. He put his hand to it and felt the cold, the bitter cold, just on the inside of the glass.

When he recovered enough to check the news, he learned that prisons, nursing homes, and all other group-living situations had become hot spots basically the world over. Jails, institutions, and death—they'd always quoted that phrase from the Big Book in meetings, everybody reciting together the short list of places where untreated addiction inevitably went, and so the line popped into his head now, amusing him somehow. Then he remembered that "nursing homes" included his mother's place.

His mother wasn't an exception to the crisis. She was vulnerable. So was Michelle, who lived with several other teaching sisters. So was his nephew, Ari, the retard, or whatever he was, who lived in a group home in Chicago. Luc spent an afternoon making phone calls and learned that everybody else in the family was already aware of all of this and that in each case what little could be done was already well in hand.

"Dammit, why doesn't anybody tell me these things!" he raged. René, the one on the phone with him at the time, hung up on him. Luc stared at his phone for a good minute after that feeling useless. He called his sponsor and got no answer. The man was probably sick.

Somehow, despite his worry, Luc still felt insulated from the crisis. He imagined gathering with his family after all this was over, amazed and relieved at the tight squeeze they'd all been through. Bad things, truly bad things, happened to other people, not to Luc. He was slick and wouldn't ever get caught. And then one of René's boys, Jo-Jo, called.

Christine, René's wife, had died. René himself was hospitalized and on a ventilator. Luc couldn't even go see him. The scientists and them thought maybe you couldn't get the disease twice, but they weren't sure yet, and the hospital was playing it safe. René died the next day.

"Why didn't You take *me?*" Luc raged, shouting at the ceiling in his apartment. "I'm the screw-up. René never did anything wrong." Somehow, even in his grief he managed to make everything all about him.

A priest said the funeral Masses with no congregation present, and the bodies of René and Christine were committed to the earth by a priest and by a small team from a funeral home, all of them wearing masks. The Cotes watched from outside the cemetery, each spaced ten feet from the next, gloved fingers hooked into the metal chain-link, breath making clouds in the silence. Philippe wasn't even there. He was an American now, separated from his family by a border closed just that week in both directions.

The world got quiet after that. Hardly anybody left their homes—there was no point as most businesses were closed. People worked from home or not at all. They were sure, now, you couldn't get the disease twice, but could you trust that? And you definitely couldn't trust anyone to be honest about their status. The police broke up groups and gatherings without bothering to ask about medical history. The American president died. The vice-president died. Several members of their supreme court, all elderly people with pre-existing health problems, died. Canada's government, having gone into isolation earlier, was faring better, but the news was full of tributes and memorials and sad stories. Luc began a portrait of his brother, from memory. He barely ate or slept. There was nothing he really wanted to do besides work on that painting. He wanted to feel René alive in his hands, if nowhere else.

"Luc, you better get down here," Célie said on the phone. "Here" was the hospital. The disease had come for his kids.

All three had gotten sick on the same day because they'd all been infected at the same time—Christine's sister had come contagious to that gathering along the cemetery fence, and those clouds of breathy steam, they had billowed along for more than ten feet. The sister recovered. Jean-Francois was dead before Luc even got to the hospital. Chloe and Rosalie were both intubated and unconscious.

This time the doctors let family in to see the dying, one at a time, provided you had already been sick and recovered. Célie and Luc split up, each to see a different daughter, intending to switch later. Of course they did not, because neither of them could bear to leave the one they'd come to first. Luc went to Rosalie, his baby, the first one of the kids who'd agreed to talk with him again, sitting down to lunch or coffee week after week, warning him not to expect too much, but she kept coming back. She looked like her mother, except for having Luc's nose, but she could paint like he could, the only other professional artist in the family. Her face had gone as slack as a sleeping child's, except where it was distorted by the tubes. A machine nearby beeped at regular intervals. Numbers and lines on a screen made no sense. There was no window, no daylight, and no sound but the harsh and muffled chatter of the busy ward on the other side of the door. He took Rosalie's hand. She was just twenty-four years old.

Afterwards, he and Célie met in the parking lot and embraced, crying, social distancing be damned.

Nothing much mattered to Luc after that. He watched the news mechanically. There were international efforts at developing a vaccine, a test, some kind of treatment. It all seemed very optimistic, except nobody was confident any of that could be ready for wide-spread use in time to make any difference. There were huge gaps on store shelves—supply-chain problems, they said, exacerbated by panicked hoarding. There were online black markets in toilet paper, hand sanitizer, macaroni, duct tape. Why duct tape?

Nothing made sense. The United States began a cold-shut-down of all of its nuclear reactors and all of its refineries and any other facilities that might cause problems if abandoned. Canada followed suit. Other countries were doing similar things. The implications were plain, but nobody said it out loud. Luc didn't much care either way. His children were dead.

His mother died, and suddenly he could care again, care about everything, but in a strange, exhausted, shell-shocked way. Maman had survived the disease, but "supply-chain problems" included medications. She was diabetic and had a weak heart. Her funeral was simply put off. It was that or mass graves, these days. Bodies filled refrigerator-trucks parked in rows near hospital morgues. Days went slowly, but weeks went fast. There was no time to respond to one disaster before the next arrived. Supposedly wearing masks would help slow transmission, and people who happened to have them wore them, but there weren't enough, and there was no time to make enough. Sewing circles and factories alike retooled and started making protective equipment, but the fruits of their labor went to hospitals and nursing homes and still doctors and nurses had to re-use the few masks they had. There was no question of protection for the man in the street. The electrical grid grew erratic. There were new faces reporting the news as the anchors sickened or left to care for the sick and were replaced on-air by producers and interns. Riots spread throughout the United States—the politics there had been becoming increasingly volatile in recent years, and now it seemed no one trusted anyone. That contagion, too, seemed likely to enter Canada.

Francine went missing. Then Andy, Philippe's other boy, the smart one, went missing. Some tired-sounding official called in the middle of the night saying something about Philippe, and Luc just about went apeshit on her ass until he realized what she was saying was true; Philippe was dead, apparently mugged for the gasoline in his car. Luc now, for the first time in his life, had no brothers.

He did not seriously contemplate drinking or screwing. Nothing is so bad that a slip won't make it worse, as they say. But he called Michelle up to ask why he shouldn't commit suicide.

"You mean, aside from the going-to-Hell bit?"

"Yes, aside from that."

"Well, it's wrong. That's the reason for the going-to-Hell bit."

"I know, but why? We're going to die soon anyway, right? There's no coming back from this."

"You don't know that. You don't know what God has planned for you. Anyway, even if you do die soon, maybe you can let Him use your death for something good."

"What?"

"I don't know."

People died at home waiting for ambulances. They died in parked ambulances waiting outside over-filled emergency rooms. They died on gurneys in the hallways of hospitals. The increasingly spotty and amateurish news coverage was full of such stories. There were no free beds at the hospitals, no available ventilators, and never enough staff because doctors and nurses were becoming patients or committing suicide. During shift changes at the hospitals, the neighbors would lean out their windows and clap and cheer, throw hand-made greeting cards or sometimes roses. All throughout the city at dusk, people would lean out their windows and sing *Gens du Pays* and sometimes also *Oh, Canada*. Birthdays, wedding anniversaries, and deaths were acknowledged by chalk drawings in the streets. Nobody ever saw the artists, only the art. There were no planes in the sky anymore, only clouds, only birds, only stars.

Luc, walking home one day from the grocery (you no longer went in—you handed a list to an employee and waited until they returned with full shopping bags and a miniature credit-card reader. Nobody was taking cash), varied his route, making his way through a lovely, upscale neighborhood where he'd never before been. The streets here had not yet been plowed, though the last snow had been three days ago. He almost didn't notice the anomaly, so common had such lapses become. He was picking his way through an icy patch when, from above him, on a balcony, came notes played on a cello, familiar notes.

Luc stopped and looked up, trying to spot the performer. He could not. The angle was bad. But while he searched, another performer, this one on a trumpet, joined in from a different balcony. Then another on a guitar and another on a violin. All around him, musicians, some talented, some otherwise, rushed to grab their instruments and join in—they were all playing Leonard Cohen's *Hallelujah*. When the song finished there was a moment of silence and then the invisible cellist started again, the same song, presumably to give the others a chance to play it from the beginning, only this time the cellist also sang, and suddenly voice after voice lifted, the entire neighborhood appeared to consist of Leonard Cohen fans, they all knew all the words, the voices of people through open wintry windows, voices of people whom Luc did not know and mostly could not see.

Luc knew the lyrics, too, and he joined in, whispering along at first, then singing, singing loudly, not caring, for the moment, about whether his voice might be good enough. He, too, had been undone by moonlight, he'd paced floors, he'd lived alone, and he expected no victory march, not for himself, not for anyone else, not anymore. He sang and felt himself heard, a baffled and a broken king alone in an empty, snow-piled street crying hallelujah, hallelujah, hallelujah!

In his voice it became an accusation. It became a plea, a question for which he heard no answer. It became his praise of God.

And Luc Cote, his fingers on the steering wheel again going numb, eyes streaming, whispered "Hallelujah." He was driving now through Ohio, his last state. None of the state borders had been watched. The barricades were all abandoned. The walls were down.

After the deaths and disappearances of his various family members, the ongoing losses of his friends, Luc found himself waiting. He didn't know what he was waiting for. He'd go out for a walk mid-day, get some fresh air, sometimes greet people out doing the same, waving and calling good wishes from a distance. There was less and less food on the grocery store shelves, less and less in the way of city services. Gas was being rationed, the price of those rations steadily climbing, climbing. If the refineries did not come back online soon, there would be no gas at all. There were people being carried out of apartment buildings in body bags as there had been nobody to even try to take them to a hospital, no one left with them to alert anyone else that they needed to be taken. A photograph he saw in the newspaper haunted him—the hand of a dead woman apparently arrested in the act of reaching for a carton of orange juice on her night-stand.

What was he waiting for?

Everybody in the city was waiting for the same thing now. They had all become very kind to each other. Nobody talked about why.

Michelle called. Always before, Luc had been the one to call her. He did not assume the aberration could mean anything good.

"Are you alright?" he asked, instead of saying hello.

"For now, yes," she replied, her voice sounding faintly, dryly, humorous. "But Luc, this is goodbye."

"What? Why?"

"I don't expect to have much time left, and I expect to be very busy until then. And I have some things to say to you before I go."

"Michelle, don't scare me like this."

"I'm not joking, Luc." Of course she wasn't joking. By and large, Michelle did not joke, though she often laughed. She wasn't laughing now, either. "We, the other sisters and I, have decided not to eat anymore. There is no more food coming into the city—you know that, don't you? We have some supplies, and people still bring us things, but we don't think it's right that we eat while others starve. So we have decided to give our food away."

"No, wait, you can't—," Luc cried. "What's the point, if we're all going to starve anyway? *You* told *me* not to off myself…." Why was he arguing, if they all *were* about to starve? But he couldn't not.

"I'm not offing myself, Luc," she said. "I'm just giving away all my food. There's a difference. It's not my responsibility to decide what happens to me or whether anything I do has a chance to succeed. That's in God's hands. My responsibility is to do the right thing at every moment. And so I will give what I have to others for as long as I can."

Luc could not speak for several long seconds.

"I should do the same," he said at last.

"No, Luc. This is what I called to tell you. You have to survive a little longer. You must get in your car and get out of the city."

"What? Why?"

"There are farms, places like that, places where they can grow food, where people might have a chance. Go find one and live there."

"You come, too!"

"No, Luc. I'm ready to meet my God. You need more time."

He could not disagree with her.

"I can't, I can't believe…" he mumbled.

"Yes, you can, it just takes a little effort and practice. Luc, promise me you'll look after yourself?"

"Michelle…."

"Promise me!"

"I promise."

"Good. That's all I needed to hear. I'm content."

"Michelle…."

"Yes, Luc?"

"I don't want to get off the phone."

"You have to. You have work to do."

"But I can't."

"I can, then. I'll see you on the other side." And the line went dead.

"Michelle!"

Luc sat in his apartment, blank and numb, for some minutes. Then he got up and set about obeying his big sister.

He packed warm clothing, his toothbrush, his razor, his soap. He packed the sleeping bag he'd bought for some of his more remote paint-ball adventures. He packed his good knife. He packed all the non-perishable food in the house plus some of the perishable stuff, as much as he thought he could eat before it went bad. He packed his two favorite copies of the Bible (the Latin Vulgate and a recent English translation with interesting foot-notes), his Big Book and his Basic Text, his men's daily meditation book. He packed his paints and brushes, a roll of canvas, his thinner, his brush-cleaner, his rabbit-skin glue. He stood looking at his finished paintings for a very long time. He could not take them, not even his portrait of René. He needed to leave half his car empty.

He spent some time printing out all the pictures he had on his phone of his family, especially his children. The ink gave out just as he finished—he could not even take and print photos of his paintings. He put all the print-outs between the sheets of a catalog left over from one of his art shows, the only collection of his own art he was able to bring. Then he went and knocked on his neighbor's door and handed over the key to his apartment.

"I'm going away," he explained. "Help yourself to whatever I leave behind. Look after my paintings and my house plants, if you can." He didn't wait for a response.

Twenty minutes later, he pulled up in front of the house that had once been his. He had barely visited the place since. It didn't look much different.

When Célie came to the door, he explained his plan, to get out of town and head south, then find a group of farmers they could join.

"You're crazy," she said. "Me go anywhere with you? Anyway, we'll freeze to death. No one will take us in. No." She started to shut the door.

"We'll starve if we don't," he said, and the door stopped shutting. "Look, I don't know if my plan is going to work, and if you have a better one, we can do that instead, but we can't stay here, you know that."

Silence for a long moment.

"How far south do you want to get?"

"I don't know. However far we can get gas to go. Virginia, maybe? We need a longer growing season, an earlier spring."

"Luc, the border's closed."

"You may remember that I'm mildly talented at getting things across borders."

"You son of a bitch." But the way she said it, he knew he'd won.

He helped her pack. She chose the same sorts of things he'd thought of, plus a few things he hadn't—more blankets, a flashlight, water bottles, several thermoses of coffee, some sandwiches. She had more emergency medical equipment than he did—blood-pressure cuff, stethoscope, epinephrine—and some medical books. She packed all that, too. The short, February day had ended by the time they got on the road together. Driving along, he felt a sense of camaraderie, of adventure, as though things were really OK between them, as though everything was going to be alright.

It wasn't.

At first he thought the car had backfired, though cars didn't really do that anymore. Then he felt the steering go funny.

"Tire blew out or something," he said, fighting the wheel to get the car over to the side of the road. He did have a spare. The muggers were on them as soon as they were both out of the vehicle.

"We won't hurt you as long as you let us get what we need," one of them said.

There were three men. One pinned Célie's arms behind her and held her at knife-point. Another forced Luc down into the dirty, re-frozen slush of the road, pressed a foot on his back, and pointed a gun at his head. From there, he could look under the car and see Célie's feet and those of her assailant, but little else. He could hear the third man getting things out of the car and taking them somewhere. The street-lights had dimmed, giving the assholes cover for their work—the rolling brown-outs and black-out had become too predictable. Nobody was around.

Luc waited quietly, mainly concerned that his face might freeze in the slush. He'd known a lot of criminals over the years, and these guys seemed amateurish, not interested in doing any real harm, but volatile and potentially dangerous if triggered. He stayed calm and waited. But Célie wasn't having it. She struggled and complained and tried yelling "fire!" like they tell you in the safety-training videos, and only simmered down when her assailant inquired if she wanted her throat slit.

But then, a few minutes later, Luc smelled gas and realized the third man was siphoning out the gas tank.

"Hey, we need that!" Célie cried out. She had nerve, he had to give her that. Nerve and *stupidity*.

"We need it, too, and there's more of us," said one of the men, but she kept complaining and yelling. He could see her weight shift from foot to foot and guessed she was struggling again. *Shut up, shut up, shut up!* Luc thought at her, as though she could hear him.

"Shut her up, will you," said the man with his boot between Luc's shoulder blades. Abruptly, Célie's voice stopped. There was a sort of thud. A large, dark something or other appeared suddenly in Luc's field of view and lay still in the wet gutter.

His throat constricted. Bone of my bone, flesh of my flesh. Some small, analytical corner of Luc's mind noted his stunned, visceral pain with interest. He'd always wondered if his marriage was real, and now he knew.

"I said *shut* her up, not *open* her up," the man above Luc shouted in English. "Idiot, the cops still care about *murder.*"

They'd shoot him next, of course. They had to. They weren't wearing masks, and so he might be able to identify them, and assholes like these had probably watched enough TV to have some twisted, erroneous sense of how hardened criminals ought to behave. He told himself he didn't care. He had nothing and no one left to live for, and the bullet to his brain would solve all his problems. He closed his eyes and tried to relax.

Except he couldn't die.

Not that he was immortal, but he found he could not *allow* himself to die, no more than he could do calculus or run a six-minute mile. He could not do less than everything necessary to stay alive.

The weight on his back lessened—the man, still arguing, was distracted. Luc twisted, grabbed the mugger's foot and levered him down, then sprang upon him and in one smooth move grabbed the gun with one hand while hammer-fist punching the guy's throat with the other. The one who had taken the gas hurried back across the street to help his companions, so Luc shot him three times center-mass. The one still on the other side of the car with Célie's body leaned up and over the back of the car—to shoot Luc, obviously, so Luc shot him first.

Silence.

Luc took a deep breath, steadying himself, then examined the man at his feet, the one he'd punched, and found him still trying to breathe a little through a crushed airway. A bullet in the head fixed that. He wouldn't have survived long, anyway. Methodically, Luc checked the other bodies, finding both men dead. Célie was dead, too, throat open, her blood still hot enough to melt the dirty snow.

Célie.

He stood, surveying the scene, for a few seconds. Ten years, he'd spent the better part of ten years trying to remake himself, to leave his criminal, sinful past behind, and here he'd killed three men. He'd killed men, and he'd allowed Célie to be killed while he lay cooperatively under somebody's boot.

"Damn me," he exclaimed softly, meaning it. Then, "fuck it." He walked over to the body of the man who'd murdered Célie. "I wish I could kill you twice," he said to the corpse. "I wish to God I could." He thought about collecting Célie's body and taking it somewhere it could be properly cared for. He thought about leaving the crime scene intact, knowing that if he did not he would almost certainly become a suspect in Célie's murder, too. He rejected both plans as impractical.

Instead, he collected all the weapons and ammunition clips he could find on the bodies. He closed Célie's eyes and said a prayer over her. He looked around and spotted a red cargo van on the other side of the street, its back doors hanging open. He investigated and found it full of stuff, much of it his and Célie's. He started to retrieve his belongings, then thought better of that plan, noting that the van's keys were in the ignition and its tires had not been shot. Besides his own goods and some electronics and other valuables doubtless swiped from another victim, the truck held several full-or-nearly-full cans of gas, precious, irreplaceable gas.

His first impression had been that the back was "full," but really it was only crowded. There was plenty of room. Luc finished transferring his stuff from his own car and drove away in the van.

About half an hour later, he passed a pharmacy glowing weirdly with emergency lighting, its windows smashed in, a single cop car parked in front, headlights on, on guard. Luc had heard about how, over the past few days, there had been a rash of break-ins all across the country as people of a certain mindset realized that most of law-enforcement had called out sick. At first, he mentally classed the sight as interesting, even vaguely disturbing, but unimportant. Then, he changed his mind. He took a right at the next intersection, then right again, and parked behind the pharmacy.

There was no cop on this side, there being no broken locks here, but the security cameras had already been destroyed. Useful. Luc armed himself, then casually strolled around to the police car.

He knocked on the window, gestured for the cop to roll it down.

"Can I help you?" the cop asked.

"I believe you can, Officer," Luc replied in a respectful tone and pointed the gun in the man's face. "I do not want to hurt you, but I need some stuff out of that store, and I will maim you if you do not cooperate."

"Store's already been robbed, that's why I'm here," the cop explained, unruffled but looking at the gun.

"I do not think they took the things I want," said Luc. "And if they did, I will not blame you. Now get out please, hands where I can see them.... Now, hands on the car roof. You know how this goes. That's it. Thank you." Luc spoke with absolute confidence and authority and, unlike the amateurs who had assaulted him, he saw no reason to be rude. He disarmed the cop, removing his radio, cell phone, and flashlight while he was at it, then patted him down to make sure there was nothing hidden. "Now, into the back seat, please."

"You're locking me in?"

"Yes, Officer, I am."

"I'll freeze."

"I'll come back and warm up the car again periodically."

Once the police officer was safely locked in the back seat, Luc walked into the store and found, as he'd expected, all the food, money, and anything that might be turned into recreational drugs gone—but everything else still present. The place looked a mess, stuff knocked off shelves and so forth, and the security cameras here broken, too, but most of the important stuff had been left.

"Idiots," Luc said.

Then he unlocked the back door and opened the van. The worthless "valuables" accumulated by the other robbers took up too much real-estate. He carried all of it, the electronics, the jewelry, the piles of cash, out to the front and shoved it into the forward passenger seat of the cop-car.

"This stuff is from somebody else's crime. I inherited it," he explained. "I have no use for it. Keep it or use it as evidence, whatever you want. I don't know anything about how they got it. You need a blanket or something?" No answer. He went to work.

He found a box of heavy-duty black trash-bags and went through the store, knocking bottles off shelves into the bag. When he'd filled the bag, he dropped it off in the van, then got another. He was not indiscriminate. He took the most important items first, unsure of how much space things would actually take, then went back for the second-tier items, then some of the third. He was not interested in resale value. He was not interested in chemical entertainment. He was interested in staying alive and in making deals with other people who also wanted to stay alive.

He checked on the cop a few times, running the engine and the heater for a few minutes as needed.

When he'd filled the van as full as he possibly could, he went around front again and siphoned almost all the remaining gas out of the cop-car, then let the air out of its tires. He opened the driver's-side door, slid into the driver's seat, and started the engine again.

"How do I work the radio?" he asked.

"Why?" The cop sounded suspicious, resentful.

"I want to call your dispatch so they can send someone to come get you."

"Why don't you let me call?"

"Officer, I am a criminal, but I am not a *stupid* criminal."

"OK, fine."

With proper instruction, Luc called and gave dispatch a message so vague as to give himself another twenty minutes before they even figured out where the stranded cop was. As to *why* the cop was stranded, they wouldn't know that until the cop told them in person.

"Listen, Officer, I mean you no harm. I hope you get through what's coming. I hope that you survive."

"I hope you go to prison," the cop sneered. "But yeah, I hope you survive, too."

Luc found that funny. He left the cop's radio and cell phone on the front passenger seat but took the gun, spare clip, mace spray, and Taser with him. He left the engine running, the heat on, as he got out. He expected the gas to run out in another five minutes or so, but at least the prisoner inside would be warm. Still laughing, he walked back through the store, back to his van, which of course the cop had never seen and so couldn't describe.

Murder, theft, threatening to maim an innocent man, how many new crimes—how many *sins*—could he lay on his conscience in one evening? He felt rather as he had that night when he lay sprawled, spent, half-naked and sweat-drenched, on Greg's couch, another man's cum drying on his skin. A line had been crossed, a mask had been ripped off, and he did not think he'd ever get that mask back on again.

Luc Cote drove through the night in a red, beat-up cargo van, trying not to think.

By late afternoon, Luc was following the Ohio river down a secondary road through a rural landscape of gray, skeletal forest and drab, open field. It had evidently snowed here, too, a few days ago—the same storm had swept across much of northeastern North America—but most of it had already melted clear before the remnants had re-frozen in the intense cold-snap of yesterday and last night. Only a few thin, crusty-looking patches, yellow in the sunlight, blue in the shade, lay upon the land.

His walls were all up again now, and he'd raised them deliberately, strategically, knowing that his entire plan, and almost certainly his life, hung on his next conversation. If the people he encountered were kind, generous, intelligent, he'd have a chance of turning 57. If not…. He didn't expect to be able to find more than one, maybe two prospects before he ran out of gas. He'd already driven through several likely sites and found no one there. If, when he finally found somebody, they wouldn't listen to him, he'd run out of gas and then starve to death in another week or two. Or if they were idiot yahoos or reactionary cowards, he'd likely get shot and die before sunset today. There would be no way to tell ahead of time, and of course how he acted, what sort of vibe he put out, would be critical in ways he could not predict, either. He needed his old self, the one who knew how to deal with lawless men, the kind of men who'd give him just seconds to prove he was not a weakling or a narc. He was getting ready.

He couldn't see the river from here, only a band of trees, but he knew it was close because he had his cell on, its GPS navigational app activated. Lacking a holder, he drove with his cell in one hand, the other hand on the wheel, and he glanced at the moving, zoomed-out map as he drove. The broad, blue strip symbolizing the Ohio lay about a mile beyond the trees, and all the space between the river and the road was public land, a park or something similar, coded green on the map. He was looking for something. He didn't know what, exactly, but he thought he'd recognize it when he saw it.

And he did.

He saw on the screen how the river up ahead bent way out, away from the road, defining a fat-ended, narrow-necked peninsula. And the end of it was a big square of drab yellow, not green. It wasn't part of the park—probably a private inholding. And the only road going into it didn't branch at all, so the private parcel wasn't subdivided.

Luc pulled over, cut the engine to save gas, and zoomed in on the yellow square. It was labeled "KanDu Equestrian Summer Camp for Girls." He looked it up online, finding that website, at least, still functional, full of gorgeous, summer-green photos of huge lawns, paddocks, athletic fields, a dock and boat-launch busy with plastic kayaks and small sailboats. According to the text, the owners lived on-site with their family in the big, old farmhouse.

Bingo.

He turned in at the sign for the camp, then drove slowly down a very long driveway. He was in no way surprised when four men stepped out in front of him. The men didn't seem friendly, but they looked like a life-preserver to Luc—they were clearly security types, and people defending land meant land worth defending. Something was going on here more important than a girls' horse camp.

He stopped the van, opened the window, and turned off the engine. The air, though much milder than what he'd breathed that morning, still smelled of snow. One of the men, a short fellow with a long beard, came close to talk.

"You can't be here," the man said, in English. "This is private land."

Of course he spoke English, this being Ohio, but Luc had not before this moment realized that he might spend the rest of his life among English speakers. He might never again talk to another human being to whom he did not sound foreign.

"I know," he said, and his accent—his own, not the mimicked American—sounded thick and awkward even to his own ears. "I have a business proposition for you."

"We don't want any," said a tall man standing several feet away. The others all looked uncomfortable.

"The camp is closed right now," Long-Beard explained.

"I know that, too," Luc told him. "Can I be frank with you?"

"Yes, quickly."

He appreciated this man's dilemma. Long-Beard didn't know Luc from John or Mathew, and the police couldn't be relied upon to come help if the visitor turned out to be a bandit. The world was becoming lawless, and everyone with even half a brain knew it—but it might not be completely lawless yet. So if Long-Beard threatened the visitor, roughed him up, detained him for questioning, the police might come after all.

"Look," said Luc, trying to make things easier, "I know you have to be careful, there are dangerous people on the loose. I had a run-in last night with..." he could not think of quite the right English word—"rough people. Do you want me to get out of the...car so you can check me for weapons?"

"Alright. Slowly, though."

Luc got out, nice and slow, keeping his hands visible, trying to be non-threatening and respectful, the way they told you to be if you were ever stopped by cops. It amused him that after all his history as a criminal, his first arrest was by outlaws.

Long-Beard glanced at the road to make sure no passing motorist could see, then patted Luc down. He found the folding knife and the can of mace and put them both on the front bumper of the van, making a respectful point of not actually confiscating them, just putting them out of reach for the moment. Luc had put the mace and the knife in his pockets to be found. When someone is looking for trouble, show them some, otherwise they won't stop looking.

"Now, who are you, and what have you got for us?"

"My name is Joseph Anatol Luc Cote," Luc explained. "And I have medicine, mostly. Medical supplies. I can see that you have defensible land here, space for a farm, for hunting, and you are in the middle of an infestation of Asian carp. They are easy to catch. I saw that on the news. I am a smart man, but I am not so smart that what is obvious to me will not also be obvious to at least some other people. We are at a dangerous time in history, and given the choice I would try to survive it in a place like this. You must have had the same idea. That's why you are here. You have...bugged off? Bugged out. You have bugged out. That is why you are defending this place. But you are going to need medicine. I have it." He indicated the van with his thumb. "That is full. I have antibiotics, statins, anti-depressants, pain-killers, shelf-stable insulin, disinfectants, over-the-counter medications, vitamins, diapers, tampons and pads, toiletries, and other things. You can have it all, to use or to trade as you like, but my price is that you let me stay with you. I want to survive, too."

"Are you a doctor?" asked the youngest man of the four. Looking at him, Luc thought he might not be eighteen, yet.

"Do ya have any rubbers?" joked a roundish, older man. Long-Beard thwacked him one, but Luc answered the question anyway.

"Yes, I have 'rubbers,' though not many, I'm afraid." He'd had very mixed feelings about taking the condoms, as he disapproved of their use. Leaving them behind would not have made the fornicators become chaste, though.

"Are you a doctor?" the young one repeated.

"No. I am a drug runner."

He let that sink in.

"Bullshit," Long-Beard erupted. "Nobody comes here offering us medications because he saw a news story about some fish. Who the hell are you, and why are you here?"

Luc shrugged.

"If you do not want my medications, I will leave and find somebody who does want them. I have the gas." He turned to go, bluffing.

"Wait!" said the young one. "What if he's legit? We need the meds. He's right."

"We do need more security guys. Can you fight?" asked Tall Man.

"I can."

"Can you really?" asked Long-Beard. "I mean really fight? We might have to kill somebody, one of these days, if someone tries to take our land. What makes you think you can do that?"

Luc faced him squarely.

"That knife you took off me," he said, quite calmly. "It's not mine. You'll find it has blood on it. My wife's blood. You think I let the man who murdered her live?"

Certain things, said in a certain tone, cannot be questioned.

In the end, they invited him in and called a community meeting. He was not surprised when the vote went his way.

There were thirty-two of them, men, women, and children. Most of them lived together in the big, old farm-house. Most of the rest lived in the dormitory built for the camp counselors, which had no heat and no insulation, but did have running water, at least for the time being.

Luc would have no running water. He (like several other recent arrivals, he was told) was taken to an empty campers' cabin. The thing was basically a plywood box with windows, though it had a charmingly rustic, cedar-shingled exterior. The whole thing was smaller than his bedroom back at his apartment. No heat and nothing even approximating a toilet. Two sets of bunk-beds built of two-by-fours and plywood, plus a pair of primitive wardrobes of similar make were all the original furniture, all of it painted pale blue, like the walls. Why blue? Why not? He imagined the box full of four giggling, horsey eleven-year-olds and was glad of its current, lonely quiet.

"We'll get you a couple of stools and a table or something," said the fellow showing Luc around. "We have a carpenter and a good supply of wood."

Luc nodded. He unloaded his worldly goods and handed over the keys to the van and its stolen pharmacopoeia. Left finally to himself, he filled the wardrobes and laid out his other things on the upper bunks as though they were giant shelves, unrolled his sleeping bag on one of the lower bunks on top of its thin, cheap, vinyl mattress, and tacked up two of his extra blankets to make of his bunk a dark, semi-warm cave. He sat on the edge of the other bunk, the one he'd decided to designate a couch, looked around at his little pale blue space, and called it home.

He settled in over the next few days without trouble. Mornings started with fishing—fishing with seining nets in the freezing, often icy river. Asian carp went in the buckets, everything else went back out to live another day. Then he would join one or another work team or train with security until dinner in the early afternoon. Sometimes there would be free time after that, but more often there wouldn't be. The community had the fish, the woods, and some apple trees and berry bushes, but it would need to grow vegetable crops, too. To that end, teams were busily building cold-frames and a small greenhouse. Plus, the entire camp had to be redesigned to work without electricity as soon as possible, and that wasn't as simple as learning to light candles. The well and the septic system both depended on electric pumps, as did the water heater in the dormitory, and of course the refrigerators and freezers where they currently stored excess fish and much else. New systems had to be designed and built, and built largely by hand by people who didn't entirely know what they were doing. The community's treasure was a solar-powered battery re-charger, but that had about all the work it could handle with the flashlights and walkie-talkies belonging to the security team.

Dinner on Luc's first day was carp. Also on his second day and his fourth. And since leftovers from dinner formed a large potion of the rations handed out after the meal, he often ate carp for supper and breakfast, too, choking it down cold in his little pale blue room.

"You wait till we run out of the perishable stuff," Long-Beard, whose real name was Josh, told him. "Then we'll really eat a lot of carp."

"Why?" Luc knew by now that there was a lot of non-perishable foods laid in, too.

"The other stuff has to last us until June or July, unless you want to eat nothing but carp and venison for a month or two. Gardens won't produce until then."

The whole concept of just not being able to buy food anymore was still hard to wrap his head around.

At first, Luc also couldn't wrap his head around eating basically outdoors—the only place all thirty-three of them could sit down together was a pavilion with mosquito screening for walls. He thought dinner, like other meals, should be served in plastic buckets so he could eat in whatever warm nook he could find. But the community needed to meet together some time to talk over work assignments and so forth, plus someone would relay whatever news had come in on the wind-up radio, and sometimes somebody would play a guitar or one of the children would recite some poetry. One of the little girls wrote and recited her own, that was cute.

And dinner was also the only time he could talk to some of these people, if they didn't land on the same work-crew, and he needed to know whom he was dealing with.

Most, he discovered, were there because they were family or friends of the owners. They had no particular relevant skill, but they were willing to learn and to work hard. Some of the friends and family coincidentally did have needed skills, plus there were also a few more distant acquaintances evidently drafted because they or one of their family knew how to do something the rest of the group didn't. As far as Luc could gather, the little community included a retired Army captain, a couple of vegetable gardeners, some hunters, some amateur fishermen, a bee-keeper, a carpenter, a chef, two nurses, and a vet. There were no animals present besides the apparently-sleeping bees and a Jack Russel mix, but as they had no doctor, the vet and the nurses would together have to do for humans.

Most of the group seemed friendly and were far more welcoming to Luc than he had expected. He figured they just didn't know him very well yet.

Days went by. Weeks. The electricity went out a couple of times, came back, went out, came back, and then went out for good and truly. They'd gotten everything converted over by then, composting privies and gray-water systems instead of the septic system, cisterns of rainwater and snow-melt instead of the well, and so on, so it didn't matter much from a practical perspective. No more news came over the little wind-up radio, only static, so there was more guitar playing over dinner. It rained and snowed and melted and snowed again. Sometimes other people came, hungry and frightened. At first they came by car, truck, or motorcycle, then later only by foot or bicycle. Some came in at the front driveway, as Luc had, while others crept in from the sides. Some were looking for people to help them, some were looking for unoccupied land they could claim, and some tried to take the land by force but fled when they realized they were out-numbered and out-gunned. No shots were fired. Everyone but the violent types left with gifts of dried fish, their water-bottles filled, but none offered anything in trade, as Luc had, and none stayed. In time they stopped coming. The work eased up some, there being little to do now besides cooking and washing and fishing until planting time. Luc got very good at cleaning fish.

Luc was pleased but not surprised to discover that being on the security team was a lot like playing paintball, except that they carried real guns and the opposing team rarely showed up. His training with guns, hand-to-hand combat, and emergency medicine proved useful, too. He had very few bad habits he needed to unlearn.

"When you told me about the paintball," said the head of the team, the former Army captain, "I thought, jeez, just what we need, some nut who thinks he's a soldier. But you're alright. I can teach you."

"You forget, sir—before I was a paintball-player, I was a criminal. If I didn't know the difference between a game and real life, I'd be dead."

Not that he'd told these people everything about his former life, but he'd thought it best to provide his resume. A few he could see opening up to at some point. He liked these people, most of them, anyway, and he was prepared to keep quiet about disliking the few exceptions. Besides the security team members, Luc spent much of his time with the carpenter, who reminded him a little of Philippe, two older children who wanted to learn French, and a rabbi named Ed who seemed very much the grumpy old man, except he was rumored to be only about Luc's age. It was the ear-hair that did it, white, cottony billows, that and a slight but comfortable paunch on a heavy, square frame, like the human equivalent of a beat-up old arm-chair. And, of course, the grumping and grumbling, always in a rumbly, old-man's voice, a get-off-my-lawn-you-pesky-kids voice. Rabbi Ed made Luc laugh.

Ed was the only member of the little community who could plausibly claim to be clergy, so even though he was also the only Jew, he led religious services every week. He was careful to allow his flock their Christianity (Protestant and lapsed, in most cases), and even held the service on Sunday, though he kept his own Sabbath as well. Luc questioned the man's theology. He answered in a rational and deeply educated way and then opined that Luc's painting, though technically accomplished, was a bit self-indulgent and often derivative. He also challenged Luc's interpretation of key passages of Scripture, pointing out, quite correctly, that Luc could not read the original Hebrew. That lead to a discussion of the role of both evolving precedent and divine guidance in doctrine and in what ways a religious life both did and did not depend on more than the written word.

Eventually, Luc realized that he was going to have to learn to read Hebrew simply so that he could argue with Ed properly.

And then there was a young woman, maybe around Rosalie's age, with whom Luc kept falling into conversation. She had a habit of turning up while he painted or split wood or sharpened tools or took his turn preparing the extra fish for the drying racks. Sometimes she'd help, sometimes not, and sometimes she brought a project of her own, usually sewing. She had volunteered to mend clothing and was good at it. He realized after a few weeks that she didn't just happen by. She was, in fact, seeking him out. Her name was Clarice.

He had no idea why she was interested in him. He didn't think he could be anybody's idea of a father-figure, and while he had some interesting war stories, he made a point of not telling them. There had been a time in his life when he assumed any young woman chasing him around must have the hots for him, but that time was long over, and he now discounted the possibility without seriously considering it. He was aware of enjoying her company.

"You're not painting *me*, are you?" she asked. Clarice was lying, head propped up on one hand, on the couch in the bay window of the living room of the big house. Luc liked working in that room. It had good light, and it was warm. He was seldom warm for long anymore.

"No, I'm not," he assured her.

"So, you don't mind if I get up and look, do you?"

"No."

She stood beside him, looking back and forth between his half-finished painting and the view through the bay window, the large patches of thin snow, fallen and mostly melted that week, the first week of March, but then re-frozen in the current severe cold-snap, the grayish-greenish lawns sloping down to the river, the still-skeletal trees just starting, in a few cases, to flower. Luc had never paid much attention to nature before, but now he was starting to like it. He kept glancing out the window as he worked.

"Your painting doesn't look like the view out the window."

"I know. I'm not painting the view. I am painting what happens in my head when I look at the view."

"Oh." She returned to her couch. He wondered if she realized that the way she was lying there counted as provocative. He wished for a moment that he was painting her—the curve of her right, currently upward-pointing breast, the wrinkles of her jeans across her hips and groin, from a strictly aesthetic standpoint they were all very interesting. "I like the way you talk about art," she added. "I just never know what to say in response. I haven't painted since I was a little kid."

"You don't have to say anything."

"I annoy you, don't I?"

"No."

"Then why don't you seem to want to talk to me?"

"My wanting has nothing to do with it. I am nobody you should be spending time with."

"Why not?" asked Clarice. He didn't answer. "Why not?" she repeated. When he still didn't answer, she added, "you know, Luc, I think you're just not giving us a chance. You brood all day, you make these dark comments like no one would like you if they really knew you, but you won't know that unless we get to know you."

He didn't respond.

"Come on, what's the worst thing you've ever done."

He quirked a smile at that.

"Alright, what's *one of* the worst things you've ever done?"

Luc went on painting in silence for a while. She waited.

"There was a girl, fourteen years old," he said at last, still painting. "She was drunk. So was I. I was thirty-two."

"You had sex with her."

"I raped her," he clarified, still painting. "I did not physically force her—she initiated the interaction, actually, and she enjoyed me, for that evening, at least. I do not know how she felt or what she thought afterwards. But I should have acted like an adult in that situation. I should have protected her. I did not do that." He spoke evenly, with no hint of either bravado or shame. He thought he had no right anymore to show either.

Clarice had sat up and was looking at him, wide-eyed. As he'd guessed, she'd never thought he might have done something actually wrong. He wondered if their friendship, or whatever it was, was now over, and if so whether that meant he shouldn't have told her—or that he was right to have.

"Woah," she said, then he saw her go introspective. "I was a fourteen-year-old girl like that. I thought I was all grown-up. I didn't know how *young* I looked to adults. I saw him again later, across the street, and I just puked, I felt so angry and so weird. But I didn't know that was rape. I guess it is."

Luc looked at his paintbrush but didn't use it. He was hoping, not for the first time, that Rosalie never met a man too much like her papa. It bothered him that he'd never know, now.

"You should talk about this with someone other than me," he said.

He didn't know whether she followed his advice about talking to someone else, but she didn't talk to him about anything for some time. The weather started to warm, and in a dry stretch in the middle of the month, one of the work teams used the last of the community's gasoline and a hand-pushed cultivator to carve large garden beds out of what had been lawns. They carted the broken sod off to make a compost pile nearby and then brought in well-composted horse manure from behind the barn to make up the lost bulk. The cultivator quit halfway through digging the manure into the soil. They did the rest by hand. Then they built a deer-proof fence while the weather turned cold.

Everything took so long with only hand-tools, but it got done eventually, and when the garden was built and waiting for the weather to warm enough for planting and transplanting, Luc again had time to make art.

His supply of paint worried him. He knew he'd run out eventually, as he would run out of canvas, and he did not want to feel constrained by thoughts of scarcity. Better to use paint freely while he had paint than to hold back, rationing himself and lose his joy in painting preemptively. So, to free himself from worry, he started to experiment with alternatives. He could make ink from lamp black and alcohol, he'd done that in an art class once, or he could draw with charcoal, but he'd need paper, or some other surface. He understood the principle of paper-making, but wasn't sure how to do it without some kind of machine to grind wood into pulp. While he thought about that, he took a magnifying glass out of the study and a pair of welder's goggles from the little machine shop attached to the barn, and began free-hand burning a vast, Hieronymus Boschish fantasmagorium all across one of the picnic tables. It was one of those warm days that feel like summer and look like winter while birds sing springtime.

"Is it a bad sign that I still like you?"

"Yes, probably." He hadn't known Clarice was behind him before she spoke—the welding goggles narrowed his mental focus curiously, almost as though they dimmed his hearing as well as his sight. He kept working. He wanted her to go away.

"It's not that I think what you did was alright," Clarice told him. "And it's not like I want to be the good woman who rehabilitates you, either, I'm not stupid like that. But everybody does something. I've done things. I don't know, I just don't think you can be the same guy, now. Just from the way you talk about it. I think you've changed since then."

"Maybe."

He let her watch him work. He was getting the hang of his new medium, feeling the way that the fluidly curving burn marks lent themselves to intricate, yet highly stylized figures, symbols, ideograms. The burning went slowly, carefully, occupying his entire mind so that he did not notice time passing at all. He thought the table might take months to complete, and that it would become a representation of the last pair of shorts from Disney's first *Fantasia*, with the demon of the mountain and his damned minions appearing to dominate the table-top but ultimately surrounded and supplanted by a long line of holy, candle-carrying supplicants. Ave Maria. When Clarice went away at last, he admitted to himself that he still enjoyed her company.

The trees and bushes started to leaf out. Seeds went into the ground.

Luc found he could sleep through the night without shivering, a great relief. The construction team finished the smoke house, built with venison in mind but tested on fish. Ed fell off a ladder in the barn, and Luc startled himself by panicking. When he learned the rabbi had suffered only minor hurts, fear turned to anger, and Luc shouted at the man for having gone up the ladder in the first place, he could have died, he had to be more careful....

"Bah," exclaimed Ed, from the bunk of his own tiny cabin, "too much noise! You think only people you *don't* care about should climb ladders? Egotistical old fart."

Luc stopped yelling, shocked into stillness. He'd encountered many reactions to his tantrums over the years—fear, fawning, reciprocal anger, self-righteous defensiveness, even stoic calm—but this absolute refusal to give a shit was new. He said he was sorry and left. Ed had to stay off his ankle for a while and baby his other injuries, so Luc helped him pass the time by sitting solicitously by his bed for some hours every day and arguing with him about what the community ought to do for Passover and Easter. In Ed's company, Luc had the curious sense of having finally come home, though he was more often conscious of feeling exasperated. The man could not be made to see reason on certain points of doctrine.

The first thunderstorm of the year moved through. The apple trees eased into bloom. Somehow, the warming weather made their whole situation, the permanence of their isolation, seem that much more real.

"You know how when something happens, you shake your head and say, 'I don't believe it'?" Clarice said as Luc and Ed played chess outside. "Well, I've finally gotten to that point. Up until now, I believed all this even *less*." Luc knew what she meant. Over the past few months, he had gradually progressed from survival mode, to disbelieving, grieving shock, to now a kind of hypothetical view of the world, an acting-as-if civilization had fallen apart and his entire family had disappeared or died, when plainly such a thing could not have happened.

"Do you keep thinking you'll wake up?" Luc asked, his hand hovering over a black bishop. He reconsidered when he noticed Ed's dark brown eyes starting to shine. Clarice had asked to play the loser. She didn't watch the board at all but instead laughed a little, almost ruefully.

"Do you think I *could* be dreaming?" she asked. "I mean, how could I really tell? The pinching thing doesn't make sense."

"I know for a fact you are not," Ed exclaimed, knotting his hairy-backed hands together casually.

"Yeah?"

"Honey, it's been a very long time since any woman your age dreamed of *me*." Not that Ed was bad-looking. He did need a proper hair-cut. The feather of pepper-and-salt hair brushing over the tip of his right ear bothered Luc somehow.

But reality was getting realer for all of them. People started breaking down and crying over nothing or everything or both at once. After the holidays, they started holding memorial services as one after another in the group finally admitted some missing person they loved must be dead. And they started holding classes, since one of the parents had belatedly realized that it was home-school or nothing now. All of the adults took turns as teachers, and most took turns as students. Luc joined the children to learn U.S. geography and history and introductory bee-keeping. He taught both Quebecois and Latin (though not to the same people) and figure-drawing—they drew with charcoal on white-painted boards and washed the drawings away at the end of class so they could re-use the boards.

"Who is that?" Clarice asked. Luc was painting in the living room of the big house again, but this time the view out the window, far from being grayish and skeletal, had gone lush with green leaves and dark with rain. He did not look at the view as he painted.

"My brother, René."

"And that?"

"My sister, Michelle."

"And that?"

"My other brother, Philippe."

"You're from a big family."

"I have another sister, too. Francine. I just haven't gotten to her, yet, or our parents. I'll have to make another picture for my children and my wife."

"Dead?"

"Francine might not be. I don't know where she is, though." He let some seconds of silence go by. "My father died decades ago. Not of this."

"Yeah, my parents are dead, too, now. You know it's going to happen someday, then when it does, you're surprised." She went and flopped herself down on the couch again, only this time she didn't look provocative.

She looked like a kid unselfconsciously throwing her body around.

"Are you doing anything to memorialize them?" he asked her.

"No. Not really. I can't think of anything. I wish I could paint."

"You can paint. Perhaps you cannot paint *well*."

"Will you share your paints with me?"

"No."

"This is funny."

"What is? You asking for my paints?"

"No. Or not specifically. I mean, us sitting around talking about ordinary stuff like this when we both know we're going to wind up in bed together eventually. I wonder how long it'll take?"

Luc's paintbrush stopped moving and hovered over his canvas. He was a good deal less startled by this admission than he should have been.

"You don't sound too happy about it," he said, wry, and continued painting.

"Oh, don't mind me, I'm being stupid. I'm plenty happy about it."

Only, she wasn't. She didn't sound happy or excited or even desirous. She sounded resigned. Why should she feel anything else? Theirs was no true sexual chemistry, more like a coincidentally shared default. If they met, it would not be a case of mutual attraction but only that they had each slumped to the shared bottom of facing hills. And yet to hear her suggest that they have sex—she wasn't his type, and he'd had kids older than her, but she was beautiful, and she could clearly have any man she wanted of any age. To hear that she, in at least some sense, wanted *him*…. He was pretty sure he knew exactly how to cheer her up. Oh, yes, he could show her a good time. He could show her a *very* good time. He could feel himself rising, and his desire felt like a kind of hope.

He shoved hope aside.

"I'm not going to bed with you," he said, evenly, still painting.

She sat up and looked at him, evidently stung.

"But I thought, I thought you…."

He could make her feel better, he really could. He could make her feel wanted.

"It's not that," he assured her, his face carefully neutral. "It's nothing to do with you."

"Are you gay? Or, what's it called, ace?"

He smiled a little, amused by how much she didn't know.

"No, I am not asexual. I've given up sex. I am celibate."

"Given up *sex?* Why? How?"

Luc again smiled. He knew that incredulousness, just as he'd recognized her resignation. He put down his bush.

"Tell me, do you actually *like* sex?" he asked.

"Of course! It's *sex!*"

"No. Not of course. Truly, think about this, how many times for you has it been *amazing?*"

"I...."

"Be honest! I do not mean how many times have you had an orgasm. I mean how many times has it been really special—or were you lying there thinking about whether you'd remembered to feed the parking meter?"

"Twice. Maybe three times."

"So, why do you do it the other times?"

"I don't know—is that why you've given it up? Because it's not amazing?"

"No. When sex is...all it can be, it *is* amazing. It is the taste of God—and God tastes *wonderful*. But to meet God just for the, the flavor? To enter that moment with another human being just for your own personal pleasure? It is a waste. It is an insult. And so the wonderful moments get farther and farther out of reach. There comes a time when you know you must no longer enter a church in which you cannot pray."

"So what do you do?"

"You enter a Church where you *can* pray."

"How?"

"I can tell you."

Luc had no interest in bringing Clarice into Catholicism—in the rooms, he'd learned to allow people their own conception of a "higher power," because more people could get sober if religious differences did not get in the way of the message. Of course he still believed that everyone really ought to be Catholic, but he'd learned there are more immediate ways of feeding His sheep. And yet he also had no interest in convincing Clarice that she was a sex addict. He didn't know whether she was a sex addict, not in the full sense of the term—probably she was too young to be much of anything, yet. But he had one thing he could offer, and he thought that maybe Clarice could use it for something.

And so he showed her his collection of pamphlets. He lent her the SLAA Basic Text. He read her The Promises from the AA Big Book

(SLAA had promises, too, but they weren't as beautifully written). And after a while they started having meetings twice a week, reading Program literature and reciting prayers and slogans according to a strict format. Using the format with just the two of them felt a little silly, but it kept the meetings from degenerating into ordinary conversation. They worked the steps together, Luc starting over at Step One. He figured if they sponsored each other, the way the early SLAA members had, she'd be less likely to start treating him like a guru. He knew what happened to gurus; they diddled their devotees, sooner or later, and that wasn't a brand of crazy he wanted to try.

Now, to sponsor a woman, or to be sponsored by her, would have struck his sponsors back home as madness. He would have agreed. Like many men of his generation, he believed that unrelated men and women could never be "just" friends, and that seeking any kind of closeness with a woman not one's intended mate was a near occasion of a relapse. And Luc, though now a widower and technically free to court, did not intend to mate with anybody ever again. Experience had shown him he simply wasn't qualified for the position. But he wasn't back home. He had to either share his recovery with Clarice or stop talking to her entirely, and he didn't think it possible to stop talking to anyone in a community of only thirty-three people.

He continued to enjoy her company. They did not fall into bed with each other nor with anyone.

Luc thought a lot about these people who seemed to like him, Clarice and Ed and some of the others, including a few of the children who now spoke passable Quebecois. They were all so startlingly kind, he wondered at times what was wrong with them. But he knew it was not the kindness of the people around him that had changed.

He sat alone one warm, moonless night on the front step of his cabin looking up at the star-speckled sky. He had lived all his life in cities, first Detroit and then Montreal, and had only seen a real night sky, a country night sky, a few times on paintball camping trips. He'd been startled then by all the stars, but this was a thousand times better because there were no artificial lights, none at all, anywhere anymore. He could see the whole Milky Way shining like a vast smear of mica dust behind and beyond the hundreds of individually-visible stars. The largest stars breathed cold fire, white and red and green. A silhouette like a mountain range blacked out the stars to the northwest. Every few minutes, lightning flashed in that direction silently. He thought about what Clarice had said about him being a different person, not being the same guy who had taken advantage of drunk women and underage girls (the fourteen-year-old was just the youngest) and done so many other wrong things...cheated on his pregnant wife, threatened or humiliated people for fun or for revenge, terrorized children who loved him....

"It was when I thought I *had* changed that I returned to the harlots and the dens of thieves," he said aloud to the night in Quebecois.

He looked at his hands and fancied he could still see the blood on them in the dark. He'd confessed his sin in private prayer many times, there being a total absence of priests. He'd told Ed and Clarice. He didn't know if his confession counted. He still wished he'd been able to kill the fucking bastard more than once—or at least more slowly, more thoroughly.

The gardens started to bear, bringing forth salads, initially, though the other crops looked promising—sweet potatoes, white potatoes, zucchini, and tomatoes, onions and garlic, green beans and kidney beans climbing up the insides of the deer-proof fence, and more. The last of the store-bought food ran out. They were running low on sugar and salt. One of the hunters brought in a deer.

And no word came from the outside world. No more visitors came begging food. The radio had long-since gone to static. No planes marred the blue sky. No boats plied the river. Occasionally they heard distant gunshots or the sound of a chain-saw. That was all.

"Do you suppose we're the only ones left?" asked Josh, whose beard had grown longer than ever.

"No. We're not that smart," Luc told him.

Anyway, there were the shots and the chainsaw and sometimes the smell of wood smoke from somebody else's fire, depending on which way the wind blew.

The weather grew hot. They swam in the river when they weren't fishing. They had to be quick to smoke the fish and deer-meat now, before it could spoil in the heat. The food driers were occupied with tomatoes and the earliest of the apples. When they cut trees for firewood, they cut young trees six feet up, using ladders, so the stump-sprouts would be safe from the deer and would give them more wood all the faster. They were all full of clever little ideas like that. They were getting pretty good at this survival thing.

In August, there was a bad storm, fierce and long with strong, almost vicious wind. There were twigs and leaves scattered all over afterwards, tangled in the tall grass that had once been lawns. The air smelled of sap, the alarm-call of damaged plants. Some of the corn stalks had been blown over and broken and now would not bear.

Three days later, one of the patrols intercepted a delegation of four outsiders. The community held a meeting so the visitors could say their piece. The outsiders might as well have been space aliens. Nobody was used to seeing strangers anymore.

They all met in the pavilion, which had become a fine place to gather, to eat and greet in the shade of a summer's day.

"It's that storm," one of them, a short, dark man said. "I'm sure it hit you, too."

"It did," said Josh. "Some wind!"

"Well, we got hail. And I'll tell it to you straight—it wiped us out. What we haven't harvested yet isn't coming. We need help. We need food and seeds."

"What do you mean, wiped you out? What do you have?"

"We have some tomatoes dried," explained a thin, tall, pale woman. "And the potatoes will be alright, just small, but they won't get any bigger, the plants being pulped, now. And we have three milch goats and some chickens. But there are *forty* of us!"

"We mostly went into corn and beans, and that's all gone," the man who'd spoken first said. "We need help."

"You'll get it," Josh said, not bothering to ask for a vote. "Let us figure out what we can spare. And let us get you lunch. It can't have been a short walk."

"About two miles," said the pale woman. The two men in the group both looked surprised and uncomfortable at her words. Luc thought it a bad sign that these people didn't want to reveal where they lived.

The visitors sat down with the community quartermaster to discuss exactly how much they had and what they needed, while a couple of people went up to the big house to prepare a hot lunch for four. Everyone else waited around in the pavilion for a few minutes until the quartermaster finished and came to report, and then, while the visitors ate some distance away (at the picnic table with Luc's half-finished fantasmagorium, actually), the community met together to finalize what it could and could not give.

Afterwards, Josh fetched the visitors and formally presented the offer—so many pounds of dried and smoked fish, so many pounds of dried apples, and a pledge to provide a certain amount of seeds of tomatoes, zucchini, popcorn, and beans. It seemed like a lot of food, just listed off in pounds like that. Luc noticed that many of the people in the pavilion had a kind of puffed-up, self-satisfied look, as though they thought they were being very generous. He thought that, also, was a bad sign. He, personally, would have slugged anyone who offered him something with that kind of attitude—any man, that is. Even in the days when Luc used to hit people, he never hit any woman except his own.

"That's half what we need!" exclaimed one of the visitors, the woman who hadn't spoken before. "We'll starve!"

"You won't starve," Josh assured her. "With what you have already, this will keep you alive until next harvest. And if you get a couple of deer and turkeys, you'll eat fairly well."

"Yeah, that's assuming nothing *else* goes wrong," said the other woman, the tall, thin, pale one. "We might not get deer or turkeys. We might get another storm. Going *into* the winter with just enough food so we don't die isn't acceptable."

"Don't complain, it's free food," shouted someone in the back.

"So we should be grateful for crumbs while you have an infinite supply of fish?" replied the man who hadn't previously spoken.

"Nothing's infinite, not even fish," someone else shouted.

"You're welcome to take a turn at the seining nets in January," shouted a fourth.

"No, they're not, not from *our* fishing place," said another, and whether it was a fifth person or one who had spoken before, Luc couldn't tell. A lot of voices sounded alike to him.

"Hey, none of that!" Josh cautioned, then turned to the visitors. "If you do run out, come back, and we'll work something out. Maybe you *can* take a turn seining. But for now, *this* is what we can afford to give you. As you say, it's not good to head into winter without some kind of buffer, and we don't know what's going to happen, either. *We* could get hit by hail. In the meantime, there have to be other people around who have found some way to live. Why don't you ask them for help, too?"

"Better us than you, huh?" muttered the tall, thin woman.

"Come on. They're right, we have other options," said the short man who had spoken first. He stood up and formally addressed Josh. "Thank you. We will send a team by with the cart and horse tomorrow morning, if that's not too soon?"

Once the four visitors were gone and everybody was starting to disperse, Josh sidled up to Luc.

"I don't like the sound of their 'other options,'" he said. "Do you?"

"I believe someone has committed a tactical mistake," Luc agreed.

"Us or them?"

"I wish I knew."

Dinner was very late that day, since the cooking crew had been busy at the meeting with everybody else, and over the meal they had another meeting. Luc and Josh weren't the only ones who had heard a threat in the visitors' words and manner, and there was some discussion of not giving them anything. Luc argued against that.

"Treat somebody like an enemy, you'll make him one," he said. "Never escalate. You never escalate. The only fight you can be sure you won't lose is the one you don't have."

"But be ready for the fight anyway?" suggested a young woman named Anita. She was one of the few women on the security team and a skilled sharpshooter.

"Oh, yes," agreed Luc.

The next day, mid-morning, six people from the other group arrived carrying large backpacks made of five-gallon buckets with rope straps and accompanied by a horse pulling a homemade-looking cart with eight bi-cycle tires. Some of them were polite and some were not. Some asked casual-seeming questions that the residents knew better than to answer, questions about guns—used for hunting, of course—and the possession of flashlights. Loaded up, the group went on their way.

"So they have flashlights, too," remarked the Army captain, after the visitors were gone. "Damn bastards."

"I call that horse, when we win," remarked the roundish man who'd joked about rubbers on Luc's first day.

"You can *have* the horse," said Anita. "I want the chickens *and* the goats!"

"We will take *nothing* of theirs even if we do win," insisted Ed, who still walked with a slight limp and could not fight. "The feud ends here!"

"We may have to take their lives, or the feud *won't* end here," suggested Luc.

"Talk to the Captain," said Anita. "He's the one with experience. I'm pretty sure we won't be honoring the Geneva Convention, though."

"We will be honoring moral law," insisted Ed, but he didn't disagree with Luc.

Luc thought a great deal about Ed over the next few days as the moon waned from full and the community prepared for battle. He thought about Ed, and Clarice, and the carpenter who reminded him of Philippe, and the children he was teaching Quebecois, and how he might have to kill again so that they all could live. He was fairly certain that if the attack came, it would not be a simple mugging operation. Had that been what these people wanted to do, they could have come armed to pick up their gift. They could have taken hostages or something, then gone away peacefully with the doubled donation they would surely have gotten. That would have threatened Luc's group's survival, yes, but not so surely as to be worth killing over. But the visitors did not do that. Instead, they had asked about guns and flashlights. They didn't want a doubled donation—they wanted to not have to ask for donations at all. They wanted access to the river, and they wanted the seining nets. They wanted undamaged crops, apple trees bearing fruit, and long grass to cut and dry for their horses and goats come winter. They would come at night with guns and flashlights to take out anyone who stood in their way.

Luc did not tell himself that defensive violence would be morally justified, that it was war and not murder and therefore did not violate the Sixth Commandment, or that God would be on his side, though Ed said all those things and was probably right because he nearly always was, that smart-ass Jew. No, Luc simply knew what he'd do if the attack came. It bothered him to know.

No one who worried about flashlights would attack when the moon was full, so they had a few days. The security team met and discussed strategy, drafting several contingency plans. Then they doubled the watch and briefed the rest of the community, including the children. They drilled several times, always during the day, everybody practicing their own designated response to the alarms, except that the security team couldn't practice all of their plays because so many of them were out on patrol all the time. Instead, they drilled each other verbally, quizzing each other at every opportunity on every step of each of the several plans.

Faced with the actual prospect of real combat, some members of the security team chickened out, but they chickened out honorably, telling the Captain what they wouldn't do and requesting new assignments. Mostly it was not the risk of dying that they minded. Others who had not been on the security team volunteered, particularly parents, mothers and fathers deciding not to leave defense of their young to others. Most of them had no training with weapons, but were willing and able to deploy as reconnaissance or as builders and minders of booby traps.

The moon waned.

Luc was on shift at the radio base one afternoon when the call came in.

"Mobile Three to Base, just saw some ducks. Copy?"

"This is Base, I copy: ducks. Where were they?"

"On the river, just below the wide place. Just sitting tight right now, paddling around…."

"I copy: river, wide place. How many? Worth hunting?"

"Two or three groups. Not many. Not worth it, I don't think they're staying. Looks like they'll leave tonight."

"Too bad. You have any important news for me?"

"No. Everything's quiet out here."

"Well, then clear the channel, will you?" Luc laughed a little as he said it. The other voice laughed, too.

"I copy that! Mobile Three, clear."

Luc took a deep breath. Then he thumbed open the channel again.

"Base to Mobile One, you awake?"

"This is Mobile One, awake and copy. Clear."

"Base to Mobile Two, just checking up."

"This is Mobile Two, just saw a few deer. Wish I had my rifle. They went towards the river. Copy."

"I copy: deer towards the river. Anything else?"

"Nothing. Too bad about the ducks not staying. I'd like to get me some ducks. Clear."

"Base to Mobile Four, you gonna babble about ducks, too?"

"No, sir, just doing my job. Mobile Four, clear."

"Base to Mobile Five, you there?"

"This is Mobile Five to Base. Of course we're all here; we're not all there."

"Don't joke."

"Aw, you're no fun. Mobile Five, clear."

Luc took another deep breath.

Of course it was all code. They had no way of knowing whether the other group had radios, and other radios might use the same channel. But it was a simple code, depending for its security entirely on the hope that it might not sound like a code at all. To that end, the jokes had all been planned. Decoding was largely a matter of reversing everything:

The Mobile Three team had seen between twenty and thirty outsiders in the woods just above the narrow part of the peninsula and thought the attack might come tonight. Mobile Two had seen an unspecified number of other outsiders headed towards the same area and noted that they were armed. All five teams had heard and understood Mobile Three's report and would be getting into position.

Luc got up, stretched, and stepped outside. The sun was only an hour or two above the horizon, already sinking into the trees, casting long shadows across the sun-lit grass and gardens of summer.

"Jayven," Luc said to the small boy sitting just outside the door, "Olly-olly-oxen-free."

The boy's eyes widened, and in a moment he was up and running, shouting the magic word, olly-olly-oxen-free! over and over at the top of his small lungs. Soon, every pre-pubescent voice was moving and shouting the same word. There was a different alarm call for each contingency plan, and each one was to sound to outsiders like a children's game. Luc waited until he was relieved by the Captain at the radio, then went back to his house to prepare.

The five teams of two already out there would converge on the neck of the peninsula and try to stop the attack, if it came. Most of the others would arm booby-traps or wait in sniper-nests with both guns and near-silent bow and arrows. A few would watch the river, although the sheer number of outsiders in the woods suggested that they had not divided their forces. Luc and Anita and one other had a little more time to prepare, because they did not need to go as far to get into position. All three would be mobile hunters, taking out anyone who got through the lines and the traps. The decision had been made to let anyone leaving the battlefield go and to not follow the strangers home—there would be no counter-attack—but there would be no prisoners taken.

Luc looked up when the door of his house opened. The light outside was already starting to fade. Clarice came in. She'd never been inside his house before, he didn't encourage visitors, so she looked around at it and at him. Neither looked as they once had.

The little room still had its pale blue paint job, and its high, narrow table and several stools had been painted to match. But with boxes and wall-hooks and hand-carved book-ends, Luc had made a place for everything and put everything in its place, except for the finished and half-finished paintings and the waiting, stretched canvasses that leaned here and there in all the corners and otherwise empty spaces of the room. And every surface but the floor, all the pale-blue wood in the place, had been doodled thick in a fine, thin, home-made, lamp-black paint, dancing figures, symbols, obscure statements in strange calligraphy, animals, botanical shapes, sections of maps, passages of text in English, Quebecois, Latin, Greek, and, yes, Hebrew, all of it woven together leaving it unclear where one piece ended and the next began. It was as though for seven months Luc had been in that room, thinking, and his thoughts and feelings and dreams had become visible and stuck to the walls. But Luc had done his best to become *in*visible. He wore long, black pants and shirt, despite the heat, and black shoes. He'd dyed his blond-and-gray hair black, and he'd blacked his face and hands, his throat and his lower arms. He looked like a blue-eyed shadow.

He had already put on a utility belt holding his knife, his flashlight, and his handgun holsters. His backpack, also recently dyed black, sat open on the table beside him revealing two full water-bottles, multiple extra clips, and a medkit. He was busy cleaning and loading his guns—an assault rifle and two semi-automatic handguns. He did not smile when Clarice came in, but his heart lightened to see her. He was glad she'd come. He was always glad she'd come.

"I wanted to see you before...before, just in case," she told him.

"You'll excuse me, I hope, for not being emotionally available just now?"

"Of course." She paused. "It's like that scene in Lord of the Rings, where they're all preparing to defend Helm's Deep. I never thought I'd see anything like this in real life."

Luc chuckled.

"I never thought I'd be going to war at all, let alone doing it at fifty-six. What about you? Are you arming, or are you a, ah, non-combatant?" He still didn't feel fully in command of English.

"I want to fight," Clarice said, in a voice that told him she would be joining the children in the big-house basement. "I don't want to be a 'helpless maiden,' waiting for.... I don't want to be some*thing* fought over. But I can't kill. And I'm afraid to die."

"You're not helpless," Luc told her, loading the last of his guns. "You have us to help you. And we have you. Everybody needs help from someone for something." He paused. He needed to be, what was that Hemingway line, *very cold in the head*, but there was something to be said in case there wasn't opportunity later. "You have already helped me. I am glad you are my friend." He saw her smile, shyly. There. He'd said it. He allowed his manner to change. "Listen, killing is nothing admirable. It's deplorable, actually, and I'm not sure I'm not damned for it. But it happens to be something I'm able to do. So I will kill for you."

He finished with his weapons, holstered his hand-guns, and slung his rifle over his shoulder. Clarice looked at him. He hoped she wasn't admiring him anyway.

"'No matter how far down the scale you have gone," she quoted the AA Promises, "you will understand how your experience can be of benefit to others.'"

Luc smiled, just for a moment, and then spoke.

"God, grant me the serenity to accept the things I cannot change, the courage to change the things I can, and the wisdom to know the difference. Your will, not mine, be done."

"Amen," said Clarice.

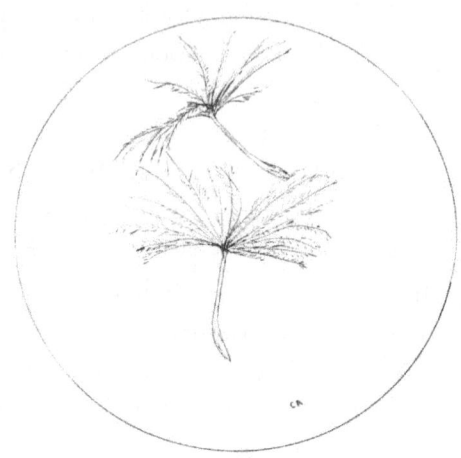

Unpredictable

On the summit of Blood Mountain, in Georgia, sits a small, stone hut. Nobody lives there but mice, and sometimes skunks. Few trees grow near it, for the soil is thin and rocky, and the place is exposed to cold winds. The views across the surrounding valleys are lovely, when not obscured by clouds. The place is quiet. Sometimes a few hikers come and sit for a while. Depending on the decade, there might be a crude sort of bench outside of the hut. Or not.

On a chilly, blustery day in early May, two men sat on the bench by that hut together.

One man was tall, slim, and handsome, with very red hair and tanned, acne-scarred skin. He wore a colorful, woolen serape. From a pocket somewhere he pulled a knitted cap with a red doodlybob on top and put it on. It made him look ridiculous, but a child he was fond of had knitted it for him, and so he wore the hat with pride. The other man was smaller, more wiry of build, with light-brown hair and smooth, tanned and windburned skin. He wore a cream-colored, cable-knit sweater, but he had no hat. Presently, he shivered.

"I could have predicted you'd be cold," the redhead said, quite cheerfully.

"Michael Estevan: show-off," muttered the other.

"Hey, my career has to be good for *something*," Michael said and wrapped his serape around both of them, making a kind of two-man burrito. Then he added, much less cheerfully, "Tristan, why did you marry me?"

"To keep from being an old maid."

Michael recognized the quote from *It's a Wonderful Life*, rolled his eyes, and paraphrased the next line from the movie.

"And to make sure your baby looks like me. Yeah, yeah. Seriously, though, why?"

"Feeling insecure, are we?"

"No. Yes. I mean, all the work I put into my education, my career, and here I am, a farmer. I'm not even a very *good* farmer."

"Everybody's a farmer, now. Or dead. It's not like the pandemic happened just to you." But under the serape, Tristan gave him an encouraging squeeze. Michael squeezed back.

"I know. It's just, it's the thing I dedicated my life to, and now it's gone. I'm just another over-educated bloke trying to learn how to use a shovel."

"I thought *I'm* the thing you dedicated your life to?"

"You, my dear, are not a *thing*."

"Nice save."

"*I* thought so."

"Why is it gone, though?" Tristan asked.

"Kinda difficult to be a broadcast met without broadcast media."

"There's still weather."

"That's true."

"And people who want to know what the weather will be."

"Also true. But with no data, no computers, no possibility of real-time collaboration... it's kinda difficult."

"The first meteorologists didn't have it any better." Tristan spoke slowly, almost sleepily, the way one does when cuddled up in a blanket with a physically larger loved one, but then suddenly he sat up, and a little whiff of cold air spiraled its way inside the serape as he moved. "Hey, that's it! Meteorology was built up from nothing before, why not do it again?"

"I suppose eventually they will," Michael agreed.

"No, not *they*," Tristan corrected, "and not *eventually*. You—us—now."

"Seriously?"

"Yes, seriously. Think about it. In another five years, we'll have computers again. Some towns already have radio. All the old tech is still there, we just need more electricity generation."

"Yeah, but human beings aren't so easy to turn back on. How many mets are still alive? How many trained observers?"

"I don't know, but let's find out. We'll look for people. And we'll train people. In five or ten years, we'll have the people and the tech to at least do better than nothing. It'll be a start."

"Bloody hell, you're serious," Michael exclaimed.

"Damn straight."

"Alright, how? We're going to need a lot more than citizen-science-level data collectors. We need people with degrees, and we need them fast, and there just aren't any more colleges."

"Yeah, but colleges can be built back from the ground up, too. They're already doing it with medicine."

"That's *if* we can find professors."

"I found one!" Tristan gave Michael another squeeze.

"Tristan, I am in no way qualified to teach."

"BS!" Tristan sat up again. "You taught at the community college--"

"Introductory courses! I can't create an entire curriculum!"

But Tristan continued as if Michael hadn't interrupted.

"—and you've been obsessed with science education as long as I've known you. The public programs you developed with me, back at the Observatory. Your social media. Everywhere you went, you blogged about it, explaining how everything worked, why it mattered. Even that year you spent in Antarctica! You were unstoppable. Remember the hate mail you used to get for talking about climate change on-air? Some of it came by snail-mail to the station. *I* was terrified. *You* corrected the spelling, graded it C minus, and sent it back!"

"Baby, you are biased. And you're letting the cold air in. Come on, snuggle up." Tristan obediently retreated into the serape-burrito again. A moment of silence passed before Michael, looking out into the cloud that had socked in the entire peak, spoke again. "I'm a two-bit broadcast met who got fired from the first decent on-camera job I had."

"Not from your second. You're worth three bits at least," Tristan said from inside the shared serape. "Anyway, that story is *exactly* why you're the right person to get meteorology going again. You were amazing. It's the whole reason I asked you out in the beginning."

"Really?"

"That, and I liked your buns."

"They are my best asset."

"Seriously, I'd heard of you, the new Day Observer coming in, the guy who'd *come out* on live TV! I thought, wow, that man must have *balls*."

"So you married me for my balls, huh?" Michael quipped.

"No, I married you for your brains. I *asked you out* for your balls. And your buns. Do not forget your buns."

"I was an idiot. I'm lucky I ever got a job in front of the camera again."

"If you'd done the 'right' thing and come out to them privately, they'd still have fired you. What you did stopped them putting out some bullshit excuse. You outed *them* for the homophobic jackasses they were. It was brilliant. Anyway, it's how you met me. Why *else* would you have taken that job on the rock pile? You were totally overqualified."

"Meeting you was worth being foolish," Michael acknowledged.

"Don't forget skiing in the Presidentials on your days off."

"Yeah, that too. Totally worth it. But I didn't know *any* of that would happen. I didn't know you *existed*. And I certainly wasn't thinking strategically about outing jackasses. I was just scared I'd chicken out. I needed a way to do it that I couldn't take back."

"I know," Tristan said. The cloud around them was thickening, condensing on their eyebrows, on the doodlybob of Michael's hat, and on the outside of the serape. They'd have to head back down the mountain before too long, back to their campsite with their friends in the valley, back to warmth and safety.

"I *had* to come out," Michael added. "How could I be a scientist and *lie* about *anything*, let alone lie about *me?*"

"I know. And *that's* why you're the right man for the job now. You don't need to know everything in an atmospheric sciences curriculum off the top of your head. Even if we *can't* find other people to teach courses, and I really bet we can, the knowledge *is* out there. We can track down textbooks, papers, whatever we need. The important thing is you know what the standard is. You know where students have to be in order to graduate. You know what qualifications people have to have in order to teach. You know who's ready to go to work and who isn't. And you won't back down."

Michael thought about all this for a moment.

"Alright," he said, "let's do this. First step is to travel around, see who's interested, see if we can find other surviving mets in the region, see if anybody else is doing the same thing. Then we start training observers, advocating for the technology we need.... Where's the money coming from though? Or, not money, nobody's using money, but you know what I mean. Resources. Equipment. Supplies. Time spent not farming."

"There'll be money again. For now, I suppose it'll be trade-goods, payment in kind. But towns'll pay. They pay doctors, because doctors save lives. We'll save lives, too. Maybe not at first, it'll take time before we can start making predictions that are really worth much, but we'll do it, and they need us to do it, so they'll pay us to get there."

"No, wait, *that* won't work," Michael objected. "We can't raise a whole industry from the dead by arranging for each met to get extra vegetables from the town council. If we're going to do this, we need full-scale, institutional organization."

"No, I know that, you don't—I didn't explain it right," Tristan said. "I mean—the *doctors* are getting organized. You know how Town Council just voted to let Dr. Katz check out all the traveling medical types?"

"Yeah, well, they have to do *something* to keep out quacks. Without certification boards anymore anybody could just come into town and claim to be a doctor, even a homeopath or a, a...light healer.... Did you know—"

"Yes, I did. And yes, that's exactly what I'm talking about. But this year it's that anybody who knows Dr. Katz can come into town and practice and get food—before too long, all the Dr. Katzes of all the towns will organize. I've heard people talking about it all over—it could be state-wide, or even beyond. They're making these guilds or clubs or whatever so that in order to practice, a doctor has to join a guild, and then the towns pay a guild to provide doctors. The guilds pay the doctors, but also source medication and equipment and supervise training, or at least maintain educational standards—there's your institutional support. And that's what we can do. We can form a guild—a meteorology guild. Towns will pay us like a, a subscription service to get forecasts eventually, and that's how we'll fund the whole project. Maybe we'll start a college or something, too. Then we'll have tuition."

Tristan was sitting up again, excited, letting the cold air in. Michael tried to catch at the serape to keep it closed.

"I don't know," Michael said. "You're still talking about something that needs a PhD, or some kind of equivalent. At this point, there's no reason a town council would vote to give me that kind of authority. I just don't have the background or the experience. And administrative skill—that's never been my thing."

"It is mine. What do you think I was *doing* the last few years before the pandemic?"

And Michael stared at Tristan a few seconds as though he had not before that moment realized that when Tristan said *we,* he meant it. A strange kind of delight bloomed gradually in his face. Michael chewed on his lip. He looked like a little boy about to try coasting down Dead Man's Hill on a bicycle. But he said nothing about that.

"How are we going to convince other people to take me seriously?" he said instead. "I don't have a PhD. You keep evading that question."

"I don't mean to. Look, Michael, you know what it takes to work on that level. So do I. We know where we have to get to. We'll teach ourselves and each other. You create an independent-study program in meteorology and science communication and put yourself through it, and I'll supervise your dissertation. You do the same for me. I'll study education. We'll make *each other* PhDs, because there's nobody left to do it for us, but nobody left to say we can't, either. *We can do this.*"

"Bloody hell, you're really serious," Michael said again.

"Somebody's *got* to."

There was a long moment while something hard to define hung, balanced.

"Alright, we're doing this," Michael announced. "We're raising meteorology from the dead."

"Good," Tristan said and settled anticlimactically back down inside the serape. Michael wrapped them both in the two-person human burrito again and kissed the top of his husband's head.

"I didn't predict this," said Michael.

"I did," said Tristan, already sounding snuggly and sleepy again. He didn't feel cold anymore.

Part Two

A Greater Silence

Andy Cote walked across the cool, slate floor of the atrium of the administrative building. Above him, the light-filled, two-story space was alive with aeromobiles—wind-up airplanes, tiny autogyros, solar-powered birds, robotic flying insects, all of them looping in loose circles all day long until their batteries or main springs wound down, or until the sun set. Then they would each glide gently to earth, sometimes bumping into walls or support columns as they went. Kaylee, the receptionist, would set them all skyward again in the morning. Andy didn't look up at the spectacle, but knowing it was there made him smile all the same.

Today, John stood at Kaylee's desk. Must be her day off. John was the dean of students, but the college was so small everybody did a little of everything. All colleges these days were small, small and new. Andy waved to John as he walked past, into the hallway where an open grid of cubbyholes pierced the mail room wall. He found three stamped letters in his—and a wooden coin signifying that he had a package. He considered. The delivery would likely be the new drone, an addition to the aeromobile flock, a present from his friend, Dashawn. He put the coin back in the cubby. He'd open the gift and set it flying with proper ceremony later, when his daughter was with him. She liked drones. He walked slowly back the way he'd come, looking over his letters—two bills and something about voter registration, nothing fun. He always opted out of paperless notifications, emails being too likely to get lost among the spam, so he often got mail, but he wished somebody would write him a real letter.

Voices caught his attention. A woman had come to the front desk to talk to John about something. She was no one he knew. Her voice sounded a little odd, almost slurred. Andy frowned, trying to figure out what he was hearing. Then she made a minor grammatical mistake that a native English speaker wouldn't.

After a moment, he noticed that she asked John to repeat himself every time he spoke without facing her. Unfortunately, John hadn't noticed the pattern, and so he kept turning away while talking to point at things or to look for something behind the desk. The woman seemed to be getting frustrated.

"Do you sign?" Andy motioned, when she glanced at him.

She nodded, relieved. John turned, startled. He hadn't known anyone was behind him.

"I'll take care of her," Andy said vocally, taking the receptionist's spot. John frowned, puzzled, then shrugged and headed to the toilet. The woman was fleshy and a little unhealthy-looking, but well-dressed, maybe in her late thirties or early forties.

"I can sign, too," Andy signed, unnecessarily. "Can I help you?"

She explained she was a prospective student, but the school website was down. Andy found several pamphlets for her and answered some questions about the application process. He wrote down the names and emails of the people she'd need to talk with. She thanked him, then paused, her hands hanging in mid-air, uncertain, before asking one more question.

"These people I need to talk to—are they like you or like him?"

"Like him? Him who?"

"Sorry—the man here before. I don't know his name."

"John Suarez. What do you mean? What was he like?"

"He...wouldn't believe that I can't hear. I told him, but he kept looking away while talking. I couldn't understand a thing he said. Then he got irritated when I repeated my questions—he didn't say he was irritated, I don't think, but I can tell, you know? How is it my fault that *he* won't talk clearly?" Her signs grew emphatic.

Andy glanced away, embarrassed for his institution.

"I'm sorry," he signed. "I'll talk to him. As to the others, I'm not in a position to know—I'm not Deaf. I have found them to be mostly helpful, personally, and you would not be our first student with a disability. But if you have any problems, email or text me." He scribbled his name, email address, and number on a scrap piece of paper. "I'm Andy Cote," he added, finger-spelling his name. He actually had a name-sign, but it was from childhood and far too cutesy.

She thanked him and took the paper. She regarded it for a long time, her face inscrutable.

"Thank you," she motioned at last. "You sign very well. Are you sure you're not Deaf?" She meant part of Deaf culture, not necessarily unable to hear.

Andy felt himself blushing, but not from the compliment. He was angry. No, he did not sign well. He used the visual equivalent of a monotone, his grammar and idiom were questionable at best, and his vocabulary was so limited that he often resorted to finger-spelling. He knew the woman must instead be indirectly praising him for taking her language seriously. But he couldn't accept praise for something that everyone ought to do automatically. That basic respect made this woman misty-eyed brought the blood to his face, and he couldn't thank her.

But he had to say something, offer her some kind of return.

"I learned to sign for my brother," he explained, instead. "He was non-speaking autistic, so we all learned. Our parents got us Deaf babysitters, and some of the kids in our Boy Scout troop were Deaf. I remember a little."

"You remember a lot," she told him, smiling.

"I like signing. It helps me remember my brother."

"The pandemic?"

"The aftermath—he starved during transition." It had been twenty-one years, now. It did not feel that long.

"I'm sorry." Her fist circled over her heart. He liked that sign.

"Thanks."

John had returned and stood behind Andy, waiting. The woman gave Andy her name and left.

"I didn't know you could sign," John said.

"Yeah, I picked it up a while ago," Andy explained, on his way out. He had worked with John for years and they knew each other's families, but John had never offered him any unexpected trust.

A Climate for Dragons

Diana Minakshi Cartwright lay at the bottom of the bowl of the sky and could not rise. Since the hang-gliding accident, nothing much below her armpits had worked. The air, for so long her friend and playmate, had suddenly—and quite literally—let her down. And yet she still loved to lie in the grass and look up at it.

But she could not lie there forever. Today was the big day, and she had to get up and be an adult in it. She turned her head, looking around for Dashawn.

He was, officially, her guild-applicant, something like what they used to call grad students, back when she was young and could still wiggle her toes. But grad schools had ended in the pandemic, like so much else. Now, to work in certain fields, you needed not a degree but a guild. And unless you wanted to start your own, to join a guild you had to be a guild-applicant—even if you were Dashawn Harris and knew more about robotics than almost anyone. So, officially he was her guild-applicant, her assistant. Actually, he was her business partner, her friend, her aid, and, on bad days, her nurse.

"Dashawn?"

He appeared, gently scooped her up out of the grass, and carried her over to an equipment tent where he undressed her and helped her put on her robotic exoskeleton. She hated to wear the thing, but it put her in command of her own body again. She put her clothes and her dignity back on and joined Dashawn at his field control center. He handed her a cup of tea and consulted a series of screens, frowning.

"How's it looking?" she asked.

"Oh, fucked up as usual," he began, then rolled his eyes and amended himself. "OK, it's not *completely* fucked up. Sections E and F aren't logging on to the cell towers, but it's probably just a relay being retarded or some shit. We've still got twenty-seven minutes before the media fucktards start crawling around. Plenty of time."

Dashawn was habitually irreverent to the point of genuine offensiveness. He would not be talking to said media.

"The, um, 'media fucktards' are here already," said a woman's voice. Diana jumped, and the servos in her exo whined as they moved her legs and recovered her balance.

"Elzy, why don't you knock?" she said and turned to face her publicist.

"Because you don't have a door," the younger woman replied. She was taller than Diana but not bigger, a girlish but athletic physical presence. This year, she'd taken to wearing her hair in dreads, same as Dashawn. They had the same hair texture and could pull off that sort of thing.

"Hey, you're a cop," put in Dashawn, still attending to his computers. "Arrest the reporters for trespassing. Fuck 'em up."

"I only fuck up bad guys," Elzy Rodriguez explained, lightly. "Anyway, I left my badge at home. I'm wearing my environmental-education hat today. Why don't you just buzz them with your toy birds?"

Dashawn tensed, then stood up slowly.

"I don't build toys," he said. He was a big man, a subtly unstable man. A lesser woman than Elzy might have felt intimidated. But when he turned around he was grinning like a friendly retriever. "I fly *dragons*."

"Children, children," Diana chided, playfully. But her accent, musical and precise, was coming out, as it always did when she was stressed. "Elzy, we're having an issue with the relays, just keep the reporters busy for the moment, OK?"

"But they want *you*."

"Tell them I'll be out when I am ready!"

"Yes, Dr. Cartwright." Elzy left the tent as soundlessly as she'd entered it.

"I've actually got things covered in here," Dashawn told her, "if you want to go out and act all famous and shit."

"I'm just not looking forward to explaining the difference between climatology and meteorology 42 times in a row."

"So, don't bother. Who gives a shit if they think you're the weather-lady? Give 'em a couple a' sound-bites, talk about the science, yada yada yada, you'll be fabulous."

"Of course I'll be fabulous," snapped Diana. She finished her tea, clipped on an earpiece so Dashawn could call her if he needed to, and walked out into the busy sunshine.

These days, the green floor of Carter Notch, in New Hampshire, was a dairy farm, but it still had wide, flat, open areas where the tourist parking lots used to be. The place made a good launch site. Today, the cows were sequestered in their barns. In the pastures rested rows upon rows of blue and white fixed-wing aerial drones, products of a resurgent, if modest, industrial capacity, small factories powered mostly by landfill gas. Each was about the size of a turkey vulture, pale beneath and covered with dark solar cells above. Retractable props provided thrust when the machine was not soaring, and a dozen tiny cameras and other sensors peered out from ports in the head and belly. Each drone sat on its own portable launch ramp, while dozens of techs moved among the rows, making last-minute adjustments and consulting tablet computers all keyed in to Dashawn's electronic nerve center.

Above, the sky warmed towards noon, and real, flesh-and-blood vultures soared upwards in huge circles. A pair of ravens gamboled, tumbling together for thousands of feet and then rising to wrestle and flirt all over again.

Diana knew each of the three hundred fliers was coming awake around her, flexing and testing various flaps. She could visualize them trying out their robotic senses, tasting the air for wind speed, direction, humidity, temperature, barometric pressure (adjusted for altitude) and trace atmospheric gas composition. She could also visualize a sixth of the machines refusing to communicate with the cell network. Without that network, the drones not only couldn't report their data and accept new commands, they couldn't correct any navigation errors. The last of the GPS satellites had stopped working years ago, just like the communications and research satellites before them. It was all just so much space-junk, now.

Those satellites could not be replaced. The new society was fossil-fuel free, a miracle, yes, but how do you hurl a payload of any real size into space without it? And without satellites, how do you collect critical climatological and meteorological data? Well, maybe if you fly enough drones along enough transects, you could do it. If today's launch went well, other launches would follow in other parts of the country. Over a thousand drones, filling American airspace. But if sections E and F would not or could not communicate, ten years of work and the best of her legacy would stay grounded with them.

In all likelihood, the problem would be fixed soon, in minutes or hours, or a few days at most. Last-minute technical glitches were pretty run-of-the-mill. The trouble was that Elzy, quite sensibly, had encouraged the project's major funders to use the launch as a publicity opportunity. A delay now would embarrass the very people whose money and goodwill Diana could not do without.

Two hours until the equivalent of a ribbon-cutting ceremony. If she could keep the reporters happy until then, maybe Dashawn would get the drones launched on schedule after all.

The stage wasn't ready yet, so Elzy was holding court from the tailgate of an empty cart. She actually had the reporters all laughing—which was part of why she made a good publicist—but she was right; it was Diana they wanted.

With as much grace as modern technology could offer, Diana climbed up onto the cart. Elzy clasped her hand for a moment and hopped down.

Diana gave the reporters an abbreviated version of her prepared statement, explaining what the drones were, why they were necessary, and what parts of the country these 300 would fly over. She graciously acknowledged the expertise of Dashawn Harris in designing and flying the drones and of Elzy Rodriguez for arranging so much of the funding and public goodwill the project required. She thanked all her institutional partners by name and then reiterated the importance of accurate climatological assessment for crafting public policy. "With these data, we will no longer have to rely on guesswork and anecdote to understand the pace of climate change." She asked if anyone had any questions.

"Dr. Cartwright?" said a very young, very freckled, man with a reddish Afro. "Did you say, 'climate change'? But fossil fuel use stopped 25 years ago." Diana fought the urge to roll her eyes. Hadn't these people attended school?

"Fossil fuel use stopped, yes," she explained, "but there are other emissions types—natural gas leaks, chlorofluorocarbons from broken refrigeration units, deforestation—these things do not stop simply because one civilization falls." She felt bad for the man-boy with the Afro; he'd probably never seen a working air conditioner in his life, but he still had to live with the environmental cost of the machines.

A middle-aged woman asked whether the drones were meant to monitor the recovery from climate change. She seemed to be having trouble with the concept that no, climate change wasn't over. Diana reiterated as gently as she could.

"But haven't CO2 levels been falling?" the woman asked.

"Yes, carbon dioxide levels have been falling, as have methane levels and some of the shorter-lived chlorinated gasses," Diana explained. "But average global temperature has not. In fact, global temperature is still rising because there is a lag in the climate system of several decades. The problem is that this additional heat could be enough to trigger positive feedback loops, such as self-maintaining forest dieback in the Amazon, or the release of the remaining methane trapped in frozen tundra in the extreme Arctic. If that happens, we will see carbon dioxide and methane levels start to rise again. That is why it is so critical that we have access to accurate atmospheric data as soon as possible."

"What will you do if those feedback loops happen?" asked the boy with the Afro, sounding desolate.

"We don't know," Diana told him. "We hope it never comes to that. But we don't have to wait for feedback loops to start to take action. These drones can identify localized methane or CFC release plumes, such as from leaking extraction sites or landfills or industrial ruins. With that information, we may be able to go in and cap those leaks. We may also be able to identify areas where planting programs or various other types of restoration can speed up natural ecological recovery and biomass build-up. All these steps can either lower emissions or enhance carbon reuptake and may be able to buy us more time."

There were other questions, all of them intelligent and well-thought-out, but most of them at least sixty or seventy *years* out of date scientifically. Why was Diana having to do basic science education for issues that should have become common knowledge a generation or two ago? The thought depressed her terribly. Worse, no one asked what should have been the obvious question; how could drones flying over the United States shed much light on what was going on in the Arctic or the Amazon? The answer was they couldn't—but the new Federal government still had not opened up diplomatic relations with any foreign countries and explicitly discouraged both international travel and the repair of international computer networks. The problem was that America still had no army, and the newly elected suits in Washington were quietly hoping the rest of the world would not notice. So, if there were scientists in Brazil or Ecuador, in Canada or the Republic of Alaska—or even back home in India—they had no way to talk to Diana Cartwright.

Finally, the reporters ran dry and wandered off to edit their dispatches. Diana sat down on the tailgate and closed her eyes. The top of her exo pinched and rubbed against her ribs and beneath her breasts. She could feel that, and the constant discomfort dragged at her. She'd elected not to wear her ugly circulation boots today and knew her moment of vanity had been a mistake. Her feet were probably swelling. She wished cacao trees grew in North America because she could really use a chocolate bar right now, but she'd happily settle for whiskey if anyone offered her some.

The cart shifted on its shocks as someone else sat down on the tailgate. Knuckles rapped on the wood—Elzy was knocking, as requested. Diana smiled.

"Nobody likes a smart-ass, Elzy."

"Good thing I don't care," Elzy replied, amiably. "How's it going?"

"If I have to tell one more bright-eyed and bushy-tailed reporter that we are all doomed I am going to have to take up drinking."

"*Are* we doomed?"

"No, but when I describe climatology to the public it always sounds like we are. Elzy, I am tired."

Elzy shrugged. She was too pragmatic to get upset about things she could not help.

"I don't think they really look like dragons," she said, changing the subject. "I still think the drones look like toy birds."

"How do you know what dragons look like?" asked Diana, opening her eyes.

"I don't," Elzy confessed. "But there was this man—you know when you've known somebody about fifteen minutes and you're in love?"

"At my age, we don't call *that* love."

123

"I didn't either, really, but I'd gone all oogly inside. We stayed up all night watching the stars and telling stories. He was a professional story-teller, and he told me about dragons. European dragons, Chinese dragons, Indian dragons, Mexican dragons, maybe even, an Australian dragon. He said that dragons embody the fertility and wealth of the land—that's why they hoard gold—but also the land's fierceness, its danger. So, dragons should look, I don't know, like a hailstorm."

"I wish I were a dragon," said Diana. "I wish I could breathe fire and protect the world. I wish I could fly."

Elzy was about to reply when Diana's earpiece came to life.

"Hey, boss-lady," said Dashawn. "I've got good news and bad news."

"Go ahead."

"E and F signed on, but I'll be damned if I know why they were off in the first place, and until I know we can't launch. If they cut out again before they gain altitude we could lose the batch."

"If they don't get airborne soon, we'll have to reschedule anyway," Diana warned. "I don't want the night glide to begin at less than ten thousand feet."

"I know, I know, I'm working on it."

"Do you need me to come over?"

"Not unless you've learned how to read relay code."

"Not in the last forty-five minutes, no. OK, I'll stay here, then. Let me know when you have a launch time."

"Will do. Later, gator." A slight click and the connection shut down again.

"Keep an eye out for the VIPs, will you please?" Diana asked Elzy.

"Do you want me to get you out of your exo?"

"No, it's too much of a hassle to get back in again. But my feet are swelling."

"Let me fetch one of the packing crates. You can put your feet up."

"That sounds good." Diana never said thank you for such assistance. Long ago she had realized that only two groups of people get to move through this life waited on by others: cripples and royalty. She had decided to be one of the latter.

She dozed for a few minutes, sitting in the ox-cart with her feet up, until a fly bit her neck and woke her. It was just as well, since the hum of distant voices and the occasional snort or nicker of a horse told her the

VIPs, the rest of the reporters, and who knows how many curious locals, were arriving. She checked her cell; one o'clock, right on time. Except, would the drones actually work?

Diana and Elzy greeted and schmoozed and stalled for as long as they could, but eventually they'd have to either begin the press conference or explain why not. Diana chose the former, hoping Dashawn would get the glitch worked out in time. But no voice came to her through her ear-piece.

She stepped on to the stage, recited her statement, and answered questions. She sat down on stage in the row of chairs set there for speakers and wondered if she was doing the right thing by acting like everything was fine. The president of Appalachian Mountain College and the directors of the White Mountain Weather Research Bureau and the Portland Manufacturing Alliance all gave professionally self-aggrandizing speeches. The director of the Mt. Washington Weather Observatory and the dean of the college's meteorology program, a couple she knew socially and had worked with closely throughout the project, also spoke and told funny stories about the years-long project. She wondered whether all of this effort would turn out to be for nothing.

Then she saw, beyond the dignitaries and behind the crowd, every one of Dashawn's techs simultaneously stop what they were doing and put a hand to an ear. Then they were off, moving again, swarming around the drones in one corner of the field, adjusting things. Her heart leaped.

"Good news, boss-lady," said Dashawn's voice in her ear. "We've got it covered. Nothing's wrong with the relay code after all—those units have an older model security card than the others, and it doesn't play nice with the new cell protocols. We're switching them out with spares. Launch in fifteen minutes, if you're ready."

"We might be," Diana replied, in a whisper. "Keep me patched in, I'll let you know."

"Okey-dokey, artichokey."

The VIP sitting next to Diana looked at her sharply, as though she were passing notes in class.

Twenty minutes later, Diana and the VIPs stood on the edge of the launch field. The rest of the crowd had turned in place to watch. Two press-drones hovered above, taking video and staying out of the way.

"Now," said Diana. Her whole career turned on this moment.

"Launching Section A," said Dashawn, and fifty propellers started to spin, every second drone in the nearest third of the field. In seconds, the light-weight machines were all airborne.

"Banking left," said Dashawn, and they all did, turning obediently in a large circle thirty feet above the spectators' heads.

"Banking right…and testing autonomous execution and crash avoidance." One of the drones broke formation and cut across the gyre, and the others neatly avoided it, turning and climbing and diving, each as its own processors suggested. The whole flock danced and spun through a series of tests and then began their climb to the heights. Some in the crowd cried out in wonder, others applauded. The press drones climbed and turned under instructions from their handlers, looking for the best shots. And Dashawn launched and tested Section B.

One after another, each of the sections took to the sky, banking and dancing. The first group were up in the thermals now, propellers retracted, turning on the rising air just like the real vultures. When they reached ten thousand feet they'd each glide out, heading to their separate transects. And still flocks of drones launched.

Diana walked out among them, and Dashawn, hidden in his equipment tent but watching nonetheless, directed the newly airborne drones to swoop down around her, curving and banking like dragonflies within a foot or two of her hips and shoulders. She threw her arms up to the sky and a drone flew right between her outstretched hands.

She laughed, giggling like a child, and spun, dancing as if she might fly herself.

I'll Be Seeing You

"There are too many people in this room," Elzy whispered. Four hundred-some sat around and behind her, most of them talking loudly. Since moving to the cabin in the woods, she'd started forgetting how to deal with strangers.

"You have never seen a train station in Mumbai," Diana, her traveling companion, replied, amused.

"I'm glad I haven't!" But she'd come to the conference to network. How was she supposed to meet people if the people had her out of sorts?

Until she just did it, without thinking.

"I like your hair," she told the stranger to her right.

"Do you really?"

"If I were going to start buttering people up," Elzy said, "why would I start with you? I don't know you from Eve."

The woman threw her head back and laughed. She was tall, slim, and slightly angular. Her hair, very short, very straight, was salt with a little pepper and a generous but irregular splash of purple.

"The cowl is new," she explained slowly, thoughtfully, lightly. "I wanted to make my hair match it, but the shade didn't come out right."

The cowl, along with black or brown tunic and trousers or a skirt, was professional dress, these days. Everyone in the room wore one, usually tipped back off the head and spread across the shoulders. The cowl's color-pattern identified the user's guild, but Elzy didn't recognize this woman's soft shades of gray, blue, and purple—quite elegant, though no, the purples didn't match.

The woman wore a senior-guildmember pin on her chest, a small, silver ankh in the cartilage of her left ear, and a gold wedding band on the ring finger of her right hand.

"How did you do it?" Elzy asked.

"Blackberry juice."

"Really? I'd have eaten the blackberries."

"Well, I'd have eaten them, too, except—" and the woman paused thoughtfully for so long that she didn't get to finish before a young man wearing a black and green cowl took the stage and called the first session to order.

There hadn't been a conference like this since before the collapse, twenty-six years ago. Maybe there had never before been one. After all, before, environmentalists of all stripes had been playing defense, fighting a long retreat. That the old way of life would itself end was inevitable—that's what "unsustainable" means—but how much of the world would be destroyed first? Conservation scientists met to discuss how much could be saved and for how long. They wanted the end to come soon, but deliberately, gently, justly. Instead, the pandemic struck, and while too many people lay sick at once, the convoluted supply chains made possible (actually, economically inevitable) by fossil fuel failed, and five billion people starved. The survivors, grieving, terrified, rebuilt on a different basis and left fossil fuel and its promises and risks behind. And the world began to green. Now, a generation later, professional scientists and educators and so forth gathered again, but the questions they were asking had changed.

These people, and the others attending similar conferences elsewhere, wanted to know, not *how can we slow decline* but *how do we aid recovery?*

But however exciting the conference as a whole, the first session was boring—introductory, bureaucratic, and seemingly interminable. When it finally ended, a mass exodus towards the toilets began.

Elzy caught at the sleeve of the purple-haired woman, asking "except what?" The question was pointless, nobody could remember an interrupted thought that long. Anybody would look at Elzy oddly even for asking. But the woman did not look at her oddly.

"Except there is a sense in which something other than the body needs to be fed," she explained. "The spirit hungers for beauty. Or silly hair. Or something." She smiled and turned again to go, but stopped when a voice called Elzy's name.

A tall, slim, long-haired, vaguely brownish man waved and called again from three rows back.

"Saul!" Elzy cried and made her way out of the chairs to meet him in the outside aisle. The purple-haired woman followed and then waited at a respectful distance as though in line.

"Elzy, I didn't know you were here," Saul exclaimed, grinning.

"I didn't know *you* were," she replied, smiling broadly back. "Not surprised, though." Elzy, a relatively young environmental educator, had gotten a spot at the conference because somebody else had canceled, but Saul was a founding senior member of a major guild. People like him got specially invited.

"Oh, everybody who's everybody is here," he said, simpering like a socialite, and then laughed.

"Have your people call my people," Elzy replied, in a similar tone. "We'll do lunch."

"Aha," said Saul, "that's exactly why I called you over—will you have lunch with us?"

"Us?"

"Andy and me."

"Andy's here?"

"Of course. Anybody who's anybody….He's the one who spotted you, actually. He was right here—he just ran off to catch somebody else, Diana somebody?"

"Diana Cartwright…." Elzy said, distracted, startled to realize she'd never even thought about whether she'd see her old college mentor here. But his invitation was even more of a sure thing than Saul's. Maybe she'd just gotten used to not seeing him. She shook her head, clearing it "Yes, of course, we'll do lunch," she told Saul, then stepped aside, letting the purple-haired woman have her turn.

"Saul Schaefer?"

"Yes?" He clearly didn't know who she was.

"We culminated together," the woman prompted. "Bernice was our advisor."

A few more seconds of puzzlement, and then Saul's face bloomed in surprised pleasure.

"Penny!" he exclaimed. "You're Penny! But you look so, so—"

"Old," she supplied, affably.

She didn't look old, only late middle-aged. Saul did, too, but his face was mostly beard, and his beard was still mostly black. He probably looked the same as he had decades ago. She beamed, enjoying his embarrassment. When he was done sputtering, they embraced.

"How have you been?" he asked, when they disengaged.

"Aside from the late, great unpleasantness, I've been good. You?" Again, she spoke with a kind of amused thoughtfulness, an irony. Saul explained to Elzy that he and Penny had gone to college together.

"So, you two know each other?" he asked.

"Oh, yes. We go back a good...two hours, wouldn't you say?" Penny looked at Elzy, who agreed it had been almost that and gave her name.

Of course, Penny, too, agreed to lunch.

A few minutes later, Elzy stood in the dining hall, laden tray in hand, looking around for Andy. Eventually, she saw him waving. Next to him sat Saul, then Penny on Saul's other side, at an otherwise empty table. She took a seat opposite them.

"Elzy," Andy greeted her, "it's good to see you." His hair was all gray, now, gray and white, but otherwise he looked as he always had, short but fit and weather-beaten. He seemed as casual and confident as ever—but his was not the affect of someone greeting a friend for the first time in five years. And he said nothing else to her at all. He looked away awkwardly. He'd once told her he wasn't very good at social stuff. She kept forgetting, and then being reminded, that he'd been right.

She couldn't think of what to say either.

They were saved from silence by Diana's arrival. She ignored Andy's awkwardness and greeted him affectionately, then introduced herself to the others. She sat down next to Elzy, which put her across from Penny. Elzy thought the two women made an interesting contrast: tall and short, fair and dark, both birdlike but like different birds, for if Penny was a heron, elongate and graceful, Diana must be a starling or a sparrow, something small, sharp, and pointed.

"Where's Dashawn?" Andy asked.

"At a wedding," Diana replied, then added "his own," letting her eyes sparkle merrily at Andy's surprise.

Dashawn, a roboticist, had been Diana's traveling companion for years, helping her design and launch her fleet of atmospheric data-collection drones.

"Well, congratulations to him!" Andy exclaimed. "Married. Hmm. I should email him…."

Two more men brought lunch trays to the table. Elzy recognized them, Tristan and Michael, as friends of Diana and Andy. Saul seemed to know them too, though he hadn't known Diana.

"Who's getting married?" Tristan asked, sitting down.

"Dashawn is," Diana explained.

"Marriage is an awful undertaking," Michael remarked, sitting down between Tristan and Elzy. He was a big, tall fellow, with snow-white hair and handsome, though acne-scarred, features. His blue and white cowl flattered him, though the cowls did not flatter everybody.

"Poor guy, he'll probably never have sex again," added Tristan. He, too, was bird-like, perhaps a dunlin or a turn-stone, one of those tiny shore-birds, affable and quick. His sandy hair and neat, brown beard were only starting to gray. He had to be at least sixty, but didn't look it.

"Oh, he'll have sex," Michael asserted, "for a while at least, but it will be pretty boring and predictable." He took a swig of beer.

"Like the weather," said Tristan, and took a big bite of beans just as Michael narrowly avoided spraying beer all over the table. Until then, they'd both been doing a good job of staying straight-faced.

"The weather is *not* boring," Michael declared in mock outrage, as soon as he'd finished laughing and coughing.

"Well, with you it's not," Tristan conceded, almost coquettishly.

The others smirked and giggled and guffawed, except for Penny, who just looked confused. Diana leaned across the table and explained.

"Michael is a *meteorologist* and the director of the Mount Washington Weather Observatory. And *his husband, Tristan,* is the dean of the associated Appalachian Mountain College Meteorology program."

"Ah," Penny acknowledged.

From there, the conversation split. Saul and Penny caught up with each other, Diana gently coaxed Andy into socializing, and Elzy talked with Michael and Tristan. Before going to college, she'd been a cop, and with her dual background she had invented a job for herself as a land care-taker and Leave No Trace educator. She now wanted to study the methods of other people doing similar work. She hoped to develop a research-based set of best practices and to design a semi-standardized training curriculum.

"You should come to us," Tristan told her, leaning backwards in his chair to talk around Michael's intervening back. "Leave No Trace is part of several of our programs."

"There's a whole chain of Appalachian Trail-associated colleges," Andy added, suddenly defecting from his conversation with Diana. "Besides Appalachian Mountain," with a nod indicating Tristan, "and Green Mountain," another nod indicated Saul, who taught there part-time. "There's one in Virginia, one in West Virginia, and another in Massachusetts. I imagine any of them would be worth talking to." Speaking professionally, he displayed no awkwardness or hesitancy. As usual, he asked some interesting questions and offered excellent advice.

Thus abandoned, Diana, a noted climatologist, cheerfully switched to talking about Rossby waves with Michael, who was so tall that the new conversation went literally, as well as figuratively, right over Elzy's head. By then, Penny and Saul had segued into a strictly amateur but still vibrant discussion of fern identification and geometry.

Afternoon brought another introductory session, then, after dinner, there were drinks and desserts in the auditorium. A trio of musically-accomplished conference participants played jazz. Elzy, who used stand-up comedy as an educational tool, put her name down on the sheet for the next night. The jazz players were good, but Elzy couldn't stay long. She was rooming with Diana, who needed help with her exo.

Diana was paraplegic. Her robotic exoskeleton fit unobtrusively under her clothing and worked so smoothly most people didn't realize she had a disability unless she told them—but she did still have a disability. The exo was uncomfortable, and she couldn't sleep wearing it, nor could she take it off without help. And once it was off, she couldn't do much of anything, for she had no trunk control, her spinal injury having been very high up, only a few inches from quadriplegia. She relaxed limply on her bed while Elzy plugged the machine in to recharge.

"Do you want anything? Water? Your laptop?" Elzy asked.

"No, I am good for now." Her cell was in reach on the nightstand.

"I was going to suggest music, but…."

Somebody in another room was already cranking out an enthusiastic drum-solo. It was only the noisiest of the many sounds in the crowded old building. People walked by in the hallways, talking. Doors slammed. Toilets flushed. Elzy lay on her bed in her purple night-shirt and shorts, looking in some fascination around the room. It had once been, and still largely resembled, an ordinary hotel room of the early twenty-first century. It was more casually luxurious and yet more generically ugly than any place she'd ever been. There was even still a corded telephone on the night-stand, though of course it didn't work.

"You're not asleep, are you?" asked Elzy, after a while.

"Why do you ask questions to which you have already created the answer?"

"So I can pretend I didn't mean to wake you up." Elzy sat up so she could look at Diana without the night-stand in her way. "Did you know Andy would be here?"

"I had not thought about it, but I was not surprised to see him."

"He didn't tell me. He doesn't tell me anything."

Diana didn't reply. She simply looked at Elzy and waited for her to continue.

"When we traveled together, you know, when I was a guild-applicant, I was so sure we were friends. Now? He won't make plans, so I try to bump into him, and mostly fail. I guess I'm just being pathetic."

"He prioritized having lunch with you today."

Elzy shook her head as though trying to clear it.

"He's so *polite* and *helpful* to everybody. Maybe that's all it's ever been."

"He is not polite to everybody."

"Oh?"

"It was after my accident—after I got home from the rehab facility. In those days there were no exos, only wheelchairs. It was…a big adjustment. My mother and father flew all the way from India to help me. And Andy and Jen—his first wife, you know—came to stay with me, too, for a few weeks. For them to come was no difficulty—they were what we called climbing bums, no fixed address. Andy's uncle called him, asking for money. Andy was…not polite to him."

"What's wrong with asking?"

"I wanted to know that, too. Andy said 'there's nothing wrong with asking, what's wrong is Uncle Luc. Everyone in my family gives in to him. Then, when he screws them over, they're surprised.'"

"I didn't know he had an uncle. He hardly ever tells me anything about his family."

"Nor me," Diana admitted. "And he has never mentioned Luc to me again. But I believe he felt the need to explain why he was shouting in my kitchen." Her eyes twinkled merrily.

"I can't picture Andy like that."

"Can you not? I do not think he understands the opposite of kindness. He does not handle it well."

Elzy had seen Andy handle cruelty and indifference with calm dignity.... But if he was so good at handling it, why had she always felt so protective of him?

"I would not worry about Andy's social reticence," Diana told her. "He does it to everybody. I have always thought of him as something like a changeling, personally."

"He's a genius," Elzy asserted, primly. She knew Andy needed no defense from Diana, but she couldn't help herself. Diana smiled.

"Half of the people at lunch today are geniuses," the older woman said, leaving Elzy to wonder which half was which. "That is not what I am talking about."

No, it wasn't.

"Can the two be separated, though?" Elzy asked.

"Perhaps not. It is the wind from a new direction that takes the sailboat to a new place. There are few such winds." She tried to push herself up higher on her pillows with her hands and succeeded to some extent. "There are winds and then there are winds, though. Perhaps his Uncle Luc is also a changeling."

"Oh?"

"Of another kind. Andy told me he thought Luc might kill someone someday and not be bothered by it. That is not ordinary." Diana frowned, puzzled or uncomfortable.

Elzy kicked her feet at the side of her bed, childlike.

"I've killed people," she said, quite lightly. "It didn't bother me." Her *voice* was light, but as she spoke her face became troubled. She glanced away. Nobody spoke for a long moment. The drum solo continued.

"You were a vigilante before you were a cop," Diana said at last, as though trying to reassure herself. By *vigilante* she meant one of those who fought to protect hoarded resources and land in the early years after the collapse. "It was part of your job."

"Yeah, killing was part of my job. But *I didn't care.* I never have. Not about anybody." She waited to see if Diana understood what she was trying to say.

"That is not true," Diana said at last. "You care about a lot of people."

Elzy smiled tightly and looked down at the floor. She could almost hear the unspoken plea, *but you care about me.* But no, she cared for Diana, and liked her, and wanted her liking in return. It wasn't the same thing.

"I care about *some* people," she conceded. "Everybody else, I mostly just want their attention. I care about justice, honor, duty.... It is my duty to protect and to serve. But most people could fall over dead and I wouldn't care, as long as it wasn't my fuck-up that killed them."

Diana said nothing, her eyes large and dark, her face inscrutable. Elzy stood up abruptly, paced around, sat down again.

"Maybe I'm a changeling, too," Elzy said at last.

"Not in the way that Luc is. Your eccentricity is useful. It has been channeled into duty. You have saved people's lives." Diana's words sounded so confident, so reassuring, but her eyes were scared, and they scared Elzy. Even lying ragdoll-helpless in a frilly, pink night-shirt, Diana usually had too much dignity to admit any vulnerable emotion.

"Luc is useful," Elzy declared, "if he's still alive. You know there was no room in the early transition for people who weren't team players."

"I remember."

"Look," Elzy said, "that I am useful is not in doubt, alright? Society needs all kinds of people, and I do things other people can't. I do things *Andy* can't. I saved *him,* once. For him I shot two men! But there's got to be more than that, doesn't there? I don't want to *just* be useful. I want to be liked."

"Plenty of people like you."

"I want to be *seen* and liked." Elzy was aware that because she was young and pretty and female, hardly anyone really believed she was a killer. Diana was going to stop believing it in a minute, in order to go on liking her, that was obvious.

"Andy knows that you shot these two men?" Diana asked.

"Oh, yes. He was there."

"Well, there you have it, then. Out of all the people at this conference, you and I are the only two with whom he made sure to meet for lunch today. He sees you."

And at that moment, the drum solo, quite politely, stopped, exactly fifteen minutes before the beginning of the posted quiet hours.

The next day, and every day after that for a week, featured three or four talks on a common theme, followed by a choice of small-group discussions on the same theme after lunch. After dinner, there would be desserts and cheap drinks in the auditorium while conference participants with musical, comedic, or other talents performed and people met, mingled, schmoozed, and hatched plans together. After a break of a few days, they'd all return for another week. Without fossil fuel, transportation had become slow and inconvenient, so once people arrived somewhere, they tended to stay awhile.

She and Andy sat together at breakfast, sometimes other meals and at the talks too. Diana or Saul or both usually sat with them. Sometimes Michael and Tristan or others Andy knew joined them. Some of these were new contacts for Elzy, people she could learn things from and might not otherwise have met. Others she already knew, such as Colin and Austin, a couple who had both once been Elzy's professors, too. Andy might be socially awkward, but he was not socially indifferent—he had dozens of friends here. But he spoke with all of them mostly about work. With Elzy, with whom he had no work anymore, he spoke very little, and yet their sitting together was almost always his idea. He'd find her in the auditorium, beckon her over in the dining hall, suggest one or another discussion group he thought she might like and that he also planned on attending. She did not understand, but she'd never wholly understood Andy. She never refused his invitations.

The first theme was physical science. Michael, the first speaker, told the story of the reweaving of meteorology and its relationship to both disaster preparedness in the age of extreme weather and the collection of climatological data. Diana talked about her drone network and the more detailed overview of the altered climate she hoped it would provide. A geologist Elzy didn't know discussed the fact that the Earth's supply of accessible metal ores and other valuable minerals is fixed within human timescales, and what taking that fact seriously might look like. Another new acquaintance discussed various issues relating to water. The next day the topic was life sciences. After that, social science and psychology. Besides the talks, each of which corresponded to a prepared paper participants could read at their leisure, there were other papers not presented as talks but rather as posters.

The whole point was to get as much relevant information and ideas out on the table as possible. Then, in the afternoon discussion groups and later in the second half of the conference, the participants could draft goals and guidelines to be integrated with those drafted by similar events across the country. For the first time since the end of the Fossil Fuel Age, everybody in several related fields would be on the same page. Healing the world could be organized.

Maybe.

"The real world doesn't agree with itself, why should we?" Andy asserted mid-week, when the subject came up over breakfast.

The talk he gave later that day—the theme being conservation and restoration planning—further developed the same point. He made a charming, dynamic, even funny public speaker, presenting his case for social, scholarly, and economic systems of the same complexity as the ecological, climatological, and cultural systems they sought to protect.

"Simplicity is seductive," he acknowledged. "It seems powerful, but it is not an effective tool for apprehending a complex reality. In *willingly* choosing models and practices and professional structures that don't reflect the real world, we will only undermine ourselves, recreating the very pathologies that we now attempt to heal from. To really move forward, we'll need to make our peace with messiness, paradox, and uncertainty. Dynamic disagreement or misunderstanding among those *who remain in relationship to each other* is only paradox embodied, the multiple tips of an iceberg of necessary human complexity."

As if to underscore that point, the very next presenter attempted to rebut, not only Andy's talk, but much of his career.

Andy, though he referred to himself as a researcher, rarely led studies himself. Instead, he advised or consulted on a vast number of other people's projects. For students, or the former students in whom he took an avuncular interest, he'd help if he could no matter the nature of their work—but Elzy knew the projects closest to his heart were big, sprawling things that combined large-scale ecological restoration, scientific research, and human community development—programs that propagated themselves into every detectable scale and every goal or priority like living Mandelbrot sets. He castigated as mere seductive simplicity not only reductive science but also any attempt to separate out "nature," "society," "public health," "economy," and so forth into separate concerns. He often said that his job was to restore the human communities that would restore the land.

This other man, whose name Elzy made a point of not learning, argued instead that the best thing humans can do for nature is to get out of its way.

"Human communities," said the man, "have always been enriched, materially and spiritually, by the presence of wilderness beyond the edge of the village—but the wilderness inevitably recedes as we move out to it. We carry the village with us wherever we go. We *are* the village. So if we truly want the wilderness, we've got to stay out of it. Our challenge now is to make the village an attractive and productive place to stay put, to stay contained."

A fair point, and he had an entertaining, conspiring manner that tended to sway the audience. But while he never referred to Andy by name, he sprinkled his talk with echoes of the language of Andy's talk and published papers, always framed as examples of what *not* to do, or be, or think. Several times the man made statements of his own opinion framed as obvious fact, then asked, rhetorically, "how is that complicated?"

"He seems to disagree with you rather pointedly," Elzy whispered, mid-talk, to Andy.

"He's not disagreeing with me at all," Andy whispered back. "He's misunderstood my whole point. He's treating *complex, complicated,* and *hard* as synonyms." He seemed unconcerned, even amused. Elzy knew she must be watching the latest iteration of some ugly interpersonal problem, and yet Andy gave no sign of even noticing the antipathy. It was as if he were above personal risk.

After the break, the organizers presented a report summarizing the first half of the event and a series of recommendations drawn from all the talks and discussions. In the second half, both full sessions and break-out groups worked on revising and amending the document.

Two days into the process, Elzy didn't find Andy waiting for her on the way in to dinner. He wasn't in the dining hall, either. She got her food, then spotted Saul, Michael, and Tristan together at a table with a few empty chairs left.

"No Andy today?" Michael asked.

"Can't find him, he's vanished," she replied lightly and sat down.

"I hate it when they do that," Michael replied, just as lightly, and took a stab at his fish. Michael knew, as she did, that Andy sometimes just disappeared.

Penny arrived with her tray of food and sat down between Saul and Elzy. Saul greeted her and caught her up on the conversation already in progress, the one Elzy had interrupted by arriving, but Penny seemed to disapprove of the topic and let the conversation go on without her.

"You have corn salad?" she observed, looking at Elzy's plate. "I didn't see any."

"Really? It's right next to the fish." The fish was Asian carp, an invasive species in the nearby Ohio River that a local fishing association had asked the conference to help consume. It was being served once or twice a day, and everybody was tired of it, but it did pair well with the corn. "You want me to go get you a bowl?"

"No, that's alright. I just want to eat at this point."

"Without corn salad, though?"

That brought Penny up short. She considered for some seconds.

"You know, you're right," she concluded. "Watch my things, please?" And she was off again.

A fortyish man with youthful, sloppy bangs sat down and greeted Saul, then nodded to the others without seeming to know any of them. But Elzy recognized him—Eric, who had moderated some of the small-group discussions. Less than a minute later, another new person joined the table.

"There you are," the new person said to Saul. "We need to set aside some time. Does tonight work?"

The newcomer looked familiar, but Elzy couldn't remember why. The combination of a sparse, Beatnik-like beard and a rather curvy figure should have been memorable, but she'd met too many people lately, and her brain lagged like an over-taxed phone app.

"You did that talk, didn't you?" she asked at last. "Something about rhetoric and disability?" She remembered mostly a humorous, erudite rage. She didn't remember hearing the presenter's pronouns, and something about the person's body language and manner kept her from even guessing.

"Ableism and the Rhetoric of the Conservation Movement," the person supplied. "Luke Moineau." Crows' feet crinkled. A smile quirked.

"Elzy Rodriguez."

"You're Rodriguez?" exclaimed Eric. "You're funny as hell, man. Eric Colbert." He reached out for a handshake. Obviously, he'd seen her comedy show the previous week, but then why hadn't he recognized her? He must be bad at faces. Some people are.

Eric ate and talked avidly. Luke ate silently, attentive to the discussion but not looking at anyone, drumming an incessant and complicated tattoo with the fingers of a free hand. Could this be the evening drum-soloist? The noise had recurred every night but always stopped at precisely fifteen of ten.

Penny returned, half-juggling three small bowls. She put down her corn salad, then gave Elzy one bowl of blackberry cobbler and kept the other for herself. "Dessert's out," she said.

Elzy, touched by her consideration, didn't reply for a moment.

"Thanks," she said at last, "but I like my hair the way it is." That made Penny laugh. The cobbler proved very good. Elzy ate half of hers before she went back to working on her fish.

"Your voice is familiar," Luke said, addressing Penny. "Have we met?"

"I don't think so...wait, you did that talk. You're Luke Moineau? Yes, we have met, but only by email and voice-call. Penny Darling."

"Oh, Penny, yes. It's good to meet you in person."

"It is. I really enjoyed your talk."

"Thank you."

"Wait," Eric interrupted. "You're *C.* Penny Darling, aren't you?"

"I am," she admitted, suddenly uncomfortable.

Michael and Tristan got up to go get cobbler, making a minor but sociable commotion.

"I'm being a yote, aren't I?" asked Eric, after they had gone. *Yote* was teenage slang, for what Elzy hadn't yet learned. She wondered if talking like that, at Eric's age, might be itself yote-ish. Nobody answered him.

"He got all excited about my name, too," she told Penny, commiserating.

"Well, you're both very exciting," Eric explained. Elzy and Penny looked at each other.

"We're exciting," Elzy said, deadpan.

"Apparently," Penny agreed.

"I didn't mean it like that," Eric protested, turning red.

"They always *say* that," said Elzy, again to Penny, watching to see if Eric turned redder.

"Unfortunately, they do," Penny said, sighing in mock-melancholy, also watching to see Eric turn amusing colors.

Actually, Elzy itched to know what was so exciting about Penny. Fortunately, Saul decided to pipe up.

"I'm going to boast a little about you now because you won't," he warned, then turned to Elzy. "ECA has twelve books in its Suggested Canon. Penny's written three of them. The latest one is the commentary on the core principles. If there are still books a thousand years from now, that's going to be one of them."

"Actually, I *compiled* the first two. I *wrote* only the third one."

"You are way too modest."

"I think I'm just modest enough, actually."

Elzy knew of ECA as an advocacy group for minority religions. The name, though pronounced as a word, Eca, was an acronym, but she couldn't remember what it stood for. She hadn't known it had a suggested cannon or core principles.

"I didn't know that," Eric admitted, "which probably means I'm twice the yote. I just don't know of anyone else who joined their first guild as a *senior* member."

Elzy stared. Making senior status without being a regular member first was supposed to be impossible, except for people who founded guilds, like Saul and Andy.

"It wasn't my idea," Penny almost mumbled.

"No, it was ours," Luke acknowledged. Luke wore the same cowl colors as Penny and had a senior guild-member pin, and so presumably had voted on her membership application.

"How? Why?" Elzy asked, hoping she wasn't being rude. Penny traded glances with Luke, sighed for real, then explained.

"I only applied to the guild last year. I wanted to travel again, and it seemed the best way. But I've been involved with ECA since the beginning, so they insisted on the upgrade. I'm not at all used to it yet."

"ECA has a guild?" Elzy asked.

Luke and Penny looked at each other and at Eric, who also wore the same cowl pattern—he wore his cowl so badly rumpled it looked more like a scarf and its pattern was hard to see. The rumples made him look handsomely roguish, so he'd probably done it on purpose. He did not have a senior pin.

"Sure," Eric explained. "Me, I'm a Quaker. We don't have clergy, so there's no Quaker clergy guild, but I do a lot of the same stuff—community organizing, teaching, and counseling—that a preacher *would* do. So ECA looks out for me."

"I don't have an *organized* religion at all," Luke said, "but I'm kind of the same deal. ECA's like an umbrella over everyone who doesn't fit anywhere else. I do what I can to serve those who don't fit. And then there are the circles—sort of like churches for people who don't want to go to church. That's Penny's gig. She helped found one of the first circles, like, twenty-five years ago."

Church for people who don't like church?

"So, don't take this the wrong way," Elzy asked, "but why are you all here? What does a non-church church have to do with conservation?" She was an atheist herself and wasn't sure what any kind of church had to do with anything.

"Well, how else can we assure ourselves of blackberries?" Penny suggested.

"ECA stands for Earth-Centered Alliance," Luke explained. "We're the *why* to your *how*." That made some sense.

"So, you're, what? A preacher or a nun or something?" Elzy asked, of Penny.

"I've never known what I am, actually."

"I always thought of you as a witch, myself," put in Saul, apparently seriously.

"Well, I hope you think of me as a good witch," Penny replied. Elzy couldn't tell whether she was serious or not.

"What are we talking about now?" asked Michael, returning laden with cobbler. Tristan wasn't with him.

"ECA," Eric explained. Michael sat down and shook his head.

"ECA's weird," he said. "A lot of it's science and art, I can go with that. But some of it's a little out-there, if you ask me." He sounded very self-satisfied.

"But we didn't ask you," Penny told him, and Michael shut up. Elzy had never seen anybody shut Michael up before and was most impressed.

Tristan returned, also bearing cobbler, but didn't sit down. He leaned over Michael and Saul.

"Do you see who's over there?" he whispered.

Elzy couldn't turn and look without it being obvious, but she watched Saul look and recognize someone.

"Holy *shit!*" he exclaimed happily, and he and Michael quickly gathered up their things and decamped with Tristan to another table.

"Who?" Elzy asked.

"No idea, and it would probably read as weird if we all went over anyway," Luke explained. "But now I need some cobbler."

"Me, too," said Eric, and they both scurried off, the one affecting a kind of cocky slouch, the other walking stiff and loose at the same time, a subtly odd physicality.

Penny and Elzy sat alone together, mutually bewildered. Penny broke the silence.

"Speaking of finding people," she said, "don't you usually eat with Andy? He's still here, isn't he?"

"Hell if I know," Elzy admitted.

"Oh?"

Elzy looked at the older woman and suddenly realized she was about to, once again, confide in a near-stranger because she had no real close friends. The nearest thing she had to a close friend vanished periodically and wouldn't tell her why.

And so she told Penny about Andy, about their work together when she was his student, about how she'd barely been able to see him since, about how he seemed to genuinely care about her but she couldn't be sure, and anyway he seemed not to know or care that she cared about him. And she did care. She had not told even Diana how truly rare that was, or what not knowing if her caring was even welcome really felt like. She told Penny.

"I probably just sound really stupid," she finished.

"No…" Penny replied, thoughtfully, but she didn't come up with anything else to say.

"Diana says he must be my friend otherwise he wouldn't bother to hang out with me at all," Elzy added. "But he talks to me like I'm some student he just met. You've seen him do it!"

"I have," Penny agreed. "Have you talked with him about any of this?"

"Of course not. I don't want him to think I'm weird."

"And so you continue not knowing. And potentially, so does he." Penny frowned to herself, perhaps saddened. "That's such a difficult place you have put yourself in."

"*I* put *myself* in?"

"Well, yes. You are the one who has the question, and you are the one not asking it."

"Asking what? How he feels about how I feel? He doesn't want to have that conversation. I don't want to have that conversation. That would be…" and Elzy stopped, suddenly self-conscious.

"Weird?" Penny supplied. "I don't really like that word. It means so much and yet so little. You know, everybody's different. Maybe Andy just has a different way of showing up for you than what you're expecting?"

"No, I know he does, it's just…."

"I don't think you need to ask about his feelings, if he's not going to want to talk about them. Just bring yours to him. Get vulnerable? If he honors that and it brings you closer, then you have a real connection. If not, then maybe you don't, but at least you'll know."

But Elzy looked at her warily.

"What *do* you want?" Penny asked.

"I want...to know what he wants of me. To know what he wants me to do." Elzy shrugged slightly, as though what she wanted were silly, trivial.

"Well, *since* you seem to be asking me for advice," Penny seemed to think this a most strange and amusing thing to do, "I think you should let yourself find out."

Andy returned from his vanishment the next day, as usual without explanation. Possibly he didn't realize anybody had noticed he was gone. He and Elzy didn't have much opportunity to talk. The conference had developed factions competing for ideological dominance, and Andy was in the middle of it, arguing in the sessions and negotiating with various people during the breaks, trying to keep the disagreements dynamic and engaged, neither prematurely resolved, nor calcified, nor abandoned. Elzy could contribute little to the process, but was busy interviewing experts for the training program she was working on and arranging mini-internships for herself with other caretaker programs. Everybody was busy doing *something* now. Everybody had an agenda or a goal.

Finally the conference finished up with no real resolution. The proceedings would be published with the contradictions and disagreements intact. Andy seemed quietly pleased.

Dinner that last night was a banquet in the auditorium with live but unobtrusive music. Then, as the desserts came out and the bar opened, the music picked up and the meal morphed quite naturally into the after-dinner party, the best-attended yet. Everybody was talking with everybody else, as people rushed to exchange contact information with, extract job offers from, or in some cases bed those they hadn't managed to connect with before. Even Diana agreed to stay up and mobile until the party ended. She liked dancing.

Then the band left and a new one took its place. A true concert had been promised, and as the musicians set up, people found seats and quieted. Elzy, sitting with Andy and Diana, recognized the players and realized they couldn't have been a band very long—she'd watched some of them meet for the first time last week.

Eric, looking more like a teenager than ever, was on bass. Saul had his violin out, though Elzy knew he more usually played only to trees. Michael had a flute. She hadn't known he was musical at all. Penny had a guitar and was discussing microphone placement and whatever else with the others as though she did this sort of thing for a living. Maybe she did. And Luke was, yes, on drums.

"Andy?" Elzy said, as the band tuned up. He was watching the musicians and did not look at her, but he tilted his head slightly to show he was listening. "Andy, for years, now, every year, I've been trying to catch up with you, to hang out with you, but—"

"Keep trying," he told her, still not looking at her, his voice quiet and unexpectedly urgent.

The first song was "Big Yellow Taxi," which Elzy had always thought was called "They Paved Paradise," and the taxi was changed to an ambulance in this version, anyway. Michael sang lead. He wasn't great, but was clearly having a good time. He led again on "The End of the World as We Know It," a better choice for his voice as it was mostly talking, except the end of the world was nothing modern audiences could take as lightly as that song did. Before the audience could sour, though, Penny sang "Something to It," a truly lovely piece that seemed to be an apology from a dead person for upsetting her survivors—and Elzy felt herself relax and actually start to cry. She glanced over at Andy and saw tears shining on his otherwise impassive face. Then Luke stepped out from behind the drumset to sing in a clear but papery tenor a love song about an Alpine flower.

"They're saying something—they're doing something," Elzy whispered, half to Andy, half to herself. She couldn't quite articulate the thing she'd noticed, but the presence of the ECA guild-members suddenly made intuitive sense. "Andy? They're telling a story, aren't they?"

"Hmm?"

"The story of the pandemic and the collapse and the transition—and everything we're doing here. It's like a sermon."

"Or a sacred play. Yes, you may be right."

Song after song traced, obliquely, the story of the deepest tragedy and the greatest miracle humanity had ever received, the possibility of a do-over—and the story, too, of the guild-members and others who had pledged their expertise and their lives to making sure the do-over was wisely done. Surrendering to the process, Elzy felt herself and her fellow audience-members being guided into a greater sense of energy, dedication, optimism, and pride than she'd allowed herself in a very long time.

"This is brilliant," she whispered. "Whose idea was it?"

"I don't know. I don't know any of them well, except Saul."

"Saul's not ECA."

"He's not part of their guild," Andy clarified.

And Elzy wondered.

After the "play" finished, Penny sang once more, a kind of farewell such as close many concerts. She chose "I'll Be Seeing You." Elzy thought maybe it had been written as a sentimental goodbye to a deploying twentieth-century soldier, and indeed Penny began in a smokey, sultry tone suggestive of a 1940's nightclub.

But as the song progressed, her voice grew naked, vulnerable, describing all the familiar places (a park, a carousel, trees) she would continue to "see" the lost someone. Had she meant to sing that way? Who was she thinking about as she sang? But then, as the final verse repeated, the mood shifted again, the whole band together gathering, rising in both volume and power, Penny making of the song now in fact *a refusal* to say goodbye, a promise to look for, to *see* a person, no matter what, everywhere, forever.

When they were done, Penny said "good night everybody. Travel safe." Her magic words ended the convention.

Elzy looked over at Andy and found him still watching the stage as the musicians took their bows and packed up their things. He seemed to be deep in thought, though what he might be thinking she could not guess. Somehow, he was very far away.

But he let her see him.

Part Three

Root Connections

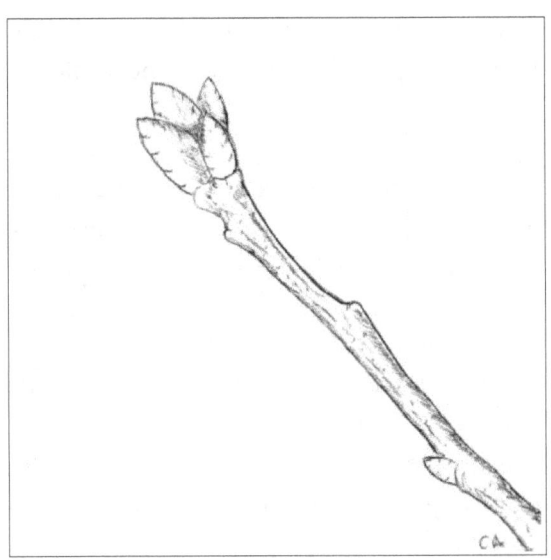

Chapter 1: Arrivals

Elzy Rodriguez checked into her favorite inn, took a shower, and got halfway through getting dressed before the lovely spring air distracted her. In sports bra and trousers, she stood just inside the balcony doorway breathing and listening to the clip-clop of horse-carts and the whine of an electric cop-car in the street. Children's voices argued from somewhere, and a crow in the winter-bare branches of the oak tree across the street cawed once, twice, three times. The deep whistle-blast of the big coastal ferry, just now leaving port, startled her but did not startle the crow. Elzy didn't like the hustle and bustle of civilization, but her contribution to the food reserve was due, and she took her responsibilities as a land-holder seriously. She held the land and the land held her. Not much else ever had.

At least civilization had hot showers.

The door opened behind her.

Elzy spun reflexively, ready for self-defense, as a young man walked in.

"Oh, hey," he said, his eyes dropping briefly to her breasts. "Is this…." He seemed to notice her defensive stance and looked around at the bed, the open bathroom door, the items of clothing and other personal gear strewn about. "Uh…."

"Why are you in my room?" she asked.

"Wow, um, I was just trying to find the balcony. I thought this was a common area. I'll just be going." His voice sounded pleasant, affable, and Anglophone Canadian.

"No, I give you permission to stay," she told him. He was slim and golden, with guileless, boyish features and short, straight, chestnut-colored hair. There was something odd about his eyes...she hadn't seen epicanthic folds in a long time, but once she knew what she was seeing, his eyes didn't look strange anymore.

He blushed under her scrutiny and rubbed the back of his head. She pulled on her tunic and beckoned for him to follow her out to the balcony. Bar Harbor, Maine, spread out before them.

"So, who are you?" she asked.

"Kevin Williams. I just got into town. I build boats."

"Oh? What kind of boats?"

"What kind do you need?" Typical salesman—except that she actually did need a boat. Come to think of it, she might need several boats.

"Kayak or canoe," she told him. "I just want something so I can noodle around on my pond. I'm the Long Pond caretaker."

"I can definitely do either."

"Do you travel?"

"Easier for you to take me home than a finished canoe." Many crafts-people worked at clients' homes in order to avoid delivery costs—without fossil fuel, transportation had gotten expensive. But Kevin clearly meant something else, too. His forwardness made Elzy cough.

"Can we just talk about boats for now?" she said.

"Of course."

But he did not seem overly chastened.

They talked business for some minutes and exchanged contact information. Belatedly, she gave him her name. He lingered. Well, she'd said he could. She finished getting ready to go out as if he wasn't there, putting on her blue and green cowl and neatly tipping its hood back off her head. She spread oil through her still-damp Afro with her fingers, then affixed a small, silver pin to her chest. Kevin's eyes widened at the sight of that pin. She turned to face him.

"Kevin," she said, with a hint of fond familiarity, "I *will* see you again. But not tonight."

He stammered and fidgeted and showed himself out.

For a moment she regretted not asking him to dinner. She had no other commitments tonight. But for the first time in a long time, she felt like a teenager. She needed time and space to decide whether to act like one.

Leaving the inn, she stepped out into the first really warm day of the year and wandered down to the water and the path that runs between the lawns of the grand, old houses and the shelving rock of the seashore. She looked out across the water that gives Bar Harbor its name. The tide hurrying to its lowest point had left behind hundreds of stranded lion's mane jellyfish like a storm of misplaced red pancakes. Sailboats, rowboats, and both electric and bio-diesel powerboats rode at mooring buoys or picked their way between aquaculture allotments. A seal lifted its head from the greenish water and submerged again. She wondered what it was like to be a seal.

And every few minutes, Kevin would pop back into her mind, usually naked. But after the naked bit her mind would run on, on to where the casual sex would inevitably become complicated by emotional attachment. And then it would all go wrong. Elzy had never had a truly bad romance, but she'd never had a really good one either, and they all ended the same way—and she never knew why.

If I'm smart, I'll stay away from this guy, she thought.

And yet by that logic, Bar Harbor and its hot showers should not exist. Thirty-five years ago, it *hadn't* existed. People always said "the pandemic," as though that explained the collapse, but Elzy knew it was dependence, not disease, that killed the old civilization—dependence on fossil fuel and its over-complicated supply chains. When too many people lost their places in the line, the whole thing snapped, and billions of people starved. Those who survived, like Elzy and her father, did so by becoming self-sufficient, defending tiny garden patches and hunting grounds, one family or several together, each group alone. Why hadn't the survivors stayed that way, isolated and safe? The new society was not as brittle as the old one, but it was hardly invulnerable. A smart people would have remained hidden under their rocks. Elzy was glad people had not been smart.

When the shadows grew long and began eroding the day's thin warmth, she headed back uphill towards the town center. At the weekend market, vendors were packing up for the day as the crowd gathered around the gazebo on the Green, but the headliner of the evening was listed as "Henry the Horrible and His Marvelous Singing Parrots," so she decided to give that a pass and took herself out to eat instead. Over a creamy sea-food chowder, she looked up Kevin Williams online.

She came to no conclusions about whether to be a teenager about him, but he seemed to be an excellent maker of boats.

Monday morning, Kevin Williams stood near the local ferry dock, lis-tening to seagulls and awaiting his newest client. They had already signed his standard contract—room and board and all necessary building supplies provided while he built two boats, one for the client and one to sell. He expected to clear a hundred and fifty shares, all profit, a *share* being what Americans used for money. That, plus a small completion bonus, would keep him solvent for five months, if he was careful. He always liked the beginning of new jobs, and this time his client—he spotted her coming towards him down the hill, and his stomach flipped.

She was slim, fit, confident, all elegant curves and light brown skin, the same shade as his but a different hue. Her black hair, threaded with silver, stood out from her head like the corona of a star.

"Hey," she greeted him, "you have the tickets? I can take some of your stuff, if you want."

"I'm good. I'd be a pretty sorry individual if I couldn't handle my own crap."

"I didn't say you *couldn't* handle it, I said you don't need to. Really, it's no trouble, my pack's almost empty now."

"Elzy, would you believe that I *know* you are a strong, capable woman? If I need help, I really will ask."

"There are men who won't."

"There are men who can't build you a canoe, either."

Actually, Kevin could barely breathe because of the weight of the portable wood-shop on his back. He wasn't going to admit that to Elzy, though.

The little local ferry, an old lobster boat with a new electric mo-tor, hummed in and tied up. The passengers disembarked, and the fa-ther-daughter crew recharged the batteries and made some minor repairs. Finally, the new passengers, including Elzy and Kevin, could come aboard, find their seats, shed sweaters and jackets and turn their faces to the sun. A few mare's tail clouds streaked the hard, blue sky. The boat headed off again, humming, but not so loudly as to overcome the warble of the green, slightly turbid water along the hull.

"Man, the sea!" Kevin exclaimed. "I can't get enough. It's like, God, it's like my soul is thirsty!"

"You're not from around here, are you?" Elzy asked. He, distracted, missed both the sarcasm in her voice and the fact that she must know where he was from, having seen his website.

"No, I'm a prairie kid. I'd never seen anything like this until a few days ago."

"It is gorgeous," Elzy acknowledged. And he suddenly realized what an ass he must sound like.

"You're used to it," he said.

"Oh, yes—but that's why I like it so much! Daddy and I lived on the island, right after the pandemic. We had to move away when he got sick, but I couldn't wait to get back."

He grinned at her, grateful, then realized what she'd said.

"Wait, you're older than the pandemic?" Almost as soon as he'd said it, he wished he hadn't. He chewed his lip. "Sorry. I know. Never ask a woman her age."

"Older is what you get if you don't die first. I'm forty-one."

"You look *good* for forty-one."

"Why are you surprised? You think people my age can't look good?"

"I *try* to flatter you…. You just look younger, that's all."

"So you *don't* think I look good?"

"Now you're just being difficult."

"Better than being easy."

"I am *not* going there."

"Smart man."

"Hey, is that a dolphin?"

"No, harbor porpoise."

"This is so cool."

The ferry took a left out of the harbor, hugging the coast so closely they could see the brown and orange seaweed on the reddish rocks and the white spray of the rising tide. Eiders fished just offshore of the broken, stone-torn surf.

"If we're lucky, we'll hear Thunder Hole," Elzy remarked.

"Isn't that what they call those openings they have in men's-only johns?"

"Those are glory holes. Do they even exist? I hope men have better places to have sex."

"I don't know," Kevin admitted. "I've never been in a men's-only. I don't think there are any anymore. And I've never tried to have sex with a dude, either."

"Really? It's quite nice. I highly recommend it."

"You!" Kevin had some difficulty coming up with a response. "You ever been with a woman?"

"No."

"That's it, then. You don't know what you're missing."

Thunder Hole is a small cavity in the rock. When the waves are high and the tide is right, the surging water traps air inside and compresses it until it explodes outwards. The noise can be heard for miles. But that day either the waves were low or the tide was wrong, as Kevin heard nothing.

A big, black-backed gull stood on the red and orange rock beside the hole and regarded the ferry without comment.

When they disembarked at Flamingo Town in Southwest Harbor, Kevin, without thinking, assumed they must be almost there. In his mind, *island* meant smallness, nearby-ness—never mind that Mount Desert is the second-largest island on the east coast of the United States, big enough for several widely-spaced towns and a respectable mountain range, and that getting halfway around it by ferry had taken a couple of hours. And then Elzy unlocked her bike from a rack near the dock, and they walked and walked and walked, through a little down-town area, then out the other side.

The problem was not so much the distance as the weight of Kevin's pack. As he trudged along beneath it, always up hill, he paid less and less attention to his surroundings and soon convinced himself that the journey would never end. He would simply keep walking until the end of time.

Then the road angled sharply downhill and abruptly ended. And there lay the pond.

The near shore, very straight and only a few hundred feet across, was low but rocky, except for a boat ramp made of sand, like a little beach. From there, the water widened only slightly but stretched on and on and out, to an opposite shore hazy with distance. A stiff breeze drove small waves crashing onto the sand and gurgling into the rocks. A mysterious mechanical hum issued from a nearby solar-roofed shed, but besides that and the water there was no sound. Herring gulls slid through the air. And on either side of the water rose high, rocky, forested ridges like a pair of great thighs—between those thighs lay the sky, streaked now with mares' tails and otherwise blue as the wind-tossed waves.

"Wow," said Kevin. "You live *here?*"

"Sort of," she told him. "I live up there." She pointed to the top of the western ridge, the one on their left.

Kevin groaned.

"I did offer to carry some of your stuff," she reminded him, smiling.

"It's OK, I can do it," he assured her. "My pack's not that heavy."

"Kevin, I don't want to carry a canoe *down* a mountain, so there's no reason for you to carry your tools *up* one. Lock your stuff up in my bike shed."

"Oh, thank God."

The bike shed was part of the pump-house for Flamingo's water supply (hence all the humming). It had a locked door and a battery re-charger, and Kevin was more than happy to use both. Without his tools, he felt so light he might float.

After a mile and a half of steep, winding, and mostly very wet footpath, they turned off the main trail on a spur marked *no-trespassing*. Soon, Kevin noticed a second sign, *beware of dog*, and then distant barking.

"It's just me, Tim," Elzy called. The now-joyous barking grew rapidly nearer. "He's kind of big," she warned, seconds before the biggest shepherd mix Kevin had ever seen rounded the bend at a gallop. Seeing Kevin, he stopped abruptly, then erupted loudly.

"Act friendly," Elzy hissed and wrapped her arms around Kevin, who suddenly rather appreciated the dog.

Tim, the dog, looked back and forth between Kevin and Elzy a few times, then all but shrugged and threw himself at Elzy's feet in abject, noisy joy. When he paused for breath, she replied "really? And then what happened?" He answered with more happy barking. She let him sniff her hands and then tangled her fingers in his dark, wiry hair. If he hadn't been crouching, she would not have had to stoop, he was that tall. He was long and lean and mostly black, and he wore a yellow vest marked POLICE that Elzy took off him before Kevin could read the rest of its lettering. The dog shook himself and trotted off down the trail, panting happily, tail waving.

"Why didn't you tell me you had a giant dog?" Kevin asked.

"I can't tell you *everything*," Elzy replied and then followed her pet.

Kevin stood nervously for a moment, then shrugged.

"His name's Timogen," Elzy added, as he caught up. "Means *wounded wolf* in some language or other."

"Is he?" Kevin asked.

"Is he what?"

"A wounded wolf?"

"Wolf? No, I don't think so. Wounded? Yes. He's a medically-retired K9—but he can still top 30 miles per hour, when he's motivated. He could be at the station in Flamingo in eight minutes, if I asked him to go."

"So he's not really a police dog anymore?"

"Oh, he is. He just has lighter duties as my deputy."

"You're a *cop?*"

"Yup. I'm a caretaker with law-enforcement powers. Why? You a criminal?"

He didn't respond.

A few minutes more and they came to a wide, bean-shaped clearing that Kevin, thinking in metric, guessed might be half a hectare. Low bushes, young trees, old stumps, and thin, winter-killed grass scattered across the place interrupted by patches of bare rock and gravel, much of it matted with thin piles of dead leaves. The surrounding forest was mostly evergreen, but two good-sized deciduous trees occupied a low, vaguely artificial-looking, earthen platform near the edge of the clearing. A group of large, winter-fallow raised beds surrounded by a tall, deer-proof fence dominated the sunny center. A few small, oddly-shaped wooden sheds crouched under the fringe of the forest. A rooster crowed from somewhere. There was a fire pit surrounded by logs for sitting. Nothing else.

"Welcome home," said Elzy. "For the next few weeks, anyway."

"You live *outside?*" Kevin asked. He didn't have camping gear.

"Sometimes," she answered. "But I do have a house." She pointed at what he had taken for another shed, a cedar-shingled triangular tube just over five meters long. Elzy gave him a brief tour of the compound, pointing out and explaining the use of the composting privy, the gray-water sump, and other features, let six or seven chickens out of a fenced run, and led him into the house.

The first meter or so of the tube turned out to be a tiny mud-room. A colorful woven rug hung in the inner doorway, like a door. Beyond that were two of what looked like built-in bunk-beds with an aisle between, except that with the walls angling in, the upper "bunks" were too narrow for human sleepers and served as pantry shelves protected by mouse-proof wire mesh. The last meter or so of the tube was a tiny kitchen, with a cast-iron stove, a tinder box, a fold-down table for one, and a wooden stool. No other furniture was present or possible. The whole interior was unvarnished spruce lit by battery-powered, honey-colored LED discs. The back wall had the only window, currently shuttered.

"Cozy," Kevin remarked, stooping. Over the aisle between the bunks stretched a kind of shelf or ceiling exactly three centimeters too short for him, but the house fit its owner perfectly.

He sat down on the bunk she indicated and took off his pack, then looked around at the house, wondering at the design. It reminded him of the shelters built during the collapse by people hoping to survive in the wilderness—weird little structures made in a hurry without much of a plan. He'd seen the ruins. But nobody still lived in those things thirty-five years later, and Elzy's house was no emergency burrow.

The little house was a sturdy, professional job no more than ten years old, as Kevin, basically a carpenter, could see. Also, the rugs and blankets were all wonderfully soft, woven works of art—probably alpaca fiber. The baskets on the pantry shelves looked like the ones he'd seen in the shops in Bar Harbor, Wapanahki-made and not cheap. Elzy could afford a house with right angles if she wanted one.

"It's weird, isn't it?" Elzy asked, biting her lip. She'd been unloading her pack, putting things away in the mouse-proof shelves, when she caught him looking around.

"It's different," he hedged. "Did you build it?"

"No." She sat down on her bed and looked around. "But it's my design, a bigger version of the house my daddy made for us. When I got back, I wanted to feel like I was really home, not in somebody else's place. And it works. It's a good place to live."

"I can see that. So, wait, you didn't get back here till you were an adult?"

"No. I didn't even remember where it was. I was too little when I left. All I remembered was the trees I used to play around. My guild-application sponsor figured it out for me."

"From just the trees? Wow, he must have been some kind of brilliant."

"He was—is—but that's not why. Any good naturalist could have done it, this area is kind of unusual. But *would* anyone else have done it? I mean, he didn't have to, and it took weeks. That's something besides brilliance, I think."

"Uh, yeah." Kevin didn't think his own memories could get even the best naturalist to within a hundred miles of home, and he'd been there far more recently. Didn't matter, of course, he knew his own address, but not knowing his own home better bothered him somehow.

Chapter 2: Root Connections

Elzy woke in the dark to the scent of cold rain. Raindrops pattered on the sloping wall inches from her ear, a lovely sound, as long as she was warm and dry. There was a man in her house. She was almost sorry, though her heart fluttered pleasantly about it. It was just that he was in her space. She'd have to talk with him over breakfast, a near stranger, in her space.

Her house was dark, but dawn had broken—she always woke precisely with the sun, though she didn't know how. She dressed in darkness, grabbed her rain poncho, and went out into a bright near-monochrome of silver-gray, silvery green, and soft, muted black. Low, fog-like cloud made everything vague and indecisive-looking. In the clearing a fine, cold drizzle fell. Fat drops shook loose from the spruce boughs whenever the wind blew.

Where Kevin had seen trees and bushes around her home, Elzy saw red and white spruces, huckleberries, spruce saplings, and thirty-year-old apple trees dwarfed by poor soil and the attentions of deer. The two bigger deciduous trees were apple trees sprouted from cores tossed into the rich soil of her father's old garden. Detail of species, of history, of relationship formed the backdrop of her mind, but she wasn't thinking consciously of tree identification just now. She was wishing she could bottle the chill and save it for the summer when everything would be too hot.

She used the privy, made sure the rain collector was working properly, and let the chickens out. They'd laid a lot of eggs for her while she was gone. She took six for breakfast, intending to return later with a basket. Back inside, she tapped an LED on. She tried to be quiet, but she had to get the morning chill off, and the door of the woodstove squeaked and clanged. Kevin groaned. He swept aside his privacy curtain and sat up, blinking. He wore only his boarding-house shorts and an elastic band that held a small, black box tight to his skin near his right hip. An artificial pancreas? He hadn't mentioned being diabetic, but then, why would he? She tried not to smile about his bare, smooth, toned torso.

"Did I wake you?" she asked.

"Hm? No, no...yes, maybe a little. Don't worry about it, you're good," he mumbled.

"I only woke you a little?" she teased.

"Huh? Oh, yeah. Um."

"You can go back to sleep, if you want."

"No, no, it's OK, I'm up." He noticed he was almost naked and quickly retreated behind his curtain to dress. "Listen, do you have any caffeine around here?"

Rather than wait for the wood-stove to heat up, Elzy brewed her favorite chicory/black tea mix on her portable alcohol stove. With Kevin properly caffeinated, she served cheese omelets and explained how to brush one's teeth and so forth without running water. Then she grabbed her green and gray caretaker's uniform—not the black guildmember garb she'd worn yesterday—and retreated into her bunk to change.

"So," she asked, when she emerged, "what are you going to do all day while I'm out?"

"You're going *out?*"

"I'm a caretaker. The job includes going out in the rain."

"I guess it would. What are you going to do?"

"Check drainage structures, see if they're working properly. Check the iron ranger at the campsite. Look for trash. I'll call in your shopping list from one of the summits—there's no cell service here at the house."

He opened his mouth as though to argue. She gave him a look.

"I guess I'll draw up the plans for the boats, then," he said, instead.

"Shouldn't we do that together?"

"Sure, if you want. So, tell me, what do you think the bow offsets should be? How much rocker do you want on the keel?"

"OK, fine," Elzy said, laughing. "You do your job, I'll do mine."

"Well, I definitely don't want to do yours," he said and retrieved a spiral-bound notebook from his pack. "Wait—what condition is your cedar *in?*"

"It's not milled yet. Do you need it to be?" Elzy grabbed her day-pack from under her bed and rummaged through it.

"No, no, I can mill it, and I only need one log. But it has to have been down at least a year, and, ideally, close to a good worksite, somewhere flat, near water. And I need a little white spruce, too, also seasoned. Sorry, I know that all sounds weirdly specific."

"No, it's OK," said Elzy, still frowning into her half-full day-pack. "Northern white cedars grow all around the edge of the pond. One fell last year that would be perfect, right next to a flat spot. And I cut a big spruce off the Great Pond Trail near the Great Brook crossing—maybe two years ago?" She grabbed a two-way radio and dropped it in her bag, then searched through her bedding for her water bottle.

"Do you remember every tree that falls around here individually?" Kevin asked, but before she could answer he added "weird that the best wood for canoe frames grows right near water."

Elzy found her water bottle and shook it.

"It doesn't always," she replied. "What cedar really likes is soil with a lot of calcium, wet or dry. Usually it wouldn't grow over our granite bedrock at all, except we get so much fog here. Each fog-drop has a piece of dust in the middle, and all that dust catches in the trees, drips down, and enriches the soil."

"No kidding?"

Elzy still had to make lunch and find her sweater, but Kevin seemed genuinely interested. She sat down on her bed for a moment of natural history.

"Northern white cedar is a weird plant," she explained. "It grows slowly, lives longer than all our other trees, and it's the only conifer around here that rots from the inside out, so really old cedar logs turn into pipes. It's also the only one without mycorrhizal associations."

"Myco-what?"

"Mycorrhizal associations. Oh, they're cool. There are fungal threads all throughout the soil, plugged into tree roots. The trees feed the fungus sugar, and the fungus becomes an extension of the trees' roots, gathering more moisture and minerals than the roots can alone. And because the same fungus can connect to multiple trees at once, even multiple species, it also helps the trees share water and sugar with each other, even communicate with each other. It's this whole big network. Except northern white cedars aren't plugged in. They can root-graft with each other, but it's not the same."

"Huh. So, wait—"

But just then, a great gust of wind moaned in the trees and a patter of water and broken twigs sounded on the roof. Something big went THUMP nearby. Kevin raised an eyebrow at Elzy.

"Screw it," she said. "I'll do paperwork and bake muffins all day. Maybe the duty officer at headquarters will take my shopping list at eight AM check-in. I can usually get radio reception at the house."

"Wait, it's not even eight, yet?"

Elzy laughed at his confusion.

"Mister, you're less than ten miles as the crow flies from the earliest sunrise in the United States," she told him. "Welcome to Mount Desert Island."

Days later, after the nor'easter cleared off, Elzy accepted delivery, by pack-mule, of paint, canvas, oil, wax, some scrap two-by-fours and one-by-sixes, and some slightly-damaged reclaimed plywood—Kevin's shopping list. Then she showed him his work-site, a flattish area off the Perpendicular Trail, just up from its intersection with the Great Pond Trail. She used her electric chainsaw to limb, top, and cut in half the fallen cedar she'd had in mind. While she was at it, she cut a cookie of wood from the cedar stump for herself and hiked off to prepare Kevin's spruce.

Kevin got to work.

All that week, the weather stayed clear, dry, and cool. Red maple, its flowers almost invisibly small but brightly colored, turned whole hillsides reddish. In the mornings, Elzy would hike down to visit the campsite above the parking lot near the little beach. She would often find one or two campers there, sometimes more. She would chat with them, collect the "suggested" donation, and answer questions. Often she'd discover that they were breaking, or planned to break, one of the rules, so she'd explain why the rule was important. She had the authority to write citations, but rarely did. Obedience is temporary while education is forever. If there were children, Timogen let them bury tiny fingers in his ruff.

That done, Elzy would take notes on campsite use, then check for litter on her way over to Kevin's work-site. There she would sit for an hour or two, watching him work while she filed and sanded the cedar cookie smooth.

That first day, she found Kevin had already made himself a work-bench from scrap-wood and used a circular-saw attachment on his power-tool to slice the cedar into long boards. Now, he was cutting the cedar boards into thin, flat strips of varying lengths, each numbered with the stub of a pencil he kept behind his right ear. He carefully cut out any knots and spliced the cut ends together with some sort of glue he kept hot in a pot on a camp stove. When she left, he was still at it, moving with careful attention, sometimes consulting his notebook or using a tape measure. The next day, she found he'd taken the blade off his power tool and replaced it with a sander. He was smoothing the strips he'd cut, one by one. He did not talk as he worked, nor did he hurry, nor did he rest much. He did not make mistakes.

The day after that was Monday, when Flamingo Town held its market, so she left Timogen in charge of the homestead, put her black guild-member garb back on, and pedaled into town for the day to lead a few work-shops. But on Tuesday morning, when she returned to her cookie-sanding, she found Kevin still working with his same, unvarying attention, this time carving some of the spruce pieces with a knife, shaping the thwarts and yoke for the canoe. He'd already steam-bent the three longest strips. They lay clamped onto the molds he'd cut from the plywood.

Every time she came to see him, he'd be doing one thing over and over for the entire time she was there—cutting, sanding, or carving. The next day he'd be on to something different, but she rarely saw the end or the beginning of any task. She only saw the repetition. He never seemed to get bored.

By the end of his first week, for all Kevin's hard work, nothing looked remotely like a boat. Elzy had once heard a wise, old trail maintenance worker quote Abraham Lincoln: "if I had five hours in which to chop down a tree, I'd spend four of those hours sharpening my ax." Abe might have meant the statement as a metaphor, but it was also the literal truth of axes. She supposed the same principle applied to canoe-building.

The next two days it rained. Elzy worked as usual, but Kevin left his material under its tarps and stayed at the house. Elzy assumed he would spend his time loafing, but when she returned the first day she found that he'd split firewood in a break in the weather, collected the eggs from the chicken house, and baked several batches of muffins. Elzy had never before come in cold and wet from work to find her house warm and smelling of food. She rather liked it.

Kevin liked Elzy's visits to his worksite. He'd had clients watch him work before, but usually if they stayed more than five minutes they'd want to talk or to help. Elzy just sat, sanding her cedar cookie. When she finished that, early in the second week, she sanded a spruce cookie.

Her silent, companionable presence, the occasional warble of songbirds, the slap of the water against the rocky shoreline not far away, the varied croaking of ravens, the slant of light in the clear, cool, dry air, they all brightened and lightened him somehow. When she got up to leave—usually without saying goodbye, so as not to interrupt his work-flow—her presence left a kind of after-image so that he kept smiling as he worked, kept smiling until he saw her again.

She spoke rarely, but her few words were absolutely unpredictable. Once, early in the project, when he was still cutting pieces, he had glanced over to find her looking at him with an odd expression. He switched off his saw and removed one of his ear-plugs.

"It's strange to watch you just...dismembering trees," she'd explained, with mild but evident distaste.

He'd looked at his saw, speechless a moment.

"I'm going to put them back together as something useful—boats," he'd managed, finally.

"Dead trees are useful," she countered, "just less meaningful to humans." She'd seemed uncomfortable, as if she wanted to argue further but didn't want to talk him out of doing his job. This from the woman he'd watched wring the neck of a young and extraneous rooster the day before. They'd eaten him with rosemary. The chicken elicited her sympathy not at all, but the cedar and the spruce were people to her, somehow.

Elzy was beginning to amaze him. Whatever moved or changed or grew in her valley, she knew. She could identify, and rattle off interesting facts about, every plant, every track, every animal sign, by species and frequently by individual. When the weather was right, she fly-fished from the shore of the pond, casting and re-casting her line in graceful, looping curves. Often, she returned from work carrying a squirrel or two, or perhaps wild duck eggs. On days when he worked late, or when he took the time to hike off in search of good cell reception, Kevin would arrive at the homestead to find her digging over her garden in the lengthening evenings of May. Or she might be hanging laundry or sharpening her tools or running Tim through his commands. She did not appear to ever stop working, yet everything she did had an element of play or rest.

She fit into her life, he decided, with an almost animalistic completeness. He did not always see any place in that life for him. Sometimes her methods for living had literally been designed for solitude, such as her outdoor shower that had no walls—just a leather bag with a nozzle hung on a pulley from a tree over the gray-water sump. Whenever either of them wanted a shower, the other had to wait inside the house.

Too bad we're not going at it, he thought. *It would be a damn lot more convenient if she'd let me see her naked.*

Kevin started work on the second boat, the kayak. The canoe was nowhere near done, but he had begun coating its partially-assembled skeleton in walnut oil, one coat per day, and he needed something else to do while each of the six coats hardened. Gradually, first one boat, then the other, took shape.

One Sunday evening in a long, soaking, cold downpour, Kevin went to the privy barefoot so as not to soak his shoes. Once outside, he could hardly see in the dripping gloom, so he pushed back the hood of his rain poncho, baring his head. He returned with literally chattering teeth. He stripped down to his shorts, hung his damp clothing up on pegs, tried to squeegee his hair dry with his hands, and almost literally dove into bed.

"The smaller your house is, the *more* clothes you need," remarked Elzy. She was sitting on her own bed finishing up the spruce cookie.

"What? Why?"

She gestured at his hanging clothes. They wouldn't dry without more airflow. The house was too small for a laundry line. A week earlier, it had rained for three days straight and Kevin had run out of dry things.

"It fucking better not do that again," he grumbled, teeth still chattering. "I thought my hair was gonna mildew."

"Mine did, one year," said Elzy, mildly. She brushed wood dust from her cookie, and looked it over, smiling.

"Why are you doing that, anyway?"

"Doing what, sanding cookies?"

"Yeah."

"I like the way they look. And maybe somebody'll do a dendrochronology project here. I have a lot of cookies sanded and oiled under my bunk."

"Dendrochronology," Kevin said, slowly, trying out the syllables. "That's where they use tree rings to study history, right?"

"You got it."

"So, what are you finding out?"

"Nothing. Most trees are pretty idiosyncratic. Each one has slightly different growing conditions, so to get anything like a bigger picture I'd have to compare a bunch of different trees and do some math, and I haven't the time. Or the interest. The cedar I sanded the other week, though? The last decade or so, the rings are really small. It worries me."

"Oh?" Kevin sat up a little, still wrapped in his blanket. He'd noticed that Elzy went into educator-mode, apparently without meaning to, every few days. If he didn't encourage her she'd catch herself and stop, so he always encouraged her. He had little interest in natural history for its own sake, but he liked listening to her talk. She'd just never mentioned being *worried* before.

She rubbed the smooth wood with her thumb.

"Yeah. A lot of my cedar cookies are like that. They've been saying for years the Gulf of Maine is warming—I mean, *puffins* used to nest here. There used to be so many lobsters, you know, Before, back when there were interstate delivery trucks, that we used to ship them all across the country. All that's gone, because the water's warmer, and people around here know it. But nobody's talking about the fog, the fog that's caused by *cold* water. And I do think it used to be foggier around here. So maybe we're losing that, too, except I can't be sure without some kind of statistical analysis I don't have the data to do. But it could be happening, and maybe the trees have noticed, and that's why the cedars are growing more slowly."

"Cedars need fog?" he asked, before remembering. "Oh, yeah, the dust in the fog droplets. So without the fog…."

"Eventually, no cedars on most of this island—and less lichen cover on the trees, too. It will just be a very different kind of place."

Kevin felt faintly sick. New England had already lost most of its paper birches. To lose both the trees of its original canoe-building tradition?

"Wow. I didn't think climate change was still a thing. I guess it is."

"Well, it's *less* of a thing than if we hadn't stopped using fossil fuels, but change takes time," Elzy told him. "The emissions already up there aren't done with us, yet."

"Man, I *like* cedar."

"I do, too. My daddy used to make me cedar tea, in the winter, to keep me healthy. In the spring he'd brew it with red maple sap—made it sweet. I loved that. Still do."

"So, wait, one cedar cookie can tell you about the Gulf of Maine, climate change, all of that? I thought you said the rings only show local conditions?"

"They only show local conditions *clearly*," specified Elzy. "It's a signal-to-noise problem. But once you know what the signal is you can see it everywhere. The world shapes everybody, so everybody shows the shape of the world."

Timogen, unconcerned with the shape of the world, began to snore.

"So, hey, what do you see in the spruce? Tell me about white spruce." He wanted to change the subject. She handed over the cookie. The wood invited the hand like a flannel sheet. It was a good sanding job. He examined the rings as though they could tell him something.

"White spruce is also called cat spruce," Elzy began, "because the foliage supposedly smells like cat pee, but I don't really get that, maybe because I've never had a cat. The sap makes good chewing gum. You probably know that already....Oh, here's something weird—you know how deer and moose don't really eat the foliage? Nothing much does, except about a billion different insects. But you know what used to? Mastodons."

"Really?"

"Really. You and I are sitting in a giant patch of mastodon food with no mastodons."

"That's kind of sad, actually."

"I suppose."

"So, tell me about *this* spruce."

"There's not much to tell. One hundred fifty-one years of slow, even growth. It's fun to map out historical events onto the rings, though. Like, what was the spot where this grew *like* a hundred and fifty-one years ago? Or a hundred years ago? What was going on in the country then? That sort of thing."

"So if we count back forty-one years...."

"We get a picture of growing conditions here the year *before* I was born," Elzy confirmed. "Remember, how much a tree can grow in any given year depends on how much energy it could store the year before." She came over and sat on the edge of his bed and showed him the rings that grew when she was a baby. She had never sat on his bed before, not when he was in it. The familiarity, apparently unselfconscious on her part, made him feel very strange.

"What happened *this* year?" he asked, pointing to another, slightly more recent, ring.

"I was seven. I don't remember much. I was living here with my Daddy. My brother had already died. I think that was the year we got our first chickens."

"And this year?"

"I was 15? No, 16, living with Mom, fighting with her a lot, mostly over some boy I liked. She never wanted me to go with boys—and sneaking around was impossible, she was head of the security team."

"What about this one?"

And so Elzy told him bits and pieces about her life. Sometimes her stories had something to do with the width of the tree ring in question—a drought she remembered, or an unusually cold year—but more often they did not. She'd never opened up to him like that before.

"That's so wild," he said, finally. "Imagine if we were like trees and could keep hundreds of years of history just in the structure of our bodies."

"I'm not convinced we don't," said Elzy.

He heard the wind start to pick up.

That night, Kevin woke, bladder full, and threw on his damp clothes in the dark. Outside, the air felt dry and still, though the trees still dripped. The storm has literally blown itself away. He watered a good-sized tree, zipped back up, and found himself wholly awake.

The night air smelled almost of frost, and the spring peepers he'd heard before the storm had gone silent. He guessed the temperature at around four degrees Celsius—in the middle of May! He'd heard spring came late to the Maine coast, despite or even because of climate change, and apparently he'd heard right. He switched off his light. Under the trees, the night was so dark he literally could not see his hand in front of his face, even after he'd let his eyes adjust. The moon must be nearly new by now, a sliver not yet risen. He made his way out to the clearing near the vegetable garden and looked up to see a night brilliant with stars, the narrow silhouettes of spruce trees stabbing black against silent glory.

The sky here was too small for Kevin's taste. The whole landscape, trees and hills, seemed crammed and weirdly vertical, as though the land itself were restless, jumpy. Though he'd been making his way through the eastern forests for almost two years, now, he still couldn't get used to being entirely surrounded by trees all the time. But this was Elzy's normal. She must know the shapes of those trees against the stars as well as he remembered his mother's face.

Kevin was 28 years old, not a boy anymore. One of these days, he supposed, he ought to see about settling down someplace and starting a family. He could have a vegetable garden and his own familiar trees…. The idea intrigued and repelled him at once.

Places, they're just places, he thought. *Why get sentimental about a place when you might have to leave tomorrow? It's people who matter, because they can come with you.* Except people didn't come with him. In five years of constant wandering, he'd met no one content to take up life on the road with him, no one who didn't want a home to return to someday. If he didn't want to be alone all his life, he'd have to settle somewhere.

I'm just the boat-maker, he thought at himself, savagely. *Don't go thinking there's more going on here than there is.*

The next morning, Monday morning, Elzy headed back into Flamingo to the market, stubbornly peddling up the hill she and Kevin had hiked down when he arrived.

Even peddling hard, she reflexively noticed the trees, recognizing species, observing the progress of the season. Spruces dominated, giving the forest a dark, brooding appearance broken by wind-storms and bug-damage. Red pine, missing from the island for a generation but lately re-introduced, was not doing well, and even the spruce could no longer make it to old age before white rot and carpenter ants took the climate-weakened trees down. But spent male red maple flowers littered the roadsides in clumps, while the females had become the small but growing red samaras hanging in bunches like weird grapes. The big-toothed aspens had gone all fuzzy-tipped with new, whitish growth, and the short, slender shad-trees were in full, delicate bloom, each thin-petaled, white flower set off against tiny, just-sprouted, wine-red leaves. Elzy thought the island looked loveliest at exactly this time, let other people wax poetic about fall foliage as they might.

She crested the hill and came out into the open, wind-swept blueberry orchard. The wooded hillsides shelved away before her down to the sea, the massed trees too distant to be more than textured color—but, just this week, the hardwood fraction had turned greenish. Spring moved so slowly, leaf by leaf, and would continue to do so until the day in mid-June when the canopy would close and spring would suddenly seem, in retrospect, to have been a single, near-simultaneous sprouting. Next year, she knew, spring would surprise her in its slowness again. Human perception never ceased to amaze her.

When she reached Seal Harbor Road, she hung a left and coasted down the steep hill past small houses, curious children, and women picking the sprouts of invasive Japanese knotweed for pickling. Faster and faster she went until she could not have stopped if she wanted to. She flew around the blind corner at the bottom of the hill, praying madly to the god that she didn't believe in that there wouldn't a skittish horse on the other side, and zipped into downtown Flamingo and its small cluster of buildings still mostly boarded up for the winter.

Her workshop went well, she got her shopping done, but then one of the other presenters asked for her to sub for him at the booth on the life-cycle of the lobster, and so she didn't leave town until almost sunset. Dark caught her partway up the mountain with her flashlight battery failing. She had to creep along in the moonless night largely by feel. Hours later, she heard Timogen bark and knew she was home at last.

Then, she saw a light.

A lit candle-lantern hung from the laundry line. Kevin had left a light on for her.

"I thought maybe you ate in town, so I didn't wait for you," he said when she came in. "But I saved you the last muffin."

"Did you feed Timogen?" she asked. She didn't know what else to say. No one had ever left a light on for her. It was always she who looked after others.

"Sure. We both had muffins, cheese, and jerky." He seemed unaware of her feelings.

She put her pack down and sat on her bed. Sitting felt good.

"My flashlight died. Why does it seem like climbing in the dark takes more energy?"

"It probably does. I mean, I always tense up, walking around at night. I'm afraid I'll bump into something."

She got up, fetched the muffin, and grabbed the honey jar, the butter, and a knife from the mouse-proof. She *had* eaten in town, but made herself a second supper, anyway. She sat on the edge of her bed to eat. Kevin put an open bottle of cider in her hand and sat down next to her.

"Drink," he commanded. "You'll feel better."

She obeyed.

She still didn't know what to say to him. She had a vague feeling that she ought to say something nice to reciprocate, but she didn't know how. She decided to ask questions, to show interest.

"So, what brought you to Mount Desert Island, anyway?"

"You mean besides the ferry?" They both laughed. "Well, I'd been working my way east for a while, building boats for people here and there, and I started seeing signs for Bar Harbor. Made me think of this necklace my mother has—it's just a little silver lobster pendent on a chain, and it says Bar Harbor, ME on the back. She used to let me play with it. She didn't know what Bar Harbor even was. Got it from her grandmother. So, when I saw the road signs, I wanted to check it out."

"Huh. Your great-grandmother must have come here on vacation. A lot of people did."

"She never said anything about it to Ma."

"So how did you get into boat-making?"

Kevin laughed, a little embarrassed.

"It's woodworking, basically. I always liked making things with my hands—even when I was a kid, helping my dad fix fences and sheds and shit. A friend of my parents made rowboats for duck hunting, and one year he offered me a little money to come stay with him a while and help out. The rest is history, I guess." He looked at his hands.

"You have that much water on your prairie?" asked Elzy, imagining endless acres of waving grass and nothing else.

"Of course we have water," Kevin said, laughing. "We just don't have trees. We use salvaged wood for everything, even the boats. There's plenty, from ruins and stuff. Or, there was when I was coming up. Eventually, I suppose, they'll run out."

She asked him more questions. As he talked about his teachers, the different kinds of boats he'd been "given" (he had an idea that boat designs ought to be transmitted teacher-to-student, not learned from a book), and all the places he'd worked between here and the prairies of Western Canada, he seemed less and less self-conscious and spoke faster and faster.

"So, I guess I wanted to see how far I could get," he was saying.

"Professionally or geographically?" she asked.

"Well, they're kind of the same thing. See, people in different places make different boats. There are different water conditions, different materials available, and in some places there are still the really old traditions, people whose ancestors have been making boats the same way for hundreds or even thousands of years. Elzy, I've been allowed to help make a birch-bark canoe! It's not that they're more practical than canvas boats, they're not. They're heavier, less durable, and harder to repair. But man, you want to talk about art? And to make *everything* that goes into a boat, even the tools, it's just incredible. I've built skin boats, too, seal-skin kayaks and umiaks, coracles that look like baskets, weigh a ton, and need the skin of an entire ox.... See, it's always a conversation. It's a conversation between my hands and the wood and the client and the water where that boat will live—and the entire history and context of the client that causes them to need *this* boat, *my* boat, *now*. So, yeah, I want to get as far as possible. I want to learn everything. Elzy, I want to put a boat in every body of water there is."

His passion was so contagious, Elzy found she had to hold on to her bedspread so she would not take his face between her hands and kiss him.

Well, why don't you? said a voice inside her head. *You're a grown-up.* But, but...she argued back. *It wouldn't have to mean anything,* the voice insisted. But, but....

"Don't you ever stay put?" she asked, without meaning to.

His body language changed abruptly. He blinked.

"Where should I stay, Elzy?" he asked. "Here?" He laughed, a single, derisive *ha!*

Then he saw her face.

Chapter 3: Getting Together

The next morning, Kevin woke up and decided to pretend he hadn't. He couldn't believe how tactless he'd been. He'd been so intent on not over-stepping his bounds, on hiding his vain hope that she might really want him, that in trying to mock himself he'd mocked her instead. She'd blown hot, then cold, then retreated to her bunk and not come out till morning. He felt terrible.

But honestly, her anger seemed disproportionate. After all, until last night, he'd have thought she was looking *forward* to him leaving so she could have her own space back. She was friendly, she was flirty, but she'd never hinted he should stay any longer than necessary. Where did she get off, getting angry with him?

His justifications did no good. There'd been a moment when he'd been sure she was about to kiss him. And then the look in her eyes had changed to hurt.

He waited until Elzy and Tim left, then packed a lunch, filled his canteen, and hiked off to build boats. He understood boats. He liked boats.

The day was cool and breezy, but dry at least. The frame of the canoe was complete, an open lattice of wood, the longitudinal stringers and thin, transverse ribs anchored to the gunnels and bow and stern stems but not to each other—the intersections of the lattice weren't glued, only tied with sinew so the boat could flex. Now, he assembled and installed the frames of the canoe seats and wove split cattail leaves across the frames for seat webbing. Then he carved the paddles, sanded them until the wood felt as smooth and inviting as cotton, then oiled them. Finally, late in the day, he gave the frame of the canoe its sixth and last coat of oil. Now the oil would have to cure for several days. He briefly considered starting to assemble the frame of the second boat, anything to avoid climbing that damn mountain and going to talk to Elzy, but as long as he wasn't *entirely* without balls, he couldn't be that much of a coward. Up the mountain he went.

He took the Perpendicular Trail, a tough route, but direct and pretty.

First there were the stone stairs, fitted together by hand from material found or cut nearby, as graceful as anything he'd ever made out of wood. Then the airy groves of now silvery-tipped deciduous trees, the open scree fields, the jumbled rock gray with lichen but pink where the hands and feet of hikers had worn. Then through dark conifer forests and, briefly, downhill along the base of a sheer cliff damp from small springs along its top, and on and on and up and up.

When he came out at the overlook just below the summit of Mansell, he stopped, as he always did, to catch his breath and to look out across the southern tip of the island. From here, he had a good view of the little boat ramp/beach and the oddly-narrow, flat-tipped end of the pond. Looking down on it over the almost-sheer slope gave the curious sensation of dream-flight. In shadow, the water looked green and deep.

But he wasn't interested in looking at the pond water. His gaze drifted further out, past Southwest Harbor and the mouth of Somes Sound to the open sea dotted with sailboats and islands. He'd lived less than five kilometers from saltwater for weeks, now, but it might as well be five hundred kilometers for all it impacted his life. He couldn't smell it, couldn't hear it, and the fish Elzy served him were all from the pond. And yet once or twice a day he could look out and see it stretch on forever, blue and glittering. He wanted to paddle out into that vastness and keep on going.

Today the horizon was not crisp but hazy, obscured by distant fog. He turned, looking out across and beyond Bass Harbor Head, and saw an arm of the fog rolling in towards land. It did not look at all like a grounded cloud, all white and fluffy, but had instead a cold, dense, dark look, its heart an inexplicable soft pink or purple.

He still had no idea what he was going to say to Elzy.

He found her in her garden, digging compost into one of the beds. Timogen lay nearby snapping playfully at the season's first flies. As Kevin approached, Tim got up and ambled out to sniff his hands and feet. Kevin felt oddly flattered. Tim didn't usually bother to greet him. He scratched the dog's jaw and received a single, polite lick in return, then followed the dog back in through the garden gate. But Elzy did not look up at all.

"Elzy," he began, "I—" but she cut him off.

"Forget it," she said, almost savagely. "It's not like I'm any good at this stuff, either."

"Oh?"

"I can't keep a man around anyway. I can't even keep any real friends, not people I ever tell what I *really* think. Which is, honestly, almost OK, because most people really do bug me, sooner or later." She stabbed furiously at the earth with her shovel, as though the crusted, weedy soil itself were somehow at fault. "I mean, I've tried. I've had other relationships." She paused in her digging and leaned on her shovel, staring out into space, angry tears glittering suddenly on her face. "All of them leave because I can't feel the right damn emotions."

"There's no such thing as a wrong emotion," Kevin objected, his own all in a roil. She'd said *other* relationships as if....

"Easy for you to say," Elzy countered, starting to dig again. "You can feel the right ones."

"OK, you've lost me."

Elzy put down her shovel, jumped down off the raised bed, and sat on its edge. Kevin sat beside her. She had dirt and composted manure caked on her hands and even smeared, absent-minded, on her face. Bits of dry vegetation stuck in her hair. Her clothes were old, stained, ripped. He could smell the fresh sweat of her labor. She was beautiful.

"Men leave because I don't care about them the way they want," she explained, simply.

"If you didn't care about them, why does it bother you that they left?"

"Because it makes me feel like an idiot, that's why!" she half-shouted, then wiped her nose with the back of her hand. "And I *did* care," she added, more quietly. "I mean, I've never dated a man I didn't like. Some of them I liked a lot. They just wanted something else."

"What?"

"How the hell am I supposed to know?" But she would not look at him.

He couldn't think of anything to say. After a while, he offered to help dig. She looked at the sky to check the time.

"No, let's get dinner. I only have the one shovel, anyway."

She got up, dusted herself off, and headed towards the house, still sniffling.

Elzy had shot two red squirrels earlier that day, and she let Kevin skin and clean the carcasses while she built the fire outside. He gave the entrails to Tim and pinned the skins out to dry while she sliced the tiny haunches and shoulders and pan-grilled them with cheese. She served them on warmed tortillas with half a jar each of pickled, sliced onion and a squirt of sunflower oil. They clinked cider bottles and tucked in while Timogen crunched happily on the tiny cut-over carcasses. And yet nothing had been resolved.

"Elzy, I'm not, I'm not going anywhere," he said, finally. She looked at him in surprise. "I mean, yes, I travel, and I...I mean my plans haven't changed." He scratched the back of his head self-consciously. "I mean metaphorically, OK? We'll stay in touch. Unless I bug you or something. You're an amazing woman, and I don't know what those other guys were talking about."

She smiled a little.

"You don't bug me—much," she admitted, then flashed a quick grin at him. But the grin faded. The air grew slightly but suddenly cooler. The sun must be setting. He wished he could see it. He wished he could say the thing that would let Elzy open up to him again, but he didn't know how.

"You never talk about your mom's place," he said instead.

"It's just a farm in Pennsylvania. It's not special to me."

"Why not?"

"I don't know. Maybe I just do better in Maine soil or something. That happens, with some people. My application sponsor told me he always felt like the Sonoran Desert was home, even though he wasn't born there."

"What was it like?"

She shrugged.

"We raised apples, geese, and hogs...vegetables, too, of course. One of the men on Mom's farm made the best scrapple. There was a grape arbor—Concord grapes, you know, the purple ones? Me and the other kids had to go out with baskets to pick them, and we got in trouble for eating so many." She smiled almost nostalgically a moment. "But I didn't really get along with those people, and Mom didn't really let me be a kid. She needed more people on the farm security team. So she trained me to kill bandits and shit. Later, she organized the town police force and trained me to be a cop. But all I ever wanted to do was talk about natural history, and they all looked at me like I was weird when I tried."

He wanted to smile at the picture she painted, the awkward young geek among the unappreciative laypeople, but—

"Did you really kill bandits?"

"Yeah. Of course. Somebody had to. I was good at it, too."

"Elzy, my father used to be a bandit."

Silence. She looked at him, and he regretted telling her. But how could he not?

"No wonder you were weird about my being a cop," she said at last.

"That's not—" He couldn't explain it. "I'm not like him. I'm not *against* cops or vigilantes. I'm not against people going after guys like him. You had to. I get it. It's just that...he's human too."

"Of course he's human. What else could he be?"

"I mean, I don't like hearing about people killing bandits and not feeling bad about it."

"What does somebody being human have to do with me feeling bad?" she asked, puzzled.

He stared at her.

"Somebody doesn't want to die, so you give a shit about that. Some woman loses her husband, you care."

"I don't, not necessarily," Elzy told him. "I don't feel things just because other people do." She paused a moment before adding "but you think I should."

He could not read her expression. He couldn't think of anything to say.

"I *do* care about people," she assured him. "Some people, anyway. There are some people I like a lot, and anyway I'm a public servant, I have been my whole life! I just don't get all wrapped up in other people's feelings. I don't feel bad just because somebody else feels bad. I don't even understand why other people do, *if* they do. Maybe they don't, and I'm just not as good at pretending? I mean, realistically, most people are basically in it for themselves."

She said that last with such casual conviction. He felt queasy.

"You really think that? Everybody?"

"No, not everybody," she admitted. "My teacher—my application sponsor, I mean—two people tried to mug him, so I killed them. There was no other way, honestly. That was back when major theft was punished the same as murder. Sentencing judges did *not* fuck around, and so highway robbers didn't, either. Those guys would've killed him once they found out how much cash he was carrying. I had no back-up and no time. But my teacher was sad when they were dead. They were strangers, and they would have killed him, and he was sad for them just because they were people. He wasn't pretending."

Kevin said nothing.

"I know how all this sounds," she said at last. "I know you think I'm a, I'm a….And maybe I am. But I'm not a monster. I don't kill people *for fun*, or anything like that. I'm an ethical, honorable woman. And even if I *am* different than most people, the world needs people like me. We do things other people won't do."

The sickness in Kevin's stomach deepened. He wanted to run away, but he'd just promised her he wouldn't do that. He wanted to ask her questions—what caring for people felt like, or even meant, for someone like her, for starters. But he didn't ask.

"The world needs people like my father, too," he said instead. "He kept my mom safe and fed when a lot of people were neither. I exist because of what he did. And he never enjoyed killing, either. He didn't even enjoy stealing. As soon as he got the horse farm he went straight."

He still felt like running away, except now he knew he wouldn't. He wanted to take her hand, but he didn't do that, either.

Kevin no longer knew what he wanted from Elzy. He at least wanted to be her friend but didn't know what that might look like. He tried starting with carpentry.

Beginning that week, he knocked off a little earlier in the afternoons to work around the homestead. He fixed the leaky laundry tub and re-greased its spinning mechanism. He carved new knobs for the chicken-coop doors. He tightened up the garden rake handle. He got over his fear of the big dog enough to help with Tim's evening training exercises as the apple trees burst into bloom. Elzy accepted his labor almost without thanks, as he already accepted hers, the way people who live together do.

Elzy hadn't sat with him while he worked on the boats in a long time, not since she'd finished sanding the cookies, so when she dropped by for a visit one day, she seemed suitably impressed by his progress. She stood beside him to watch for a few minutes.

"What are you doing?" she asked.

"Waterproofing the joints with beeswax."

"Why?"

"The joints are glued. Hide glue's not waterproof."

"Why not? Can't you make waterproof glue?"

"Sure. Just add alum. But waterproof glue's a bitch to clean up, and it leaches poison into the water. I won't mess with it."

"The boats look like boats now," Elzy remarked. She was right. Both frames were complete, open lattices of aromatic cedar. Once the oil on the kayak finished curing, he'd waterproof its joints, too.

"I'm almost done." The fact should have been a source of pride, but he felt only sadness.

"Can you make a kayak for me?" Elzy asked. "Not for fishing, I can fish from the canoe. I mean something small and fast."

Another boat might add weeks to the project. The sadness receded.

The trees all had little baby leaves, now. The garden yielded turnip tops and nasturtium leaves, the first fresh greens of the year. The apple trees bloomed and buzzed with bees. Less idyllically, the mosquitoes attacked. At least the weather was still cool enough for long sleeves. He stretched canvas over the canoe, tacking it in place and cutting and sewing it to shape, then painted it with glue. Overnight, the glue shrank as it dried, pulling the canvas taught. Then he waterproofed inside with wax and outside with marine-grade vegetable-based paint. Suddenly, pollen was everywhere. Though not seriously allergic, he sneezed and sneezed and sneezed again. Elzy, of course, did not even sniffle.

Finally, on a clear, cold, blue morning, he invited Elzy to come inspect her new canoe.

They left Tim at the house. The dense screen of cedars along the shoreline prevented launching from the work-site, so Kevin got the boat up on his shoulders and set off. When they arrived at the little beach, Elzy got her fishing gear from the shed, then inspected the boat carefully.

"What's this?" she asked, noticing the symbols in black near the stern.

"A Japanese approximation of my name."

"Why? Are you Japanese?"

"No. But my family's part-Japanese on both sides. I think the other part's English or Scottish? Anyway, my Dad taught me how to write my name. It's my trade-mark."

Elzy took her inspection so seriously that Kevin almost got nervous. Finally, she lifted the boat up on her own shoulders, strode into the water, and set the canoe upon the waves. The onshore breeze pushed it against her legs almost affectionately. She wrapped its painter around her hand and splashed ashore to fetch the two paddles, leashed each of them to a thwart, and stepped in, balancing well.

"Hey, it works!" she cried.

"Don't sound so surprised!"

She paddled around for a few minutes, testing speed, stability, and turning radius. Then she stood, legs wide and braced against the back of a thwart, and put the boat through its paces again. Of course she *would* be an excellent boatwoman. She returned to shore, and Kevin climbed aboard so she could test it as a two-person boat. He realized that despite living and breathing boats for weeks, he hadn't actually gone for a paddle in far too long.

They returned to shore, and he used his phone to take photos of the boat on the sand, on Elzy's shoulders, and on the water with Elzy paddling and the blue, shining pond and the spring-green hills in the background. He'd put the images, minus Elzy's face, on his website next time he got a good signal.

"Hand me my stuff, will you?" Elzy asked. "I want to find out what's biting."

Late in the afternoon, he heard Elzy's voice. He found her floating just off-shore of his work-site, under the imperfect shadow of the cedar trees. Reflections from sunlit patches of water played on the underside of the flat, green foliage and on her dark skin.

"What's up?" he asked her. In answer she held up a dripping-wet cloth bag that wiggled.

"Keep a hold of these, will you?" she asked. "Do anything you want with them for dinner. I found a couple of stealth sites I have to naturalize, so I'll be out late. I'll get left-overs or something." By *stealth site* she meant a campsite made by hikers against regulations. He tied the bag to a tree and dropped it back in the water, then went back to work.

Elzy watched him disappear among the trees, then shoved off again, skimming across the water under the blue, gull-visited sky. She had no real reason to work late, the stealth sites could wait till tomorrow, but she had no intention of getting out of the boat before she had to.

She'd never seen her pond and her hills from this angle before, nor had she ever been able to move so quickly from one side to the other. She could smell the water, green and living, see pine needles, bits of dislodged algae, and unlucky insects floating in columns of sunlight lancing down into the slightly silty depths...and then a wavelet would pass, changing the angle at which the light hit the water, and she would see nothing but brilliantly reflected sky. She would have to buy sunglasses.

Why did it take me fifteen years to get a boat? she asked herself.

When the shadow of the western ridge started to climb up the opposite slopes and cliffs, Elzy beached her boat on the sand. Her legs ached from disuse. Her arms ached from overuse. She didn't mind. But where was she going to *put* her canoe? *Dumb-ass,* she accused herself. She leaned the boat against the pumphouse wall, right under the sign that said GOVERNMENT PROPERTY DO NOT DISTURB. She'd have to find a better solution, something more secure.

She headed up the mountain. Her stomach grumbled. *I should have brought a burrito for dinner,* she thought, but of course she hadn't known she'd be out so late.

She found Kevin relaxing beside an overly-large fire with Timogen, who of course jumped up and ran to greet her. The dog hadn't seen her *all day* and had missed her terribly. To her surprise, Kevin also got up, almost as excited. When she went inside, man and dog both followed her.

Once inside, her first thought was that she wished Kevin had held dinner for her after all, because whatever he'd made smelled delicious. Then she saw she'd gotten her wish.

"I did what you told me," he said, sounding almost embarrassed. "You said do what I want for dinner, and I wanted to make you a feast. Tim's already eaten, but I haven't."

"Um...." She didn't know what to say. Nobody had ever made her a feast.

Set out on the various horizontal surfaces of the kitchen were bowls and plates, all of them covered by other bowls to keep their contents warm. She looked under one of the bowls and found a vegetable and mushroom soup in fish broth. The next was a platter of sliced polenta, each slice piled with slivers of fish, onion, egg, and some of the dulse she'd bought at the market months ago. Another platter held meadow mushrooms sauteed with the last of last year's onions, sunchokes, and winter squash. On yet another, she found samples of all five kinds of pickled vegetable she'd put up last year. She found one covered plate that wasn't warm and looked inside.

"Did you forget to cook this part?" she asked.

Kevin laughed.

"Sashimi is supposed to be raw! Try it, it's good. Here, dip it in this sauce."

"Hey, that *is* good!"

"Just like Gramma used to make."

"It must be nice to have known your grandparents."

"Actually, I never met her," Kevin admitted. "She taught my Dad to cook, though. I don't know what she would have thought of all this—substituting polenta for rice? And I don't even know what *this* is. Sort of reminds me of octopus...."

"You've got the right phylum," Elzy told him. "It's a pickled wrinkle—a sea snail. Same thing as a dog winkle, I think? But pickled *winkle* is almost impossible to say....Lobstermen find them in their traps and pickle them for emergencies. Sometimes someone sells a few jars."

Kevin placed the item, which was small, pink with black speckles, and rubbery, in his mouth and chewed. A look of surprised pleasure lit his face.

"Huh. I've never tasted a wrinkle before."

"There's a joke in there, somewhere."

"I admit nothing. Or I'm guilty as charged, depending on what joke you had in mind."

"This is really good." She was still nibbling at the sashimi.

"I made a pot of the cedar tea you like."

"Mmmm. I don't have any sake. I'm sorry."

"Let's make do with your applejack."

They carried the food outside and lit a couple of citronella candles to keep away the bugs. Night settled as they ate and talked about childhood, mostly Kevin's.

"What's your mother like?" Elzy asked.

"Not as good a cook, for one thing." Kevin said, amused. "Dad says she's the brains of the family, which isn't exactly true. I mean, my dad's brilliant and I'm...not that dumb, anyway, but she handles the business side of the business, finances and client relations and records. She's also about half a vet. I mean, she was partway through school when the pandemic happened. Mom's easier to deal with. Dad acts like he likes horses better than people."

He poked at the fire with a stick. Sparks went up. The flames had died down, yielding just enough light, with the candles, to ruin Elzy's night vision. Everything beyond the fire pit, including all of Kevin except his shoes and his poking stick, were lost in the blackness.

"I used to ask him to show me how to do shit just so he'd talk to me about something," he continued. "That sounds fucked up, doesn't it? But it never felt that way to me. I guess I always figured he liked teaching me stuff for the same reason I liked learning, so we could connect. It's the one way he knows how. I think that's why he learned to cook, so he could connect with his mother. She got him into horses, too. She was into horses. He's never said so, but I think Dad was real close to his mother. He learned everything he could from her."

He seemed to be in a mood to talk about his dad and would not be diverted.

"Has he ever shown interest in learning from you?" Elzy asked. "Like how to build boats or something?"

Kevin shifted a little in the dark, as though he'd been struck by a new thought.

"Not before I left. Now, maybe he would. If I ever go home, maybe I'll teach him."

He poked at the fire again and added a log. He seemed unaware that fires can burn un-poked.

"*If* you ever go home?" Elzy asked. "Won't you eventually?"

"I guess I will. At least to visit. I don't know. Maybe I'll settle somewhere else. Maybe I won't settle at all. You were right, the other week. I don't really stay put."

"Why not?"

Kevin shrugged.

"I don't know, I guess I've never thought it's all that important. The way I was raised, where we lived was just never a big deal. It was only where we happened to be. Mom says it's a mistake to get too caught up with stuff you can't carry, anyway."

The fire suddenly flared up as the new log caught. Elzy could see the light shining on Timogen's face, paws, and eyes. Normally, when Elzy built a fire, the dog watched the flames. Now he was watching the humans, his eyes shifting back and forth as he tracked the conversation.

Later, after they'd done the dishes and given whatever scraps wouldn't keep to the chickens, Elzy gave Tim a long twist of jerky, made another pot of tea, and she and Kevin sat together on the same log, close but not touching, staring into the flames and not talking.

Kevin took Elzy's hand. He did it casually, as though he did that sort of thing every day.

She flinched a little in surprise. She was not a touchy, affectionate person, but decided she liked the feel of his hand in hers. It could stay. She watched shades of red flicker and move through the charring wood.

Kevin began to caress her hand a little with his thumb. She liked that, but when he lifted her hand and turned it over she glanced at him almost sharply. What was he doing?

He was inspecting her hand, turning it in the meager firelight, running his hands along her fingers and over the hard little bulges of her wrist bones. It felt nice, so she gave him her other hand to examine, too. He grinned and bent to his work, looking over her hands as though he planned to sculpt them later from memory—and maybe he did.

Why was he doing this? Elzy turned towards him, straddling the log so she could face him comfortably and examine *his* hands, find out what the fuss was about. And they were fine hands, much larger than hers, the fingers long and narrow, the muscles at the base of the thumb and little finger well-developed, the skin not soft but smooth, except for the callouses along the upper palm and the little scars all along the fingers and the top of the hand where tools had slipped and bit, just a little, over the years. He had even trimmed his nails, maybe filed them, each one a smooth, neat oval, the hands of a meticulous, artistic man.

She turned his hands and caressed them as he caressed hers, not looking at him but only at their joined hands, the fire warm against her back and shoulders. Timogen looked on with interest, and she ignored him.

The caresses expanded from hands to arms to shoulders, Kevin leading and Elzy following—but it was Elzy who kissed first, kissed his mouth.

Then his hands were on her hips, her back, her breasts, her neck and collarbone, her face. His shirt wrinkled under her moving palms across his back, his sides, his shoulders, her fingers in the fine, short hair on the nape of his neck. His body was solid, lithe, muscular, and very real in her arms. They kissed for a very long time, just kissed, until Elzy felt the fire die down beside her.

"It's time for bed," she said, pulling away slightly.

"I thought you'd never ask," he exclaimed.

"No, I mean to sleep."

Kevin opened his mouth to respond, perhaps to protest, but yawned instead. They both laughed.

They doused the last of the fire with the dish-water, locked in the chickens, put the applejack and the cups away, took turns using the privy, brushed their teeth, then closed up the house for the night, except for the back window, which they left open so they could hear frog song. Elzy was just drawing aside her privacy curtain to get in bed when she turned to look back at Kevin. He was looking at her from beside his own bed, his gaze dark and urgent. She sat down on the edge of her mattress.

"There's condoms in the mouse-proof, in a jar behind the extra match-es," she told him.

Chapter 4: Reasons to Stay

Elzy woke. Her body felt odd. Good-odd. But she wasn't in her own bed? Oh, right; she was in Kevin's bed because he had fallen asleep in hers. She stretched luxuriantly and looked over at him. He lay sprawled, naked (except for the band and the box he still hadn't explained), his limbs long and lean, his skin goose-bumped by the morning cold. Beautiful.

She lay for some minutes watching the indirect but strangely bright sunlight from the open window illuminate naked Kevin until she suddenly realized why the light was strange—she'd slept in several hours.

"Eight AM radio call!" she shouted, sitting up so fast she almost bumped her head.

"What?" shouted Kevin, who did bump his head. "Dammit, Elzy, what the fuck?" He rubbed his crown.

"Sorry. I think I missed radio call. What time is it?"

"I don't know." But he found Elzy's phone between her mattress and the wall. "Eight-ten," he reported.

"Shit. I'm gonna have to call them. I *never* miss check-in. I can't believe I slept so late." She held her head in her hands, wondering how much she could get away with not explaining. She'd had sex with Kevin. She hadn't planned on it, they hadn't discussed it, they'd just fallen into bed, a lack of discipline she had thought she'd grown out of. She groaned a little and clutched at her face.

"Oh, don't fuckin' tell me you're hung over," said Kevin. "I really don't want you to have been drunk last night."

"What? Oh, no. It's just that I stayed up half the night with some handsome boat-maker...." Her head did feel muddy, though. Maybe she just needed some caffeine. Or some more sleep. Belatedly, she realized she needed to address the question he wasn't asking.

"Last night," she admitted, "was weird. But I liked it." She glanced over at him. He was looking at her with a kind of eager conspirator's delight.

"Does that mean we can do it again?"

"Well, not before breakfast, I don't think."

Kevin whooped and kicked his legs in the air.

"You go radio your people, I'll make the chicory. And I've got to find my clothes somewhere, it's goddamn freezing in here."

An hour later, morning chores finished, Elzy served out left-overs and jerky. The chickens, released to forage at last, stalked clucking across the clearing on their dinosaur legs, while the mosquitoes floated just on the edge of the clouds of repellent. Bees hummed in the apple blossoms. The early chill gone, the air warmed rapidly. In some undefinable way, the season had changed.

"It's *so* late," Elzy said, turning her face to the sunshine. "I think I'm just gonna pretend I took the day off on purpose."

Kevin, on his second cup of chicory, stretched out beside her, laying his head on a sitting-log.

"This place is finally beginning to grow on me," he said.

"Yeah? Only now?" As if she didn't know what had changed. "What was wrong with it before?"

"It's too enclosed. All these trees, they're...it's claustrophobic."

"It's not your natural habitat. I'm the opposite. Away from the canopy, I feel...exposed. I guess I'm just a timid, brown, forest creature?" She remembered a cartoon rabbit had once used a similar phrase.

"Timid, my left nut! You're a predator, *that's* why you like cover."

"I suppose," Elzy said, a little uncomfortably. "But if you dislike the forest because it isn't the prairie, that must mean you *like* the prairie. You're not indifferent to place."

"I guess."

"You said this place is growing on you. How?"

"What? Oh, I was just smelling the pine trees and shit. It's pretty. Clean-smelling."

"Those aren't pines, they're spruces. Anyway, I think you're actually smelling balsam fir. There's a little of it on the edge of the clearing."

"Same difference. A pine is a pine."

"Yes, but firs aren't pines. Neither are spruces. I mean, they're all in the pine *family*, they're Pinaceae, but they're different genera. There aren't a lot of pines here in my territory, but there are a few. White pines, mostly. The pitch and jack pines like the other side of the island better, where it's more fire-prone. The way you tell the difference—let me show you, actually."

And she got up and ran back to the house to grab some botanical specimens.

"I collected these for my workshop on Monday," she explained. "I don't know why I still have them." The twigs were starting to dry out, but the needles were still green. He sat up, and she showed him the white pine twig, how its long needles grew in bunches while the short ones of the other conifers grew singly. Then she held up the twigs of white spruce, balsam fir, and hemlock in one hand like a group of playing cards. "Do you see the difference?"

"No. Yes. Sort of? They're, um, the needles are different shades of green?"

"They are, but there are other differences. Look at where the needles meet the twigs? Spruce needles sit on little wooden pegs. When the needles fall off, the pegs remain, leaving the branchlet bumpy. Fir and hemlock both lack pegs. Also, spruce and fir each have even-sized needles. Hemlock needles are variably-sized—their twigs are thinner, too. And spruce needles are square in cross-section. Fir and hemlock both have flat needles."

"So, if you squint you can see the difference, and that's why they're categorically distinct?"

"No, once you're used to it, you can see the difference from 500 feet away without even trying. It's a visual texture kind of thing. But learning detail sensitizes the eye, teaches you what textures to look for—and the detail requires a bit of squinting. Or a hand-lens."

"Huh."

"Look at that tree over there and that one. Are they the same?"

"No. That one's kind of bunchy-looking and narrow. That other one's,

I don't know, smoother, and the branches go like this." He made J-shaped motions with his hands.

"Exactly. You're seeing it. That one's a white spruce, the other is red spruce. Tree ID is less about memorizing details and more about learning to *see*—which you do by memorizing details, but the point is that once you *can* see, the differences become obvious, and you know why fir isn't a pine. It just doesn't look like one anymore. You can see what makes it *itself*."

"This is nuts," complained Kevin, scratching the back of his head. "I make my living knowing the difference between different kinds of wood."

"Well, now you have the opportunity to get to know the living trees, too."

"Opportunity, my ass. You're just showing off how much smarter you are than me."

"Maybe I *am* smarter than you. You got a problem with that?"

"Of course not! A brilliant woman like you picks me, you think I'm *complaining?* I just don't want you to think I'm stupid, is all. I mean, I'm not a naturalist, but I can notice things."

"OK, you can notice stuff. Prove it."

Kevin smiled a little and then closed his eyes. She could see his eyeballs moving under the lids as he almost literally looked around at whatever image he had on his mind.

"Your hair," he began, and a strange little ripple went through her, "stands out from your head like a halo, deep enough for me to bury my fingers and not reach your scalp. It looks black from a distance, but up close it's very, very dark brown, like the earth in your garden, and the silver threads in it shine in the light like tinsel. Your skin is perfectly clear, no freckles, no zits, nothing, except you must have had chicken pox when you were a kid because you have a little round scar on your jaw just near your left ear. Your earlobes are free, not attached, it's that genetic thing, and you'd look great with earrings but they're not pierced. Your eyes are so black they reflect light easily and look white sometimes, it's weird. Your teeth really are white, not stained at all, and you have nice teeth, except there is a chip off the end of your right upper incisor, and there's a bit of a gap between your lower incisors where one of them turns in slightly, and every time I look at you I want to put my tongue in that gap, especially when you smile, because you have a wonderful, big smile. Your nose is straight and a little narrow, almost a European-type nose, but the curve of your cheek down to your jaw is African. You have a heavy, strong jaw, but it's curved like a, like a, well, it's feminine, anyway, and I like it, it suits you. You've got these lines on your neck, horizontal lines, two of them, about three centimeters apart, and your eyebrows are pretty wide, you don't pluck them, which is good, because plucking eyebrows is stupid, and the curve of the underside of those eyebrows matches the shape of your eyes exactly."

He opened his eyes and smiled.

"Wow, you could talk a woman into bed like that," Elzy said, with feeling.

"Aren't you glad we've already been to bed, then? Otherwise, if *this* were our first time, you'd always wonder."

They did not return to bed that morning. Elzy got busy with chores, starting with laundry because of the dry weather, while Kevin hiked off to give the frame of the fishing kayak its coat of bees' wax. But there was a next time a few days later, and then another a few days after that. And then after that again.

Sex changed nothing and everything.

Elzy found Kevin gorgeous and eager and considerate, but she'd never bothered with men who weren't, and he was good only in the normal way. In fact, after the first several trysts, she realized Kevin made love the way he made boats—skillfully, attentively, and careful to do what worked *exactly the same way* every single time.

It took her a little longer to notice what he didn't do. He didn't pout when she said no. He didn't get weird and self-conscious the few times he couldn't bring her to climax. And he never asked her to "act all hot and horny" in order to turn him on. She'd always thought stroking a man's ego—and worrying over whether she could stroke it properly—was simply part of sex. She had never realized before Kevin that sex could be so *relaxed*. It was as though he'd opened a door inside her, just by being in her life.

Elzy didn't want that door to close. She didn't want to go back to how it used to be, not having anyone to come home to, not having anyone to look out for her and help her with things. But she didn't want Kevin falling for her, either, because she knew how that sort of thing always ended. She just had to get Kevin to stay for some other reason.

Kevin, for his part, spent the days after their first encounter walking about six feet off the ground. It wasn't just the sex but the fact that Elzy had said yes to him—anything was possible. He might jump straight from Mansell to Beech Mountain. He might even settle down, though that still seemed a stretch. He might....

After his initial euphoria faded a little, Kevin started to wonder just what Elzy had said yes *to*. More than just sex, surely? But it wasn't the sort of thing he was used to talking about.

"Have you ever been in love?" he asked, quite casually. They were sitting at the fire pit on a warm, mosquito-filled, late afternoon. He was sharpening the teeth of one of his power-tool attachments while Elzy plucked another extraneous rooster. She glanced over, and he regretted asking.

"I don't even know what that means," she said, then paused and frowned. "That didn't come out right. I've had the feelings. It's just—if you're *in* love, does that mean it's *right,* you're getting the fairy tale? Are emotions predictive? Or if it doesn't work out, do your feelings change retroactively?" She shook her head and stuffed a handful of feathers into a sack.

"Alright. Have you ever *loved,* then?" he asked.

"Timogen," she said, continuing plucking. The dog heard his name and opened his eyes a moment. "My parents, I guess. My brother." She wouldn't look at Kevin.

"No men?"

"My father was a man."

Alright, then.

But Elzy did seek his company. Not during the day, of course. He had to work and so did she. This being well into June, she had little time now for trail maintenance or the slow contemplation of flowers—half of Flamingo seemed to come for a swim or a hike every day. If Elzy didn't mingle with them, offering what she called "stealth education," there would be dogs swimming next to the intake pipes for the town water supply or some other problem. That she knew most of these people and issued the same gentle corrections to them every year irritated her no end, but she complained only to Kevin.

But later, when the crowds thinned, she'd come find him at his worksite and they'd go swimming with Tim off the big, sloping rock at a bend in the pond trail. Or she'd show him the purple-red rhodora flowers now just past their peak, or explain the geologic history that made the rock pink, or take him to see the bats emerging from their roosts in the tiny voids among the jumble of fallen stone at the base of the slopes that give the Perpendicular Trail its name. Her face shone as she showed him these things, and for a moment he could see her valley, her pond, her hills the same way she did.

And then, finally, the fishing kayak was done. He and Elzy tested it on the pond and took pictures, which he posted to both his website and the town's commerce page. Then he got the fourteen-foot boat up on his shoulders and carried it into town. Elzy went with him. She was headlining at the market that day and had gotten them a room together at the bed-and-breakfast in case the boat didn't sell the first day.

Walking along, Kevin could hardly see anything but the inside of the boat. Elzy guided him. He knew when they got into town by the noise, weirdly muffled as it was by the kayak. Sometimes he caught glimpses of people's feet, too many feet. The market crowd unnerved him. He felt as though he'd spent years, rather than weeks, living with only Elzy and her dog in the woods.

He spent all day hawking his product, buying lunch from a food cart when he got hungry. He got several good offers but didn't settle on any of them before the market closed for the day. He stowed his boat in a locker, picked up his order of shelf-stable insulin from the pharmacy, then found the stage where Elzy was to perform.

Her talk surprised him. He had known she was brilliant and knowledgeable, but he hadn't known she could be funny.

Afterwards, they met for dinner at the town's one real restaurant, then went for a walk. It was after eight by then, but the day, the longest of the year, wasn't over.

Together they wandered along the main road, away from the music of the market grounds, through the center of town and out the other side to where the road ran along the water. Elzy told him to stop and turn and there, in the distance, loomed the high domes of the mountains on the eastern side of the island catching on their bare granite the last light of day.

At ground level, everything seemed to be in flower. Though the rhodora was done for the year, Elzy pointed out the smaller, white flowers of the closely-related Labrador tea. Wild irises bloomed in the wet ditches, and the aptly-named rabbit-foot clover (the flowers did resemble furry little paws) made their scraggly living along the dry road shoulders. Invasive but still lovely lupines in blue and pink spread through any old field. A hedge of rugosa rose bushes crouched dense, thorny, but scattered with huge flowers, some red, some white, guarding the top of a high earthen embankment that sloped down fifty or more feet to the mud and stone beach of a cove off of Southwest Harbor. A family of ducks, the ducklings as big as their mother but not yet independent, paddled around the pilings of a long private dock wobbly with age. The tide was out. Kevin and Elzy literally stopped to smell the roses and then stood looking out over the water as the sunset turned the almost mirror-slick water pink, yellow, and purple. Dozens of small boats bobbed at their moorings. The air, quite suddenly, turned chilly.

"It's gorgeous," said Kevin.

"Yes," agreed Elzy.

"I could almost imagine staying here, on this island. There's plenty of work."

Elzy said nothing.

"I've never thought of myself as the type to settle down, though. Not in one place, I mean. I've always wanted to know what's around the next bend in the road. I've never wanted to miss out on the next thing."

Elzy said nothing.

"I guess what I'm saying is I might stay—if I had a reason. I need a reason." He turned towards her, intending to tell her how he felt, to ask her how *she* felt, *if* she felt, but then he chickened out. He looked away, out over the water. All of this had happened very fast—he hadn't even known Elzy for two whole months yet. He wasn't sure what he even wanted, he just wanted more time in which to figure it out—assuming there was anything to figure out. It suddenly occurred to him that maybe Elzy wasn't being reticent out of caution or because she didn't know how to talk about emotions—maybe she just thought of him as nothing more than a good fuck.

Self-conscious, worried he was acting a fool, unable now to ask his question, he began to babble.

"I can't just settle someplace without a reason because what if it was the wrong place? What if there's a better place? I don't want to just *settle*.... How could any place be important enough to stay in when it could just be gone tomorrow?"

Just tell her how you feel, urged some wiser part of his psyche, but he couldn't. Suddenly, none of his options seemed safe. Did he want a home because Elzy might be in it, or did he want Elzy because she embodied having a home? Either way he felt, with a blooming, bald clarity, that whatever he allowed himself to need might at any moment turn to ashes.

Why was he afraid? Why was he suddenly so sad?

Elzy said nothing. He turned towards her and cried out "what the hell is wrong with me?"

He could still smell the roses. Their scent and the scents of the low tide and of the marshy ditches and the wet meadow across the street mingled weirdly but not unpleasantly together.

"Never mind," he mumbled, turning away. "Don't tell me."

The next morning, after a very quiet breakfast, Kevin spent some minutes texting with a buyer who'd put in a bid overnight, then went off to deliver the kayak to its new owner, leaving Elzy alone with her thoughts.

At first she thought she wasn't reason enough for Kevin to stay. That hurt far more than she'd expected. But then she remembered that she didn't want him to stay *for her* and realized what he really meant—he would stay only if she asked. And she knew what would happen if she did.

Why couldn't he just like the island and stay? Plenty of people did. Something about the idea of staying put seemed to attract and repel him at once in a way she couldn't understand.

She checked out, then wandered disconsolately back to the market grounds where some vendors were already starting to pack up. The second day of a two-day market is never well-attended. She didn't need anything, but picked up a few other odds and ends anyway. She got a samosa at Sakshi's, then meandered over to a booth selling goat dairy products where she ate all the free samples.

"Those are for customers!" objected the proprietor, whom Elzy had known for 14 years.

"I *am* a customer," retorted Elzy.

"Oh yeah? Prove it."

"What do you have left for fudge?"

The proprietor, whose name was Anne, rummaged among her coolers. She was tall, thin, and knobby, and her pigtails had gone a sort of dirty dishwater shade years ago. She had a smile that looked very much like squinting in the sunlight, and she was either squinting or smiling now.

Elzy asked for both the butterscotch *and* the butterscotch/peanut-butter swirl.

"Feeling extra-gluttonous today?" Anne asked, wrapping up the order in wax paper.

"What? Oh, not really. I'm not by myself. See, there's this man…" Elzy admitted.

"Oh? Do tell."

"Well, see, I hired him to build me a boat a month or two ago…."

"Oh, yeah, the cute Asian boy, he was selling a kayak yesterday?"

"He's not—" Elzy almost said *he's not Asian, he's Canadian*, before realizing what Anne meant. "He's not a boy."

"Sorry. OK, man, then."

"And I…like him."

"Does he like you, too?"

"I guess so? Yeah, he does. I don't know. These things never seem to work out for me."

At that moment a half a dozen people all converged on the booth wanting tubs of soft, herb-infused cheese packed in oil and jars of flavored, honeyed goat yogurt. They chatted and joked and gossiped while waiting their turn, and since Elzy knew all of them she had to join in and act sociable, although she was not in the mood.

"Anne, why bother?" she asked, once the crowd dissipated.

"Why bother with what?"

"With…men, I guess. Dating." She started to lean on Anne's table-top, but stopped when she realized customers might not appreciate it. She felt tired and awkward and didn't know what to do with her hands.

"Well, there's sex," suggested Anne, starting to pack up her wares.

"Yeah, but there's something else, too, isn't there?" Elzy insisted. "I mean, friends-with-benefits isn't the same as having a partner, is it? There's something else. Romance, I guess. And I want that something, it just always turns out wrong for me."

"Nah, you don't mean romance."

"I don't?"

"No. Romance is…melodrama. It's fun, but it doesn't last. Not usually, anyway. Love, though, partnership—you used to serve on a vigilante team, didn't you? You know that feeling of always having each other's back? It's like that, except there's usually only two of you, and you get to have sex on the job." Anne would know, having been married to the same woman for 25 years.

"Sounds nice."

"Oh, it is."

"I don't think I can do that, though. I think something is wrong with me inside. Guys say I, I, don't love them, even when I think I do. Maybe I don't. Maybe I don't know how." She and Anne didn't normally talk about anything deeper than goat cheese, but she had to talk to somebody.

"It's not complicated," Anne explained. "You give a shit. That's all love is, you just give a shit about someone, even when it's not fun, even when you don't feel like it. It doesn't have to be self-*sacrificial,* it just can't be selfish. Care about the other person *for themselves,* even if there's nothing in it for you."

"I don't know, it sounds like an awful lot of work...." Elzy said lightly, as if she were joking.

"Price of admission, my friend. Would you want to be with someone who didn't give a shit, who saw you only as a means to an end?"

"No."

"Well, neither does anyone else."

It was a long, hot, awkward walk back to the pond. Kevin, though cheerful when they met up—he had paddled around in the harbor, his first time on salt water—gradually became less so as they walked along. And Elzy had a lot on her mind.

She thought several times of asking him to stay, at least long enough that they could figure out if this thing between them was worth keeping, and she would open her mouth but then close it again. She wanted him, but she wanted him for herself. Even just his walking along beside her, lithe and solid, nibbling with boyish seriousness at peanut-butter fudge, was a pleasure. And according to Anne, if she couldn't feel the right feelings for him, the selfless ones, she couldn't keep him. He wouldn't stay.

When they finally arrived back at the pond, they found Timogen there on the little beach, playing with a group of children on the sand. The children called to the dog and to each other in Spanish, in English, and in both at once, and he chased and ran and play-bowed and wrestled, absurdly gentle with their tiny, human bodies. Watching the happy tumult could cheer anyone up, at least a little.

The dog noticed his people and threw himself at Elzy's feet with his typical abject joy.

The mother of the children approached, smiling.

"*¿Tienes ganas cambiar pañales?*" she asked Elzy, which means, roughly, you want to change diapers? She glanced at Kevin. He gazed back at her, uncomprehending, handsome and charming, and young enough to be the woman's son. Or Elzy's son, actually.

Elzy rolled her eyes.

"Es una manera de mantenerme jovencita," she managed, after a moment. It's a manner of maintaining my youth. But Elzy didn't think that way, not really. She switched to English. "Kevin, this is my friend, Amarita Martinez. She and her husband manage the campground at Seawall. Amarita? Kevin."

"Um, mucho gusto?" he ventured. "I remember you—you were selling tortillas yesterday."

"Someone has to sell them," Amarita explained. "Anglos like 'em, but they can't make 'em worth a damn."

"Speaking of which," said Elzy, "I think Miguel gave me the wrong change today. I owe you two tenths."

"Agh, that boy can't subtract. Don't give it to me now, I don't have my wallet."

"I'll bring it next week."

The women chatted a little longer until Timogen barked, impatient to get going.

On the way back to the homestead, they stopped to check on the work site. Some animal had scattered a few of the tools. Elzy's kayak, a slim twelve-footer, existed now as an almost-complete skeleton, a row of ovals linked by transverse stringers and interrupted by the collars of the cockpit and the well. It needed only the seat and stirrup assembly and the well-basket before it would be ready for its skin.

"Almost done," said Elzy.

"Yep."

"So, I'm wondering if you could make me another boat."

There was a very long pause before Kevin asked what kind?

"A portable little sail-boat? Something I could put on a bike-trailer and take over to Southwest Harbor or Echo Lake. Or use on the pond here, of course."

"There are sail kits you can get for kayaks, you know."

"Yeah, I know, but my kayak's not designed for the ocean, and I'd like to try that, too."

"If you want to learn something new on this boat, better make it a two-seater."

"Alright."

They talked business for a few more minutes until Tim grew impatient again. Elzy turned back to the Great Pond Trail, which would curve around past of the hidden approach trails to the homestead. She wanted to go let the chickens out while Kevin stayed to put away his tools.

"Elzy," Kevin said, and she turned back to look at him. His eyes had gone dark and pleading.

"I know," she said.

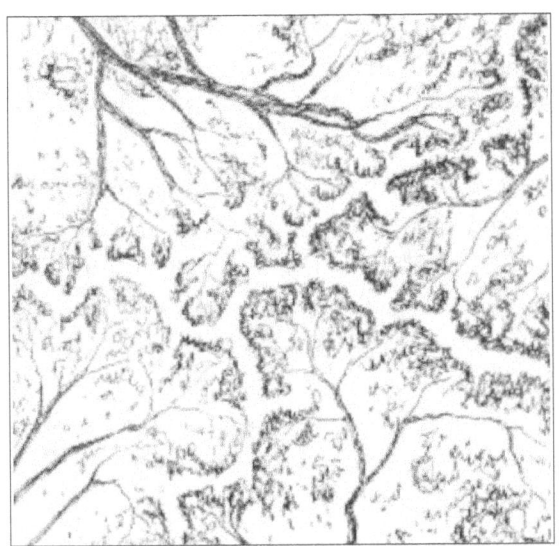

Chapter 5: Island Afire

M oving fast down a paved road, the trees between him and the water, the fire in the trees illuminating the night, fire shining on the water, he had to get off the island, the island on fire....

"I need a boat!"

"You've just built three of them," said an amused voice from somewhere, and Kevin found himself in his bunk in the dark, safe.

"Elzy?"

"I'm here." He heard her privacy curtain sweep open. He opened his. Not that he could see anything.

"Did I say something? Out loud?"

"Very."

"Shit. What time is it?" He saw the glow as she checked her phone.

"Just after three."

"Shit, shit, shit. I'm sorry."

"Never mind that, tell me the dream! You can't wake us up screaming and not tell me the dream!" She tapped a light-disc on, fetched him a mug full of water from a bucket, and sat on the foot of his bed. She was naked but so unselfconscious it almost wasn't sexy.

He drank and started feeling better. He told her about the dream, the dream about the island afire and how he couldn't find a boat to get away.

"That's really weird," said Elzy, thoughtfully.

"Yeah, some dream, right?"

"No, it's weird because it really happened. And it happened here."

"What?"

"In 1947, there was a very bad drought. There were a lot of forest fires all across Maine. One almost burned up Bar Harbor—both the roads out of town were cut off, and so everybody evacuated down to the dock, but there were thousands of people, there weren't enough boats for them all. The town was saved only at the last minute."

"Wow, you're serious?"

"Sure am. There are still signs of the Bar Harbor Fire across half the island, if you know how to look, just like our half has evidence of the June Fires from when I was a little kid."

"Wow. That is a seriously weird coincidence. You don't think I build boats because of that dream, do you?"

"No, I don't think the human psyche is that simplistic. I also don't think it's a coincidence."

"How could it not be?"

"Your great-grandmother had a lobster-charm from Bar Harbor, didn't she?"

Kevin stared.

"No, that's not possible," he insisted. "There has to be some other explanation. Maybe I'm reincarnated from one of the fire victims?"

Elzy didn't laugh, just reminded him that nobody died waiting for a boat on the dock.

"Hardly anybody died in that fire at all. One man went back into his house, looking for his cat, a girl died in a car-accident.... Why *can't* your great-grandmother have been in the fire?"

"She lived in Kingston her whole life, married some government official, inherited a boat-load of money.... I mean, we have stories about her. If she'd lived through this monster fire, why don't we have stories about it?"

"I don't know, I had a whole *brother* my parents didn't tell me about. He died in the pandemic. I blocked that memory for years, and they just let me forget about him. I'm telling you, people are weird. They just don't talk about some stuff."

"OK, but, so, like, how did I end up dreaming about it?"

"I don't know."

"I don't know, either."

"What I *do* know?" said Elzy, "is radio call is gonna come *awful* early if I don't go back to bed. You gonna be OK?"

"Yeah, I think I can get back to sleep without a cookie and a glass of milk."

"Closest we've got to that is a tortilla and a piece of cheese, anyway."

Kevin woke up the next morning and went for a long paddle. He had nothing else to do while the kayak frame cured. The supplies for the sailboat hadn't come in yet. He might have hung out with Elzy while she worked, but things had been awkward between them since that day in town. He came home for lunch alone and borrowed one of her books, *Backcountry Ethics,* by Guy and Laura Waterman, one of the few in her small collection that didn't look like you needed a college education to read. Reading in the hammock under a tent of mosquito netting, Kevin realized he hadn't heard frogsong in a while, even at night. The afternoon was warm and bright. Summer had begun.

And somehow, when Elzy and Tim returned from work hours later, the awkwardness was gone. Elzy acted as though nothing had ever been wrong between them. He didn't understand, but he went with it.

"How much do you weigh?" she asked, handing Kevin a jar of pale green liquid.

"I dunno. About ninety kilos?" He frowned, trying to remember the conversion. "Two hundred pounds?"

"Good enough," she replied and climbed into the hammock facing him, their legs tangled together. She raised her own jar of greenish liquid to him in a toast.

"What is this, wood sorrel?" he asked. His jar smelled earthy and sour. He knew the plant as a garden weed.

"Waste not, want not," she replied.

Kevin read. Birds sang. Elzy stared at something. Eventually, Kevin noticed, closed his book, forefinger marking his place, and followed her gaze to where dozens of yellow-jackets flew around a spruce branch for no clear reason, but Kevin had no eye for "bugs" and didn't notice them. Instead, he looked at the trees themselves.

"That's weird," he said.

"What?"

"Those trees, their branches almost touch but don't, like they're avoiding each other."

"Maybe they are," Elzy said. "Usually you see it in old-growth forests, trees holding back from shading each other."

"Why? I thought trees competed for sunlight?"

"Oh, they do, but they work together, too, especially in the older forests."

"Work together?"

"Yeah. They avoid shading each other, use various chemicals to send messages through the air, warnings about insect infestations and so forth, share food and water through their roots...."

"Right. Myco-ryco-whatsits."

"Mycorhizal association and root-grafting, yes."

"You make it sound like they're doing it on purpose," Kevin observed.

"They are. Plants aren't self-expanding green rocks. They sense and respond to their environment just as animals do."

"Yeah? I never thought of it that way before."

"I don't have to *think* of it," Elzy told him. "I've seen it. It was back when I lived with my mom—I saw a bittersweet vine growing straight, no twists or turns, unsupported, for about four feet. They do that when they're trying to find something to climb on. But it wasn't growing just *up*. It was at something like a sixty-degree angle. It looked weird. And following that angle another three feet from the vine tip, there was the end of a low-hanging maple branch. That vine was *pointing* right at the branch tip, just *reaching* for it. There is no way that bittersweet didn't *know* the branch was there."

"Wow."

"Yeah, it was creepy as hell."

"You're saying the vine could *see* the branch?"

"Or sense it somehow. Anyway, plants probably don't have very *good* vision, but of course they're sensitive to light. They're plants."

"Oh. Right. Duh."

"So, yeah, they're aware. They're deliberate. When they help each other, that's gotta be deliberate, too."

"What you're telling me is that trees have, like, friends?"

Elzy grunted, amused.

"I'm not sure I'd go that far. You can't....You can't be friends without caring for each other." Just then, the chickens erupted in indignant clucking. Elzy sat up to holler at the dog, who tore himself away from the game and slunk over, lowering his body submissively as he approached Elzy. She let him in through the mosquito netting and let him sniff her hands. She patted him gently and spoke to him kindly until he understood he'd been forgiven. He lay down in the duff, and she gave him a twist of jerky from her pocket.

"I don't know," said Kevin, once she was settled in the hammock again. "It sounds like they care. It sounds like love."

"Trees can't feel love, they don't have brains."

"So? They don't have dicks, either, but I spent, like, a month sneezing pollen. Maybe they have some tree-way to feel things? Anyway, love isn't an emotion."

"It's not?"

"Well, it's not *just* an emotion," he amended. "It's not *mostly* an emotion. I mean, there was this girl, she was really into me emotionally, but the way she treated me was really messed up. I want a woman who *acts* like she loves me."

"Don't you want her to feel for you, too, though? Don't you want to be important to someone?" As if the topic were purely abstract for either of them.

"Well, yeah, if I can have both! But if I had to choose, I'd rather be with a woman who *does* love and feels *squat,* than someone who *feels* love and *does* squat."

After a moment, Kevin went back to reading. Elzy watched him.

"So, about your dream of the Fire of '47?" Elzy asked.

"Huh?"

"Your dream last night. Where did it come from?"

"What do you mean, where did it come from??"

"What inspired it? Originally, I mean. You said you'd had it before."

"Oh. Yeah, my mother had a dream about fire when I was a little kid. She told me about it, and I was so scared I started having my own."

"OK, where did your mother get it?"

"From a stall at the market, I don't know, it was just a dream!"

"No, seriously, where did she get it?"

"I don't know."

"So, let's call and ask."

Kevin dismissed the idea, but Elzy persisted, and soon he was hiking up to the summit of Bernard with her for good cell reception. He'd never been up there before and found it quiet, densely forested, with just a sliver of a view out to Seal Cove. Kevin called, thumbed on speaker-mode, and just before the call connected realized he was introducing Elzy to his mother. If Elzy noticed that aspect of things, she didn't say anything about it, only asked his mother's name.

"Tricia."

"Kevin?" said his mother, sounding confused.

But when Elzy asked, she said her fire dream had been inspired by her grandmother. Kevin almost fell over in shock.

"I'm the one who took care of Grandma," Tricia explained, "before we had to put her in the home. She'd tell me stories, not like she meant to, more like she just said whatever. Mostly about the fire, over and over."

"So it wasn't a dream for her, then, it was memory?" Elzy asked.

"Well, I don't think there was much difference at that point, but yes, there really was a fire. I don't know anything about it, besides what she told me, and she wasn't super-coherent. She said the tree burned or exploded—I don't know what tree, it was always just *the* tree—that the gardens were gone, the water was cold, the firelight was bright through the blanket.... She kept asking if Chubby had gotten on a boat. She was very worried about that, there weren't enough boats for 'all those people,' and Chubby might not get on a boat because he wanted to be a hero. I don't know who Chubby was. She talked a lot about a Mrs. McCarthy, too. And something about hoping Chubby didn't think the girl in the car accident was her. That's about it, I think. She talked a lot about the gardens, the gardens and the tree. They bothered her."

"Not looking for a boat while driving through trees?" Kevin interjected.

"No. That was the way you dreamed it, right?"

"Yeah. There's firelight on water through trees. And no boats."

"My dream was never exactly like grandmother's story, either."

"Where was this fire," Elzy asked. "*When* was it?"

"Oh, I don't know. She said it was on the island, before Chuck. Before Chuck what? My grandfather's name was Charles, so maybe he's Chuck.... But I don't know what any of this means. She never talked about her past, before she got sick. And I didn't think to ask. I was just a kid. And then there was no one left *to* ask."

"By sick, you mean she had dementia?" Elzy asked.

"Alzheimer's, yes."

"Losing her like that must have been hard on you." Elzy could at least mimic sympathy.

"Pf. She was a racist, crazy-ass *bitch*. Spending time with her felt like being hit upside the head with a rolling-pin. But there was no one else. My parents both worked. Ma said she'd heard that Gramma wasn't always like that. I mean, I assume she always was racist, but she wasn't born a bitch. The fire did something to her, I guess."

Elzy grinned, vindicated.

Later, over dinner, she told Kevin her idea.

"It's your mother who doesn't think having a home is important, right? Maybe she got that attitude from her grandmother, along with the dream? Something happened in the fire, like she lost something. Maybe, if we find out what, *you* can get it back. And then it would be easier for you to settle down somewhere. If you want to."

Kevin stared at her. Obviously this research project was Elzy's latest ploy to get him to stay. But why? The sex couldn't be *that* good. She must like him after all—but then, why didn't she just say so? And yet, if she thought tracking down his family's mental problems would help her be with him, then fine. And maybe she was right. He *wanted* to want to belong to someplace. He wanted to be like her.

The materials for the new boat came in, and he got to work cutting, sanding, and bending cedar strips. He'd decided to adapt an outrigger design he'd learned on Lake Michigan. The main hull would be shorter than the fishing kayak and very narrow, so with the side-floats and the mast removable, it would fit on a bike trailer. In the evenings, he and Elzy would talk, trying to work out a research strategy. He called his mother again. He called his cousins, since they had the same great-grandmother and might know something. Elzy asked him to make a dock where she could lock up her growing flotilla, so they drew up *another* shopping list and called it in. On the Fourth of July, he and she lay together in the hammock reading aloud from the Declaration of Independence and the New American Constitution while fire crackers popped above the market grounds of all the towns on the island. The next day, Monday, they both walked into town, Elzy to work the market, and Kevin to go to the library to learn about his great-grandmother, Rose Marks.

One of Kevin's cousins had emailed him a copy of an old genealogy report, and so he spent the morning reaching out to relatives he hadn't known he had, looking for information, feeling optimistic. Then he checked phone books and census records for Bar Harbor for the relevant time period, all digitized and searchable online. A hit would at least prove Rose was in the area during the fire. But there were no hits, and Kevin's new-found relatives either knew nothing or their emails bounced. Some searching revealed they had died. So did his optimism.

They stayed in town overnight and Tuesday afternoon had a strategy meeting with the librarian, but all her suggestions required information about Rose they simply didn't have. The market was over, and they were out of ideas.

It was a long, hot walk home. Elzy seemed even more dejected than him.

"At least you got to see your friends again," Kevin offered. "I used to think you were some kind of hermit, but you talk to everybody, every chance you get."

"Caretaking is mostly talking," Elzy acknowledged. "It would be a bad job for a hermit. Are they my friends, though? I was thinking, the other week, when Amarita made that crack about me changing your diaper or whatever?" What crack? Kevin realized that must have been the Spanish bit, and that Elzy had forgotten that it was in Spanish. She continued. "I was thinking, another few comments like that and I'm done with her. Over-reacting, but at the time I meant it. Kevin, I've known her almost fifteen years. I trained her and her husband as caretakers. That's what they do now, because of me. They would've made me Miguel's Godmother, except I'm an atheist. And I don't care about her if she's not fun to be around. Is that normal? Maybe I *don't* have any friends. Not around here, anyway."

She glanced at Kevin. He didn't know how to respond. He asked if she were lonely.

"I can't tell," she said. "Is that a bad sign?"

Chapter 6: Another Arrival

Tim met them on the trail and joyously led them up to the homestead. The dog was covered in mud, tree sap, and ticks, so while Elzy attended to the chickens and put away the groceries, Kevin got a bucket of water, an empty jar for pouring, a flea comb, and a pair of tweezers. He sat by the fire-pit cleaning up Tim's wiry coat. He'd gotten to like Elzy's giant dog.

Elzy came back out of the house with a jar of pickles. She drank the juice but left the pickles behind. The first real heat of the summer was on, and her clothes were damp with sweat. Kevin had a headache himself and didn't feel good.

What Elzy said about not having friends had shocked him, but should not have. She'd said almost as much weeks ago, when she'd told him about not being able to keep boyfriends. He kept forgetting, and she kept reminding him who and what she was. Why did she keep reminding him? He thought that today, especially, she'd done it on purpose. She'd warned him off. Why? If she really only liked people as entertainment, as she'd strongly implied, wouldn't the smart thing be to lie about it?

So she had to care about him at least a little, enough to warn him about herself. There had to be some exception to her limitation, right? Someone she cared about for real? Maybe he was it. A cicada, the first of the year, began to sing.

Then Tim alerted.

At first the dog only raised his head and stared, ears cocked, towards the access path, the one that came in behind and to the right of the little house. After a few seconds, Tim barked. A few seconds more and he jumped to his feet and erupted in a series of rolling barks, the canine intruder alarm, which Kevin had not heard since his own arrival. Elzy reflexively checked her gun. She always wore it, concealed if necessary.

"Elzy?" called a distant and uncertain male voice.

"ANDY!" she cried, her face utterly changing, and ran off down the trail. Timogen leaped to follow, but Kevin grabbed his collar. The animal pulled him halfway into the fire-pit before acquiescing. Man and dog sat up together and looked towards the path as Elzy returned. She had a man with her.

He was shortish and oldish—droopy, spotted skin, white hair—but he moved easily and wore a respectably-large backpack. Around him Elzy gamboled and chattered, greeting this man exactly the same way Timogen normally greeted her. The visitor seemed slightly flustered by the attention, or maybe he was distracted by Tim's barking. He spotted the dog from fifty feet away and stopped moving, staring at the animal.

"Let him go," Elzy called to Kevin. "He's barking more because you're restraining him."

Tim ran forward. Elzy hugged the new arrival, and the dog stood down, giving a cursory sniff before leading the way back to the fire pit, tail waving.

Kevin stood up as they approached. He could feel the newcomer studying him, assessing him. Whoever this man was, he had expected to find Elzy alone.

"Kevin, this is Andy Cote...my friend," explained Elzy. "And this is Kevin Williams, my...friend."

The pauses weren't lost on either man, nor was the fact that they weren't the same pause. They shook hands, and Elzy urged them both to sit, then rattled off a long list of available beverages. Andy clearly needed a drink, the heat was getting to him—his European-type skin made his flushing obvious—but still Elzy's hospitality seemed a little manic.

"And don't worry about the dog," she added. "He likes cats."

Andy gave her an odd look for that last comment, but when he took off his pack and sat down, Tim didn't bound over in the normal canine way. Instead, the dog approached gently and—carefully and with great delicacy—sniffed the man's nose and mouth. It was exactly the same greeting that cats give each other, and that some dogs learn to offer cats they respect. And, incredibly, Andy returned the gesture. Kevin could see the quick movements of his breathing as he sniffed the dog's breath and offered his own. Ritual complete, he very cautiously rested his hand in Timogen's ruff and regarded the animal gravely.

"I'll have some of your cider, thank you," he said. His voice was dry, somewhat nasal, and curiously softened around the edges, like the feathers of an owl.

Elzy rushed off without waiting for Kevin's drink order, leaving the two men to regard each other across the empty fire pit.

"You're him, aren't you?" Kevin said, without preamble.

"Excuse me?"

"The one who found this place for her."

"She found it. I taught her how to look."

"You taught her well. She loves this place."

"Yes, she does."

"I'm the boat-maker," Kevin explained. "And, um…. Well, she keeps asking me to build her more boats, so I won't leave. And so now here I am." He rubbed the back of his neck, embarrassed. He might as well have said *we're banging*. It was obvious. And, really, what else was there to say? He and Elzy had never figured out how to talk about their relationship. Andy regarded him with a hint of humor.

"You must be very good at making boats," he commented.

"I do try," acknowledged Kevin, modestly.

Elzy returned, bearing a large, wooden tray piled with an extraordinary variety of foodstuffs—pickled eggs, a jar of apple butter, two different kinds of cheese, crackers, honey, the now juice-less pickles, venison sausage, dried fish jerky and a pot of sour cream dip—and three bottles of hard cider. She set all of it up in bowls and on cutting boards laid across the fire-pit, handed out the cider, and finally sat down. Andy carefully selected an egg, a couple of crackers, and a slice of each kind of cheese. While he was preoccupied and not looking at her, Elzy stared as though he were a miraculous creature who might evaporate if she didn't keep an eye on him.

"Nice pin," he said at length, a little archly. Elzy looked down at herself and touched her guild-pin, the only item of jewelry she had on.

"Did you not know I got senior status?"

"Colin told me," he explained, around a mouthful of egg. His generation was always pre-occupied by food. They had lived through not having enough of it.

"But I didn't tell Colin," Elzy objected.

"Or me. But you told Aaron, and he told Colin."

"We always wondered if you professors gossiped about us."

"I wouldn't say gossip, more like sharing news. There are people who would like more news from you."

"I'm sorry. I thought you considered academic rank pretentious."

"I consider the *symbols* of rank to be a bit much, yes, but they go with the territory, now. Your advancement in your career—you're allowed to celebrate that."

"You don't give me any of your news."

He seemed somewhat taken aback, as though he hadn't realized he'd been unforthcoming.

"There isn't much," he countered, "and you don't ask."

"You don't ask, either."

"I don't want to pry."

Elzy huffed her breath, the way Timogen did when he was frustrated, but said nothing. Kevin made a little sandwich with two crackers, a slice of sausage, and some cheese, and he watched the conversation go on without him.

"I don't have any other news," Elzy said. "I got a dog, but you've met him. What about you?"

"Were you still in touch with Saul?" he asked, though that didn't seem to answer her question.

"Not recently, no. Why?"

"He died."

"Really? How? When?"

"He had cancer. It was just a few months ago."

"I'm sorry to hear that. You were friends."

"Yeah, we went back a long ways."

Elzy let the silence lay there for a few seconds. Timogen licked his paws. He seemed to be getting a touch of arthritis. The resident red squirrel loudly ran off an intruding squirrel.

"How long can you stay?" she asked, finally.

"I don't know how long I am welcome," Andy replied, "I don't want to impose."

Elzy stared at him as though he'd said something bizarre.

"You're welcome to stay...much longer than you ever will. Didn't you know?"

Andy looked away a moment and grimaced slightly.

"I appreciate that. I'll stay for a week, then. Maybe two. I do have other things to do."

"Great, I'll make up the guest-bed."

Kevin noticed, but decided not to overtly react, as his bed was given away without his input. Andy glanced at him occasionally, but Elzy never did.

Andy finished his cider, several more eggs, a handful of crackers, and a pickle. He went to use the privy, then doused his head in cold water from the cistern spigot. Returning to the fire-pit, he offered to go fetch more water. Kevin tried to tell him they didn't need any, which wasn't true—summer had turned the weather dry—but Elzy showed the man the buckets and their yoke, and he set off down the path to the stream.

"You shouldn't let an old man carry water for you," Kevin protested. "Not after he hiked all the way up here."

"Must be nice."

"What?"

"To be so confident in your usefulness."

"Huh?"

"You can't imagine how it would sound to him—telling him his help isn't wanted?"

Kevin chewed on that.

"You left one off," he said, after a while.

"Left one of what off of what?" Elzy asked.

"Your list of people you love."

Elzy went very still.

"It's not anything romantic," she said at last.

"And your love for your dog is?" he demanded. Elzy grimaced, but she said nothing. "Look, for the record, I believe you, OK? It's Platonic. But so what if it wasn't? So *fucking* what? I'm not the first hot guy you've ever met. You're not with me by *default*. You *chose* me. Someday you might choose somebody different. That's up to you. Just don't blow smoke up my ass."

"What happens if I do blow smoke up your ass?" asked Elzy.

"I'll get a smokey ass," Kevin told her. She leaned against him, laughing helplessly.

Together, they moved Kevin's stuff into Elzy's bunk and re-made his former bed with fresh sheets. When Andy came back with the water, Elzy showed him how to use the cistern pulley. Then she showed him his bed and offered him a tour of the compound. Of course, Andy had been here before, he had helped Elzy discover the site, but from the way he remarked on the "new" house, he must not have been back since. Why not? Who was this man who made Elzy tumble all over herself like a love-struck puppy, who felt free to walk right into her home without calling first, and yet hadn't bothered to visit in, what, fifteen years?

Whoever he was, Kevin remained a third wheel in the man's presence. After a while, he stopped trying to tag along. He collected the latest batch of eggs, refilled the chickens' little water trough, and unpacked his bag from the trip to town. Elzy had left all the food from their late lunch on its tray on her bed with only upside-down bowls to keep the flies and the mice away. He noticed that the sour cream dip had hardly been touched, though now that it was unsealed, it wouldn't keep till morning.

He brought the dip and the bag of fish jerky and some other supplies out with him and built up a small fire, then set the fish in a pot with a little water to re-hydrate. While he waited, he fetched what he needed from the garden, where he noticed Elzy and Andy meticulously checking the potato plants for beetles and talking about something or other while Tim snoozed in a freshly-dug dog hole nearby. None of the three noticed Kevin, who returned to the fire pit, where he mashed up the fish, then mixed in two raw eggs and a little salt, powdered mustard seed, and ground sumac. Then he set aside a quarter of the mixture and minced some green onion to add to the rest. Then he set a cast-iron fry-pan over the fire to warm. He had to keep feeding the fire and blowing on it to keep it hot, as he had no intention of waiting hours for a true coal-bed to set up.

When the pan was hot enough to sizzle oil, he fried up patties of the fish mixture, doing Tim's first to keep it away from the onion. Then he warmed up some of the tortillas they'd bought yesterday. He took the pan off the fire, put the tortillas and patties back in it to stay warm under a lid, and put a pot of water on to heat. While he waited for the others to notice and come over, he shredded bowls full of cheese and lettuce. Timogen arrived first, following his nose.

"Tim, down!" Kevin ordered amicably. "Stay, please."

The dog obeyed him with only slight hesitation (he obeyed Elzy instantly), and Kevin set out the sour cream, the lettuce, the cheese, Elzy's home-made hot-pepper sauce, a little bowl of minced sun-dried tomatoes, various serving implements, four plates each already garnished with nasturtium leaves and flowers, three bottles of cider, three clean handkerchiefs to serve as napkins, and the little bottle of rubbing alcohol from Elzy's med-kit so everyone could disinfect their hands before dinner.

"And what do you call this?" Elzy asked, suddenly standing above him.

"Um, fish tacos?" he ventured.

Kevin did not mind being temporarily sidelined. Andy would not be here long, and Elzy obviously trusted that Kevin would be. What bothered Kevin was knowing that he'd been right—there was an exception to Elzy's pattern of uncaring—but Kevin wasn't it.

That night, in the house, she and Kevin found themselves alone together while Andy was off brushing his teeth.

"Elzy, what are we?" he asked.

"Humans. *Homo sapiens sapiens,*" Elzy replied with a straight face, folding an extra blanket. "Recognizable by our high foreheads, mostly bare skins, and an inability to stop chatting with old friends while someone else makes dinner and entertains the dog."

"No, you and me. I didn't know how to talk about us to Andy today. Neither did you."

She laid the blanket down at the foot of the now-shared bed.

"We're fucking," she said. "But yeah, that doesn't really work for introductions...."

"I think he figured that part out, anyway."

"I think you're right. What's wrong with 'friends'?"

"Nothing. Except it sounds like a euphemism when you say it about me."

"It does?" Elzy took advantage of their temporary solitude to strip off her tunic and bra and put on her night-shirt.

"Yeah. I'd like to be your friend, for real, or your partner, or *something....*"

Elzy was massaging her newly-freed breasts through her night shirt. She always did that at night, both to re-establish proper lymph drainage and to check for lumps. Belatedly, she realized the conversation deserved a greater decorum and stopped.

"You are. You are my friend or my partner or something."

"Elzy...."

"If we're not careful," she said, trying to sound light-hearted, "my life is going to end up sounding like one of those novels." She struck a dramatic pose and declaimed in suitably purple tones; "Elzy, the spirited and beautiful caretaker of a lonely mountain preserve, has everything she's ever wanted—until a handsome artist arrives to hint at life's other possibilities. Will he enter and warm her cold ivory tower?"

"Sounds like someone is familiar with the genre," Kevin remarked.

"Takes one to know one," she replied.

"Would it be so bad if I did?"

"Did what, read romance novels?"

"No, warmed that ivory tower of yours." His eyes had gone dark and insistent, and while he still wore half a grin, he wasn't joking.

"What do you want from me?" Elzy said, not laughing anymore. But Andy returned and of course Kevin could no longer answer her.

Elzy had shared sleeping quarters with Andy many times before, mostly in communal dorms in hostels, but some subtle formality remained. To get in bed with Kevin in front of him felt very weird. She lifted the corner of her privacy curtain and saw Andy standing there beside his bunk in boarding-house shorts and a t-shirt, knobby-kneed and older-looking, fiddling with his tablet computer, like an ordinary person.

She let the curtain fall and turned toward her mate. They could not even talk without being overheard. In silence, Kevin traced the side of her face and the line of her jaw with one finger. In the dim light filtering through the curtain, she could barely see his features. He and the sheets and the sloping wall behind him all took on a duotone quality, a study in shades of honey and black. And then the light went out as Andy went to bed. Kevin, knowing how Elzy felt about cuddling, rolled over and away. Soon his breathing became slow and regular.

Elzy had trouble dozing off. Tim, finding the bed too crowded, slipped out through the privacy curtain. She heard his nails click on the wooden floor, then a surprised human murmur from the other bunk. Soon she could hear Andy sleeping, too. He wasn't snoring, exactly, but some of his breaths were faintly audible. She smiled.

Elzy hadn't had a bedroom of her own until she was ten years old. Later, in college dorms, shared campsites, trail shelters, and countless hostels, she'd always been near other sleepers. To hear others asleep as she slept was a comfort, a return to the best parts of her strange and abortive childhood. But to hear these two men breathe, out of all the possible people in the world…?

Next morning, Elzy was busy re-building the outdoor cook-fire when Kevin joined her, eyes still bleary. Timogen thumped his tail in greeting.

"Any chicory yet?" he asked, petting the dog.

"Early bird gets the caffeine," she replied, without looking up. "I saved you a cup, but it's probably cold by now."

"Fair enough. What's for breakfast?"

"Cheese omelets with fresh puffballs and the last of last year's dried bell peppers."

Kevin took a sip of chicory and black tea, made a face, and took the pot to get more water from the cistern.

"Where's your friend?" he asked when he got back.

"He's not in bed?" Elzy asked. Actually, she knew he wasn't. She'd spotted Andy, when she first came out, paying his respects at a small graveyard behind the house, but she didn't want his privacy interrupted.

"The curtain's drawn, but I don't think anybody sleeps that quiet," Kevin explained.

She chanced a look around. Andy was now on the far side of the clearing, looking up at something in the trees. He seemed to hear them talking and moseyed over.

Timogen stood to greet him as he approached, but the man held back, looking uncertain and awkward.

"He won't hurt you," Kevin put in, evidently unaware of where Tim had spent the night.

"I'm not afraid of being hurt," Andy corrected him. "I'm…I don't want him to lick me."

"It's a scent-thing, isn't it?" Elzy guessed. Andy had always had a thing about scents. She could never predict which ones would bother him. Feces elicited only mild distaste, while a certain fragrance popular in laundry soap would prompt him to hold his breath until he could get away. Dog breath might well be on the list of problem odors. But Andy would neither confirm nor deny, only shot her a warning glance to the effect that she ought to mind her own business.

This was how it was to be with Andy, this maintenance of an arm's distance away from everybody else, this constant refusal of sympathy, of familiarity, a kind of repeated alienation. She had almost forgotten. She should not have. He rarely emailed her, did not call or write. The man was impossible to make social plans with; one had to bump into him, and though she visited campus almost every year with him in mind, in fifteen years of trying she'd succeeded in bumping into him just twice. A third encounter, at a professional conference in Ohio, really had been an accident.

And yet when she emailed him he always responded, his sentences courtly, considerate, often humorous, more reliable than most of her ostensibly closer friends. *Write again,* he would remind her. *Keep in touch,* or, often, *it's good to hear from you,* and *thank you for thinking of me.* No one else ever thanked her just for her friendship. If he didn't want her closer than arm's distance, he didn't want her any farther away, either.

Once, he and his eccentricities had been part of the daily rhythm of her life, but this visit was already the most time they'd spent together in years.

She broke eggs into a bowl and whisked, watching him without seeming to.

He'd always described himself as old, but he never had been, merely middle-aged. Now, though, some line had been crossed. His hair had gone all white. His face and body had thinned and softened just slightly, and he walked now with a subtle stiffness. Had all this happened in the few years since their last dinner together, or was she only just now noticing slower changes? As he chatted with Kevin across the fire-pit, she could hear a slight coarsening of his voice. She dropped a pat of butter in the pan, tilted the pan to spread the melting fat, and poured in a thin layer of egg. She added slices of cheese and a layer of sliced puffballs and rehydrated peppers and noticed her own sadness.

He spoke and moved and existed, and the forest seemed more real now that he was in it.

The men did not talk much over their food, though Andy complimented her on her cooking and briefly inquired about the species of mushroom, and Kevin exclaimed "hot dog!" when the water came to a boil and he could make more chicory. Elzy had nothing to say either. A hermit thrush sang. When Kevin wasn't looking, Andy watched him thoughtfully.

Elzy's phone beeped.

"Eight AM radio call, gentlemen," she excused herself and went inside.

By the time she came back out, she'd changed into her uniform and had filled her day-pack. "Kevin, your stuff is coming in today," she announced.

"Good. When, abouts?"

"They said sometime between ten and noon."

"Wow, that's almost entirely unhelpful," Kevin grumped. "I can't sit around by myself for two hours doing nothing. My brain will get up and walk away."

"Well, we can't have that," Elzy agreed. "Brains are to be accompanied at all times by bodies. Says so in the manual somewhere."

Andy, who had been watching the conversation go back and forth like a tennis match, smirk-snorted into his chicory.

"I know, I know, you have to work," Kevin said. "I wasn't going to ask."

"I wasn't going to answer." Elzy tried not to smile and failed. "You want me to lend you Timogen?"

The dog, hearing his name, looked at her.

"Sure, if you think he'll come with me."

"Tim, you want to spend the day with Kevin?"

The dog thumped his tail twice agreeably, not that he had any idea what he was agreeing to.

"Go with you where?" asked Andy. "What's happening?"

"I have time on my hands while the oil on the frame of the fourth boat dries," Kevin explained, "so Elzy asked me to build a dock. I've ordered lumber and whatever else. I'll cut everything to size today at the boat-building site and move it over tomorrow."

Andy nodded thoughtfully and finished his chicory.

"I have to go to the Beech Mountain fire tower today," Elzy told Andy. "Mostly to talk to tourists there. You want to come with me?"

"Sure."

Elzy, not wanting to ignore her partner for a second day in a row, waited until Andy went inside to get ready, then kissed Kevin well and thoroughly. Then she packed lunch for four.

"Which way did you come up yesterday?" Elzy asked Andy as they left the clearing together.

"Gilly Trail to Great Notch Trail."

"Then we'll go down Razorback, get you some variety."

"Alright."

Once, Andy had made all their plans—and hadn't always waited for her assent. Though capable of deference, never before had he deferred to her. But he'd never been the guest of the noted naturalist, Dr. Elzy Rodriguez before, either. She had very mixed feelings about the shift.

As soon as they set out, she started second-guessing herself. Razorback? It's the second-hardest way to get to the valley. There's a cliff-like slope up just to get to it. Andy had to be at least seventy by now. But he would not thank her for doubting him, so she said nothing. He climbed slowly but well, and soon they were up on a gentler slope in an airy spruce grove—no understory, except for a few spruce saplings, because of the dense shade, but everywhere thick, green moss. Patches of whitish reindeer lichen an inch or two tall showed where rock lay just under the surface. Then the trees opened up a bit, letting in a little more light, and Elzy and Andy passed through great patches of waist-high huckleberry bushes, then clamored up out of the forest over huge fins of lichen-gray stone exposed to the sky. There, the trail divided. The Perpendicular Trail went left up over Mansell and then down to Kevin's boat-building site. They went right on Razorback, following the crest of those granite fins sloping away to the south. Andy stood a moment, balancing easily on the narrow rock, looking out over the small trees below and around him. The pond wasn't visible, Mansell being in the way, but he could look down the valley between the great mountain ridges and out to the southern tip of the island and on to the great blue sea. He said nothing, and she watched him look and said nothing either.

Eventually, the fins flattened to slabs mostly green with map lichen, but streaked black with moss where rivulets of rainwater had run. The trail plunged back into forest, descending steeply over well-made stone steps, along small streams, then finally down to the flatlands just to the south of the pond.

Elzy usually talked natural history while walking with others, a perpetual expert guide, but she'd learned natural history from Andy in the first place, so now she stayed silent. Andy didn't talk either. Maybe he didn't know she still wanted to learn from him. Maybe he was just tired of being on the job around her.

At the pond, she detoured up to the campsite and found two families there. Andy waited as she schmoozed professionally, collecting visitor-use data. Then he followed her up the next trail.

The day was getting hot by then, so Elzy went up Beech Mountain on the shady, eastern side. The footing was easy, the trail actually graveled like a sidewalk in places, and it gained elevation only by means of beautiful-ly-made stone steps just one or two together at a time. The well-watered forest, spruce, cedar, and pine mixed, stood dense, moss-covered, and rel-atively cool.

At the next junction, they went left. The trail grew steeper, but still gentle, cool, pleasantly damp. They came out on the summit quite sud-denly, a long, narrow, irregular oval of bare, blond rock in shelves and cuts and slow, smooth curves, perhaps a half-acre. Trees rose around it like the rim of a bowl. The summit was not above tree-line, but it had been cleared, probably to build the fire tower, and then the thin, unprotected soils had quickly worn away down to bedrock, bedrock that could not now gather new moss because of all the foot traffic. Mountain cranberry and three-toothed cinquefoil crouched in protected crevices, but on the open flats not even lichen grew. The tower, a squared-off, open lattice supporting what looked like a small hut at the top, cast black shadow on its concrete pad.

A young family wandered around the bare rock. Two men stood on the landing halfway up the tower. Elzy didn't know them, they were summer people, but they all recognized her uniform.

"Hey, the top of the tower's locked!" called one of the men.

"I know, I locked it!" she called back.

"Can you unlock it?"

"Not only can I, I even will!" She trotted up the stairs, the heavy metal mesh of the treads and the landing clattering under her feet. The stair wound upward inside the tower, a squared helix, but the wire mesh platform at the top formed a continuous ceiling, blocking the stair. Elzy reached up and unlocked a padlock, then pushed up, and a big trapdoor opened in the ceiling, rising easily, counterbalanced by two long, white weights. She trotted up through the opening. The men followed. The fam-ily, their interest hooked, came up behind. Andy stayed below.

"Why did you lock it?" one of the men asked.

"There's equipment up here," she explained, "both historical and mod-ern. I don't think my supervisors want any of it to walk away." She un-locked and removed the protective panels from the windows.

"Why are there two different kinds of equipment?" one of the children asked, standing on tip-toe to look in a window. The door to the hut would stay shut.

"When this tower was built," Elzy told her, "people watched for wild-fires in person, with binoculars. There were lots of towers like this. But then they invented satellites—you know, orbiting in space?—that could send back pictures of big parts of the Earth all at once. Somebody still needed to look at the pictures, to see if they showed any smoke, but they didn't need the towers anymore. So when a tower broke, nobody repaired it. Only a few of them are left. But since the pandemic, we haven't been able to put up any more satellites, and the ones that were up there got old and broke. So now we're using the towers again, but we have computers and infrared cameras to look for fires, so nobody needs to actually be in the towers any-more—and all the old equipment is just for show, like a museum, because computers can't pick up binoculars, right?"

"But you said the towers broke. Are they building more of them?"

"In some places, yes. Other places, they look for fires with drones." She took children's questions seriously, having once been a child with ques-tions herself. She explained wildland firefighting and the various pieces of equipment in and on the station. From the tower, visitors could get a clear view out over the trees. When the adults asked her which mountains they were looking at, she pointed out and named each one.

When the little crowd trickled back down the steps, she followed them, leaving the trap door open. A troop of Boy Scouts came up the mountain. Elzy knew these boys; the littlest one liked to talk with her about botany. Then one of the families from the tent-site emerged from the woods, recognized her, and greeted her pleasantly. All these people had taken the tour before and didn't climb the tower but instead wandered over the rocks, looking at plants and eating trail mix. With an almost furtive glance at Elzy, the mother of the tent-site family carefully picked up and pocketed the crumbs her children left behind. She'd been lectured before.

People trickled in and out along various trails, the summit being a kind of crossroads. Some visitors wanted directions or minor first aid. Some wanted a tour of the tower. Some had questions about history or natu-ral science. Some didn't want anything except to chat amiably for a few minutes.

On the edge of all of it floated Andy. He explored the summit, exam-ined plants and insects with a hand-lens, and closed his eyes to listen to the cicadas and the occasional bird. He wore ordinary clothes, not guild-mem-ber garb, and most of the visitors seemed to assume he was a fellow tourist and left him alone. Sometimes he chatted with Elzy, and then visitors approaching her also greeted him, shaking his hand and asking *how 'bout the weather?* Some, especially men, would ask, *have you been following the AR games? How 'bout that Tyrell? Think he'll make MVP?* Andy was personable, even charming, and chatted about the old days when sports teams could travel and professional-level ice hockey was on television. He agreed the weather was nice, but should not get any hotter.

Don't you know who this is? Elzy felt like shouting. *He's ten times the naturalist I'll ever be!* Some of them had probably even heard of him. Andy had been a dominant figure in the reweaving of science after the pandemic, and he still traveled the country, almost literally keeping his hands on the pulse of half a dozen interrelated fields. Many of the brightest lights in environmental education, ecological research, and conservation science credited him as a teacher, an influence, or a friend. But Andy had not come here to be treated as a celebrity. He disliked attention categorically and was capable of recommending a book or a paper and neglecting to mention he'd written it. The tourists left unaware of whom they had entertained.

Two women arrived, obviously in love with each other but paying little attention to their off-leash dog. He, being a friendly sort, trotted off to play with some small children, who started screaming. Soon, the women and the parents were shouting at each other. The dog sat nearby and hung his head, acutely embarrassed by his people. Elzy had to go mediate.

After all the combatants were out of earshot, she sought out Andy.

"Dog people are *the worst*," she complained. "Everybody thinks their dog is special and the leash regs shouldn't apply to them. I can sometimes get through about leaving trash or stepping on plants, get them to understand *why* they shouldn't do it, but in fifteen years I haven't found any way to convince people to leash their dogs in the woods except to threaten to cite them—and that only works when they know I'm watching." Only with Andy could she indulge in childlike whining.

"You keep your dog off-leash," Andy pointed out.

"Yeah, but my dog's special." Elzy grinned. "Timogen is an intensively-trained, multi-purpose K9. The leash regulations really *don't* apply to him. And he lives here. Over 90% of his food comes from this watershed and the next one over, so he's not a subsidized carnivore—or a subsidized pooper. He's local wildlife, same as me. And I keep him on leash when we patrol, just to set a good example."

She accepted Andy's offer of a drink from his water-bottle but didn't see his fond, amused look.

"You want to have lunch?" she asked. There was nobody else on the summit now. "My bag is up top."

Elzy headed for the tower stairs, but Andy laid one hand on a support girder and looked up. She stopped and turned to him. He glanced at her, his eyes suddenly dancing.

She nodded, just once, and so slightly he could pretend he hadn't asked her permission, that hers wasn't the higher-ranking authority on this ground.

She'd watched Andy climb before—up trees, rock faces, dilapidated shopping centers, any vertical or nearly-vertical surface would do, for any reason or none. He was a serious rock climber who played around on lesser problems without safety equipment, flowing up cliffs almost without apparent volition. But that had been almost twenty years ago. Today, Andy climbed with no less skill, but that liquid quality was gone. Solid now, he had to move his limbs with effort, struggle against gravity and steel. Any stranger watching would have been amazed by his athletic prowess. He was very, very good—for an old man.

She picked up his daypack from where he'd dropped it, mounted the stairs, and waited on the landing while her friend and teacher clambered over the safety rail and joined her, the clatter of metal at his feet sounding alien in a world of rock, sunshine, and birds. He might have climbed farther, she could see him considering it, but the upper half of the tower was complicated by a skin of wire mesh and by the lip of the catwalk. Instead, he followed her up the stairs.

Andy sought the cooler, shady side of the tower. Elzy followed him. He stood at the rail and looked eastward to where ridge after ridge fell away in forest and rock, across narrow Echo Lake, then over the heads of Acadia and Flying Mountain and down to the blue and busy Somes Sound. On the other side of the sound rose the higher, more dramatic ridges of the east side of the island—Parkman, Pemetic, Cadillac, and Champlain. Mount Desert Island is a row of high, rounded, granite ridges separated by the parallel, sometimes pond-filled, valleys where the great continental glacier raked its fingers to the sea. Now the sky, too, featured long, thin streaks, the white mares' tails that foretell rain. The air was warm and heavy as syrup. Andy looked tired, damp, and flushed.

She handed him her water-bottle. He thanked her and drank deeply. After a moment he walked around to the other side of the tower. Elzy followed him, and they looked west together. They could barely see Long Pond, because of the trees, but could look over to Mansell and Bernard. She sometimes fancied she could see her homestead from here, but she could not.

"I shouldn't have done that," Andy said.

"Did you enjoy it?"

He nodded.

"Well, then."

Andy grimaced and looked away. Then he looked out over the ridge to the mainland in the blue distance, over the shoulders of hills.

"This is my last long trip."

Confused and alarmed, Elzy looked at him. For a moment she thought he meant their hike today. He continued.

"When I was younger, I might have needed twenty or thirty percent of my energy to hike a hill like this. Now, I can feel it's taking double that. If I'm wearing a full pack, it's more like triple. If a storm comes up, or if somebody I'm with gets injured, I won't have any reserves to draw on for the emergency. I won't be able to help anyone. It wouldn't be fair."

"Life isn't."

"No, but I try to be." Silence returned for a moment, and he crinkled his eyes against the glare of the sun on the rock and the mountains and perhaps the air itself. Any hotter and the day could not have been pleasant. "I'm retiring," Andy added. "Semi-retiring, anyway. I'm still going to teach part-time, but I'm resigning my leadership positions on campus. And there'll no more of this." A wave of his hand took in the whole wide world and the semi-professional travels he had indulged in every summer of his career.

Elzy stared at him, unable to name her tangle of feelings to herself, much less speak. Andy retiring? The sun might as well have decided to quit. And almost as strange was the possibility that he had taken the time to visit her now *because* he was retiring and wouldn't be able to visit later. He might have planned this entire trip, no matter its other objectives, around a visit *to her*. On the other hand, maybe he'd simply found himself in Flamingo for a week with nothing better to do—after twenty years she still could not be sure. He wouldn't say. And she wouldn't ask.

Instead, she offered him lunch—fresh, chopped strawberries, honey, soft goat cheese, and tiny, roasted beech-nuts all packed in a light-weight titanium tin. He hadn't known she'd packed anything for him and had brought his own, some granola bars he had left over from traveling. He accepted her offering, gave her a granola bar in trade, and they clinked water-bottles. After lunch, she returned to work as the crowd swelled again. Andy watched her unobtrusively, just as he had when he was her teacher.

Another hour and a half and Elzy decided to call it a day. She took Andy down by a different route, heading around the north end of the mountain ridge and then across its dry, rocky, pine-dominated western face, both to show him some variety and so she could check for blowdowns and other issues. She found none, though the terrible footing on this side embarrassed her.

"It's not my fault," she protested. "I've been asking for a crew to come in here to build steps for fifteen years."

"I doubt you're the first to ask," he replied.

As they approached the little beach, Elzy glanced at the sun, not her cell, to check the time.

"You want fish for dinner?" she asked.

"Uh, sure."

"OK, I'll get our gear out of the bike shed."

She'd never seen Andy fish before, nor had she ever heard him mention fishing, but she assumed he'd be good at it, and she had two rods. She was not disappointed. The clouds had started to thicken, and a stiff breeze had risen down the length of the valley, as it did most afternoons, turning the pond water gray and choppy and pushing the small bait fish south. The larger fish would follow. Andy and Elzy took off their shoes and socks, rolled up the legs of their trousers, and waded in just off the boat launch beach side by side. In the distance, they could hear the high whine of Kevin's electric saw.

"Kevin said something interesting the other day," Elzy remarked, after a bit.

"Oh?"

"I mean, he says interesting things all the time, but this one particular thing….He said love isn't a feeling, it's an action. We were talking about mycorrhizal networks and everything, and he called it love. I said plants can't feel, and he said they don't have to."

"Well, he's right," Andy replied, surprising Elzy. "I mean, that's what makes marriage possible."

"Hmm?"

"I can't tell you what I'll feel like having for breakfast tomorrow, let alone who I'll want pushing my wheelchair twenty years from now! It's—" His lure was drifting towards the shore, so he reeled in a little line to keep it from tangling. Then his brow furrowed slightly as he tried to think what he'd been talking about. "It's a safe bet it'll be my wife. I've been more than happy to be married to her every day for almost thirty years. But a bet is not a promise, and feelings can't be willed. Actions are willed, and so I can promise to love if love is an action."

Elzy had a bite, but the fish spat the hook out. She drew in her line, checked the lure, and recast. She'd never had a conversation like this with Andy before. He rarely even mentioned the fact of his marriage, let alone his feelings about it. She'd had no idea Alejandra, the literature professor back at the college, was anything other than Andy's colleague until Andy invited her to dinner with his family and there Ale was. The whole evening Alejandra conversed volubly and warmly while Andy, quiet as ever, nursed a brandy, watching his wife with a fond, undemanding, yet unquenchable desire.

"Andy?" He tilted his head slightly to show he was listening. "How did you know you wanted to get married?"

His eyebrows went up, but he didn't look at her, only his line in the water.

"The same way I've known I wanted anything else. Not that no thought went into it."

"I'm not sure how to think about Kevin, then, I guess," Elzy confessed. What she really wanted to know was how do you decide whether to even try for long-term when everything you know suggests it won't work? But she had no idea how to have *that* conversation with this man.

An odd tremor of surprise ran through Andy, though his face remained impassive.

"You might want to consider why you want to marry," he suggested, as if they were discussing the methodology of some research project, "and whether the things you seek are available with this person. Marriage means different things to different people."

"I should find out what he wants, too, I guess."

"Yeah, except that won't help."

"Oh?"

"He's not going to tell you. He may not know himself. He might also lie or change his mind."

"That doesn't sound like a good basis for a lifetime commitment."

"What does?" Andy said, chuckling, adjusting his line. But a moment later he'd grown serious and turned towards her. "Yes, it seems like if you just ask the right questions, if you just understand completely and prepare everything properly, you'll get what you're after. But life doesn't work that way. You know my history. In the end, the promises you choose to keep are the closest thing you can have to certainty. *Anything else* is *beyond* your control."

Elzy could think of no response. But then a fish bit. She landed this one, a good-sized bass, and then Andy re-cast and almost immediately hooked and landed another. By the time they decided to call it quits, they had caught six between them. They took the Great Pond Trail back to the homestead but didn't speak much on the way. Andy seemed lost in thought.

That night, Andy volunteered to cook. Elzy salted the extra fish he didn't need. Kevin put Tim through his evening training regimen, then harvested salad greens and the day's strawberries. By the time Kevin returned to the fire pit, Andy was heating the Dutch oven over a nice bed of coals while a couple of fillets marinated nearby.

Kevin looked at Andy. He looked at the strawberries.

He spent a few minutes carrying supplies out to the fire-pit and then swiped the butter from Andy's pile. Andy frowned slightly.

Kevin cracked a few eggs, mixed in a little sugar, and whisked the mixture stiff. Then he added vegetable oil and dried lemon zest and—carefully—folded in some flour. He set the batter to cook in a covered, buttered fry-pan over a cooler part of the coals and sliced up a couple of cups of strawberries. By mixing them with sugar he softened the fruit and released its juice, making a kind of syrup. and mixed them with sugar. He added cornstarch for thickening and a touch of Elzy's hot sauce.

Andy said nothing but assertively reclaimed the butter. He dry-roasted ginger, sumac, dill seed, celery seed, and mustard seed in a small fry-pan then, as these became fragrant, added the butter, a generous splash each of apple cider vinegar and moonshine, and a truly remarkable amount of chopped garlic.

Kevin eyed Andy's progress while whipping a can of heavy cream, then got up and went inside to fetch even more ingredients. Returning, he swiped Andy's knife and used it to chop fine a bowl-full each of anchovies and hard, well-aged, sheep's milk cheese, as well as a separate bowl-full of garlic that he drenched in vegetable oil and set aside.

Andy frowned, went inside to get more supplies, then swiped the knife back and rolled up several tortillas in a cigar-shape that he sliced into thin strips. He set the strips aside and retrieved the marinating fish, arranged them in a single layer in the bottom of the Dutch oven, and poured most of the butter and mustard mixture over them.

Elzy checked Tim for ticks, combed him to keep him out of trouble, and watched.

Kevin reclaimed the knife, then retrieved his egg-and-flour mixture, now baked into a light and fluffy sponge-cake. He squared its edges, cut it into quarters, and stacked the quarters layered with the strawberries and whipped cream. Then he frosted the whole with more whipped cream and, with an aggressive flourish, placed four whole strawberries on top.

Andy took the knife back and attacked a mountain of garlic and dill. Then he retrieved some mushrooms he'd set to re-hydrating, used the small amount of excess mushroom water to moisten the tortilla strips, and fried the mushrooms with the garlic and the dill in quite a lot of butter. He also turned the fish fillets over carefully, without breaking them, and added more sauce. Tim began to whine, smelling the fish.

Kevin hardened his expression, then added raw eggs, a little vinegar, some lemon zest, some salt, some ginger, all of the anchovies, and half the cheese, to his garlic-and-oil bowl and whisked the mixture up. He got some left-over home-made tortilla chips from his backpack and fried them with butter and garlic to make a stand-in for croutons, just as Andy was frying *his* tortilla strips in with the mushrooms, butter, garlic, and dill. The two men eyed each other over their fry-pans.

After the chefs put their things away and brought out plates, they watched the dog while Elzy fetched three bottles of cider. When she returned, Kevin was mixing Caesar salads "table-side" as per tradition, and Andy was artfully plating baked fish in mustard sauce with buttered-and-herbed tortilla "noodles" and wild chanterelle mushrooms on the side. Kevin's Japanese-style strawberry shortcake sat nearby at attention, though starting to slump a bit in the heat. Elzy rolled her eyes.

An hour or so later, Elzy leaned back and sighed with ostentatious contentment.

"Well, *that* was just about the most *delicious* pissing match I've ever tasted," she announced. "Thank you, gentlemen."

The two men looked at each other. Andy blushed. Kevin did, too, but his complexion made it less obvious. First Andy and then Kevin began to laugh. Neither stopped laughing for a very long time.

Later, Andy surprised the others by casually asking Kevin if he could help with the dock.

That night, while Andy was again off doing something or other before bed, Elzy urgently sought Kevin's attention.

"Kevin, you can't take Andy with you tomorrow, you use walnut oil on everything!"

"So?"

"I think he might be allergic."

"You *think* so? You traveled with this man for *how* long??"

"He doesn't *tell* me these things," she explained, as if it were self-evident. "I didn't even know whether he had a family for the longest time. He *avoids* walnuts. Not other nuts. That's all I know."

"Can you ask him?"

"I did ask him, about the walnuts. He avoided the question, talked in circles until I let it drop."

"That's bizarre."

"That's Andy." But her tone suggested correction, not agreement. She gestured at him to get on with it before Andy returned and found out she'd interceded. Kevin thought Andy wasn't the only bizarre one.

"I don't use *culinary* walnut oil," he explained. "Woodworker's oil is made from the shells and husks, not the nuts, and doesn't have any of the proteins that trigger the allergies. Every second person is allergic to nuts, do you think I'd make boats no one could touch?"

Elzy didn't look entirely assured.

"I'll make sure he doesn't handle anything oiled till it dries, OK?"

The next morning, Andy helped Kevin load the canoe full of tools and some of the dock pieces, then paddled off. Kevin walked to the new worksite and waved him in.

"Why is the dock going to be *here?*" Andy asked as they unloaded.

"Officially or unofficially?"

"Uh, both!"

"Unofficially, she wants an out-of-the-way place to lock up her boats, and this spot's the closest water access to the homestead. Officially, she sold it to her bosses as an ADA fishing pier. Not everybody can use exos, apparently." *ADA* stood for the name of a piece of legislation that had once required public places be accessible to the disabled. Both the law and the legislature had since been replaced and updated, but the phrase had stuck.

"I hadn't thought the trail between here and the beach was accessible."

"I didn't either. There's that giant rock. But apparently there's some hut in New Hampshire that needed a wheelchair ramp even though it's on top of a mountain—"

"Galehead!"

"Um, yeah." Kevin felt rather deflated that Andy already knew the story, but the older man apologized and gestured for him to continue. "Apparently, the law said that when they rebuilt the hut, they had to put in a wheelchair ramp. But there's no road access, not even bike paths, so everybody acted like it was a big joke until a couple of wheelchair users got themselves up the mountain and rolled on in."

"Yes, exactly. And then they spent all night drinking Champagne," Andy finished, grinning.

Kevin wanted to avoid both glue and rust-prone nails, so he'd already cut the wooden pieces to intricate shape with mortis-and-tenon joints that now only needed assembly. But since Elzy couldn't use horses to pull the dock out in the fall, he'd designed a sectional dock she could disassemble. If he'd known he'd need to explain the plan to an assistant he'd have designed something simpler, but Andy got it pretty quickly. He held his own athletically, too, to Kevin's surprise, working with the casual physicality of a practiced laborer.

The two men did not talk much, working in silence but for the slap of water or the dull thud of the mallets. Birds spoke occasionally. But whenever Andy took a break, Kevin did too, and then, passing the trail mix back and forth, they asked each other the sort of mildly personal questions most people use to get to know somebody—what do you do for a living, where are you from, how did you get into this type of work, and so on. Andy answered without much detail, but without hesitation. Somehow, listening to Elzy, Kevin had expected him not to.

They did not take a lunch break but pushed straight through, assembling all the material they had brought over. The day warmed. The bugs got bad. They each had to keep stopping to re-apply repellent or pull off wandering ticks. The ticks seemed to like Andy especially. Kevin thought about how long it had been since he'd last worked with someone else like this—not domestic stuff with Elzy, and not being instructed in some new skill by another master, but just building something with somebody. He was startled to realize it had been years. On the job, he was habitually alone. He found now a kind of short-term brotherhood working alongside another man—another presence, a weight and a sweat-scent besides his own.

Now and again, hikers passed. They had passed the old worksite too, but Perpendicular was a less-popular trail, and few people on the nearby Great Pond Trail had noticed Kevin unless he was running the saw or the sander. Here, people passed in ones, twos, or larger parties every few minutes. They never spoke to the two men, but some spoke about them, asking each other what the work was for as though Kevin and Andy could not hear. Some watched the local human wildlife with brief interest.

"Don't think of them as tourists," Andy suggested.

"What?"

"Don't think of them as tourists. Think of them as visitors, or even guests. Think of them as people you're making something for. It'll give you a sense of agency, so they'll piss you off less."

"Thanks."

"Yeah, it's an old trick."

Andy's old trick worked.

Finally, when there was nothing on hand left to assemble, they had lunch.

Kevin found in his box a hard-boiled egg, a tortilla, and a little jar of porcinis and onions fried together with garlic, mustard seed, and salt.

"What did you get? Did she give us the same thing?"

"I doubt it. She knows *I* like hot sauce." But Andy did seem to have the same general sort of meal.

"I *like* hot sauce," Kevin asserted, then blushed, embarrassed by his reflexive, defensive competitiveness. Andy looked at him without comment, amused.

Kevin watched the other man eating, though he was careful not to stare. What else, besides who had trouble with spicy food, did Andy notice? His face was always quiet. Not inexpressive—in fact, Andy often seemed startlingly unguarded—but subtle, undemonstrative, as though he didn't realize other people could see him.

"Andy?"

"Mm?"

"You've known Elzy a long time, right?"

Andy finished chewing his mouthful and swallowed.

"Yeah, we go back a ways, now."

"And you know her pretty well?"

"I guess so." He took another bite.

"I can't figure out how she feels about me."

"I used to wonder the same thing," Andy admitted, after some thought.

"Oh?"

"I used to take on a student or two to assist me on trips. In return, I'd supervise their pre-application work directly, show them the ropes. It was a good deal. Elzy applied that year. We'd always gotten along. She was a good student, knew how to backpack, knew how to handle herself in an emergency....She'd TA'd for me a couple of times. But she was...limited. I simply assumed that no personal friendship would be possible."

"But she loves you," Kevin said.

"Yes, as it happens. I was surprised." Andy smiled, remembering, then quickly added "it's not—"

"I know."

Kevin saw Andy relax slightly. A bird sang. He didn't know what kind.

"How she feels about you is not the right question," Andy said, suddenly.

"Oh?"

"No. Provided she wants to continue, her private feelings are not your business. Do you want her? Limitations and all?"

"Uh, yes!"

Andy gestured towards him with an open hand, as though inviting him to continue, or as though ceding him ground.

That afternoon, Elzy was picking up micro-trash in the campground when she heard the canoe beach against the sand. She got down to the pond shore in time to see Kevin and Andy haul the boat up out of the water. Both men were barefoot, it being difficult to get out of a canoe without stepping in water. Kevin left his footwear in the boat and came to give Elzy a proper kiss. Andy took his shoes and sat down near the water so he could rinse the sand from his feet and then carefully dry them with one balled-up black sock.

"How goes it?" he asked, still drying.

"Good," replied Elzy. "Nobody's at the campground tonight. The Great Notch Trail looks good, though in two or three years the bog bridges will need replacing again. I'll put in for the crew now, maybe it'll get approved and funded by then. Oh, and I found a nice flush of peppery bolettes. I left them back at the house."

"I thought they were western?" asked Andy.

"No, we get them, too, they're just not as common."

"Do they taste like peppers?" Kevin wanted to know.

"Not really. More like black pepper, I assume." Black pepper hadn't been available in North America since the pandemic. "How goes the dock?"

"One more day of assembly, then we wait for the oil to cure, then we install."

Andy, shod again, stood up to ask about the rest of the day, but an anxious voice interrupted him. He and the others turned to see a middle-aged, comfortably-plump man standing in the parking area above the beach, holding a large, partially-unfolded, paper map.

"*Parle l'un de vous français?*" he asked, without much hope.

"*Oui. Un peu,*" Andy replied, his accent tolerable but inconsistent. His companions stared at him. The plump man smiled, relieved and joyful.

"*Tiguidou! Là, je parle pas anglais. Mon mari le parle donc je pensais pas je devais le parle, mais maintenant...?*" He gestured, almost apologetically, towards the empty space beside him, the space normally occupied by someone who could speak English.

"*Ton mari a-t-il disparu?*" Andy inquired, concerned.

"*Non, j'suis. Peux-tu m'aides avec ma carte? L'impression est trop petite.*"

Andy grinned, relieved, and stepped up beside him. Together they consulted the map, discussing and pointing, before Andy stabbed at the map decisively with one finger, speaking one final sentence in imperfect but confident Quebecois.

"*Merci!*" the man told him, and meant it.

"*Pas de problem. Bonne chance pour trouver ton mari.*"

"*Je te l'ai dit, il n'est pas perdu,*" the man corrected him. "*J'suis.*"

Andy laughed.

"*Bonne chance d'être trouvé alors,*" he said.

"Toi aussi!" the man told him and turned and headed quickly up the hill.

Andy watched him go, then murmured, more to himself than to the man's receding back, *"mais j'suis déjà trouvé."*

He turned and found the others still staring at him. He grinned a little, self-consciously, then stepped back down onto the sand.

"He was lost," he explained. "The print on the map was too small for him. He said he's 'missing.' He was probably joking, but maybe you should call it in, just in case?"

Elzy nodded and retrieved her portable radio from her backpack. In a moment she had ascertained that no missing-persons file existed for an amiable and monolingual French Canadian.

"I didn't know you could speak French," she said, putting her radio away.

"I learned it from my cousins. They didn't speak English back then. I don't remember much."

"I didn't know you had cousins!" Elzy exclaimed, prompting Andy's grin.

"Oh, there used to be a pile of us. My Uncle René had five children. Luc and Francine had three, each."

Luc. She hadn't heard that name in a long time. She was fairly sure Andy didn't know she'd heard it at all. The men didn't notice her reaction.

"Your Dad had *three* siblings?" Kevin was asking. Since the pandemic, most families had been small.

"No, four. Aunt Michelle was a nun. No children."

From there they segued somehow into sea vegetables, which are only digestible by people with an unbroken maternal lineage back to Japan, something to do with probiotics. Kevin said his maternal grandmother's ancestry was English. Andy speculated, rather drolly, that Japanese identity, like Jewish identity, comes through one's mother.

"I didn't get any special digestive powers, though."

"Yes, you did. Milk."

"That's true, I can digest milk. My wife can't. She's mostly Indigenous."

Elzy put the canoe away while the men talked. Tim paced after her, never far from her heels. She remembered a story about Andy getting angry and shouting at his Uncle Luc. She had trouble picturing Andy shouting, but he *had* been much younger then. She'd always wondered, from the details of that story, if maybe Luc was like her, missing something inside. Well, she'd been taught to compensate through discipline, duty, and honor—what she'd told Kevin about the world needing people like her, she still believed that. But what about Luc? Was "useful" really the best a misfit could hope for? Andy never said much about his family, but over the years he'd given her bits and pieces about his first wife, his children, his parents…. But about Luc, he'd never even bothered to complain.

All her attempts to protect Kevin—and ultimately herself—from her shortcomings, to keep him from caring too much, what kind of personal connection had that left her with?

Doing love, Andy had said. *Price of admission,* Anne had said. Well, it beat becoming just a foot-note in somebody else's story.

The next morning during eight AM check-in, Elzy learned that the weather would go to hell later in the day. The weather went to hell often, and, as she told the men, today's trip could begin as early as noon. She advised not going to work on the dock at all. She would spend the morning in her garden—weirdly, she had to water before the storm hit because the plants would need to be covered, protected from the down-pour. Kevin volunteered to weed. Andy announced he was going for a walk and would not be back "for at least two hours."

"By yourself?" Elzy asked and wished she hadn't.

"Timogen can come with me, if he wants to." Andy looked at her, his chin raised slightly. A few seconds passed.

"Well, have fun, then," she told him.

Andy nodded, satisfied.

It took him only five minutes to get his pack together. On his way out of the clearing, he called the dog. Tim vacillated and looked at Elzy, wagging his tail almost apologetically.

"It's alright," she told him. "You can go."

Just before they left the clearing, once the dog's choice was clear, Andy attached the leash, just to set a good example.

"That's weird," Elzy said, gazing after them.

"What, that he might want to go for a walk by himself?"

"No, I—" she shook her head as though shaking away the misunderstanding. "What's weird is that he told me he's going. Usually, when he wants time by himself he just vanishes."

"Dude, he was telling us how long we have."

"How long…?"

"'At least two hours.' In which to have sex."

"What?" That Andy would provide for such a thing on purpose had not occurred to her.

"Come on, he may be eighty-whatever now, but he wasn't always. He knows we haven't gone at it for like a week." Kevin's grin grew.

"First of all, I don't think he's over eighty. Second, it hasn't been a week."

"OK, fine. Whatever. Well?"

"Oh, hell, yes."

When Andy returned, he found them weeding and watering as before. Without a word as to their lack of progress, he unclipped Timogen and set about checking the potato plants for beetle grubs.

"The clouds are building, but I doubt the first storms will strike us," he reported.

Elzy went to refill her buckets. She'd already rigged up the tarps to catch as much rain as possible—a good storm could yield fifty gallons or more, assuming the tarps didn't blow away. She could hear the men talking, though she couldn't tell what they were saying. She frowned, noticing in herself a stab of…jealousy?

No, not jealousy, exactly, but she had not thought Andy talked so readily to anyone. She'd always assumed that his reticence, his reserve, was just *him*, how he was with everybody, except possibly his family. She had allowed herself to feel special because he communicated with her at all. But she didn't know that. She *couldn't* know that—when did she ever see him in a purely social context, this former professor whom she now knew mostly through email? Theorizing without data. What if he was chatty and forthcoming with everybody *but* her?

She filled the buckets from the cistern's filtered spigot and stewed, mentally muttering *how dare he?* But what had Andy done—existed as someone she cared about? Surely it wasn't *his* fault if she were a fool?

But walking back, laden, she had another thought. Suppose Andy was reserved and reticent with everybody *but Kevin?* But why?

Because Kevin was Elzy's boyfriend. Because if Kevin did not think well of Andy, did not identify with him and perceive him as an ally, he might get jealous and hostile. He might forbid Elzy to talk to Andy.

The thought made her stop walking.

Andy was making himself into a social human being, an almost normal person, strategically, in order to keep her friendship? She didn't know whether to feel special—deeply special, specially-special—or to get pissed off that Andy might think a man could forbid her anything. And no man who would make her choose would ever be chosen—didn't Andy know that?

How dare he? she muttered mentally again, walking back towards the garden.

Thunder peeled, distant. She saw Kevin and Andy look up, though Timogen ignored the noise. He was asleep again in a dog hole. The sky was still mostly blue above the clearing.

"I wish I could see," Kevin complained. "In these trees, I can't see what the weather's doing until it's doing it on top of us."

"The air will change," Elzy told him. "We'll know when it's time to go in.`"

"This isn't the greatest place to shelter from a wind-storm," Andy commented. He didn't explain why. Plainly, he knew Elzy could read the signs of site history as well as he, that she knew this clearing had originally been opened by wind, that its position on a ridge top left it vulnerable. His implicit recognition of their shared expertise warmed her.

I am way too old to be this emotionally needy, she thought.

"It's not," she agreed, aloud, "but my house is built of triangles. I think a tree could fall on it and not punch through."

"Maybe."

"Best we've got," pointed out Kevin.

"You've got hornworms," Andy announced. He had moved on from the potatoes to the tomatoes. "Do you want me to kill them or leave them?"

"Leave them, unless they're excessive," Elzy decreed, then filled the watering can from a bucket and sprinkled another bed.

Kevin watched her go, then wrinkled his nose in disgust, asking "who leaves hornworms?"

"Well, maybe if you want the acquaintance of butterflies..." Andy began. He gave an awkward almost-laugh. Was that a *Little Prince* reference? Then, more seriously, "parasitoid wasps control hornworms, right? But if you kill all your hornworms, you don't have any food for the wasps. The next infestation will have no control. You'll never find *all* the hornworms then. They'll eat all your tomatoes."

"So, in order to control the pests, you need wasps," Kevin replied, "but in order to have wasps you need pests? You need a certain minimum population of pests in order to control the pests?"

Andy didn't answer verbally, only grinned, quick and almost feral, then returned his attention to his work. He was crawling carefully through the jungle of growing tomato plants, searching for and pinching off extraneous suckers. Watching him move thus, dappled in green and fragrant shadow, Kevin found himself mentally reciting the half-remembered lines of "Tyger, Tyger," without fully understanding why.

"What you're telling me, then," Kevin ventured, "is that this ecology stuff is *useful?*"

Andy looked up and cocked an index finger at him, making a *tk!* noise with his lips against his teeth, the universal gesture for *you're getting it.*

They finished work and got inside before the first storm hit. The lightning didn't last long, but a couple of strikes sounded very close, the thunder exploding and echoing weirdly among the hills. A couple of big branches broke loose and came down, and one did indeed strike the house, though it did no damage. Once the storm eased up a bit, Kevin opened the window and the door to let the rain-cooled air freshen the house. He couldn't see the other side of the clearing, only a dull, faintly luminous wall of white rain.

Two more storms rolled through that afternoon while other small but vicious cells rumbled from other parts of the island, leaving still other parts to bake in continuing drought. The three humans and the dog ate strawberries and lazed about. Elzy cleaned and sharpened her tools. Kevin read. Sometimes he and Elzy talked.

Andy did not talk. He lay on his bunk writing on a beat-up red tablet computer or staring thoughtfully into space. Kevin looked at him, thinking about their conversation about Elzy the day before. Could it really be as simple as that? Could he really let Elzy *do love and feel squat,* as he'd once said? If only she'd at least say something definite.

Towards evening, the storms cleared off, though the air remained cool and the forest drippy. Elzy went out to check on the garden and to boil a couple of eggs at the firepit. She used the little alcohol stove, her wood being wet, but she never cooked indoors in the summer—once the house heated up, there was no quick way to cool it. Andy also left the house, vanishing as was his daily habit. When Elzy came back inside, bearing the hard-boiled eggs, some green onion, and the last head of lettuce that hadn't bolted yet, Andy still wasn't back.

Kevin took advantage of their temporary privacy to ask if researching his great-grandmother still seemed worth it. Elzy went still for a moment, then continued peeling the eggs.

"Yes," she said. "But I don't know how. I thought it would be easier. Maybe the librarians in Bar Harbor will have some ideas, or the Bar Harbor Historical Society? I don't know. We'll figure out something."

"Will we?"

"I don't know."

"In another few days, Andy and I'll have the dock ready. And then I'll finish the sailboat. Are you gonna ask me to build something else?"

Elzy glanced at him, embarrassed.

"If I have to," she said, as though joking. She peeled a bit of egg-white away with the shell and cursed mildly. She put down the egg for a moment, resting her hands in the bowl of wet eggshells. She seemed to be gathering herself. "Whatever I have to do, I guess."

"Elzy," Kevin said.

She took a deep breath.

"Kevin, I *want* you to stay," she announced. "I want you to stay *with* me. This place is more of a home with you in it."

"Elzy!" he exclaimed. He would have swept her up and kissed her, like they do in the movies, except her hands were full of bits of eggshell, and anyway she looked far from amorous. Perched as she was on the edge of their bed, knees clasping the bowl of broken shells, she looked tight and small and very frightened. She did not smile.

"I'll stay, then," he said. He'd been standing, but he pulled the stool in from the kitchen and sat down facing her. "Not all the time, I mean, but I'll make this home-base. There are plenty of people who need boats up and down the coast here. I'll stay. I'll learn to paddle in the ocean and everything." He glanced away a moment, imagining, and when he looked back he caught a glimpse of a wide, relieved, joyous smile, but for some reason she put her smile away as soon as she saw him looking.

She said nothing.

"I still kind of feel like caring about a place is stupid, though. I mean, I want to, I start to see this place the way you see it, and then, I don't know, *something* comes up in me. It's weird. Maybe you're right. And if you are, then I think we *have* to find out what happened to my great-grandmother. I mean, I want to be part of your world, Elzy, and I don't think I can until I know why I was taught not to even want that."

"We'll figure it out," Elzy replied. "I just don't know how, yet."

"Figure what out?" asked Andy from the doorway. He came in and sat down on his bed. Tim set his huge head on the man's knee and earned a pat.

"Kevin's great-grandmother survived the Fire of 1947," Elzy explained. "We know that. But we don't know anything about why she was here or why she left. We don't know what happened to her."

"Your great-grandmother?" Andy asked, surprised. "She must have been a child, then. That was a long time ago."

"No, she was an adult. I come from a long line of old parents." Kevin explained his situation, how he needed to find out what happened so he could stay with Elzy.

"We've tried, and we've hit a dead-end," Elzy added. "Neither of us know where to look next."

Andy looked Elzy to Kevin and back, strangely shocked, then seemed to get a hold of himself. "Why didn't you ask me for help?"

"I didn't think you *could* help," admitted Elzy.

"Any time you're involved in an ongoing project, it's important to tell everybody. Precisely because you never know who is going to have something you need." Andy spoke as though reminding Elzy of some principle, some long-ago lesson, that she ought to have remembered.

"I know," Elzy said, hanging her head for a moment. "But you're an *ecologist,* not a local historian!"

"Actually," put in Kevin, "he wrote a book about Mount Desert Island."

"He *what?* How do you know that?"

"I looked him up online," Kevin explained. "Last night, when I went to call my parents. What? Clearly he's some kind of big-shot, I knew there'd be stuff on him. I wanted to know who I'm sharing a tiny house with. You didn't know about the book? He's written a couple of them."

"No, I didn't know! You wrote *a book* about this place?"

"Edited a book, actually. Three of my students wrote it. We did the research...the summer before you and I hiked together, something like that."

"Oh, Karynn, Enizah, and John—what was his name? There were, like, five Johns in that cohort. Ah, John Palladinetti."

"That's right, Johnny Palladinetti. You have a good memory. We surveyed the White Mountains and Mount Desert Island. We weren't able to publish the White Mountain material, though."

"*That's* why you knew all about the island. You'd just been here. And that's how you knew Michael and Tristan and the others at the Observatory, too."

"Actually, Tristan and I knew each other from grad school. Saul, too. We all used to hang out." His face became sad and troubled a moment, mentioning Saul. "I'm surprised you didn't know about the book."

"No, I didn't *know*. I looked you up online twenty years ago, but I didn't think I needed to do it *again*. I thought you'd *tell me* when you published something. You normally do."

"I guess it came out just after you and I got back. Back then, I didn't know you were interested."

"Didn't know…." Elzy seemed flabbergasted.

"So you *can* help us?" Kevin asked, bringing things back to the subject.

"Oh, yes, I believe so. But not so much because of the book. Elzy can tell you I spent a lot of time after the pandemic looking for people. I got pretty good at it."

"But you're an *ecologist*," she protested again.

"'What's more, baby, I can cook,'" he told her, half-grinning. As usual, Elzy didn't get the reference. Kevin did and laughed.

Chapter 7: The Game Afoot

Clearly, the next step was to go back to the library, but the dock and sailboat still needed a few more days of work until they were ready to be left alone for a while. And so, by the time Elzy, Kevin, and Andy finally walked into town together, the Flamingo Festival was in full swing.

The Festival was like a weekly market on steroids. There were the stalls and tables selling everything local farmers and artists had on hand, the food carts, the tents where various traveling professionals offered their services, the paid entertainers and educators and the buskers hoping to be paid...but there were more of all of them than usual, and everything was decorated in flamingos.

There were realistic flamingos, cartoonish flamingos, surrealist flamingos, flamingos made of wood, metal, plastic, paper maché, and repurposed trash. There were flamingo cookies, flamingo sandwiches, flamingo cocktails, and people wandering around wearing pink feather boas and vintage plastic pink flamingo sunglasses. There were more people than Kevin had ever seen in town before—every town on the island had its own summer festival, and many of the island's residents, both seasonal and permanent, would converge on whichever town happened to be celebrating that week.

"I'm surprised they still do this," Andy asserted. "Forty years ago, the locals all hated the Flamingo Festival." But he seemed upbeat, happy.

First, Andy and Kevin had to rent bicycles.

"I should have thought of that!" Elzy exclaimed.

"Thinking different thoughts is the whole reason we have different brains," Andy told her.

Next, they sat together on stone benches around a tiny outdoor court with a sailboat bas-reliefed into the floor and reviewed the known facts of the case over pink-bunned burgers and a basket of onion rings.

There weren't a lot of known facts—mostly just scraps of family legend and a list of the places where Kevin's great-grandmother's name wasn't. Andy agreed that they had to confirm her presence in Bar Harbor before they could do anything else, but he didn't say how.

"Wait," he said suddenly, so startled by an idea that Elzy jumped, "what was her name?"

"Rose Marks," Kevin told him. "Spacy was her maiden name." But they'd told him that already.

"No, what was her name *then?* Was she married more than once?"

Kevin slapped his forehead.

"Yeah, you're right," he acknowledged. "We don't know anything about what she was doing while she was gone. We don't even really know how long she was gone. Nobody who's still alive knows anything. She *could* have been married before my great-grandfather. She *could* have been banging six guys every Thursday, for all I know."

"What happens in Bar Harbor stays in Bar Harbor," Andy muttered.

"So, she had a different last name," Elzy said, "that would explain our not finding her in the census. But how do we find out what her other name was?"

Andy suggested looking for the records associated with the known marriage—the forms that listed her name-change ought to list what name she'd changed it *from.*

"But how do we do that?" Kevin asked. "I don't know anything about my great-grandfather, except that he was named Charles Marks and did something or other in the provincial government. I don't know when or where they got married."

"We don't need to," Andy assured him. "Those records are digitized and mostly archived at the state or province, or sometimes county level. Some are even searchable."

Andy and Elzy both had to teach workshops at the festival—being guild-members, they had to work a minimum number of billable events in order to retain their salaries—so they would be in and out of the research effort all day. Kevin would stay at the library, nose to the grindstone, on a loaner machine. Elzy headed to her first work-shop before the men had even finished their onion rings. An hour and a half later, when she got to the library, she found Kevin in a foul mood.

"He emails off questions and then just *leaves* for his workshop, so I have no idea if there's an answer yet or not. I can't open his email." Kevin gestured at his computer screen as though it were, like Andy, somehow at fault.

"What questions?"

"His Canadian cousin has good internet at home. We only have to check the American records."

"You expect this cousin to have anything to report yet? Canada's kind of big." She signed out a loaner for herself and started combing through marriage records. Soon, she was heading towards a foul mood herself.

She was irritated at having to spend so much of the day inside, though the library's insides were lovely, all white walls, hardwood trim, and graceful doorways. The main reading room had a high, skylighted ceiling, with shafts of dusty sunlight reaching down across a space structured by quilts hanging mid-air from bamboo poles. Above a generous stone fireplace stretched a portrait of a stone bridge done in colorful, looping yarn. A well-made but hobbit-sized canoe hung on a nearby wall adorned with commemorative plaques. Intricate model sailships and plaster busts of important or semi-famous people rested on the tops of bookshelves and other horizontal surfaces. Light-filled windows looked in on couches, chairs, and tables, all of them both tasteful and comfortable.

And all of it cool. The interior of the library was a good fifteen degrees lower than the outdoor air, which had become oppressively soupy. Elzy liked the cool air, but her attention kept wandering to the Juneberry trees outside, one at the front corner, the others along the strip of garden on the side of the building, all of them bearing now a weight of fruit almost but not quite yet ripe. She wished she were a bird in those trees.

She didn't feel like helping. It had just occurred to her that since Kevin had agreed to stay, she didn't need to get him to fall in love with the island anymore. But she couldn't simply abandon Kevin's quest. To do so would violate the decision she'd made to *do* love, to *act* as though Kevin, his feelings and his welfare, were intrinsically important, irrespective of her own still quite selfish impulses. It was on the basis of that decision that she'd finally been able to risk asking Kevin to stay with her.

She'd paid the price of admission, as Anne had put it, and she intended to continue paying it, to pay it genuinely and in full. And that meant reading indoors when she wanted to be playing outside.

Not that she was finding much. She'd try a search term, read through some ancient newspaper clippings, find nothing, then try again with a new search term. But she wrote down citations and notes for everything she read, even if the note was only "found nothing," because once, long ago, Andy had told her that discovering where the answer *isn't* is just as valuable as discovering where it *is*.

By the time Andy returned, she and Kevin could tell him, with at least some confidence, that no Canadians named Rose and Charles Marks had gotten married in the United States between 1947 and 1962, the year Kevin's grandmother was born.

"I have a positive result, too," Elzy added. "It may or may not be pertinent."

"Oh?"

"A politician from Ontario named Charles L. Marks showed up in gossip columns several times for attending parties on Long Island in 1959 and 1960."

"OK, stick a pin in that," Andy told her, sounding impressed. "It'll be useful later."

Elzy and Kevin had already read most of the library's material related to the fire. Now they checked the catalogs of every other library on the island to see if anyone had anything different. Andy spend a while talking by phone with staff at the Bar Harbor Historical Society and the Abbey Museum, both of which had collections that included 1947. Just as he got up to go prepare for his second workshop, Kevin stopped him.

"Don't take this the wrong way, man, but why are you helping us so much?" It had become obvious that he planned to stay much longer than the original week or two, if that's what it took.

And Andy looked at Kevin in a way that suggested he had a great many reasons and didn't plan to reveal any of them.

"I'm a scientist," he explained, after a bit. "I'm curious. I want to see how things turn out."

"He's changed," Kevin commented, as soon as the older man was away.

"No, he hasn't," said Elzy.

"Yes, he has. He's, like, in charge now."

"He's always in charge. When he lets you make a decision, it's because he's delegating."

That evening, Elzy walked home alone through the lovely, cooling air and the green of the trees and gardens, eating a samosa on the way. The men stayed to read more and have dinner, then biked back, getting home not long after she did.

While Tim greeted his people, she set out cheese, a bowl of chips, and three bottles of beer.

"So, what have we got?" she asked as the men sat down.

"What we've got," began Kevin, "is half-remembered family legend, her obituary, a scan of her birth certificate, and a biographical paragraph on that Charles L. Marks you found in the gossip columns—I looked him up on a provincial history website, and he's our guy, but we still don't have the name-change forms. We also have a bunch of those pertinent negatives you like." He took a swig of his beer. "She's missing from the 1941 census in Kingston, Ontario, so she must have left by then. Likewise '51 and '61, but her daughter—Ma's mom—was born in 1962 *in* Kingston, so that narrows her return down pretty well. Looks like Rose was just rich for a living—we didn't find anything about her having a job—but she was a big-deal philanthropist, especially with women's science education. She and her husband endowed a couple of scholarships for women in botany and plant ecology. She must have loved plants, Ma remembers she had all these books on botany and gardening, even brought some of them with her to the home. Anyway, she was widowed in 1998. A decade later, she 'retired from public involvement,' whatever that meant, and died of the flu in 2016. Weirdly, there's no mention of dementia, anything like that, except for Ma's stories. But what we *don't* know is why she left home or what she was doing for twenty years. Or, of course, what happened in the fire."

"Sam says he'll get back to us when he has anything," Andy added. "It should be a couple of days. And Kevin is expecting calls from two more libraries."

Kevin sat up suddenly as though he'd just remembered something.

"Tell her about the book," he prompted.

"You found a new book?" Elzy asked around a mouthful of chips.

"No, no," said Andy, "you've read it, it's...." but the name eluded him. He waved his hand around some, as though trying to grab the word. "It's on the tip of my mind. I know what it is, I haven't forgotten," he insisted, shamefaced.

"*I've* forgotten," admitted Kevin.

"Anyway," said Elzy, "if I've already read it, it doesn't mention Rose."

"The book doesn't, no," said Andy, "but it says, and I confirmed this today, the author left all her research materials—all her interview notes and the original documents she'd gathered—at the Bar Harbor library. Somebody may have mentioned Rose in an interview, and it just didn't make it into the book."

"And they'll let us read it?"

"Oh, sure. As long as we don't take it out of the library."

Elzy considered.

"We're going to have to go to Bar Harbor to solve this anyway," she said. "We might as well do it sooner rather than later. But listen, my contribution for the county is about due. Let's take a few days to give your cousin and everybody a chance to report back, and I'll get my stuff together so I can take it in when we go."

"Your contribution?" Kevin asked.

"Yeah...."

"What contribution?"

"Oh. You mean you...? Oh, you don't have them in Canada, do you?"

"Not by that name, anyway."

"It's, you know, it's just the...." Elzy had trouble explaining something she normally took for granted. "Well, you know how each share is worth one day's food, water, and shelter? That's because there's a day's worth of food and other supplies in a stockpile somewhere for each share. In case of famine or something. Landholders have to send in a certain amount every year. The receipts you get are shares. That's how they enter circulation. That's why each issue of shares is good for only two years. Whoever has the shares at the end of the two years can redeem them for the food and stuff. The whole stockpile is continually renewed."

"Yeah, that's not how we do things," admitted Kevin. He considered. "Wait, so, what if—"

"Look, it's complicated," Elzy told him. "The important thing is that I bring in stuff three or four times a year to the depot in Bar Harbor—that's what I was in town for the weekend I met you, actually."

"Well, thank goodness for high finance, then."

Elzy spent the next week, when she wasn't attending to her more ordinary responsibilities, gathering and processing food and deciding which
of the things she'd already put by to take. She kept the strawberry jam and
the pickled chanterelle conserve for herself, but the dried strawberries and
boletes, the salted and dried fish, and the powdered eggs all went into sacks
for transport. Kevin and Andy both helped where they could or kept her
company as she worked, though they were seldom both with her at the
same time. Andy still spent a few hours a day on his little computer, while
Kevin had a sailboat hull to cover with canvas, glue, and paint.

Midweek, Andy took a trip alone to the eastern half of the island and
its system of scenic carriage-roads. He took his rented bike and was gone
for two nights. On the third day, Elzy got back from fishing and found him
sitting in her garden with a sketchpad, drawing the portrait of a flowering
potato plant.

"I didn't know you could draw," she said, coming up behind him. She
was gratified to see him startle, just slightly.

"Hmm? Oh, yeah. Well, I hardly do it anymore." His style appeared
simple, unpolished, almost artless, but precisely accurate. The plant
bloomed on the page.

For the next few days, it rained. After that, Elzy, with the others' help,
began harvesting beets from her garden and Juneberries from the small
trees scattered through her territory. One evening she announced that the
strawberry season was over.

"Tomorrow, or maybe the next day, we'll harvest the last of it. The
plants haven't made any new flowers in a while."

"I don't know whether to be relieved or sad," said Kevin. "I've been
eating strawberries every day for like a month."

"There's always jam."

Andy looked from one to the other, following the conversation while
eating boiled beets so flavorful that they needed no seasoning at all.

The next morning, as usual, Elzy set out with Tim to work, but after
only an hour of picking up trash on the road, she returned to the little
beach to meet the others. She was surprised to find Kevin alone.

"He'll be down," Kevin assured her. "He wanted to call Sam from the
overlook."

"He brought his tablet?" She knew Andy didn't have a phone. His tablet could handle voice calls, on the rare occasions he couldn't avoid them.

"No, he borrowed my phone."

In a few more minutes, Timogen barked, high and eager, but as a well-trained dog on duty, he remained at heel. Andy ambled up and, understanding the protocol, formally asked Elzy's permission before kneeling to greet the dog.

"Any news?" she asked.

"The woman who married Charles Marks," he answered, "was named Rose Spacey *Stone.*"

Elzy spent a few seconds confused, thinking they'd been tracking the wrong Rose, before she realized what he was talking about.

"Who's Stone, then?" asked Kevin.

"Christopher Stone, an American. They were married in Montreal, in 1938. A notice in the paper listed him as a gardener, but didn't name his employer. Christopher and Rose Stone are on the 1940 census in Bar Harbor." Andy stood up and handed Kevin's cell phone back as he spoke.

"So, you're saying she ran away with the gardener, eh?" Kevin asked. He pocketed his phone.

"Most likely, yes. My guess is that he had to leave, for whatever reason, so she decided to go with him."

"Huh. So what happened? Why was she available when Marks came around?" Kevin's affect was casual, almost jocular, as though he suspected some sordid melodrama. His smile dropped when Andy explained that Chris Stone was also on the list of Bar Harbor residents who were killed in World War II.

"Rose Stone is *not* in Bar Harbor in the 1950 census," Andy added. "I've just asked Sam to check Long Island for me."

"Long Island?" Elzy asked, surprised, but after a few seconds she made the connection. "Because that's where she met Marks!"

"Yes, exactly."

But they hadn't come to the beach to discuss Rose but to get the boats. Elzy carried the canoe down to the water while Andy brought the kayak. Kevin followed with an armload of paddles and the cable and lock—the boats would not be coming back that night. Andy set the kayak on the water, accepted the paddle from Kevin, and climbed in. Elzy and Kevin took the canoe with Tim as passenger. The dog spent much of the trip gazing intently into the warm, green water. When he saw a school of baitfish flit by a foot or two below the surface, he barked.

Kevin showed Elzy how to assemble (and disassemble) the dock while Andy sat and communed with the dog. The process didn't take very long. The structure wasn't very big, just a T-shaped deck linked to a short ramp on the shore, plus a kind of hitching-post on land where Elzy could lock up her boats. That anybody would ever get to the dock by wheelchair seemed doubtful, but a wheel-chair user could paddle up, and the trail for be rolled-upon before some distance.

Elzy inspected the dock critically and appreciatively, as any new owner might.

"It's a whole, new *thing*," she exclaimed, then felt herself blush for sounding ridiculous. "You've built a whole new part of the shoreline," she clarified. "The pond is different now."

"I hope that's good," Kevin said.

"*You* are a whole new thing," she told him. "And that's *definitely* good."

He kissed her nose. He kissed her mouth.

Elzy still had to paddle around to check for new stealth sites and then patrol a few trails. Tim and Andy opted to go with her, but Kevin had to stay and clean up. He said that afterwards he'd hike to some suitable high-point to make some phone calls and that he'd meet them back home for dinner. But a few hours later, when the others paddled up to the little beach, intending to lock the canoe up and go patrol the Valley Trail, there Kevin was, waiting for them.

"What's wrong?" cried Elzy, seeing his eyes.

"I talked to Ma," he explained. "Dad's dead."

Chapter 8: Tell the Story

Elzy and Andy quickly beached the canoe and hurried over. Kevin, barely coherent, explained that his father had been found, broken-necked, in the corral with a young horse, but whether the fall had been the cause or the result of death, no one could say. Elzy made him sit down. He sat, pinching the bridge of his nose. Timogen carefully sniffed Kevin's face. The dog could smell the tears Kevin wouldn't let himself shed.

"I don't know, I don't know," Kevin said, after some moments. "There's no doubt, my mother's seen him, *seen* him, dead, actually dead, there's no doubt, but I don't believe it. I mean, I'm gonna go home someday, and he'll be there, right? There are things I have to tell him—not anything dramatic, it's not like I never told him I loved him or anything like that, but stupid stuff, like, hey, I designed and built a dock! And it turned out pretty cool!" His face crumpled, but he pulled it together again.

"It's difficult," Andy acknowledged, sitting on the sand beside the younger man. "When my father died....We hadn't seen each other in months, had not spoken at depth for—perhaps years. We were never fully estranged, but...we were *not* close. He was *not* kind. Yet—it's been thirty-five years and there are still time times I want to tell him things and forget why I can't."

"Your father died in the pandemic?" Kevin asked.

"In it but not of it, yes. He survived the disease itself."

Kevin nodded, acknowledging.

"I just....There are things I want him to tell *me*."

Andy lifted his hand as though to touch Kevin, but he hesitated and spoke instead.

"The conversation is always limited, and it's always over too soon."

Kevin nodded again, and this time Andy did place a hand on his shoulder. He would not have touched Elzy like that—he knew she disliked social touch. But she'd noticed he often clapped Kevin on the shoulder or back in passing, or traded mock-punches with him, the playful aggression men use for affection among themselves. She remembered that he hugged friends, shook hands with colleagues—or elbow-bumped with the more germ-phobic pandemic survivors. She'd noticed, too, how little he ever said, and how every word seemed to come thoughtfully, deliberately, out of a great and private wordlessness. She thought for the first time that maybe *touch* was a language, *his* language, and wondered what it meant that she could not speak it.

She saw that whatever Andy's hand on Kevin's shoulder said, it made the younger man draw a ragged breath and relax a little.

"I've gotta go," Kevin said. "I've got to go into town so I can make more calls, look some things up....My phone's about out of juice."

"You could borrow mine, while yours charges," Elzy offered, feeling utterly inadequate, wishing she could think of something better to offer than the loan of a cell phone.

Kevin shook his head, just slightly, and within a few minutes he was pedaling off towards town.

"Damn me, I didn't say *anything*," exclaimed Elzy once he was gone. "What kind of girlfriend am I?"

"What do you think you should have said?" asked Andy.

"I don't know. The only thing I could think of was 'just be glad you're not ten, like I was.' That wouldn't have *helped*. I can't think of anything useful to say in these situations."

"I'm not sure I ever say much that is useful at all," Andy admitted.

Elzy thought that was very odd, coming from him.

They patrolled the Valley Trail as planned, and Elzy thought about the death of her own father, how the event divided her life into before and after, creating a brokenness that had never really healed. Instead she'd gotten used to it, grown across it, the way lichens grow gray and black and green over the blocks of stone on the slopes above the pond, stones levered off from the higher cliffs during the dramatic freeze-thaw cycles right after the glacier or, more recently, in one or another of the earthquakes that still sometimes shake New England as the land continues its slow rebound from the weight of ice. Given enough time, soil collects and trees grow over the rockfalls, but the stone never knits itself back together. The voids among the blocks could still snap the leg of the unwary.

She didn't exactly feel bad for Kevin. She understood, but didn't empathize. Frankly, she was irritated by this intrusion on his emotional life, because the loss of his father would inevitably make him less emotionally available to her for a while. It would make him require things of her instead. Because this was it, the thing she had feared, the moment when Kevin would need what Andy could offer intuitively but she could not.

She'd have to fake it, that was all. Not to deceive Kevin, but simply to be the tree root she had promised to be, a root growing over the gaps to form solid ground for its companions.

She wished Andy could teach her how. He obviously knew, but he couldn't pass along the knowledge, not any more than she could teach him how to give up his armor of distance that anyway left his real vulnerabilities all too exposed. She watched him walking ahead of her, his shirt starting to cling oddly as sweat and humidity dampened it, his hair flashing white suddenly as he passed through a fleck of sunshine under the trees. He stumbled a little over a water-bar with a loose stone. She'd have to come back and fix it. He could not teach her how to be a different person.

That night, Elzy made dinner, beets and beet greens scrambled with eggs, plus a pan-cooked sponge-cake with shadberries, honey, and whipped cream, her homage to Kevin's Japanese-style strawberry confection. But she delayed serving. Kevin wasn't back yet.

"I wish I knew what kind of comfort food Kevin likes," she said, sitting by the fire-pit with Andy. "Think we should have dinner or wait longer?"

"Whatever you think is best."

"I wish he could call."

But there was no reception at the homestead.

A few minutes later, Tim barked happily and ran to greet a very tired and oddly old-looking Kevin.

"You're dehydrated," Elzy pronounced clinically and got him first water, then beer. She was out of cider until the apples ripened. He inhaled two helpings of cake and then started in on the beet scramble. Elzy and Andy ate rather more sedately. Timogen got whipped cream on his nose. It took him a long time to notice and lick it off.

"So, what did you do in town?" Elzy asked. Kevin looked at her, his last forkful of egg paused mid-air, and said nothing for a moment. Then he took his bite, chewed, swallowed, and spoke.

"I made travel plans," he said.

"You—"

Elzy felt herself go cold.

"My mother needs me, Elzy," he pleaded. "It's not what I want to do."

"What do you want to do?"

"I want, I want...I want to find out how you live here in winter—and how I can help. I want to find out if every spring is as cold as this one was, or if this year was unusual. I want to see if that...damn...red squirrel survives till next summer. I wanna learn how to paddle in the ocean with the waves and the tides. I want to go from island to island, visiting, and I want to see whales breech from the cockpit of a kayak I made with whales in mind. I want to find out what this thing is between us and what happens when it really has time." He drew a breath and glanced away. "But Ma can't run the ranch by herself. She has friends and neighbors helping now, but they can't keep doing that indefinitely, and it's not fair to make her figure out the next steps alone. I don't know. I just.... I need to go be with my mother."

"Are you coming back?"

Again silence.

"I don't know," he said at last. "I can't think that far ahead. I want to, but it could be a couple of years. Anything could happen."

"You mean you could fall in love with someone else," she supplied. She wasn't accusing. It was just a statement. Her voice sounded in her own ears like leftover oatmeal. They had never before used the words *in love* with each other, for each other.

"Or you could."

"We could just decide not to. Not with anyone else." She was peripherally aware of Andy sitting nearby, tense and uncomfortable.

"Elzy, that's not the only thing that could happen, though. Really, *anything* could. One of us could die. Something else could go wrong. We could have a giant fight over the internet. We've never really had a fight, what if we're no good at it? If I've got to lose you, I'd rather say goodbye in person than online. I'd rather come back when we thought I might not than think we have more time and then not get it." Another moment passed. "I don't suppose you'll come with me?"

"No, I can't. You know I can't, not if it might be forever. I'm rooted here."

"Well, then."

Andy started to get up, to clear away the dishes and escape a conversation more intimate than any he wanted to witness. Kevin stopped him.

"Wait, would you do something for me? Both of you?"

"If possible, yes," Andy replied. Elzy didn't speak.

"Help me figure out what happened with my great-grandmother. I don't have to leave right away—it's such a long trip that an extra week or two won't make any difference. And I want to know. I might not have another chance. And if....If I do end up having to stay out there, I want to be able to embrace it. I want to *be* home. And that's never going to happen unless I can resolve whatever happened with Rose. I just need to find whatever it is that she lost."

Elzy wanted to say no. She knew what would happen. Her real rival was not some floozy he might meet on the road or some home-town old flame he might decide to rekindle, but the Canadian prairie—the wind in the grass, the scent of horses and of saddle leather, the wideness of the sky. She'd seen him trying to find the sky through the trees here, paddling out to the middle of the pond or looking out over the ocean, a prairie of water....He loved his home as much as she loved hers, only he didn't know it. And if he ever found out, he would never leave it, not permanently. If he reconciled the memory of his great-grandmother and *then* went home, there would be nothing to keep him from finding out. And he wanted her to help him?

She wouldn't. She couldn't. And yet she must because she'd promised—taking advantage of his unresolved issues in order to keep him would not be doing love. Anyway, Andy was already saying yes, and he was the one whose help Kevin really needed. Elzy's refusal would be meaningless, except to piss everybody off.

So she said yes. Of course she did.

Elzy didn't know how long they'd be in Bar Harbor, so she asked

Amarita to come look after the place and Timogen. Amarita didn't have law-enforcement authority, but she could do everything else and do it well. From the ferry deck, Elzy kept looking back and up towards her hills.

"Worried you left the stove on?" asked Andy, dryly.

"I don't want to miss the beginning of blueberry season," she told him. He smiled a little ruefully, perhaps recognizing his own evasiveness. Kevin said nothing.

The ferry crossed the mouth of Somes Sound and put in for a few minutes at Northwest Harbor, then pushed out into open water bound for Seal Harbor and then Bar Harbor after that. Once a day a ferry stopped at the largest of the Cranberry Islands, but Elzy had made sure to board one that wouldn't. She didn't want to be too late getting into town.

"There used to be a great little book-store in that town," said Andy, of Seal Harbor.

"I know. You told me," Elzy replied. She knew he could not help seeing the past wherever he went.

A young woman who had boarded at Seal Harbor spotted Kevin and must have thought him cute because she plopped herself down next to him and started chatting him up. He responded politely, but then warmed to the conversation, and was soon compulsively telling his new friend all about his father and the recent tragedy. The young woman nodded and murmured sympathetically, obviously trapped. Elzy smirked, thinking that some people get what they have coming.

"Man, I talk too much," said Kevin to Elzy, when they got off the ferry and left the young woman behind.

"You have to talk to somebody," Elzy told him. "You're not talking to me, so what do you expect?"

"I expect to not act like an idiot."

"All grief-stricken people are idiots." But she meant it fondly.

The air at the town dock was hot, hard, and heavy, smelling of pitch and of the potatoes frying at a nearby food cart. There was little scent of the sea, since the tide, pulled up to its extreme by the new moon just past, covered the odoriferous intertidal zone. Gulls sat on the dock pylons, heads hunched into their shoulders, eyes half-shut against the sun. All colors were very bright—the green of the lawns and trees, the blue and white of the sky, the yellow-white sparkle off the green and blue water of the bay. Elzy looked at Kevin, the way he glanced around everywhere but at her, the way the sweat collected under the straps of his knapsack and darkened his shirt there. The last time she arrived in Bar Harbor she hadn't yet known he existed. The thought of him leaving hurt.

Bar Harbor marketed on the weekends, so there were crowds to push through on the way to the county land office where Elzy could drop off her contribution and lighten her pack. Then they bought bread and cheese and a jar of honey, so they wouldn't be entirely dependent on restaurants during their visit. Elzy's favorite inn had no vacancy, so they got two private rooms at a hostel. They reconvened in a nearby bar over a basket of sweet-potato fries.

"OK, I'm brain-dead these days," Kevin admitted. "Can somebody tell me where are?"

"Bar Harbor, Maine," Andy replied.

"Dude, anyone ever tell you nobody likes a smart-ass?"

"Yes, but never accurately."

Elzy flagged down a server and ordered a glass of sumac tea. The pitcher of beer they'd ordered with the fries wasn't doing it for her. She wanted something sour she could guzzle, the day being so hot. Then she addressed Kevin's question.

"We know your great-grandmother, Rose, left home to marry the family gardener, Chris Stone, an American. We know that by nineteen-forty, they were living in Bar Harbor. Stone died in the war, and by nineteen-fifty, Rose had left Bar Harbor and was probably living somewhere on Long Island, where she met Marks. They married, in Ontario, in nineteen-sixty. We still don't have independent confirmation that Rose was in Bar Harbor in nineteen-forty-seven, nor do we know what she was doing here if she was."

"She's in the nineteen-fifty census in Cove Neck, on Long Island," Andy put in. "I heard from Sam this morning."

"Great," Elzy acknowledged. "So now we're going to go to the library and read--"

"You didn't let me finish," Andy chided, then paused as the waitress arrived with the tea. "Census records don't just record individuals, they also record households. In nineteen-fifty, Rose was living in the household of a woman named Kathleen McCarthy, as an employee. A lot of wealthy people owned property on both Long Island and Mount Desert Island in those decades. It's possible her employer in nineteen-fifty was also her employer in nineteen-forty-seven."

"Kathleen McCarthy?" Elzy said. "That's familiar.... I can't place it."

"OK, but how do we find out?" asked Kevin, a little annoyed. "Do we just grope around until we get lucky?"

"If we need to, yes," admitted Andy. "But if we search fire insurance records for Kathleen McCarthy, they should tell us what property she had on the island, if any, its address, and its layout. I'm willing to bet there was a large garden. You know what Rose probably did for Kathleen, right?"

Kevin looked at him a little stupidly for a second. His brain was still foggy with grief. At last he grinned, realizing.

"She was the gardener!" he exclaimed.

"Bingo. It wasn't unusual back then for women to marry men who had the career they wished they could have—or to find ways to take over that career once they were widowed."

"Or when the men went to war," Elzy added. "Rosie, the Riveter. Rose, the gardener."

"Yes, quite likely."

"So that fire insurance map will show us where Rose's exploding tree was," Kevin concluded. "*If* we can get confirmation that she was the gardener there. And to do *that*, we read that author's research notes."

"Yes."

"Let's hit the library."

They finished their drinks and their fries and argued amicably over who would pay the bill (Andy won and paid). But they found the library was about to close.

"I thought they stayed open until eight!" Elzy complained.

"Not on Saturdays," Kevin said, tapping on the sign on the door. They went in and spoke to the librarians about their project, hoping to at least locate the resources they expected to use.

"Rose Stone?" one of the librarians said. "That's familiar. Hang on." He tapped something into his computer and grinned. "Yes, here. Her book. You want to check it out?"

"She wrote a book?" said Andy.

"I can check it out?" Kevin exclaimed, eager. The librarian grinned.

It was very much an antique, its pages faintly yellowed and smelling of caramel and dust, and though it had been professionally-bound, something about it looked amateurish.

"It's signed," Kevin commented. "'To the librarians—thanks for all the help!' Well, that's why it's here but never came up on our searches. They probably only printed fifty copies."

"Let me see it," Andy asked. He read the title aloud. "'The Phoenix Garden or The Entwife's Reconciliation.' Interesting."

"Why?" asked Elzy. The librarian was still hovering around, curious.

"*Entwife* is a Tolkein reference. Ents were the shepherds of wild trees. Entwives, the female ents, were into gardening. They couldn't live together anymore. The entwives left. An entwife's reconciliation—could mean gardening for wildlife habitat value? Saul had a friend who studied it—there's been some really cool work, but none of it as old as," he checked the copyright date, "nineteen-fifty six. Huh. That's only two years after Lord of the Rings was published."

"Phoenix garden—the garden reborn after burning," Elzy commented.

Kevin buried his nose in the book while the others oriented themselves to the library. When the librarian gently kicked them all out, Kevin kept reading.

"Good book?" Andy asked.

"Um, what? Yeah, it's good, I guess."

Elzy took Kevin's arm and suggested he look where he was going and not fall and break his nose. "Though you might look pretty handsome with a broken nose," she added.

He laughed and put the book in his day-pack.

That night, over pizza, Kevin read aloud passages from his great-grandmother's book. It was mostly a guide for how to design and plant gardens for maximum habitat value—not that Rose used the phrase. Instead, she explained that "if we men and women can have our cottages and camps out in the forest, certainly we can grant our animal neighbors space to come visit in our world? And they will come—if we can make places hospitable for them." She provided native species lists, range maps, notes on habitat value, and extensive notes on design, layout, how to source plants, how to care for them, and how to find more information.

But there were little drawings, cartoon-like and whimsical, mostly of plants and animals, but a few showed a man—always the same man, young-looking, with a floppy hat and a shovel or a pair of gardening shears, drawn with a great, amused fondness. There were snippets of poetry, mostly sentimental doggerel, but suggesting a keen awareness of plant and animal interactions and the growth requirements of various plants. There was a moving passage on the friendship possible between a person and a tree—she never came out and said she was the person, but her description of the joy of sitting among the branches of a field-grown white oak and reading there were too detailed to be made-up.

"The tree that exploded," Kevin guessed.

In the introduction she rather obliquely referred to not one garden but two. The second one seemed to be somewhere on Long Island, but she said that in planting it she had drawn from what she had learned somewhere else, a garden whose location she never gave except to say it was farther north on another island. There was something dreamlike in her mention of it. She wrote of her hope that by planting again and by writing about it for others she could make that first lost garden "rise, phoenix-like, from the ashes of memory."

She dedicated the book to "Chris, my favorite gardener," and to Beatrix Farrand.

"Who's Farrand?" asked Kevin. Andy and Elzy glanced at each other. Andy nodded fractionally, yielding the floor.

"Oh, she's cool," Elzy exclaimed. "She was one of the first landscape architects to really get into using native plants and naturalistic styles. She had projects all over, but she lived and taught here, on Mount Desert Island. One of her biggest projects—in the nineteen-thirties, she landscaped the verges of the carriage roads, around the bridges, the whole system. I've seen copies of her notes and plans, she used plants like paint, arranging everything so it would look just right, but it was all natural-*looking,* so you'd see it and never know it was all on purpose. There are gardens of hers that still exist, but that's not one of them—the carriage road plantings mostly burned in the fire. So she and Rose had that in common, too.... But Rose wasn't just using native plants to *look* natural, was she? She wanted them to *act naturally.* She was trying to create functional habitat. But you just said that wasn't a thing back then?" She looked to Andy.

"It wasn't," he replied. "Except obviously it was." He gestured towards Rose's book. "Some of the ideas were in the air. Wilderness conservation was definitely a thing. *Sand County Almanac* was published in nineteen-fifty—no, nineteen-*forty* nine, right after Leopold died. She could have read it. Heh. She was thinking like an island." An Aldo Leopold paraphrase, as Elzy knew but Kevin did not.

"We're building a picture of Rose's life," Elzy commented. "When her book was published, *Lord of the Rings* was new. Ecology was, what, an established scientific idea but only starting to sort of trickle out into general consciousness? What else?"

"The Montgomery bus boycott was in the news," Andy supplied.

"Yeah. And what's-his-name, Emmet Till, he was...."

"Murdered the year before, yes. And his killers were acquitted."

"Acquitted because the victim had skin like mine...." Elzy looked uneasily at her brown hand a moment. She glanced over at Andy again, wondering if he remembered how little she'd known about American history when they first met. She'd made a point of learning certain things since then. She returned, with an effort, to the subject. "And the nineteen forty-seven fire was only nine years earlier."

"I bet that seemed like a long time," said Kevin.

"And not long at all," added Elzy.

"There are times," said Andy, "that separate the world into *before* and *after*. For people on Mount Desert Island, that October in nineteen forty-seven was one of them."

"Like February, thirty-five years ago," said Elzy, "for the whole world." Andy nodded. After a moment, Kevin nodded too. He hadn't been alive, yet, but he knew—February was the month of collapse.

"Like this month, for me," he said.

Elzy rubbed his shoulder and tried to make gesture seem natural. He sighed.

"Bifurcation events," she said, before realizing she ought to have said something sympathetic instead. Kevin looked at her blankly, but Andy frowned, interested, thinking.

"Well, metaphorically, yes," he concluded.

"No, literally," Elzy replied. Andy stiffened ever so slightly at her disagreement. To Kevin, she explained "bifurcation events are when a complex system—like, you know, me or you, or an ecosystem, or the atmosphere or something—switches from one mode of behavior to another. The switches aren't predictable from prior conditions."

"So, like, a fancy term for 'life is surprising,'" Kevin concluded, sounding irritated.

"Well, no," Andy told him. "It's more specific than that. Bifurcation events aren't random, just unpredictable." The paradox made one corner of his mouth quirk up. "They're not something that happens *to* a system, either. They're an inherent part of a system's development or an *active response* to outside stimulus. Something that was stable one way becomes stable in a different way."

'Exactly!' exclaimed Elzy. "That's why it's not a metaphor. It's what we all do."

"Well...."

Kevin rolled his eyes and went back to reading. Sometime later, his companions surfaced from their arcane digression and noticed him again.

"Your pizza's getting cold," Elzy remarked, teasing.

Kevin chuckled, realizing he had gotten distracted from eating. He looked at his book.

"It's weird," he said, "my family's smaller now, but it's larger, too. My great-grandmother is real. She was a real person. I read this and...she's family. I guess that's why I can't stop reading. Her life doesn't seem like it was that long ago."

"It wasn't, really," said Andy. "When I first started coming here, in grad school, there were people on the island who still remembered the fire. I met a woman bird-watching in Seawall Campground who told me her father went to fight it. She remembered looking up and seeing the sky to the east glowing red. Almost the whole eastern half of the island was on fire that night."

"The night the tree exploded," said Kevin.

The next morning, Andy and Kevin started on the collection of research notes, while Elzy checked digitized, but not searchable, insurance records for Kathleen McCarthy. She didn't find anything. After an hour or so, she and Andy both left to teach at the market. When they returned, Kevin caught both of them up on his lack of progress. After lunch, they all went back to reading. This time, Kevin, tired of finding only pertinent negatives, helped Elzy, leaving Andy to work alone.

An hour later, Andy appeared behind them.

"I found her," he half-whispered excitedly. Kevin and Elzy jumped. Andy tried not to grin and failed. He showed them a passage in a typed transcript of an interview. The paper was very old, very yellow, and stained on the corner by ancient, spilled coffee. The interviewee, a firefighter, was talking about a friend of his, another firefighter.

Chubby couldn't find his girl. She lived and worked up at Cranberry Ledge, and he'd promised to go get her if it came to that, but by the time the evacuation blew, Cranberry was gone. He thought she might have come into town on her own, but she wasn't there, and we had to get back to the line. I said maybe they got out before the road was cut off. The next day, I went with him to Trenton and asked around. A lot of people had gone there. You could see furniture and things, stuff people had taken with them when they left, all along the sides of the roads. We found some of the others who'd come from Cranberry, but they said Chubby's girl hadn't gotten out with them. You could tell they thought she'd burned, and Chubby didn't know what to think. I told him we'd just keep looking. Eventually, she turned up in the hospital in Ellsworth. She'd been in the fire, alright, something about a tree falling and blocking her way, but she'd grabbed a cotton blanket and jumped in the pond, kept that blanket wet with cold water. When the fire front passed, she walked out to the road. Some smart, that girl."

"Cranberry Ledge?" Elzy exclaimed. "But Kathleen McCarthy didn't own it! I just read that one! That was…Marsh or Mars or something."

"March?" asked Kevin. "Was it March?"

"I don't know, I've read ten zillion names today. I'll look it up again." And she did. It was David March.

"That's her brother."

"What?"

"David March was Kathleen McCarthy's brother. This morning, I got tired of finding nothing, so I looked up Kathleen McCarthy in the 1940 census on Long Island. She was a widow living with her brother, David March. I was going to look up *his* name in the insurance records, but I didn't know how, and by the time you got back I just forgot. I'd forget my butt if it wasn't attached, honestly. I'm telling you, I can't think straight."

"At least you have an excuse," Elzy said. "I just remembered—why the name Kathleen McCarthy is familiar." Kevin and Andy both looked at her. "*She's* in that book about the fire. There are so many names in that thing, and I was really only paying attention to see if Rose came up. But McCarthy was in there. I think there was a whole, long story about her. I forget the name of her house—it *could* have been Cranberry Ledge. I'm such an idiot."

"I didn't remember, either," Andy admitted. "I remember Cranberry Ledge, but not the name of the person who owned it."

"The library's gotta have a copy," Elzy said, half to herself, and ran off to re-read the relevant chapters. The others moved outside to a picnic table to wait, and twenty minutes later, she found them there.

"I am officially an idiot," Elzy announced. "Rose *is* in here, she's just mentioned only once and only as Mrs. Stone, no first name. When I read the book before, I thought we were looking for Marks or Spacey."

"She's there?" Kevin asked. He wasn't interested in Elzy's shortcomings. "Where was she? What was she doing?"

"She *was* the gardener at Cranberry. But she worked for McCarthy—David March owned the place but almost never went there. Anyway, the short version is that when they evacuated the house, Rose wanted a minute to say goodbye to the garden, so the others drove to the foot of the driveway and waited, but she never came out. They thought she was dead and left. Later, she turned up at a hospital in Ellsworth. She had been trapped by a falling tree, so she hid in an artificial pond. The fire went over her."

"Wow," pronounced Kevin. "That's intense."

"That would certainly explain her trauma," Andy agreed.

"What's the long version?" asked Kevin, eager.

"Well, you could read the book...."

"No, I mean...how does it all fit together? Everything we've found? I'm just all jumbled up with details right now, and I'm still not really thinking straight. I want to hear the story."

"OK, let me think a minute."

And so Elzy told Kevin about how Mount Desert Island was once just fishing villages and loggers, just like the rest of Maine, before being discovered by painters of the Hudson Valley School in the middle of the nineteenth century. They would rent spare bedrooms from families and spend their days painting the scenery. Soon, it became fashionable for all sorts of people to come "rusticate" on the island, first at Southwest Harbor, where Flamingo Town would someday be, then at Bar Harbor, to hike and to hunt and to party. Soon, hotels started springing up, and over several decades Bar Harbor developed into a resort town where the super wealthy would spend their summers. Their fondness and enthusiasm for the island created a network of some of the best-constructed hiking trails in North America and, later, Acadia National Park.

The invention of the automobile and other changes began to erode the "scene" in the early twentieth century, but the outskirts of Bar Harbor still boasted the enormous summer "cottages." Kathleen McCarthy was not super-wealthy, but the Cranberry Ledge property she managed and loved, though modest, was acknowledged one of the *nicest* summer homes on the island. How or when Christopher Stone and his young bride came to work at Cranberry seemed lost to history, just as no one living could say whose idea it was, Kathleen's or Chris' or Rose's, to redesign the garden. But somewhere along the line, Rose took charge, having come under the twin influences of Beatrix Farrand and wildlife conservationists such as Aldo Leopold. At Cranberry Ledge, Rose Stone planned and planted the first, perhaps imperfectly realized, version of a garden concept sixty or seventy years ahead of its time. And there she made friends with a tree, a field-grown white oak.

Elzy told Kevin about how the spring of 1947 was abnormally warm and wet, how plants across Maine responded by growing strong and well, but by autumn, all that lush growth was drying up in the worst drought in the state in thirty years. The fire wardens knew what was coming, but the farmers were preoccupied trying to save their crops and their animals, while town-folk simply enjoyed the sunny weather. Maine hadn't had a really big fire in about a hundred and twenty years. Nobody put in place any sort of fire bans. Nobody said you can't smoke cigarettes and drop your matches in the woods. And everybody smoked back then. By the third week of October, small fires were springing up across the state. And some of those small fires quickly grew very large.

"The Mount Desert Island fire began in a cranberry bog north of Somes Sound," she explained. "That was Friday afternoon, October seventeenth. By midnight, they got the fire contained, but it smoldered until early Tuesday morning, when the wind picked up, and the fire jumped the line. By ten-thirty that morning, every fire company on the island, plus a convoy from Bangor, was on the job, but the fire was crowning, headed east, and considered probably unstoppable."

Much of the story Elzy told was material she'd picked up over the years, either for one or another of her talks about the island, or out of simple curiosity about her home. History in general still wasn't her strong suit, but the specific history of Mount Desert Island had become almost as familiar to her as its plants and animals. But she wove into this material everything she'd learned over the past few weeks about the fire and about Kevin's family. He listened, entranced. Andy, who knew most of the tale already but not all of it, leaned forward, attentive, smiling slightly.

Elzy told them about the fire, the alarms and reprieves and alarms again as the wind changed this way and that, but always Mrs. McCarthy knew, and so Rose Stone must also have known, that if the fire came to-wards Bar Harbor, Cranberry Ledge would be the first house in town to burn.

She told them about the huge column of smoke as the fire crested McFarland Hill late Tuesday afternoon, how from Great Hill, to its east, just above Cranberry Ledge, the setting sun shining through the writhing smoke and fire must have looked like even greater flames, the onrushing and beautiful end of everything. She told them about how that night the fire ate the electrical transformer, plunging the whole island into darkness, except where the fire burned. How Wednesday it looked like Bar Harbor might be spared but nobody in town trusted that, and everybody spent the day packing and making plans. How, as dramatic and fast-paced as the story was, the actual experiences of the islanders that day, in Bar Harbor, in Somesville, in Hull's Cove, all the threatened places, were dominated by the detailed, the prosaic, the slow—what to do with a favorite vase, how to save the furniture, where to put the car, and, above all, where to go if the fire came and how to get there.

And she told them about the gale-force winds of Thursday, October twenty-third, the day fires across Maine leaped over the land, destroying whole communities, whole towns, and how on Mount Desert Island it looked as though Hull's Cove would be lost as the wind-driven fire focused on it, as some said, like a blow-torch.

But then the wind stopped. Utterly stopped. And the fire stopped, too, for five long seconds. Then the wind came back as strong or stronger than before, but from the other direction. Now what had been the side of the blaze, a relatively safe place for firefighters to work trying to prevent lateral spread, suddenly became the front. Men had to run for their lives.

"A couple guys ran a mile to Duck Brook Bridge," Elzy said. "You know, one of the bridges for the carriage roads? It's narrow and low down under there, and the fire went by above them, roaring and spraying sparks. They survived. But one of Farrand's plantings was there, too. Incinerated, I'm guessing. Another gone garden. All these stories are connected."

She told them about how everyone had known from early afternoon on that the wind would shift, so when Mrs. McCarthy, in town at the post-office while her friends and servants packed, saw dry leaves go danc-ing suddenly down the street around three PM, she knew what it meant. And she drove home, towards the fire, to get her people out.

She couldn't save her gardener.

Her gardener saved herself, as Elzy explained.

Just after four, the final evacuation siren blew for Bar Harbor. The road north to Hull's Cove was cut off, so evacuees went south then west towards Somesville. Just before five, that route, too, was cut by fire. Twenty-five hundred people were trapped in Bar Harbor as night came on, the temperature dropped, and the fire swept into town, eating its way down Millionaire's Row through the houses and hotels of the richest people in the world.

But the wind was pushing the fire south. The spread east into town was lateral, slower. Firefighters made their stand in the streets, Rose's boyfriend, Chubby, among them, while a call went out on the one remaining phone line out of town, the one to Southwest Harbor, to the Coast Guard station there, which relayed the call to Rockland, Portland, and Boston, the call for boats.

Twenty-five hundred people stood at the municipal pier, their backs to the sea, watching the fire come in, knowing that if the oil tanks just seven hundred feet from the pier caught, they would all die.

But none of them did.

There were fatalities on the island, but none on the pier that night. The firefighters stopped the advance and saved the center of town. Four hundred people were evacuated by boat before the road north opened up again, around 9 pm, though the bluffs on either side of the road were still afire. One of those fleeing vehicles, there was no record of which one, picked up a hitch-hiker. She was dangerously hypothermic, but with burned feet and singed hair and clothing from running through the still-smoldering forest. She was taken to the hospital in Ellsworth, where she was found the next day by Kathleen McCarthy. The fire never seriously threatened any of the island's other towns. Rain, a few days later, dampened it, but it was November before it finally went out.

"McCarthy never went back to Bar Harbor," Elzy said. "Cranberry Ledge wasn't rebuilt. None of the grand vacation homes and hotels were. Bar Harbor recovered, but as a tourist town for middle-class vacationers—a totally different scene. Nothing was ever the same. As far as we know, Rose Stone never went back, either. We know she never talked about it. She went with McCarthy to Long Island and worked for her as lead gardener and landscape designer there for almost fifteen years, until she married again and went back to Kingston. But she never really recovered. When her mind started to go in extreme old age, that's where it went, back to Mount Desert Island. She was finally institutionalized because she kept trying to get in cars and drive. She was trying to get away from the fire."

Silence.

Noises, ordinary street noises. A hot, summer afternoon. Bar Harbor of the present day. No cars, no fires. Daylight. Normality.

"Wow," said Kevin, his face streaked with tears. "That is *intense*."

"Nicely told," exclaimed Andy.

Elzy smiled, a little self-conscious. She'd fallen into her story far more than she'd expected to.

"Where is Cranberry Ledge?" Kevin said, suddenly. "I have to go there."

Chapter 9: The Phoenix Garden

They had an address, but the road, Cleffstone, had no houses any-more—any built after the fire had been abandoned after the pandemic and recycled. There was no way to tell where along the road a given house number might have been.

They discussed various possibilities and options. Maybe maps at the Historical Society might show Cranberry Ledge? Maybe a pre-pandemic street map could allow them to orient themselves and figure out where the missing address ought to be? Finally, Kevin spoke up.

"Let's just walk Cleffstone," he said. "Bar Harbor is not that big."

So they did.

It looked like a typical rural lane, with oak forest on one side and a savanna of cow pasture on the other. The forest looked very lush and wild. For anybody but a serious natural history geek or ecologist, it would have been hard to imagine any buildings ever having been there. On the pasture side, a few weedy black-topped driveways and broken hints of foundations remained, ruins, not from the fire but from the post-pandemic collapse. Kevin looked at the former house-sites as he walked, distracted by a strange double-vision. Abandoned houses or their remnants were as common in the modern world as occupied ones, but somehow he'd never realized before that these were *homes,* places people had called theirs and lost, one way or another. He trailed a little behind, thinking about vanished families, while the other two peered into the woods, searching for ruined walls, overgrown driveways, any kind of sign. But young trees, shrubs, and low branches, all taking advantage of the light along the edge of the forest, formed a kind of green skin, obscuring the interior. He had a hard time believing they would find anything.

"You passed it," said Andy.

"What? That's a driveway?" exclaimed Elzy, retracing her steps a few paces to stand near Andy. Kevin joined them without speaking. He didn't see the driveway, either.

"Sure. Look a little farther in."

"What about those rocks? You couldn't get a car in through that."

"I'm betting they moved the rocks there after the fire so no one would drive in."

"Oh. Right. Makes sense. Oh, you're right—this is a driveway!" Elzy had stepped into the woods. Kevin followed her, and once he got through the green "skin," he saw what she'd seen—a flat track, covered by fallen leaves, interrupted here and there by sticks and branches, but overall still quite plain. It ran off far back into the woods, up the side of the hill, curving to the right to keep its grade gentle. They all followed the track, Andy and Elzy pointing out and discussing their discoveries while Kevin followed, silent, the non-expert, not seeing much of anything until it was literally pointed out to him. He learned everything he could.

Thanks to Elzy's tutelage, he could recognize most of the trees, at least in a general way. Most were oaks, something in the red oak group—their leaves had pointy tips. There were lots of red maples, too, some big white pines, and a few smaller spruces. The ground was rocky and scattered with bleached white tree stumps, badly eroded by time but still recognizable, all cut off at about waist-height. A bird, possibly a red-eyed vireo, he wasn't sure, sang. The setting seemed peaceful. Cheerful. Very green and lively. Surely, no nightmare could have happened here? Kevin knew better intellectually, of course, but he found it difficult to believe viscerally. He could smell no smoke, see no charcoal, feel no damage.

What if we're in the wrong place? he thought. *What if we've got it all wrong and we have to start over from the beginning?*

"Ork! Ork!" cried a raven nearby, the sound that in a crow would have been caw. "Ork!" the bird repeated, its grunting, grating cry sounding almost musical this time. The humans all turned to look, and Kevin saw the bird, a great, black, hulking thing sitting on a low, broken-off dead spruce branch, looking at him. "Ork! Ork! Ork!" it said yet again, insistent, then flew, its great wings beating audibly, rowing itself hugely through the dense trees. And then Kevin saw the stone foundation.

It was small, no more than twenty feet on a side, a low stone wall that turned and turned and turned and turned and met itself, enclosing a square.

"That's her cottage, isn't it?" Kevin asked. He remembered the gardener's house at the foot of the long driveway from Elzy's story. All the details matched. "The gardener's cottage," he stammered. "She lived here."

"'Cottage' means something rather larger, hereabouts," said Andy, with a quirk of a smile.

"Whatever."

"This driveway's still graveled," observed Elzy, toeing gray pea-gravel half-buried by duff.

"Driveway's long, that matches the book. The house must be pretty high up," added Andy.

"What's that rock wall?"

"Must be some kind of flood control—see how the water comes down here? It's rutted out the road." No water flowed today, but the leaves had darkened along a dip in the ground.

"The drive is stone-lined."

"Well, of course it is."

"Look at all these multi-trunked oaks and maples! Stump-sprouted after the fire….This was forested."

"And those cut stumps—Rockefeller's crews were here cleaning up."

"But they left the stumps so tall! I'd have low-stumped them."

"Low-stumping wasn't common then."

"Is it my imagination, or were the pre-fire trees all about the same size? An even-aged stand? You can't plow here, clearly, so was it an old pasture, grown into forest?"

"Quite possibly. Most of the island was cleared at one point."

"Speaking of which, where was the garden? If this was all forested, what was she growing?"

"Well, up here was all open. See? No multi-trunked trees, and all the white pines seeded in here. There are none over there." Andy waved vaguely, indicating up- and then down-slope, respectively.

"I guess it is flatter, fewer rocks—except what's that? It's a channel, a stone-lined channel. That's not natural."

"No, that's intentional. Somebody did an awful lot of work."

"But why? Here's another one. How was there this much water here? It slopes down again over there."

"I've found your garden—or an escapee from your garden anyway."

"Ugh, what are all these things! They're not native."

"Lily-of-the-valley."

The whole top of the site, a great bench of flattish ground, was covered ankle-deep in the low, spreading plants, large, oval leaves and thin stalks bearing still-unripe berries. They looked out of place, yet defined the place, greening the ruin oddly.

For there *was* a ruin. Here on this flat, clearly artificial bench of land, the driveway hung a right and passed across the back of a low, undramatic, stone terrace. And inside that terrace, dominating it, lay the cellar hole.

Kevin walked around near the top of the driveway, getting the lay of the land.

He hadn't looked at a contour map, and it was hard to see far through the trees, but the hill seemed to become steeper and taller towards its north end. The house had stood near that end, just below the crest, about a hundred feet (or, for Kevin, about thirty meters) above Cleffstone Road, with commanding views on two sides. The driveway had to come in from the side to take advantage of a longer, less steep, part of the hill.

A natural drainage crinkled the hillside between the house and the driveway—the driveway crossed the drainage as it turned right towards the house, the culvert beneath it disguised artfully by naturalistic arrangements of native stone. Both the top of the driveway and the side of the terrace were held up by retaining walls of rough stone, exaggerating the small gully of the drainage between them. In that gully lay various piles and lines of stone that Kevin, with an eye for construction, soon realized would have caught and retained water coming off the hill. Elzy noticed them, too.

"Mini-wetland gardens?" she suggested.

The largest of the structures seemed not to depend on runoff, though—it had pipes and a cement lining and was big enough to contain a small pool, though cracks in the lining must long since have drained it. It was roughly circular, its artificial nature camouflaged by an outer rim of rocks, and about four and a half meters in its inside diameter. Kevin and Elzy climbed down and examined the structure together, finding that it had an inner circle some two and a half meters across that was quite deep, though exactly how deep was difficult to say because the bottom was piled up with rotting leaves and needles and other detritus. The outer part of the pool was shallower, probably not more than a meter.

"Fish-pond," Elzy judged. "And bird-feeder. A heron could hunt in the shallow bit. Deep water's a refuge from ice, too." Kevin remembered plans for water-gardens from the book, with areas of different depth for different types of aquatic plants.

Meanwhile, Andy had found that the driveway continued on past the house to a three-sided concrete structure built into the side of the hill. Kevin and Elzy stared at the thing, confused, but Andy, who remembered the days of personal automobiles, recognized the remains of a two-car garage.

"Ha! Bring the car around, Jeeves!" he snarked.

The cellar hole was some fifteen meters long, nine wide, and three deep or so, stone-lined and rectangular, its bottom lumpy with chimney bricks, other debris, and drifts of newly-developed soil and duff, its edge complicated by cut-outs for half-sunk windows. A massive fireplace and the base of a wide chimney dominated the southern half of the structure. Elzy had mentioned that Mrs. McCarthy had sat alone by her lit fireplace on her last night in the house, her way of saying goodbye to her home, but surely that fireplace had not been in the basement? Perhaps this one had something to do with heating or cooking? Kevin had no clear idea of how wealthy Americans over a century ago lived. What he did have was a strong understanding of all the different ways things could be built and had been built, and he suspected the house had been an example of the Arts and Crafts movement, perhaps made during the nineteen-twenties in the last hurrah of mansion construction on the island. The lack of any remnants of the upper part of the house suggested an all-wood design.

Andy stood, somewhat precariously, on the crumbling top of the cellar wall, looking out over a row of short stone columns parallel with the front wall of the cellar and of the same height.

"You can see whoever comes up the driveway from this porch," he remarked. "Oh, yeah, that's the point. It's a commanding view." He climbed around to the far north side and looked out over another set of short columns. "And this, *this,* is why this house is here. Without the trees in the way, you could see all the way to Hull's Cove. You'd have a view of the water."

Andy and Elzy clambered around exploring, slipping on loose mortar and warning each other of animal holes, deducing the architecture of the structure. Looking at the lay of the land and discussing wind direction on that fateful Thursday, they determined how, exactly, the fire had entered the site. Andy, who had spent part of his career in Arizona and understood fire behavior fairly well, decided that the flames had come, not straight down-slope, but from the north and west, sweeping around the contour of the hill and coming in and down at an angle.

"That puts your fish-pond in the lee of the foundation-wall," he explained. "That would protect it, provided none of the burning timbers fell this way. On the other hand, the rock wall would retain and radiate heat. It would depend. But she could have survived there, since this was all open." He went on talking about fire behavior. Kevin listened carefully, learning whatever his companions had to teach, while he explored what had once been the gardens, his great-grandmother's gardens.

He could see what Andy meant about the pine-dominated half-hectare around the house—it was clearly different than the surrounding forest. He imagined it mostly in grass. The rock structures were the planted beds, the mini-wetlands and water-gardens below, in the drainage, the upland plant-ings above, on artificial ledges and cliffs and in soil held in place by walls and piles of lichen-covered stone. A few blueberry bushes, huckleberries, and fragrant sweet-fern plants survived among the rocks, though the shade of the trees wasn't doing them any favors. Whether they had, like the pines, seeded in after the fire or if they, like the lily-of-the-valley, descended from survivors from the garden, Kevin could not say. He hoped the latter. Some of the blueberries were ripe, so he ate them, hoping that the afterlife existed because he really wanted his great-grandmother to be able to see this.

He looked around, seeing more plants out of place.

A large flower spike, something like a cross between a mullein plant and a hollyhock, bloomed yellow from debris drifted against the inside of the cellar wall. A large flowering dogwood—that is, a dogwood of the species called *flowering*, not one in flower at the moment—grew in a sunny spot down in the cellar hole. It wasn't native, even Kevin knew that, but it was a common ornamental. Birds could have carried the seeds, but then why hadn't more of those seeds grown in these woods?

"They like rich soil," Andy explained, noticing Kevin staring. "I guess the ash from the house must be what it needs."

The tree must be lovely when it flowers, Kevin thought. *All white against the surrounding green, alive inside the old ruin.* By an effort of will he visualized it, and then, looking around once again, he visualized the gardens, the house, the open places, the shrubs and trees, the whole aesthetic that he knew from the book that his great-grandmother made. The large open area would not have been lawn, it would have been meadow. Native grasses of a dozen different kinds and twenty or thirty species of wildflower, though only a few would be flowering at any given time. In October, what, it would be the fading stalks of yellow goldenrod and the blue and white of asters? There would probably have been curving, winding footpaths mowed through the tall grasses for human convenience, but also used by deer and snowshoe hares. Interrupting and encroaching upon the meadow would be those rock gardens, large and small, round and long, the ones built up by added rock difficult to distinguish from those on natural slopes and promontories with paths cut into the earth and stabilized with stone, the gardens grading almost imperceptibly into the surrounding forests.

What were in those beds, besides blueberries and lily-of-the-valley?

Purple-flowered rhodora, surely, and also white-flowering Labrador tea, huckleberry, and sheep laurel (purple again), each arranged so that as one after another bloomed and faded the whole remained visually balanced and lovely. Snowberry, crowberry, mountain cranberry, and crow broom must have crept like green throw-rugs over the stones that made up the bones of this place, and three-toothed cinquefoil and black chokeberry sprouted from the soil caught in the deliberately incompletely-mortared joints between the stones. Multiple species of arching fern fronds, crouching juniper bushes, dark-leaved witherod, young northern white cedars with their flat sprays of aromatic foliage, all provided contrast and enriched the visual texture of the whole. Small, slim shad trees provided color (white flowers against wine-red spring foliage) at the beginning of the growing season, while young sugar maples did the same at the end. Rose had written extensively about the importance of painting with plants not only in space but also in time—and for multiple audiences, for the human eye and also for the needs of mammals, birds, and insects, so they would have food, cover, and places to raise their young throughout the year. The multiple water-features, mostly small, shallow pools but also winding, intermittent streams, accommodated frogs, toads, salamanders, newts, turtles, and the nymphs of dragonflies. The gardener, Rose, painted with animals as well as plants, in sound as well as in color, aiming for frogsong in May, fireflies in June, Monarch butterflies in July, deer gamboling through hoarfrosted grasses as autumn came on.

From that house you could see all of it. From that brooding, simple, yet grand wooden structure with a stone foundation, brick chimneys, and multiple porches, you could look out over the water gardens and the rock gardens and the deer-haunted meadows, look deep into the surrounding forest that largely screened the road from view, look out across the green and sloping land to the northeast out to the blue and shining sea.

Only the land wasn't green today, not *all* green. It was orange and yellow and brown and winter-gray, the bare or autumnal deciduous trees peeking through, scattered among, the dark pines and spruces, because it was October. It *is* October. It is 1947. It is Thursday, between three and four in the afternoon.

Half a dozen people are carrying armloads of things out of the house and packing them in a large station wagon. The wind has just changed, they can hear it, a rising gale out of the north, and they know what it means, yet now they stand irresolute, each frozen in place by a different set of uncertainties. They can't all fit in the already-loaded vehicle. To drive away to safety, they need Mrs. McCarthy to come back. She went to the post office to mail out a box of her most precious things. She's not back yet, and anyway, not everything the people had meant to take has been loaded. Should they abandon their employer's things and run? What about their own things? What about the house and the gardens and the woods, their own attachments and loyalties? Is anywhere going to be safe? Already they can smell the fire on the wind.

Gravel sprays as another car, an altogether nicer one, tears up the driveway, turns around in front of the garage, comes back, and brakes hard behind the house.

"Drop everything! Let's go!" shouts Kathleen McCarthy before she's all the way out of her car. "Come on!"

"Dot won't come," says Mr. Stevens, coming out of the house. He and his wife are the only two in the group who don't work for Mrs. McCarthy but are instead her dear friends. Dot is the maid. She is very young and doesn't think clearly when she's frightened. She has just run back into the house. Plainly, Mr. Stevens wants to be gallant and go in after her. There is no time.

"Augh!" cries Mrs. McCarthy, exasperated. "*You* make sure everybody gets into the cars. *I'll* go get Dot." And she runs into the house. The others finish loading whatever they're carrying, but a few things don't fit and must stay. The people get in, Mr. Stevens at the wheel of one car, the other's driver's seat empty. But one woman, her arms full of botany texts and notebooks, still hasn't gotten in. The others are calling to her, but she ignores them.

She looks around wildly—the trees! The shrubs! The sitting areas mowed into the grass, each one with its own wooden benches and tables, like favorite rooms! The fish, the poor little fish! The wind is carrying sparks now. Thick smoke, the column of it unbelievably huge seen this close, leans up over the house and then blots out the sun. The others call again. She's not listening. Rose Stone stares in longing horror at her gardens, the closest thing to a child she and her dead husband will ever share.

Mrs. McCarthy comes out of the house, pulling the weeping Dot by the hand. She shoves the girl into the car and the care of Mr. and Mrs. Stevens, who will make sure she doesn't get out again. Rose dumps her books into the foot-well of the front passenger seat of the other car as Mrs. McCarthy jumps in behind the wheel.

"I can't go," Rose tells her employer, stammering but decisive. "I, I, need a minute. Chris's garden…. I'll meet you at the foot of the driveway." The two women look at each other. They are not of the same generation, and despite Rose's moneyed upbringing, they are not now of the same social class. And yet they are alike.

"Hurry," Mrs. McCarthy tells her. "We'll wait as long as we can." Rose shuts the door and the cars speed off.

She looks around one last time and the roar of the coming fire fills her ears. It has crested the hill above her and to the immediate north. She has seconds, she knows. Her eyes fall on the white oak, a field-grown tree as out of place and yet as at home here as she is, her vegetative friend. She has always felt safe with him, and she fights an urge to hug the trunk, to climb up into the spreading branches and hide.

The tree explodes.

It was the sparks, the red sparks filling the darkening air, that caught in the debris collected in an upturned scar where a branch came off in a storm two years ago. The fungus feeding on that exposed wood had, against all odds, held a little water through the long drought, and it was that water that flashed to steam and blew the tree apart, cracking it down the middle, opening it like a blooming flower. The clinging, lavender-colored autumn leaves, the drought-crisped twigs, they're all on fire now anyway. The debris, the remains of her oh-so-comforting friend, lie burning across the driveway, blocking her way out.

Is there another way? She looks around. She had expected the fire to come in all at once, like a tidal bore, turning life to flame as surely as a wave turns dry to wet—but that's not what's happening. Rose lives, so the fire can't be here yet, it is still coming, but the air is hot and fast and full of sparks, more and more sparks, and wherever the sparks take hold small fires burn, more of them all the time. The cedar shingles on the roof of the house have already caught. The fire is all around her, and though she cannot see the sky through the black gloom of smoke, everything here at ground level is plain in the hellfire glow—and yet the fire is still coming, still has not arrived, because she can hear it, roaring as it eats whole trees, still coming.

Should she run through the woods aflame and try to make the road? It's two hundred feet horizontally, if that, but the slope is so steep, the ground rocky and thickly vegetated. It would not be a quick or easy run, with more small fires taking hold every second, and if she tripped and fell.... She imagines stumbling out of the woods into that narrow, forest-arched road and the safety of Mrs. McCarthy's car—but she can't see the cars. She runs a little higher up the driveway for a better view. No cars. She ought to be able to see them. The forest trees and the fires and the smoke all complicate the view, of course, but in this gloom the cars' lights must be on, and she sees no lights but the fire. They must have heard the oak explode. The trees along the road are starting to burn, becoming a death-trap, and no one could live up here anymore anyway, they must know that. Except Rose does live. She stumbles a little, sobbing into the back of her hand.

There is no time for self-reflective thought. Chubby, her fireman boyfriend, has taught her some things. She can see where the fire will not be survivable and where it might be. The ground slopes quickly away from the house on the south side, putting the fish-pond in the lee of both the stone foundation of the house, almost ten feet tall there, and of the retaining wall of the driveway. The fish-pond is close enough to the walls for some protection, but far enough not to collect burning debris from the house. The meadow and gardens stretch all around, and though they will burn, they will burn fast and relatively cool. There are no trees here to carry the really hot flames. Her eyes fall on the pile of abandoned possessions—a few toys that had once belonged to Mrs. McCarthy's now-grown son, kept for sentimental purposes until today, a couple of blankets, a thirty-year-old bridesmaid's dress the color of a rhodura flower. Rose grabs the child's baseball bat and a big, soft, cotton blanket, then runs for the fish-pond. No sooner has she gotten away from the house then all its windows explode outward in a shower of crystal winking red in the firelight as the shards fall.

The coldness of the water makes her gasp.

Water, wetness, guarantees no safety, for hot water turns to steam and kills all the faster, but water takes a lot of energy to get hot, it's something to do with physics. If the fish-pond is big enough, if it's deep enough, if the shelter of the rock walls is real enough, the water will not receive enough energy to heat up before the fire front moves on. Until then, she'll need air cool enough to breathe. She wades through the tangles of emergent vegetation, jumps into the deep, waterlily-filled center, and feels her feet come to rest in the soft, nutritive ooze on the bottom. She can just stand with her head above water. She holds the blanket under the surface until it stops bubbling and she knows it is soaked through. Then she doubles the blanket over longways and uses the baseball bat like a tent pole, holding the edges of blanket down under the water with her feet and hands, trapping a pocket of air around her head. The soaked cotton will be air-tight until it dries.

Until it dries. How long will that take? How long will whatever will happen take? Not long. She hopes not long. Because there isn't anything she can do about it anymore. Everything she can do is done.

She can see the glow of the fire through the cotton, hear the hiss of sparks and cinders landing on the water and the wet cloth. She splashes water upwards, hoping it will help. Large branches, or maybe whole trees, fall not far away. She can feel, as much as hear, the thudding through the water, through the ground. The muck at the bottom of the little pond oozes into her wet shoes and numbs her feet. Fish nip at her legs and arms. There is no noise except the roar and hiss and thud of the fire and now the chattering of her teeth. Rose is cold, very cold, though inches away are gasses capable of incinerating her lungs should she only emerge from her tent and breathe.

Have Mrs. McCarthy and the others made it? They must have. They have to have. But where are they now? Rose visualizes where the fire front must be as it races south and, more slowly, spreads east into town. She didn't hear the siren blasts, two sets of seven she'd been expecting, the signal for the final evacuation, but they must have blown, inaudible under the roar of the fire. Everybody must be withdrawing downslope, into town. Chubby had said there would be trucks to take people out from the Athletic Field. That was the plan. But out *how?* The way the fire was going, Bar Harbor must be cut off, all its ways out severed by flames by now but one—the sea. How many people must still be trapped downtown? Two thousand? Three thousand? There aren't enough boats in the harbor to take that many off. Where are they going to get the boats? How fast is the fire moving into town? Will the boats come in time?

Chubby! she cries out in her mind. *Where are you?* The worry, the complex knot of fear, anger, and pride, is familiar, would be familiar to any war widow. She had always believed that allowing her man to face certain danger was just her part of the war effort. She hadn't wept when her husband deployed, never asked for reassurance in her letters to him, never betrayed any indication that she was not as brave as he was. Her bravery had not saved him. Now she just wants her man to get on a boat and get away.

The sound of the fire eases, diminishes, dies away, though the wind still whips through the dead and dying trees. She can no longer see the glow of flames. She doesn't dare come out yet, but soon. Minutes pass. It's getting hard to breathe. Carbon dioxide, her own exhalation, fills her bubble. She is cold, dangerously cold, now, all her muscles stiff and clumsy. She must get out of the water soon, if she's ever going to. She reaches out a hand from under her tent to test the air and finds it merely warm. Safe.

She climbs out, crawling through the heat-wilted aquatic plants, picking her way over the still-hot boulders where the wild irises used to grow. The ground smolders. She's glad of her wet shoes. Fire lingers on some of the trees. The crumpled skeleton of the house, like a giant, broken umbrella, still burns, belching black smoke from the tips of huge flames. Everything is simple, now, no green, no life, just black char, white ash, and red and orange fire. The sun is going down. It's going to get very cold, and she's soaked through. She stands near the foundation wall, the stones radiating like an oven. The heat feels good.

What next? She can't stay here, she'll freeze. She can't walk into Bar Harbor, either, for though she's now behind the fire front, surely the fire still burns. She might be able to make her way north, then east, get to the road to Hull's Cove. The fire came from that direction, and it can't go backwards. Stay in the black, Chubby would say, the black, charred places where the fire has already been and so cannot be again. It's the burned places that are safe. Only the living are vulnerable.

Rose is starting to think she might really survive. Driven no longer by terror, by immediate urgency, she starts to think again, to feel. She feels a great weight of futility. She knows now that anything she sets her heart on can be taken, anything she tries to build or accomplish may be turned to ash. Nothing, ultimately, will survive for long. The fire is *not* over, it can *never* be over, because the thing it has taught her can never be unlearned.

She stands, dripping, lifting her feet alternately so they can't get too hot, shivering uncontrollably now and sobbing in relief, fear, and unending grief. Maybe the wind, and hence the fire, will die down, soon. She's not sure if it matters.

More than anything, what she feels is a sense of betrayal. Nobody stayed to save her. She could save nothing but herself.

"Look at this!" cried a familiar voice, and Kevin snapped back to himself, his own time, his own life. He wasn't cold, it wasn't night, it wasn't autumn, and he wasn't his great-grandmother. The living forest surrounded him. Light. Green summer. A hermit thrush sang. A phoebe sang. In the distance, a robin. "Come here, look at this!" Elzy repeated. He approached her.

She and Andy were standing beside the driveway, before the only multi-trunked deciduous tree among all century-old pines at the top of the site. Kevin recognized it as an oak, but it was not like the other oaks lower down on the hill. They all had dark gray, almost black bark, ridged and rough, but this one had blond bark, checked and cracked. High up, in the upper branches, the bark seemed to loosen up, become shredded, peeling, almost like that of some hickories. It was big, too, each of its two trunks at least fifty centimeters across. A third trunk, much smaller, dead for years and now broken off near its base, lay in pieces, sprouting mushrooms.

"What is it?" he asked.

The other two looked at each other, as if deciding which one of them should say it.

"It's a white oak," Elzy explained. "It's *her* white oak, her tree-friend. It stump-sprouted after the fire. It's still alive."

Chapter 10: Holding On, Letting Go

Kevin barely spoke the rest of the day. What he was thinking and feeling, Elzy could not guess, though he seemed sad or stunned. To her he only said "I thought I'd feel better. I thought I'd understand why she was the way she was. But all I know now is that she didn't have to be that way. Some of the garden survived. She was wrong."

"You could probably claim the property, you know," Elzy told him. "No one else seems to have. And unless some McCarthy shows up, you're the closest thing the place has to an heir."

But he just shook his head.

"That wasn't the point," he said, and did not elaborate.

What Andy was thinking and feeling seemed a mystery to her too—usually she could read him fairly well, at least up to a point, but today he seemed to be playing something or other very close to his chest. Why *had* he gotten involved in this little detective-story? What did he feel now that it was over? Triumphant? Sad? Something else?

As for Elzy's own feelings, once the excitement of solving the puzzle and actually seeing Cranberry Ledge faded, she felt very little except a small, dull resentment that everybody had gotten what they wanted except her, and she did not even have the luxury of complaining about it.

She suggested backpacking home, up and over each of the mountain ridges of the island. She wanted to show Kevin more of the place while she still could. Of course, Andy might not see the island again, either, but he never let her give him gifts openly. She knew he wouldn't let her openly consider his age, either, so she made up excuses to go slowly and stop often, and he pretended not to know why.

The trip went well, and the weather was lovely, except that Kevin tripped and fell badly against a rocky slope. He skinned his knees and one elbow and bruised one hip, but he wouldn't let Elzy fuss over him much and insisted he could walk off the pain in his ankle—which he did. Andy muttered something about envying the young.

Timogen was glad to have them home.

The next few days were mostly rainy. Andy rested and worked on his little red tablet, while Kevin wrote up a detailed account of his great-grandmother's story, both for his own family and so he could donate a copy to the Bar Harbor Historical Society. Once the weather cleared again, they launched and tested the little sailboat, which performed admirably.

Elzy vacillated between pretending Kevin wasn't leaving and panicking because he was. Her moodiness and clinging triggered several actual fights. Discovering that they *could* fight and make up made Elzy want to weep. What Kevin might be thinking and feeling, he would not say. He seemed to have closed himself off. He spoke to Andy more than to her, even when all three of them were together.

"I *still* feel like staying in one place is stupid," he said, one evening. "Like, it's a missed opportunity, a smallness, a sentimental attachment to something transient. And it is transient. My great-grandmother was right. But she was wrong, too. If she'd only gone back. If Mrs. McCarthy had gone back, if Rose had gone back, they could have replanted the Phoenix Garden on site. Some of the plants were still alive. Her tree *lived*."

"Almost nobody went back," Andy reminded him. "The reasons were economic and cultural as much as they were emotional. The era of the big cottages was ending even before the fire."

"I know. But it didn't have to be like this."

"A lot of things didn't. Then again, it's hard to say what's necessary before it happens."

"Three generations of nightmares. Feelings aren't always the way the world is."

Over the next week or so, Elzy noticed Kevin becoming irritable, sometimes overly emotional. He never had been before, but she assumed he was upset for the same reason she was, plus of course he was still grieving his father. He tired easily. The heat bothered him—he seemed to be sweating more than usual. He ate a lot. She could think of reasonable explanations for all of this. These days, she was easily distracted, easily upset, herself.

One or two nights she actually thought Kevin might be drunk, though she hadn't noticed him drinking. She thought about asking him about it, but decided it wasn't her business. Andy went on lots of walks or paddles by himself, giving them time to be together alone. They tried to enjoy it.

One morning, Kevin seemed groggy and clumsy. He rebuffed her attempts to find out why and announced his intention to go down to the work-sites and clean them up and pack his tools. He had his ferry ticket already.

"Do you want me to come with you?" she offered.

"Will you quit worrying about me?" he half-shouted.

But when Timogen insisted on going with him, he didn't say no.

"Timogen is a smart dog," Andy commented, after they'd left.

"He certainly knows something's up," she replied, frowning.

Andy headed into town to spend some time online. Elzy sat around the house alone for a bit, worrying. But worrying could do no good, so she got up, got her stuff together, and went out to patrol the Mansell Mountain Trail.

For thoroughness, she went up and tagged the summit, though she'd just been there the other day. She was on her way down when she heard an odd, distant noise.

She stopped, held still. She heard it again. Was that…?

Timogen howling! He almost never howled. Why do dogs howl? She tried to think.

"TIMOGEN!" She shouted. "I'm over here!" But would a human voice carry as far as a howl could? "FOO!" she shouted, a high-pitched, explosive sound she'd learned from trail crew members in New Hampshire years ago, the sound they used to call each other across distances, through trees.

Distant barking.

"FOO! FOO! Timogen!" No use trying to find him, he could get to her a lot faster than she could get to him. Already he was sounding closer, the sound coming from the northeast. She retraced her steps and followed the connector west, downhill, towards the intersection with the Razorback Trail. Soon, she spotted him a few hundred feet away, just above Great Notch.

"Tim!" she called.

He looked around, saw her, and barked. Then he wagged his tail, almost apologetically, and barked again, this time sharp and demanding.

"I'm coming, Tim!"

But if Tim had found a hiker in trouble and come to fetch her, as per his training, why didn't he seem proud of himself? He seemed anxious, whining and fidgeting and impatient.

It can't be Kevin who's hurt, she told herself. *It just can't be.*

But it could.

She followed the dog, walking fast rather than running. No sense breaking an ankle on the way to a scene—the first duty of a first responder is not to become an extra victim. But she wanted to run.

Tim led her to the place near the boat dock where Kevin lay sprawled in an odd position, his bag open, his lunch gone. He'd spilled his water bottle when he passed out.

For some seconds, she could not speak or move. Then she took a deep breath, put Tim in sit/stay, ignored his anxious whining, and got to work.

She had a protocol to follow.

Scene safety. Could whatever hurt the victim hurt her? Nothing looked amiss. She grabbed her med-kit from her pack and put on a pair of rubber gloves. She knew by now that Kevin had no blood-borne illnesses, but her habit was to wear gloves on-scene, and she did not wish to weaken that habit.

Next, *get consent to treat (assume consent if the victim is unresponsive), then check the ABCD and E.* That is, Airway, Breathing, Circulation, Disability, and Environment, the four types of problem that might require the most immediate action. Emergency medicine is as methodical in its own way as Kevin's boat-building. There are steps to take, and none can be skipped or taken out of order. Elzy had known that and practiced it—and occasionally taught it—for over twenty years, ever since she'd been a cop, but now, for the first time, she understood why.

She didn't want to check Kevin's ABCD and E. She wanted to flail around gibbering.

"Kevin! Are you OK? Kevin!" She squeezed his shoulder, then, getting no response, rubbed his sternum with her knuckle hard enough to hurt, if he could feel pain, a standard assessment of responsiveness. Nothing. "Kevin, it's me, Elzy, let me help, OK? Hang on, I'm going to help you."

She spoke as if he could hear, as some unresponsive people can. She put a hand on his forehead to minimize neck movement (another good habit, just in case his spine might be injured), and used her other hand and her eyes to go through an initial assessment.

Finding no immediate threat to life, she straightened him out, took off his shoes and used them to stabilize his head and neck, then carefully examined his entire body, head to toe, looking for bruises, injuries, bite marks, dents, swellings, odd scents, or anything else out of place. The whole time she explained what she was doing and why, so that if Kevin could hear and understand he wouldn't be surprised or frightened. She hoped at least he could recognize her voice.

He still had the scrapes and bruises from his fall the other day, of course, and the one near his hip looked particularly nasty, as bruises do several days into healing. She palpated his belly, forcing herself not to avoid the bruise, and nearly panicked when she felt an odd, hard squareness. After a moment, she realized it was just the implanted part of his artificial pancreas. She'd always assumed it was right beneath the external component, but apparently it wasn't. As familiar as his body had become, he'd never let her examine or ask questions about his hardware. Odd, the implant was right under the bruise.

Crap.

If his implant wasn't working, then his blood sugar was probably way too high, given how much he'd been eating lately, and that could explain his unconsciousness. But even if she'd been able to give him insulin, she would not have—calculating the dose is no job for a novice, and the wrong dose can kill. Maybe his blood sugar was too low, though? That, too, could cause unconsciousness, but is easily treated with honey. Even giving honey to someone with high blood sugar wouldn't make things much worse.

She grabbed the honey-tube from her med-kit, opened it, and rubbed some of it into his gums. She waited. Nothing happened. Well, his sugar must be high, then. But her job wasn't to diagnose, only to gather information and get appropriate help.

She finished her examination, found no other problems, wrote down all his vital signs and the time, and pulled out her radio. But she could get no signal.

"I can *see* the repeater-tower on Beech from here, why can't I get signal?" she asked nobody in particular. Timogen wagged his tail. She ignored

285

him, not wanting to tempt him to break out of Stay and get underfoot. She wandered around a bit, trying to find signal. Sometimes a few inches could make a difference. But she found nothing. She tried her cell, but of course it had no signal either; it never did here in the valley. She huffed in frustration, the way Tim sometimes did.

Giving up on her radio, she sat down next to Kevin, tore out a couple of sheets from her notebook, and started writing. When she'd written down everything she knew about the case except Kevin's name—protecting the privacy of a patient is standard procedure—she took another set of vitals, wrote them down with the time and her current location, and looked for Tim.

"Timogen, at ease." She let him get up and shake himself. "Come! Now, sit!" He sat before her, panting a little and smiling. She put her note in the pocket of his vest, snapped its flap closed, and sat back. "Tim—*get help!*"

He stood panting and staring at her for a long moment, indecisive, then wheeled and leaped down the path. In a few seconds, he was out of sight.

Elzy watched him go, then watched where he had gone a little longer. He'd be at the police station in eight or nine minutes, give them fifteen minutes to get the drone off…. She could expect the airborne cavalry to arrive in no less than half an hour. An entirely acceptable response time, if the patient had been anybody but Kevin.

She turned and settled in to wait, watching Kevin breathe.

After about ten minutes, she took a third set of vitals, wrote them and the time down in her notes. She wanted to provide Kevin's doctors with as much information as possible. His vitals weren't changing, and most of them looked pretty good, except for level of consciousness. She tried to tell herself that there was nothing to worry about, that reestablishing Kevin's blood chemistry should be fairly straight-forward, once he got to the hospital, but herself wouldn't listen. Looking at him lying there, face slack as if in sleep, bangs slicked to his forehead by sweat and already getting too long again, she could not ignore his beauty, his endearing boyishness, or the fact that he couldn't wake up.

She touched his shoulder and then straightened his shirt, pulling it down to cover his belly again. She sat with one hand resting on his chest, the other on his abdomen, feeling the heat of his body through the thin fabric. She could not help imagining the worst. What if he was permanently damaged? What if he died? She was startled to realize that thinking about him dying felt the same as thinking about him leaving—a great, frightening loneliness. It was her access to him that she cared about, not Kevin himself. She still could not feel the feelings she thought she should.

But she had made a decision, no matter her feelings, and so it was Kevin himself, for himself, she would fight for. As she waited for the medivac drone to come save him, she spread her hands across his body as though she could grow rootlets from her fingertips, willing, if such a thing can be willed, for any nutrient or bodily substance she had, sugar or insulin or glycogen, whatever he needed, to flow across the gap.

She heard the rhythmic *thwak thwak thwak* of the approaching quad-copter drone.

Elzy splashed out into the pond to wave the drone in. It set down on the water and a paramedic named John Kasem—she knew him slightly—emerged from its carry-pod and got to work.

He didn't bother repeating Elzy's exam—he trusted her—and instead he introduced himself to his unconscious patient and then did things Elzy couldn't, starting with taking a little blood and injecting it into the several different ports of a hand-held multi-purpose tester. While he awaited results, he opened the external control box of Kevin's pancreas, revealing a tiny display. Both machines agreed Kevin's blood sugar was low.

"But I *gave* him honey!" Elzy protested.

"I know," John told her. "Something's off. Let's give him more honey and watch to see what's happening."

What happened was the display showed Kevin's blood sugar start to spike upward, then quickly even out and return to its previous low. John cursed, apologized to Kevin for cursing, and explained that the implant was malfunctioning badly.

"Damn thing's *keeping* your blood-sugar low. Its set-point is wrong, probably been drifting lower since you fell."

"So, what, you have to turn it off?" Elzy asked. "Manage his blood-sugar the old-fashioned way?"

"Can't. There's no off-switch for these things. I can disconnect the external reservoir," he did so, "but there's probably enough still in the implant to keep him under for hours. It'll have to come out. Mr. Williams, you just won a non-stop flight to the OR. Elzy, help me package him, OK?"

There being only room for one man in the carry pod, John sent the patient off alone, hooked up to various non-invasive monitors. Elzy watched the drone fly off, imagining the noise of its rotors disturbing the diners in the restaurants along the harbor as it headed for the little clinic that served all of Flamingo Town.

"He's your friend you've been living with, isn't he?" John asked, when the drone was out of sight. That she was living with a man had spread by rumor all over town. "Are you OK?"

She didn't know how to respond. She wasn't used to such questions. She wasn't used to caring enough about anybody to be asked such questions.

She gave John a lift by canoe back to the beach and let him borrow Kevin's rented bike. She biked into town, too, stopping only briefly once she had reception to call Headquarters and ask them to keep Tim for a few days. Then she headed for the clinic.

The receptionist told her Kevin was in surgery. He would tell her nothing else because she wasn't family.

"But he has no family here, just me. His mom is in Canada, in Alberta. His dad just died."

"Really?" the receptionist looked up, suddenly attentive.

"Yes, really."

"No, I didn't mean...." The man looked around, possibly checking to see if a supervisor was within earshot, and then spoke quietly. "Listen, do you know anything about Mr. William's finances?"

"Sure, a little. He's my employee, as well as my friend."

"Is he going to be able to cover his bill? Because if his parents can't.... There are things we can do to cut costs, but only if we know ahead of time to do them. And we can't ask the patient about this, he's gonna wake up without a functioning pancreas, dude doesn't need to worry about money right now."

Elzy digested this. No, Kevin's mom couldn't pay his bills, there still being no straightforward way to transfer wealth internationally. She hadn't thought about medical bills in a long time—as a guild-member, hers were always covered. But Kevin had no guild, nor was he entitled to the substantial discount due a town resident. In this day and age, the entire healthcare system was more or less non-profit and costs were kept fairly low, but a big bill could still set a laborer back a couple of years.

"What's his bill going to be?" she asked. The receptionist looked around again, uncomfortable.

"Well, obviously we don't know yet, but he'll need a new AP, those run about a hundred shares, this surgery, obviously, plus the other one implanting the AP, and the in-patient care...that'll come to another hundred, hundred and twenty, unless they get creative. He's looking at around two hundred shares, more or less."

"How much less?"

"I don't know. They might get it down to somewhere around one-seventy. We do have payment plans."

Elzy thought about this. A weird thing was happening inside her chest, a light, happy, relieved glow. Kevin didn't have that kind of money. He'd have to arrange a payment plan, and since money couldn't be sent across the border *he wouldn't be able to leave.* He'd have to stay for months while he worked to pay off his medical bill. His mother would have to muddle through without him, and by the time he could afford to go, she wouldn't really need him anymore. Kevin could stay.

This was the best news Elzy had had in weeks. She felt the way she'd always imagined a prisoner granted a stay of execution must. Kevin didn't need to know she had enough to cover the bill herself. Her happily-ever-after was saved!

Except that taking advantage of Kevin's finances and lying about it wasn't really *doing love.*

Elzy had kept her elation carefully away from her face, and she kept her rather more complex knot of feelings now just as hidden.

"I can write you a check," she said. "Just please don't tell him. I don't want him feeling obligated."

Later, alone, Elzy cursed and kicked and threw things, but she never went back on her choice. Nor did she ever tell anyone. The receptionist and one of the clinic's accountants were the only people who ever knew, and they did not know why it was important.

She texted Andy from the clinic. When he met her back at the homestead that evening, he smiled, embarrassed and sad, and showed her his freshly-printed ferry tickets. He would leave the day after next.

"I got Kevin's refunded, while I was at it," he said.

"I wish you could stay until the tomatoes started coming in," she said.

"Yeah, your plants are looking good."

The next day, Andy and Elzy walked into town together. He walked his bike. He had to return it to the rental shop, and couldn't do it on his day of departure because the shop wouldn't open in time. That taken care of, they went to visit Kevin, who was alert and recovering well but had to stay in the hospital until the new artificial pancreas came in. He didn't know how to manage his diabetes without one. Elzy stayed with him several hours, even sitting beside his bed while he napped, but Andy vanished. She met up with him again at the homestead late that afternoon. He was busy packing.

"So, this is it," Elzy said. "You're leaving tomorrow."

"Actually, I was thinking of heading out tonight, maybe sleeping in the campground? My ferry leaves early, and it's a long walk even if I don't have to hike down a mountain."

"You mind if I camp with you?"

The offer surprised him. His surprise surprised her. After all this time?

"Yeah, I could do with some company," he admitted.

She packed her bag.

No one else was in the campsite when they arrived, and none showed up while they unpacked, fetched water, and fixed dinner. That suited Elzy, who didn't want to have to deal with The Public just then.

"It's weird not having Timogen around," she said, wiping up the last of her stew with a piece of tortilla.

"Yeah, I'm gonna miss having that beast under foot."

"He'll miss you....You ever had a dog?"

"No. I've thought about it. I guess I don't really gravitate towards the standard pets."

"You have lizards, right?"

"My first wife had a black widow named Arania. I wonder whatever happened to her? She wasn't in her jar when I got back to the house—it was broken open, empty."

"Did you sleep in that house that night? I wouldn't have."

"She wouldn't have still been there. Black widows are long-lived, but not that long."

Elzy set about doing dishes while Andy sketched the view from their tent platform—the long axis of the narrow pond framed by the knee-like ridges of the low mountains, the water reflecting the pinkish sky as the sun went down, a few wisps of young aspens starting to intrude on the view in the foreground. Elzy cut those aspens every few years to keep the view open, but they always grew back. Dishes done, she went and sat beside Andy and watched him sketching. He never used to sketch. When they'd hiked together—over a hundred campsites with dishes to do and hammocks to hang and lovely environs to look at, just like this one—he'd spent all his down-time typing into his little red notebook, working.

"That's pretty good," she commented.

He paused in his drawing a moment and frowned inexplicably.

"Every time I come to this pond, I see something new," he said.

"Same here," she told him.

After he finished his sketch, they strung their hammocks from the provided stands, put their breakfast things in the raccoon-proof box, and packed up their other gear nice and neat and out of the way. They both brushed their teeth so they could put their toiletries in the raccoon-proof, then rigged lines in case it started to rain and they had to put up the tarps in a hurry—though the sky was clear, the few wisps of cloud gradually evaporating into the dry sky. By the time they were done, night had almost fallen. Elzy lit a couple of sticks of mosquito-repellent incense. She did not bother to light any candles. They both knew where their flashlights were, and her night vision was still good.

"I'm not used to going to bed at sundown anymore," she admitted.

"Feel free to stay up, then. I plan to. I can sleep tomorrow on the ferry."

They sat together for a while, wordless, watching the sky deepen from green-blue to clear, clean cornflower blue, to midnight blue, to black. Presently, the moon, a day or two before full, rose clear of the eastern ridge and washed the western ridge, and then the pond, silver.

Elzy stood up, trying to get a better view of the pond between, over, or around the aspens. The moonlight glittered yellowish on the water. A dock light on the very far end of the pond, beyond the boundaries of Elzy's water protection preserve, glowed like a star for a while, then went out. A cricket sang, then two.

"When I see the pond like this," she said, "all stretched out and shining, I want to run across the water."

"Thus the appeal of boats," Andy commented, invisibly, from the shadows.

"Hey, you want to—but the boats are off by the dock."

"Come on a walk with me," Andy said, imperious, eager.

They ambled along the shoreline path, Elzy walking slightly ahead and shining her flashlight on the ground for both of them. Had he used his also, the light would have cast shadows of her legs, making the ground in front of her a flickering, striped impossibility to walk on. When she came to a root or a rock or some other tripping hazard, she warned him verbally or sometimes turned to shine the flashlight on it until he caught up. The moonlight cast weird, silver zebra stripes through the trees on the edge of the water. When they got to the big outcropping, she took a position just above the trail, shining her light down so he could pick his way across the nearly-smooth, sharply sloping, gray stone. They both got the giggles because taking this route in the dark seemed such an ill-advised thing to do, yet they were doing it anyway.

When they got to the dock and walked out on it, Elzy turned her flashlight off. They no longer needed it. The moon rode high, now, turning the sky a deep, silvery blue. Few stars could compete. Andy sat on the edge of the rail and looked out. She copied him.

"Andy?" she asked. He turned his head slightly, not looking at her but listening. "What's it like to be a parent?"

He chuckled.

"Scared half to death all the time and glad of it," he answered. He seldom spoke of his children, but she had met his living daughter once, then a self-possessed and pragmatic twelve-year-old. The girl would be nearly twenty by now.

"I always thought I'd have kids someday," she admitted. He looked at her then. She couldn't make out his expression in the dark, but since Andy often didn't have an expression, that wasn't anything new. He probably didn't understand why she'd spoken with such finality, and she blushed, realizing he was probably wondering whether she still got her period. She saw him nod a little to himself as he realized what she'd meant.

"I wouldn't discount Kevin just yet," he said.

"I'm not. But he says it's better to prepare to not see each other again, and then maybe get to, then the other way around. He's right."

"Yeah, he probably is."

"It's just that I guess if someday were going to happen, it would have already."

"Well, we're not an endangered species yet."

"No."

A few minutes went by in silence except for the gurgle of water against the shoreline and the singing of crickets. The night was warm but cooling now.

"Thanks," Andy said at length. "I needed this." But whether he meant the walk in the dark, the playing hooky from sleep, the entire adventure of searching out Kevin's great-grandmother, or some other thing, he did not say. "Beech mountain must be beautiful right now," he added, after a while.

"We could go up there."

"The days when I could climb a mountain at night and get up to catch a ferry in the morning are over." But he said it lightly, amused rather than mournful. "You wanna go for a swim?"

"Sure!"

They stripped off their shoes, socks, and outer clothing, she in her bra and panties, he in a pair of boarding house shorts. It struck her as odd that in the twenty years she had known this man, she'd never before seen him without a shirt.

They climbed out beyond the railing, then stepped off into the shallow water, the sand and the muck and the rocks of the pond bottom, then waded out to where they could swim.

The water was still warm from the heat of the day—in an hour or so, a mist would doubtless start to rise as the air cooled, but even with her eyes mere inches above the surface, treading water, Elzy could clearly see the moon and the few, brave stars. She tried submerging, eyes open, and could still see a glimmer of moonlight from under the small, lapping waves. But swimming now in deep water, every now and again her feet reached down into the layer of the pond the sun did not warm, the colder, denser water that resisted mixing with the layer above it. Every foot-full of cold thrilled and frightened her deliciously, as though there were a monster down there in the hidden dark, a monster that might grab her by the foot.

Elzy had not swum in her pond by night in a long time, since normally she'd be up at her house well before dark, but she had done it before. She'd even done it as a child, when she and her father had spent summer nights crashed out on blankets wherever in their domain tiredness happened to overtake them. In those days nobody came to Long Pond, nobody but them at all. She remembered him life-guarding her from the moonlit shore, keeping her talking as she played in the water so he would know where she was and that she was alright. She wondered now if he had been scared half to death all the time and glad of it. He must have been. But she was in no mood to try to think like a parent tonight. She dove, slapping her feet on the surface of the water as she went under, feet like tail flukes, for she had become a mermaid.

But if Elzy was a temporary ten-year-old, so was Andy. When she came up, he gave her just enough time to breathe before dunking her. And he kept dunking her, laughing triumphantly, until she, shrieking in mock outrage, counter-attacked. They play-fought until Andy inhaled water and bolted for the shallows so he could cough and breathe again.

"You alright?" she asked him. In answer, he splashed her. But they both got out of the water, using their shirts as towels before putting on their pants and foot-gear. Shirts are not terribly absorbent, though. By the time they got back to camp, the mist had begun to rise and their teeth were chattering. They were glad to climb into their sleeping bags at last.

In the morning, Andy was all business, packing up his things quickly and efficiently while Elzy cooked up a pot of grits with nuts and dried blueberries and honey, plus their traditional chicory. He ate quickly, without wanting to talk much, and insisted on doing the dishes before he left. She had her things packed up and ready to go by the time he was done.

The little campground connected to the Valley Way trail on one side. She walked Andy down the broad, neat steps of that trail to the little beach and watched him gaze out at the pond and up at the hills one more time. He looked, apart from age, so much like the backpacker she'd had for a teacher so many years ago—but it didn't seem like many years. She wanted to offer to walk him up to the road. But then, she also wanted to walk him to the edge of her territory, or to the ferry dock on the other side of town. She wanted to board the ferry with him and travel the world with him, just as she used to. But she had a life to live, and her life was here, and anyway she hadn't been invited.

He looked at her, his face unreadable.

He was probably trying to decide whether to hug her, or even just what to say. She didn't know either. She had a sudden feeling, the kind that gets forgotten unless borne out by later events, that she would never see him again. Elzy didn't credit such feelings, but she knew not to rely on the future too much, either.

Making an executive decision, she hugged him, getting her arms around him awkwardly, because of his backpack. He clung to her a moment, and she held him, held him for as long as he'd let her. And then she let him go.

Suggested Readings

*B*ifurcation Events is fiction, so while it touches on a lot of interesting science and history, it may be difficult for the reader to be sure which is real and which is made-up. Some of you are doubtless OK with that, saying "it's just a story." But some of you are geeks, like me, and want more. I am happy to provide.

First I will direct your attention to the essays at the back of *Ecological Memory*. They all apply here, too, and summarize (with citations!) why I made the decisions I did in world-building. Next, let me provide you with an annotated reading list. These are books I used as resources while writing, and you'll be able to find the facts behind the fiction if you want them. The list is thematically organized—books related to each other in some way are grouped together.

Spillover: Animal Infections and the Next Human Pandemic
2012. David Quammen
W.W. Norton & Company

I wrote *Ecological Memory* (a novel whose backstory involved a pandemic) before COVID-19, a fact that has led some readers to jokingly accuse me of clairvoyance. Nope. I just read up on the warnings of experts—*they* predicted the disaster because the disaster was predictable. The evidence of our vulnerability was extremely clear. In this second book in the series, I have added some detail from the real pandemic in some places, but basically I'm still using what I learned from *Spillover*, an engaging and accessible exploration of an intricate topic, just like everything Quammen writes.

By the way, there's nothing dated about Quammen's warning, now that COVID has happened—there is no reason whatever another terrible pandemic couldn't start tomorrow, and as of this writing, we're still not prepared.

Dire Predictions: Understanding Climate Change, the Visual Guide to the Findings of the IPCC, 2nd Edition
2015. Michael E. Mann, Lee R. Krump
DK Publishing

This book provides an actual ink-and-paper summary of our knowledge of climate change as of its publication, written for a general audience. Its publication is getting to be a while ago now, but as of this writing, the picture is still pretty much the same.

The World Without Us
2007. Alan Weisman
St. Martin's Press

Literally a description of Earth without humans, as though we had all suddenly vanished one day—what would happen to the stuff we left behind? Although the premise of my books is quite different, I used Weisman's work to get a sense of how the abandoned and ruined areas might be faring decades later.

Newcomb's Wildflower Guide
1977. Lawrence Newcomb
Little, Brown, and Company

There are a lot of field guides out there, and for the most part I leave readers to find their own favorites, if they even want field guides, which not everybody does. But I recommend *Newcomb's* because it will teach you a better way to look at—even think about—flowering plants. If you want to see New England the way Elzy does, learning to "think like a Newcomb," as one of my own teachers put it, is a good way to start.

The Book of Forest and Thicket: Trees, Shrubs, and Wildflowers of Eastern North America
1992. J. Eastman
Stackpole Books

and

The Book of Swamp and Bog: Trees, Shrubs, and Wildflowers of Eastern Freshwater Wetlands
1995. J. Eastman
Stackpole Books

and

The Book of Field ad Roadside: Open Country Weeds, Trees, and Wildflowers of Eastern North America
2003. J. Eastman
Stackpole Books

These three are not field guides. Instead, they are collections of essays on the principle ecological relationships of various plants. Once you identify a plant, you can look it up here to find out what it's doing ecologically. Alternatively, if you notice something happening, say, an odd sound coming from inside a tree, you can look up the plant and possibly find out what organism is making the noise. I really did this once—it was a sawyer beetle. Again, this is knowledge that my characters have and it informs the narrative voice of the story.

Reading the Forested Landscape: A Natural History of New England
1997. Tom Wessels
The Countryman Press

and

Forest Forensics
2010. Tom Wessels
The Countryman Press

Continuing on with the theme of seeing the world as Elzy does, these books will teach you how to see forests not merely as they are at the moment, but as the products of processes unfolding over dozens—or sometimes hundreds—of years. With a little practice, you can deduce the history of a site in remarkable detail. *Reading the Forested Landscape* introduces the technique and takes the reader through the analysis of several sites. *Forest Forensics* covers the same material but in a field-guide format.

Becoming Native to This Place
1996. Wes Jackson
Counterpoint

A thorough exploration of the idea that each human culture needs to adapt to the reality of the place it inhabits. The book is not well-written, but the dense and erratic text hides some important material that is worth reading several times, if that is what it takes.

The Geography of Childhood
1997. Gary Paul Nabhan
Beacon Press

Gary Paul Nabhan is one of my favorite writers, both for his ideas and for his ability to evoke a place in full sensory detail with just a couple of words. He is an ethnobotanist by training, and writes about the connections between humans and their landscapes. Here, he discusses the connections of very young humans, arguing that there is a distinct developmental phase when children bond with their land—and that the loss of a place a child learned *during that developmental window* can cause lasting psychological scars. Elzy's deep attachment to her home must be understood in this context.

Granite, Fire, and Fog: The Natural and Cultural History of Acadia
2017. Tom Wessels
University Press of New England

It's what the title says it is—a thorough and very readable introduction to Mount Desert Island, where the entire later section of the book takes place. Acadia National Park covers much of Mount Desert Island, and so the name of the park has become a kind of nickname for the island as a whole (though it's a nickname locals rarely use, and Tom, as an adopted local, doesn't use it in speech, either).

Guide to the Geology of Mount Desert Island and Acadia National Park
2016. Duane Braun, Ruth Braun
North Atlantic Books

As of this writing, the Brauns' book is the most up-to-date treatment of Mount Desert Island's geology I know of, plus it is quite accessible to non-geologists.

Wildfire Loose: The Week Maine Burned
2014. Joyce Butler
Down East Books

Mount Desert Island's fire was part of the terrible week of this book's title, and I drew from the relevant chapter heavily. When you read that chapter, you'll find that the final moments of a place called Barberry Ledge bear a striking similarity to those of my fictional Cranberry Ledge. Of course that's not a coincidence, though I hasten to add that my fiction is not meant to depict or in any way comment on any real person or place. What is extraordinary is that I had the basic outline for that sequence in place—including the critical detail of the gardener's reluctance to leave—before I chose Barberry Ledge as a model or learned that its real gardener was also reluctant to leave! The gardener of Barberry did make it to the waiting car, though, and a good thing, too. The differences between Barberry and Cranberry are such that that a burnover at Barberry would not have been survivable.

Noah's Garden: Restoring the Ecology of Our Own Back Yards
1993. Sara Stein
Houghton Mifflin

and

Planting Noah's Garden: Further Adventures in Backyard Ecology
1997. Sara Stein
Houghton Mifflin Harcourt

There are actually a large number of books and websites available on wildlife-friendly landscaping. Just over a decade ago, I read most of them, as I wrote my master's thesis on the subject, and these two were among the best. I imagine *The Phoenix Garden*, the (imaginary) book that makes an appearance in my story, as rather like a combination of these two, only with more whimsy, and written forty years earlier.

The Public-Spirited Beatrix Farrend of Mount Desert Island
2016. The Beatrix Farrand Society
Beatrix Farrand Society Press

Although Beatrix Farrand gets only a brief mention in my story, she is important to know about. My character, Rose Stone, would have known about her, admired her, and perhaps been her student. Plus, Mrs. Farrand was a dominant figure in landscape design in her generation and a leader in the movement towards naturalistic designs. She and her colleagues also demonstrate something that may surprise us all these years later: although sexism did make things difficult for female landscape designers and gardeners and certainly prevented some from getting the recognition they deserved, a large minority of the leadership of the field were always women. By the 1940's and '50s, a gardener like Mrs. Stone would have generations of women behind her.